Greater
LOVE

Greater LOVE

Blake Lorenz

XULON PRESS ELITE

Xulon Press
2301 Lucien Way #415
Maitland, FL 32751
407.339.4217
www.xulonpress.com

Paperback ISBN-13: 978-1-6628-3182-9
Hard Cover ISBN-13: 978-1-6628-3183-6
Ebook ISBN-13: 978-1-6628-3184-3

CONTENTS

Greater Love *is dedicated to my Lord and Savior and soon coming King, Jesus Christ.*

To Chris Bright, Tom Lorenz, Stan Moore and my wonderful wife, Beverly.

All stories and characters in Greater Love *are* fictitious, except those who are of the tribal lands of Zambia.

PREFACE

"Now as Jesus sat on the Mount of Olives, the disciples came to Him privately, saying, "Tell us, when will these things be? And what *will be* the sign of Your coming, and of the end of the age" (Matt. 24:3, NKJV).

Two major events impacted my life. One was when I met Jesus as my Lord and Savior. The other was when the Spirit told me the return of Jesus is imminent. Both of these Damascus Road encounters propelled me to travel to five continents to tell of Jesus and His greater love.

Right before the Covid-19 pandemic hit, I asked God to enable me to write a novel that would be my legacy for Jesus. This story would help fulfill God's vision for my life, to awaken a world asleep in sin that Jesus was coming soon. Out of that prayer I took the prophecies of Jesus in Matthew 24 and 25 and stories of my world adventures in missions and evangelism to create *Greater Love.* Never has the world experienced deception, terror, and confusion on such a massive scale as in the last hundred years when we began to think as a global community. Now these global prophecies of Jesus are unfolding before our eyes on the nightly news and over the internet.

This fast-paced thriller of Jesus's love and return to claim His throne is a call to action for us in these prophetic days. "And do this, understanding the present time: The hour has already come for you to wake up from your slumber, because our salvation is nearer now than when we first believed" (Rom. 13:11 NIV).

The main character is an Indiana Jones persona, who becomes a time traveler in the Spirit for Jesus because I believe that a life lived for Jesus becomes an adventure of faith. His marriage with the love of his life becomes a romantic expression of God's greater love. They become the dynamic duo that God chooses to prepare the way for Jesus's second coming.

I have seen in the past forty years the miracle-working hand of Jesus give sight to the blind, hope to the hopeless, and life to the dead. His greater love has captivated me. It is my prayer that you will have your spiritual eyes opened that the return of Jesus is imminent.

We are all on a hero's journey. May we be inspired to be about our Father's business so that in the glorious return of Jesus, we find ourselves rejoicing that our labor was not in vain.

Chapter 1
CONFRONTED WITH DEATH, AD 2019

I love Jerusalem, I thought to myself as I stood in line waiting to buy some morning coffee for Marie, my wife. The quaint local markets, the ancient history, and the stone beauty of its buildings sparked my imagination. The City of God, the very meaning of its name, abode of peace, brought me that inner oneness that we so easily are robbed of these days.

I scanned the ancient stone walls that rose to an almost impenetrable height to protect this treasured city. *Solid as a rock* came to mind. I could not imagine storming this fortress. It would be futile to even try. Still, how many armies through the centuries had taken Jerusalem? I began to name those conquerors—Babylonians to Alexander the Great to the Romans to the Muslims to the Crusaders, back to the Muslims, to the British, to Jordan, and finally back into the hands of the Jews who vowed never again to lose control of their capital.

Not much of a history of peace I thought. Yet, for Marie and me, we were desperate for some tranquility and rest after our last adventure in Jerusalem, having been kidnapped by Islamic terrorists, the fruit of our harboring a young girl who was to be honor-killed.

The very thought brought chills to the point of panic as I remembered the cold knife pressed against my throat by the young Arab. We had dared to rescue Fiza from her brother who had been given the task of murdering his sister for denying the faith and giving her life to Jesus. That cold steel, sharp as a razor, drew my blood without pain. I had wondered if, when they slit my throat and cut off my head, I would feel much pain as he looked into my eyes like a crazed killer. Marie was held back by another terrorist, but I could hear her prayers whispered under her breath. I agonized that she too would suffer my fate. I prayed fervently for God to intervene. He did deliver us.

As I stood in line, post-traumatic stress disorder was all too real in my life experience. These thoughts made me want to hide to escape the anxiety that tormented my mind. I wondered how many people around me experienced such panic because of the trauma Israel lived with each and every day.

Strange, how we were back in the hornet's nest of strife and hatred between Jews and Muslims. Both claimed the title to Jerusalem. History was on the side of the Jewish people since they were here almost two thousand years before Islam and Allah were ever invented. In Islamic thought, once a land had been conquered by Muslims, it was permanently their rightful territory. Therefore, there was little hope for peace.

Suddenly, I heard the ear-shattering rapid fire of an AK47! Then screaming and yelling, the fruit of fear and death resounded around me. More explosive, deafening shots sounded, and I realized there was a gunman somewhere near. I turned to see a terrorist with an AK47 aimed at the mother and baby beside me. Instinctively, I dove in front of them as I felt a heavy impact strike my chest. I fell instantly to the ground. Dazed and confused, I sensed my life blood oozing out of me.

More fire power and then quiet. The mother was crying as the baby stirred, screaming for her mommy. I seemed to be drifting. I heard someone say in Hebrew, "Hold on." Funny, I did not know Hebrew, but I understood what he said. I tried to see what surrounded me. People hovering. A man placed pressure on my chest. Pain started to build where I was wounded. I could see the red stain of blood covering my shirt.

Where was Marie? I thought to myself. She will not know what happened to me. Today was going to be our day of rest, I told her as I left the Airbnb. I would be right back with her coffee that she loved every morning. We would relax and enjoy the shalom of Jerusalem.

I began to lift, to float upward. Bright figures surrounded me. Angels I thought as I looked into their faces glowing with the light of heaven. They seemed joyous in the midst of this brief battle. They even smiled at me as though to say I would be fine.

A peace settled over my entire being. No more suffering. They were taking me home to heaven. I looked down, and there I was lying in a pool of blood, but here I am awake and alert with glorious angels. I could not be in better hands. I smiled back at these messengers of God.

Outstretched before me was the City of Zion, the capital of Israel. I remembered three nights ago how on our terrace Marie and I had overlooked this ancient capital of the Jews. It was night and the city was bathed in a beautiful red glow from the blood moon. We both had looked at each other and said together, "Jerusalem is covered in the blood of the Lamb."

As Marie and I stood on our apartment terrace overlooking Jerusalem, the Spirit of prophecy lay heavy upon Marie. She spoke in the Spirit, "Jesus longed to gather the chicks to Himself. These days are upon us. Blessed is He who comes in the name of the Lord." She began to pray for the people of Jerusalem that they would come to their Messiah. Her emotions were deep in this prayer, believing for their salvation in Jesus, the descendant of Abraham and David.

The sky was lit in a red haze by this unique crimson moon. We thought of the blood of Jesus that covers this ancient city. His blood shed for their sins, our sins, and the sins of the world. To be covered in His blood is to be forgiven and reconciled to God, as well as to have eternal life, an intimate love with the Creator God. God's wrath passes over us. We are free from His judgment to walk in the liberty and power of the Holy Spirit.

We had just finished an amazing night with six leaders from a church in Ramla. We talked about what God is doing throughout the world, preparing it for the return of Jesus. God had a vision to impart to them. God is looking for men and women who will offer themselves to be available to be used by God to fulfill His vision for Israel. We shared how God is looking for lightning rods, these poles of metal that catch the fire from heaven and channel it into the earth. God has called us to be His lightning rods, to receive His fire from heaven, tongues of fire, in other words, the baptism of the Holy Spirit. Wherever we go we are to take that fire and spread that flame that consumes the sin in us and empowers us to proclaim the good news of Jesus Christ and perform signs and wonders to witness He is the anointed one of God.

These leaders were hungry to be those men that God will use to bring about His vision for the salvation of all Israel. We went into an intense time of prayer as God poured out His Spirit upon us. Truly, there was fire from heaven, filling us with His glory, power, and vision. Our prayers grew so loud that the residents below us came up and knocked on our door, curious and disturbed by this raucous noise that literally shook the walls. We assured them all was in order as we quieted down from our intense prayer. This was just a glimpse of our beautiful day with God in Jerusalem. Earlier, God showed up in His love that touched one of the leaders as only the Father's love can heal, restore, and transform. So many are in need of a father's love. God is our Father.

We had just read in Jeremiah, "I will be a Father to them." God poured out His fatherly love on this pastor, who had never known his earthly father. Words cannot describe the wonder and beauty of that moment of healing and restoration. The majesty of God and the mystery of His plan produced the emotional peace he had longed to know his whole life. He wept tears of life as he forgave his earthly father. That deep void in his soul was now filled with his Father's love sent down from heaven. It was as though the burden of sorrow and rejection that had plagued him was lifted, and he was free to know that peace of God that surpasses understanding.

God had us anoint these leaders' feet, as we were led last Sunday in our service in Orlando. Wherever these leaders go, they are to go as Joshua who was given the promise of God that wherever his feet trod, it became their inheritance. This is Israel and the covenant promise being fulfilled in our day.

"Keep us in prayer," we emailed to our friends in America and around the world, "as His prophetic Spirit continues to be released as we minister in four churches Friday and Saturday. May we all become His lightning rods in this land of Promise. May the fires of the Spirit spread in this continued Pentecost that will shake the land of Israel as God promised in the last days to pour His Spirit on all Israel that they may be saved. We believe! Come Lord Jesus come."

As I rose with the angels, portions of my life began to flash before my eyes. This floating was different from what I had experienced as a time traveler for Jesus. Yes, I am a time traveler. I know the past, and I know the future. I know the present. I travel through time with God and His revelations. His Word teaches me our past, tells me our future, and reveals to me our present. I can go back to the beginning of creation. I can comprehend the history of humanity. I know our destiny. I know our struggle today.

I visit with kings and prophets. I ride with armies. I hear the truth and foundation of life. I see empires rise and fall. The mysteries of time unveil themselves in the wisdom of God. I listened to the voices of great men of the past. I walk with Jesus along the Jordan and in the wilderness. I see Jesus in the Garden and on the cross. I weep knowing the love of God and the betrayal of men. I rejoice in the redeeming grace of God.

I see the gathering storm of the future. The evil and deception of men will grow stronger. Authority and power will corrupt the world governments and media. Technology will become rebellious man's gateway to the heavens to reach the very throne of God. Satan's hand will appear to rule the earth. Persecution will torment those who know the truth of God. The very core of this world will be shaken with earthquakes and signs and wonders in the heavens.

I can tell you what is happening today. Humanity will reject the laws of God and replace them with the new laws of secular humanism. The philosophies of men will seek to rob human beings of their souls. Evolution and the deception of half-truths will cause us to lose our concept of being created in the image of God. Personal sin and responsibility will be lost. Thus, personal salvation will no longer be needed by humanity. Jesus Christ will be relegated to just another prophet and teacher.

Our love for Jesus for who He is will be swept aside by the cultural collective of the postmodern world. The concept that Jesus was the Word who was God and became flesh to dwell among us will be rejected by the elite educators and religious leaders of our day. Any god created in the image of man will do, except Jesus.

They will redefine the family and marriage so the sins of humanity will become normal lifestyles. Wickedness will become the heart of humanity as in the days of Noah. As we transcend the laws of God to please our lusts and misguided logic, what humanity intends for good will create much evil. The collapse of marriage and family will be the Humpty Dumpty of our inability to restore godly civilization.

We will see a world without borders. Nations will exist in name only. Yet, the dreams of men and women will turn into nightmares, which bring about war and destruction. Division and chaos will destroy any hope of oneness and unity. The vainglory of men who believe they can save the world will bring us to the eve of destruction. Our education system will be used to indoctrinate us into the new ways of secular humanism. The media and social media will give rise to an intolerant world where only the elite and their false ideals will be tolerated. Those who control the mass media will control humanity and feed us with a deception that will leave us empty and our love will lose its power.

As a time traveler, I have experienced our past and know our future. I can unveil the present to give warning that we live in an age of deception. The ultimate deception will be who is the Christ, the God-ordained one who alone can save us from ourselves. There is only one Jesus, God's Messiah. Yet, many will proclaim His title and lead us into war and destruction against each other and against God.

Look to the heavens and the Word of God. Only in the Spirit of God can you see and know what is rising out of the sea and out of the earth. Babylon will fall and the one who is faithful and true will come in the clouds of glory. He will end humanity's rebellion against God, defeating Satan and the kings and their armies. Jesus Christ will rule the nations to make all things new.

We will see the personal salvation of souls, the restoration of family, and the healing of the nations as promised by God millennia ago. All of God's promises to humanity are and will be fulfilled in Jesus Christ, as it is plainly written. What was lost with Adam, what was lost in the generations of Noah, and what was rejected by the nations of the earth at Babel will be restored through Abraham and his Seed, the Lord Jesus Christ.

As I looked over this ancient city that would become the center of humanity's future, I was comforted by these prophetic thoughts. I began to think of the time God stirred my heart to love this treasured city and her people.

Chapter 2

LOVE FOR ISRAEL, AD 2000

My love for Israel began in the most unexpected way. As I was preparing a sermon message, the Spirit nudged me with an announcement that our church would begin to visit Israel and have some wonderful adventures. I would be given a new heart for this Land of Promise. Rather stunned by these words, I was instructed to share this word when I preached the following Sunday. Our people had never had any special affection for Israel, but there was a core group that were almost fanatical about the Jewish people. I was often put off by their rabid insistence on us celebrating the Hebrew ancient feasts listed in the Bible, but every once in a while I would surrender to their pleas to have a Messianic Jew come and sing or speak to us about our Jewish connection. After all, Jesus, our Savior, was Jewish.

Little did I know, God in His mysterious ways, had already planted the seeds for the fruit of this prophetic word to be reaped. Months earlier, God had sent one of His *aliyah* leaders to our church to contact me. Terry's efforts to meet me had come at a time when I was traveling to several parts of the world to preach and plant churches. Thus, when he would come to church to see me, I was gone. He would later remark to me that he almost gave up on his mission from God for me. He had moved himself and his wife to Orlando from the state of Washington, based on the word he received from the Spirit that he was to go to Orlando and visit my church and begin a relationship with me. Quite a step of faith, since he did not know me or my church. After several visits to see me as I was absent from the pulpit, he said what kind of church is this that the pastor is always gone traveling to be an evangelist and missionary. Yet, God's direction was true.

On the Sunday I shared that God was leading us to embark on a new connection with Israel, Terry was sitting in the congregation. His eyes lit up when he heard my announcement. He now knew he was sent to Orlando to educate me on what God was doing in the Promised Land to prepare the way for Jesus's return. Immediately after the service, he made an appointment to see me the next day.

As we sat in my office, Terry began to share about his ministry of *aliyah* and how his team had helped thousands of Jews return to their homeland from the nations of the earth. This would be the first of many stories he would relate to me of the miracles of God that he had experienced in his calling. Terry had been a very successful and prosperous businessman before God grabbed him by the scruff of his neck and turned him into a champion for Israel. His goal in life had been to make as much money as possible and retire in the luxury of America's prosperous lifestyle. Yet, one day, God showed up at his house. Late at night, he could not sleep, so he was downstairs looking for something to watch on television. He flipped through the channels and found nothing of interest until he saw a strange man with a long white beard speaking on the miracle of *aliyah* happening around the world with the Jewish people. This was the hook that snagged this great fish from the waters of his small pond into the deep seas of God's redemption plan for Israel and the nations. As he listened to this remarkable prophet tell tales of the miraculous work of God in rescuing Jewish people from the poverty and persecution of the lands like the Crimea and Russia, he realized God was calling him to become part of this fascinating saga that began thousands of years ago in Ur of the Chaldees when God called Abraham to follow Him to the Promised Land.

Suddenly, the Spirit of God came upon Terry and brought him to his knees in tears. His selfish pride was broken. His trail of sins humbled him before the eternal one. God spoke to him in the Spirit to his spirit that He would teach him all he would need to learn about *aliyah* and the work the Master had called him to do in these last days. In that instant, the list of his sins were erased, and his name was written in the Book of Life. He was a new person in Christ, and God had work for him to do. God sent Terry up to his attic with a Bible he found stored away in a closet. This former agnostic wiped the dust off of it and began his journey with the Spirit as a new believer in Jesus and His mystery plan of salvation for the Jew first and then the Gentile.

In the morning, his wife, Linda, found him alone at a desk in the attic studying the passages of Scripture God began to reveal to Terry in the education he would need to do his job for God. He looked at his wife who stared at him in disbelief that her husband had found God and was reading the Bible. Without explanation, he gave his wife the keys to his business and told her to go and run it. For the next six weeks, Terry met daily with God to learn of *aliyah* and his mission.

As Terry shared with me his story, I sat confused by his language of *aliyah*. Afraid to show my ignorance, I listened intently until I could not stand it any longer and confessed my stupidity. I had to interrupt him and ask him what in the world does *aliyah* mean. He stopped and took a breath realizing he was like a doctor using medical terms to his patient, but instead of helping his student he was confusing him with his medicalese, in this case his *aliyah*ese. With a smile he explained to me that *aliyah* was the Hebrew term for going up to Jerusalem. Since the sacred city sat atop Mt. Zion, from whatever direction you came to visit, you had to climb up to the city David. Jews would sing psalms in celebration as they climbed up to Jerusalem in the joy of their return home. Today, most of them come from the nations of the earth on their winged chariot. When they land, they kiss the holy ground after their feet touch the pavement in Tel-Aviv.

Terry continued to tell me that all of these Jews coming home are the fulfillment of prophecy given thousands of years ago by the prophets Isaiah, Jeremiah, and Joel and, of course, the greatest prophet of all Jesus. He showed me in the written word of Scripture where these prophecies were. A day would come when the Gentiles would no longer trample the city of Jerusalem under their feet. The city of Zion would be liberated and given back to the Jews as their capital, after Israel would be reborn in a day. This took place in 1948 by the edict of the United Nations and then the liberation of Jerusalem in the Six Day War in 1967. A trickle of Jews had begun in the 1880s, but after World War II and the Holocaust, the rebirth of Israel and the retaking of Jerusalem, the mass movement of Jews flooded into Israel, especially after the fall of the Iron Curtain and collapse of the Soviet Union.

I remembered hearing an amazing violinist at our church from Norway, who had been a concert violinist for the communists tell of why the Soviet Union dissolved. I was impressed by what he said. Historians and politicians tried to explain this historic collapse of the USSR, but none knew the true reason. It was because the Soviets would not allow the Jews to leave their homes from the communist empire for Israel. So, God brought this collection of nations to their knees and ended her reign over the Jews. The new Russia and the new nations birthed from the end of the USSR, freed from the vise of communism, now allowed the Jews to come home to Israel. No one can stop the plans and will of God when it comes to His people and their redemption.

I was truly being educated concerning the Jews and the season of Jesus's second coming that began with the rebirth of Israel as a nation. Except for a brief period in the Maccabean revolt in 167 BCE to 160, Israel had been a conquered nation. The Jews had been the people of God without a country to claim as their own for over 2,500 years. The Babylonians had begun their siege of Jerusalem in 597 BC. From the conquest of Judah by Babylon to the English rule in the 20th century, Israel was not a nation. Its people scattered to the four corners of the earth as promised by God for their rejection of His covenant.

God never forgot His chosen people, as He promised to gather them home to Israel and rebirth the nation as prophesied by Isaiah and Jeremiah. This *aliyah*, going up to Jerusalem, began to build with the Zionist movement in the 1880s. Actually a trickle began twenty years earlier as Jews started their homeward journey. This redemptive plan of God gained momentum in World War I, and then the miracle happened. The horrors of the Holocaust in World War II with the extermination of over 6 million Jews by the Nazis and the dislocation of millions more in Europe, the time for a new Jewish nation had come.

Led by the USA and President Truman's support, the UN voted in 1947 to grant the Jews their own land in Palestine. Then in 1948, the nation of Israel was born in a day. This became the strongest sign that the age of the Gentiles was ending. God's focus would now be centered in Israel, and the coming of the Messiah's clock reached five minutes to midnight. Within this generation, He would come in His glory with His followers to become the king of Israel and to rule the nations of the earth.

For to us a child is born,
>to us a son is given,
>and the government will be on his shoulders.

And he will be called
>Wonderful Counselor, Mighty God,
>Everlasting Father, Prince of Peace.

Of the greatness of his government and peace
>there will be no end.

He will reign on David's throne
>and over his kingdom,

establishing and upholding it
>with justice and righteousness
>from that time on and forever.

The zeal of the Lord Almighty
>will accomplish this. (Isaiah 9:6-7).

Now the signs of His coming had multiplied across the earth as He predicted in Matthew 24. The age of deception and lawlessness would overtake the world. Humanity would replace the laws of God with the laws of men. Our love would grow cold. Jesus warned in His prophecy not to be deceived by the claims of false Christs and the deceptions that would lead humanity into rejecting the Bible and the God of creation and especially the deity of Jesus Christ of Nazareth. Nation would rise against nation, and kingdom would war with kingdom. Earthquakes and famine would multiply on the earth. Signs in the heavens would increase. The climate of the world would drastically change. Governments would seek to control the climate and the lives of every living being. Famine and disease would grip the nations. Terrorism would arise. The killing of the innocents would become a mass business in the name of compassion. Sexual perversion would once again become the norm and idolatry, and witchcraft would regain popularity.

Marie and I would later be led to work with the Knesset in supporting prayer meetings and conferences to bless Israel and influence the nations to move their embassies to Jerusalem. President Trump led the way for the USA to establish our embassy in Jerusalem. Other nations followed, like Guatemala and Moldova. Business leaders were encouraged to expand their business with Israel, in opposition to the BDS movement against Israel, which seeks to boycott, divest and sanction Israel around the globe.

World religious leaders gathered to pray with rabbis and pray for God to bless Israel. We even sang "Amazing Grace" in the Knesset. A new sense of unity and oneness between Jew and Christian arose. Barriers and prejudice fell away as we joined together in God's plan for Israel and the nations of the earth.

The curse of Babel was being broken by the blessing of God. At the same time, this ancient judgment on the nations increased in the different worldviews and philosophies of men. Technology became the new gateway to God. The battles raged within the human soul and in the nations of the earth for our destiny. Our only hope was in the truth and revelation knowledge that the Messiah would come to bring God's peace. Every knee would bow and every tongue would confess Him as Lord.

Terry insisted I go to Israel on one of their tours. How could I say no, when the Spirit had already told me I was to travel to this exotic and beautiful land of the Messiah! My heart now yearned to walk where Jesus walked and to learn more of God's design for Israel and the nations of the earth. My first trip came just six months after Terry and I began our divinely inspired friendship. In that time, I studied and learned much more than I had ever known about Bible prophecies and Abraham and the Hebrew people.

When I landed on the sacred ground, my love for the Jewish people had already been planted in my heart and grown into a reproducing olive tree. So, my first act with my team of twenty-four that came with me on this adventure was to plant an olive tree in the mystical "Garden of Eden," on a Jewish hillside. This is a newly established tradition for anyone who visits Israel to plant a tree to bless these hearty and enduring survivors of ages of persecution. Now, they would be rooted and grounded in the Promised Land, never again to be removed from their God-given soil.

Terry finished our first meeting by telling me of his vision he received from God. He could see the whole nation of Israel, and within its borders were tiny but brilliant lights shining within her cities, towns, and villages. They continued to multiply through the land in this vision. The Spirit informed him these were the small groups of people He was planting to prepare for the Messiah to come and rule in Israel. We were on the verge of a new beginning that would usher in and restore the glory and perfection of His creation.

As I rose higher into the heavens beyond the sacred walls, my thoughts now turned to Marie and her love for Israel, which flowed from a far different fountain of God's grace then mine.

Chapter 3

MARY, AD 31

Slowly, my eyes focused as I awakened from my time travel. I heard voices and then I thought I discerned a woman crying. I looked around the household and then around the table where I sat. I was clearly back in Jesus's day. The humble rock dwelling with its one large open room and high ceiling told me it was the home of a man of some means in the town. Then the men who sat across from me were dressed in robes and turbans. Pharisees, I believed.

There, a few seats down was Jesus. How He seemed to love being in the midst of trouble. He amused Himself with the tests of these religious leaders, pious and smug legal scholars about the Word of God, yet so far from true faith. Over the centuries they had erected laws upon laws to protect themselves from breaking God's Word, that the very thing they feared had come upon them. Their rigid system left little room for love or faith. They had become self-righteous and proud of their position and power. Jesus often exposed them for the hypocrites they had become in the eyes of God. They prayed to impress and took the most prestigious seats at the celebrations of weddings and feasts. They were seen by the masses as close to God, but Jesus said their hearts were far from Him. They could not understand Jesus and His ways. He healed on the Sabbath and allowed His disciples to gather food on the Sabbath. When they challenged Him, He told them He was the Lord of the Sabbath.

One time, He brought a man with a withered arm before everyone in the synagogue and asked whether it was right to heal him on the Sabbath. Their silence angered Him because they treated their animals better than their neighbors. When Jesus commanded the man to stretch forth his hand, He was instantly healed. No joy or celebration was heard among them. How hard their hearts were toward the Messiah and His God. Instead, they were insulted and realized they needed to kill this rebel who exposed their false religion that had lost its way in the maze of human tradition.

Suddenly, I realized I was with Jesus at Simon the Pharisee's house. There, at the feet of Jesus, was Mary. A joy that broke all boundaries leaped within me when I realized who she was. I knew her name because she was the woman I had known intimately from one of my travels. It was a low point in my life. I found myself alone in her village without food or money. I was hungry and cold. I had suffered a terrible rejection in my life 2,000 years in the future. The love of my life had called off our engagement. The pain was sharper than any sword that could pierce my soul. I had never known such a wound. My failure in love caused my heart to crumble like a smashed cookie, tossed and thrown away. "How could she do this to me?" I cried to God. Her rejection was like cancer hidden in my body and now exposed the fraud I was. That cancer spread throughout my being until I died inside.

That night I could not sleep. Waves of anxiety swept over and over through my mind. I had to get up from bed and from the dizziness that swirled within me. No matter how hard I prayed, I could not make my suffering stop. How could I face my congregation after such failure in love? They would lose all respect for me. I was a disgrace. I was supposed to be a leader in love, but I was a fool.

Then God in His mystery plucked me up and sent me back in time alone and without any means of survival. I had expected God to lift me up, to bind my wounds, and mend my broken heart. When I needed God the most I was left in despair and deserted in an unknown town. I could not bear my sense of aloneness. Loneliness was bad enough, but aloneness, that sense of having no one to comfort me or to share with me my sorrows and grief, was too much to bear.

As I walked the streets of the village in that darkness, I began to panic. Where would I sleep? How would I eat? I had denied my trust in God and was focusing on my problems instead of looking to Him for direction. No, self-pity consumed me, for even God had deserted me. Then I saw that dim light in a small hovel of a hut. I sensed a pair of eyes searching me, following me as I wandered to who knew where. I must have looked like a lost dog who had been separated from its master weeks ago and now was on its last legs. I was hunched over with the weight of failure bearing down on me.

Her voice whispered to me in the blackness of my soul. It was sweet and inviting, although any voice would have sounded as a call of rescue from my dilemma. I looked earnestly with a deep longing for any kind of hope, but saw no one. Again, she beckoned to me. I moved toward the door. There she stood like an angel to a forlorn stranger. Yet, I knew she was no angel. Only a prostitute would be awake at this hour and alone in a hut with one room with a bed and small fireplace.

Why not? God had brought me here. Where was my Deliverer? I knew I should run, but my mind agreed with my eager flesh. Why not? Where else can I go? It is a lighthouse in the stormy sea of my troubles. At least I can get warm and have a place to sleep and maybe get some food. I don't have to do anything with her. Just talk to her and go to bed.

As I walked to her, I heard a slight jingle near my belt. I felt for what it was. A pouch with some coins attached at my side suddenly appeared. Maybe God had not deserted me? How foolish one's thoughts get when one is desperate; we love to rationalize away our sins. *Now you have a way out*, my inner spirit said. But my carnal voice was quick to respond. *No, now you can pay her for the bed and food. You do not have to sleep with her. Go in and rest.* Ah, the ancient war rose up in my flesh against the truth of God. How many men had fought this battle and lost down through the centuries?

As I approached the rickety door, her warm and caring hand touched me. I saw her smile. *Maybe she is just a kind woman looking to help me,* I thought. Yet, I knew that was a lie. I sensed that sensual connection a man feels with a woman who attracts his attention. My flesh rose up. I wanted her. Why not? If at any time I had needed comfort, it was in this alone moment where my world had collapsed all around me.

I had never been in such a position since I met Jesus. Before I had given my heart to Jesus, I had known many women in high school and college. That fire was still there in me to touch her and caress her and lose my soul to her seduction. I needed a moment of pleasure to ease my pain. In that surrender I lost the battle. I would play her game and satisfy my lustful desires. That night, I delighted in this foreign woman with no name. She gave herself to me with a disguised passion that made me feel loved and wanted. I knew it was false, but I did not care. I imagined it was my beloved Jennifer who had cast me away. What was one more lie added to my fornication with a prostitute?

Yet, when it ended, I felt worse. My soul cried with an empty wolfen howl that knew I had given myself to the devil. I turned away from her. This woman I had used and abused for my own pleasure meant nothing. She was only an object that could meet my needs. Besides, I would pay her. She was an adult who knew what she was doing, and in our silence we agreed to the bargain.

Still, my remorse now tormented me. How could I have been so weak? This failure was worse than my failure with Jennifer. I had let down my church and betrayed my God. How could I ever serve Jesus again, especially as a pastor? The men in my church could be forgiven for their adulteries, but not me. I was to be above such sin and wickedness.

Now, the goodness in me would not allow me to hide from her. I resisted to turn back to look at her as though she was real and a human being of worth and value. My act had condemned her as a woman of no value. She was not precious to me or God. Why try to make up for my evil abuse of a woman created in the image of God? Pay her and be on your way. Guilt is a terrible master and motivator to hide one's shame.

No, I had to see her face and know her name. I needed to ask her forgiveness for what I had done to her like all the other men who used her for their pleasure and counted her as a piece of dung when they saw her in the village. The sickening irony of human existence rose like a battering ram in the hands of a demon to strike the door of my soul and leave me open and vulnerable to the taunts of his fellow dark spirits. I jumped to my feet and startled the woman. My longing for righteousness awakened me from my vile thoughts. Like a man stirred from a trance, I knew I had to speak to her and beg her forgiveness. She would probably laugh at me and tell me to be on my way, but my consciousness was seared and the fire would burn a hole in my soul if I did not quench its flames with an act of kindness.

Looking into her face for the first time, I saw the pain of human existence written across her brow. Her eyes were dark like shadows. She turned away from me, but I discerned she was young and fragile. How could I have done this to such a woman, frail and alone in a world that scorned her, but allowed her to exist within their walls so she could be used by men.

Gently, I touched her shoulder. "What is your name?" I asked. She remained silent. "My name is John," I said as if to open a door of hope.

"Why do you ask?" she spoke with a whisper, implying, "No one cares about me; why would you?"

Somehow I found my footing. Yes, I had sinned terribly, but God would forgive my transgression. I had a choice to continue the charade and worsen my sin or be used to speak the truth that could set us both free. I struggled to answer her. My actions had said I did not care. She was right, and that shot an arrow into my heart. I had acted the beast. Can I now express some genuine love to her? It was like moving a boulder from my mouth even to speak, but I did.

"You are correct. I have treated you without care. Please forgive me for how I have used you."

Her face hardened. She knew men like this. Once their lust was spent, they became sorrowful, but they never changed how they treated her in the daylight. She expected the same from me.

Feeling like a hunter who had found a wounded animal in the woods, I tried to help her, but she withdrew in fear and terror as though I would kill her. As much as she longed for love and kindness, she could not receive my offer of gentle warmth. We had done the deed; now leave her to rest and sleep in peace. But she knew there would be no peace, only deeper sorrow buried farther down in the recesses of her mind. One act of kindness could not heal her years of wounds.

"Please get out and leave the coins on the bed," she said as her back turned from my gaze.

"I do not know what you have suffered, but I believe it has been more than I can imagine," I continued to try to soothe the wounds of her soul. "I have added to your hurt and pain. I am wrong and need to ask for your forgiveness. Please forgive me." The strange irony unnerved me as I said those words and placed the payment for my sins on the bed. She looked to see if it was the right amount. She marveled that she saw twice the amount I should pay. Then, the wounded animal in her came back to haunt her. *Guilt money*, she thought, *only to relieve the weight of his shame.*

I realized what she was thinking. "No, it is not to make up for my sin," I stated. "I know this sounds hollow to you, but I do care about you. I want to share with you about Someone who cares even more for you."

She turned to see this man who expressed a kindness she had rarely experienced in her life. Our eyes met for an instant. She saw in me a hope that she craved, a lifeline that could save her soul for at least this night. Then she turned away once more. There was no hope. She had chosen her path, and she would suffer for a few years then die, and no one would care or remember she had ever lived.

A love and boldness arose in me. I could not rescue her, but I could plant a seed that God could nurture to sprout a stalk and one day produce the fruit of her salvation. The spirit of prophecy came upon me.

"One day a man will come to this village. He will be like no other man who ever lived. His name is Jesus. He comes from Nazareth, and He is the promised Messiah. His heart is full of love for you. In Him you will find hope and forgiveness for all of your sins. His love is the love of God beyond the love of men. He alone can heal your soul and restore you to wholeness and awaken you to the love you have always sought for your heart."

A moment of silence as she pondered my words. Then, "Can such a man exist who loves the unlovable? If He does, He is not a man."

"You are right. He is God who has become a man to dwell among His people Israel. He has come to reveal to all of His sons and daughters who God is. He is the one true God who loves and forgives all sins to those who seek Him and fall at His feet in love and repentance. When you hear the crowds greet Him, go to Him. He will not turn you away. He will welcome you home to your Father. He will give you a new life and an everlasting hope that will set you free to live for the glory of God, to love Him, and follow Him."

She could not respond. My words were too good to be true. She wanted to believe in this light of revelation that opened a door into the heavens. *Could this be true*, she questioned herself.

Her silence caused me to think she wanted me to depart. I did not know what else to say. I finished by offering her a challenge. "Remember, He will come, and His name is Jesus," I concluded as I opened the door to leave.

"My name is Mary," she replied as I left.

Chapter 9

REDEMPTION, AD 31

Oh, the joy I knew as I realized the woman at the feet of Jesus was Mary. I had no clue how long it had been when I was with her until this day of her salvation. A week? A month? A year? What mattered, she had come to Jesus. Her sobs were genuine cries of repentance for her life, expressing her love for this unique man called Jesus. I earnestly looked to make eye contact with her, but she never lifted her head.

Her tears wetted Jesus's feet as they streaked through the dust on his ankles and toes. More tears came, so many tears of cleansing and restoration. When His feet were clean, she undid her hair and dried His feet with every soft strand. She then began to kiss His feet in adoration and worship. I could hear the angels in heaven singing and rejoicing. She had come home to the Father through Jesus. She really believed in Him and His forgiveness. She would be a new person after today, I knew without a doubt in my mind.

Then she took a vial and broke it open. Fragrant oil spilled out onto Jesus's feet. She anointed Him with the oil of her salvation, filling the room with its aroma and wiping away the stench of rejection and the evils of the Pharisees' false religion. The beauty and holiness of God's redemption covered her in the perfume of her restored intimacy with God. It was as though the oil released the fullness of God's love and covered her with its divine protection.

For the first time in her life she knew genuine love. The divine love of God in Jesus poured over her like a warm light. In this aura of God's love, all the abuse and rejection that had scarred her soul melted away the black wound of human suffering. Her value as a human being was now stamped into her image. She truly believed she could be loved and give love. The night of hopelessness that controlled her destiny had been driven away in the light of this new gift from Jesus's hand. This brought forth an ocean of cleansing tears that washed Jesus's feet and brought living water to her spirit.

Now when the Pharisee who had invited Jesus to eat with him saw this, he said to himself, "If this man were a prophet, he would have known who and what sort of woman this is who is touching him, for she is a sinner."

And Jesus answering said to him, "Simon, I have something to say to you."

And he answered, "Say it, Teacher."

"A certain moneylender had two debtors. One owed $10,000, and the other fifty thousand. When they could not pay, he cancelled the debt of both. Now which of them will love him more?"

Simon answered, "The one, I suppose, for whom he cancelled the larger debt."

And He said to him, "You have judged rightly." Then turning toward the woman, he said to Simon, "Do you see this woman? I entered your house; you gave me no water for my feet, but she has wet my feet with her tears and wiped them with her hair. You gave me no kiss, but from the time I came in she has not ceased to kiss my feet. You did not anoint my head with oil, but she has anointed my feet with ointment. Therefore I tell you, her sins, which are many, are forgiven—for she loved much. But he who is forgiven little, loves little." And he said to her, "Your sins are forgiven."

Then those who were at table with him began to say among themselves, "Who is this, who even forgives sins?"

And he said to the woman, "Your faith has saved you; go in peace."

Mary rose to her feet as if she could soar. The weight of her shame, sorrows, and condemnation had been lifted by the love of Jesus. Her head was bowed to the ground, but her heart was rejoicing with praise and adoration. Jesus was the Savior, the promised Messiah who had given her a divine liberty that cleansed her so clean she felt whiter and purer than any washing she had ever known. She had a new life, and her past was dead. The chains and bondage were no more. Jesus had imparted into her soul that she was a woman of value created in the image of God. She would never doubt this sacred truth throughout the rest of her life. It would inspire her to love God and love all she would meet in her new journey of life.

She was leaving the house of Simon where Jesus remained, but she knew she would follow Jesus and serve Him as a holy woman of God. Gone were her thoughts of death and darkness. Somehow He had healed the deep wounds of her soul, and she realized for the first time in her life God loved her and Jesus loved her. She had found her reason for living and discovered her purpose in life. Everyone would hear from her lips how He had saved her from her own self-torment and fires of hell. No one could do what Jesus had done. She owed Him everything. Oh, to be free from the prison of death in which she had lived. She had a fresh, righteous vision for living now. She could love and give authentic love to others without prostituting her body. That way was buried in her past, never to be resurrected. She was dead, but now she was alive. This new beginning was tied to Jesus. She was connected to Him with a holy bond. In Him was life that was filled with love. She quickened her pace with joy as she made her way into the street. I had done my best to let her see me, but it all happened so fast and I did not want to embarrass her or disrupt the meeting. When she did walk past me, I reached out to her, only to find myself in that dimension between time. I was hurling back to the 20th century.

YEAR 1981

When I arrived in the year 1981, I was full of joy like I had not felt in the year since Jennifer had left me. God had given me a gift of unbelievable celebration.

My words that night of the forgiveness of her sins had planted a seed in Mary's soul. Jesus had come to deliver her from the horror of her suffering. She loved Jesus, and that love would change her life and her destiny. She would become a world changer for Jesus.

A peace that had evaded me for months now reigned in my mind. It was as if my failure with Jennifer had been erased. The heartache that plagued me vanished. The aloneness that gnawed at my soul slipped away. I still felt lonely because I wanted a soul mate, but that was bearable until that one came into my life. I had to be about my Father's business, and that purpose satisfied my soul. The next day I received a phone call from a frantic friend who needed help. I noticed her emergency did not bother me. The weight of ministry seemed to have lifted from my mind. The return of joy from knowing that Mary had found her way, restored that fire in me to serve Jesus. I just felt plain good about life. My vision for living had returned to me as it had for Mary.

Now I needed to go see this street walker who visited my church from time to time. Perhaps it would be another Mary encounter but without the sin that had beset me. I went on my way, believing the best would occur for this broken woman who needed to discover her value and worth as a child loved by God. Jesus could do that in an instant. I prayed that would be the case. I didn't want to go by myself, so I stopped to pick up Bart on the way and shared with him that we were going to see the prostitute who often visited on Sunday morning. She sounded in trouble, but she had not told me what was the matter. I asked Bart if he knew a female who could help. It was best to involve a woman with another woman, and no one had come to mind.

Bart was a street-wise young man who grew up without much of a home life. His father was shot and killed by drug dealers when he was two. His mother had become an alcoholic. Bart was left to fend for himself and learned quickly the ways of the world. He joined a gang at thirteen and got his first demonic tattoo at fourteen. He became a runner for the Diablos, his gang, and shot his first victim at fifteen. He was arrested and sent to juvenile but was not tried as an adult. He was sentenced to the state-run juvenile prison where he stayed until he was eighteen. He was hard as a rock when he was granted his freedom. Then the miracle of Jesus happened to him and He broke him out of that shell of sin that held him in bondage. One night shortly after his release, he was running from the cops when he holed up in the only place he could find—my church. The side door had been left unlocked, and he ducked in, not knowing this warehouse was a place of worship. I found him asleep early that morning. Bart had no place to live. He needed to lay low for a while, so he conned me into letting him sleep in my office. The next evening, Bart came back to his new home early to discover a service taking place.

The presence of God was mighty that night, and His glory hung heavy in the room. I preached on Mark 10:46–52, the story of how Jesus healed blind Bartimaeus and gave him a new vision for living. The divine encounter for Bart took place that night when he was overwhelmed with the love of God. Now he was truly free to live for Jesus. After the first week I realized Bart was someone special when he came to me with a question.

"Preacher, can I ask you something?"

"Anything Bart," I replied.

"I have been reading the Bible you gave me, and it says if I do not forgive people then God will not forgive me. I know God has forgiven me of my sins. I have the gift of eternal life. I have forgiven everyone I know, except one person. I hate him, and I am so angry with him when I think of how he tormented me. I try to forgive him, but I can't," he cried somewhat puzzled at his predicament.

"This guy was a cop. He hated my dad, and I think he would sleep with my mom when we were low on money as she worked the Trail. When

I was with the Diablos, he chose to harass me unmercifully. The night I shot that man, I envisioned it was this cop. What should I do?"

"That is a tough one. First, 99 percent of the police are good people, but like all professions, there are a few bad apples. This one, being a cop, that makes it worse because they have this power and authority over us," I began to say, trying to get my thoughts together. I prayed for guidance. "This is what I have learned the hard way. I had a man who made my life miserable at one of my churches. He would write half-truths and lies about me in emails and even threatened me with harm. People believed him because, unfortunately, people love to believe lies more than the truth. It got so bad, the Spirit led me to leave and go to another church. It was really hard because I loved those people and the vision God had given us, but when trust is broken, it is nearly impossible to restore.

"So, every day I would forgive him over and over again, but it wasn't real. I still was angry and, like you, hated him for what he did to me. One morning I was in prayer, and the Spirit spoke to me. You have forgiven him, so stop repeating his actions over and over in your mind. Begin to bless him every time you think of him. Pray that God will bless him and for his work and family to be blessed, and that the deep wounds in his soul that produce such terrible fruit be healed. After a few days of doing that, I noticed my anger and hatred were gone. He pops up in my mind every now and then, and I pray for him to be blessed. I am free from that bondage of unforgiveness. By praying for him, God healed my wounded soul."

"I will try it and see if it works for me," Bart concluded, unsure if he could do that.

"Trust God to do this in you," I assured him. "God will do it. You will see."

Two weeks later he came to me and said he was free. We rejoiced and prayed together and thanked God for the victory.

"By the way, that guy I struggled with was a cop too!" I told him.

Bart hung around after that life-changing moment with Jesus and became a worker with me and eventually my partner in ministry.

"You need a woman," Bart teased me, bringing my thoughts back to the now. "That would solve all of your problems," he insisted.

"Yeah, I need a wife like Teresa," I replied, implying that Bart had married a wonderful woman and now had three kids and an amazing home.

"There is no one like Teresa, man, but there is one for you," he added. Then he remembered he heard of a new woman in town who had started a street ministry to the prostitutes. "You know, there is this lady who began to help the prostitutes a couple of months ago. Maybe she can help us."

"Wow, I had not heard of her. Where can we locate her?"

"She ministers down on the Trail. I think she opened a storefront near Michigan Avenue. Let's swing by there and see if we can find her. I hear she has quite a gift in helping set these girls free."

"The Trail it is." Off we went.

Chapter 5

INTO THE FIERY
FURNACE, AD 2019

Alone in his room, the angry, drunken man sat at his computer, his finger on the send button. He savored the moment as he was about to end the life of his enemy. Full of hate, he wanted to hurt him in the worst way. He knew the perfect one to destroy, the pastor who had ruined his life. This broken loner blamed me for his misery. It was my false preaching that caused his parents to divorce, which led to his mom's suicide, he reasoned with himself.

His reasoning was: "This pastor was the one who ratted him out to the police, which caused him to be quietly asked to resign. He had taken liberties with the street girls he was supposed to protect on the Trail. That moved him to get a cut of the drug money being sold to the addicts. If it was not for this phony man of God, none of this would have happened. He was the reason people walked away from Jesus. Now I have him." That is why he gave up on Jesus and religion.

So, the former police officer, turned Neo- Nazi, white supremacist would get his revenge. He had investigated where I was on my trip to Jerusalem. Then he thought, *One press of the send button, and his life was toast. Those Islamic terrorists do not mess around. Once they know there is a fatwa on this preacher, they will capture him and torture him to death. Just what he deserves,* he smiled to himself.

How could he be so stupid as to be staying at the National Hotel in the Muslim section of Jerusalem, he mocked me. *God's wrath will consume him and his wife. Their heads will be cut off and seen across the world on video.*

It was so easy for him as he pushed send. He thought his life would turn around, as he took another shot of whiskey.

Marie and I did not know if we would live or die. We huddled close in the room. There were no windows and only one door. We were closed in like two lambs waiting for the slaughter. We prayed to God for Him to deliver us from our Islamic terrorists, but even if He did not, we would still praise Him like the three Hebrews ready to be cast into the fiery furnace. We trusted in God. He was our only hope.

"I am afraid," Marie whispered. "Afraid I will not stand to be a witness for Jesus."

"God will give us the grace to be strong. I can hear His angel saying to us, 'Fear not.'" I assured her even though I doubted in my own mind whether fear would not overtake me. Emotions often exceed our faith in our frail human bodies.

"I am so sorry for putting us in this place. Please forgive me," she whispered again.

"No, no, no. You are not responsible. We prayed and believed God called us to stay at the National Hotel. This is all of God. Hey, the good news is we will be with Jesus probably tomorrow. He will give us the strength to see this through to the end." I squeezed her tight to let her know I would not fail her. I was with her in this hour of our greatest trial.

When we planned our trip to Jerusalem, Marie felt led to book us into the National Hotel in the Muslim section of Jerusalem. We knew it could be dangerous since we had been put on a fatwa list by radical Muslims to have us killed.

Several years before, Marie was with a prayer group on the internet and had contact with a teenage girl. It was through this relationship we came to harbor Fiza who was to be murdered by her family for converting to Christianity. Marie had gotten up at 3a.m. as was her routine to intercede on the prayer watch. She went to her computer to check if any new prayer requests had come in so she could lift them up in prayer that night. Yes, one had come in from Fiza, a Muslim girl in Ohio who had been baptized and become a follower of Jesus. She requested that Marie call her because she needed someone to talk with her and pray. When Marie went to call her, the cell phone had been disconnected, so she emailed Fiza her phone number to call her, which she did. That began one of our greatest trials as followers of Jesus. When Marie answered the phone, Fiza was distraught and hysterical. "Please pray for me that when they come to kill me, I will not deny Jesus," she cried as she stood on the balcony of her apartment.

Her parents had found a Christian book in her backpack several weeks earlier and scolded her for her interest in Jesus. They did not know she had already given her life to Jesus and had been baptized. They forced her to go to extra Muslim classes at the mosque in Dayton, Ohio, to restore her to the true faith. While at the classes she wore her hijab and had her earphone plugged into her iPod under her garments. She would listen to teachings about Jesus as she sat in the classroom. Fiza had come to love Jesus and given her heart to Him.

Marie began to calm Fiza down with prayer and soothing words of protection and love. She feared that the next day she would be honored killed or sent back to Pakistan to be enslaved or murdered if she did not give up this Jesus and return to Islam. She was determined to run away and asked if Marie would take her into her home. Marie knew time was short for Fiza, so she said she would talk to me in the morning to see what we could do. That morning Marie told me of Fiza's dilemma and insisted we had to do something to save her life. I said I would call our friend Tom Stanton, who was a lawyer, and he would have good advice for us. It was Saturday when I called Tom, thinking he would not answer, but he picked up right away. When I told him of Fiza's situation, he said we could not transport a minor across state lines as we lived in Orlando, Florida. If she ran away from home and came to our house, we could take her in as a runaway. He also said he would call his friend, who was a former Muslim but was now the head of the seminary where Tom worked as dean of their law school, to see what he thought.

Within two hours, Tom called me back and said she would be killed within forty-eight hours if someone did not help her. His friend told him it was a matter of honor with many Muslims. The family had been shamed by her conversion and the only way to restore the honor to the family was for her to convert back to Islam or be killed. This event happened before most Americans had ever heard of honor killings by Muslims. It was difficult for us to believe a family could do this to their own daughter. Tom had impressed on us the seriousness of the situation. So, Marie called Fiza and told her if she ran away from home, we could take her in to protect her life.

Two days later this brave young woman showed up on our doorstep late at night, having traveled by bus from Dayton to Orlando. When we first met this wisp of a girl, I was amazed at how petite she was for her age. She wore a Yankees cap and normal teenage dress. We soon learned she was a mighty woman of faith and loved Jesus, and the threat to her life was real. To me she was a modern day Joan of Arc, whom God had raised up to help set free so many young people held in the bondages of religion, not just Islam. She would eventually fulfill that prophecy as her witness helped set many free from the tyranny of twisted religion. I spent the next ten days calling everyone I knew from politicians, to judges, to lawyers, to the chief of police trying to figure out what we should do with Fiza. I got as many answers as I made phone calls. No one really knew what to do as this was so foreign to our culture and system of law.

One thing we determined, she could not go back home, for many former Muslims told us of their friends who had been honor killed in Lebanon, Syria, and Egypt, and some even in the USA. One former Muslim had me listen to a 911 tape recording of two sisters in the trunk of a car, screaming for help as their father shot and killed them just a few months earlier in Texas. Eventually, the police tracked Fiza to our house, and we had to hand her over to the police authorities and the juvenile system in Orlando. It became an international story full of lies, deception, and intrigue. The governor of Florida stepped in to protect Fiza, but she would be sent back to a foster home in Ohio before she received her freedom from the courts right before her 18th birthday. What a celebration that was!

For Marie and I it became a grueling year and a half of persecution, betrayal, and the rebuilding of our lives. Not only were we threatened to be killed, but most of the news media sensationalized the story in such a way we were portrayed as child molesters, brain washers, and kidnappers, and her parents were the innocent victims of our evil plot. There were moments I would throw up my hands in disgust when I would read an article about us. We were the ones who helped save her life, but we were the bad people, all for just trying to save a young girl's life.

Some of our church leaders turned on us. We showed up at church early one Sunday morning only to be locked out of our building. They took all of the church money and equipment and shut the church down. Fortunately, our people stood with us, and we met in a testing laboratory for a year. We had no heat in the coldest winter I think ever in Orlando. People showed up with ear muffs and gloves on. Some called me and said, "Preacher we love you but it is too cold to come this morning." We had no A/C in the summer heat. I would be drenched in sweat by the end of our service, but we were bonded as one in unity in our faith in Jesus and fellowship together.

Every so often a news reporter would show up at our service and write an article, mocking us as we worshiped with our keyboard on a saw horse and our projector on a ladder. Behind where I preached was the wall scarred with projectiles used in our friend's business to test the strength of materials against hurricane force winds. My missionary friend from Zambia, Dexter, loved coming to visit our humble house of worship. It reminded him of the early believers worshiping in the underground catacombs of Rome. We were truly tested for our faith.

Our people rallied behind Marie and me in love and support. To this day, the ministry continues to touch tens of thousands of lives all around the world. God was faithful that not one hair of our head was touched, even though warrants were issued for our arrest but never acted upon. We were told the police would show up at 6 a.m. with the news people and arrest us. That was a heavy burden we carried for over a year and taxed us to the max at times. It was a fearful season for us. I discovered how weak my faith was—but how faithful God was. I struggled with fear inside of me almost daily. I did not want Marie to be arrested and to go through that humiliation of arrest and jail. I knew Jesus taught we should rejoice when we are persecuted for His namesake, but I truly struggled to rejoice. Fear would grip me, and I spent hours on my knees in prayer, seeking God and asking for courage.

The hardest part was friends who deserted us and believed the lies told about us. Several men had told me previously before the Fiza situation they would take a bullet for me, but when the hour of trial came, they sold us out to the Muslims. I forgave them, but not after much agony and emotional trauma. I had to realize they were in a spiritual battle over their heads. They were good men but not up to the warfare we endured. Of course, I had to confess I was not up to the task as well. Only Jesus carried us through this dark season.

All these thoughts had been stirred up by our captors and the interrogation we endured several hours previous. We had left our hotel that morning to go visit the Garden Tomb where many believe Jesus was buried and rose from the dead. We almost walked to the tomb because it was so close to where we were staying, but we decided to drive as we would go up to the Mount of Olives later that day. It was early morning as we sat in the beautiful garden that many believed was where Jesus was buried. The sun shone brilliantly without a cloud in the sky. The birds were chirping songs of delight that brought a gentle peace to my soul.

It was still cool as we studied the "Skull of the Rock." This was the face of the hill where it was also believed Jesus was crucified called Golgotha. It was not a serene view as before the skull-like face was now a bus depot with lots of noise and traffic. Above the Skull was a Muslim cemetery. It could barely be seen over the crest of the bluff. I thought the likeness of the skull looked different this year. I asked a guide about it and he said part of the nose-like feature had fallen off during a storm. It did not appear as a human skull now. I laughed to myself inwardly, that someone would take this as a sign of Jesus's return and write a book on it. I looked to Marie to share my satire, but she was deep in prayer, so I left her to meditate and ponder the death of Jesus.

Mary was unique to the human race in that she had stood at the cross with Jesus's mother as He suffered and died for our sins. I tried to imagine what her tears meant as her memory visited this sacred site.

God had chosen this place as the center of human history. It was perhaps where the Garden of Eden had been, where sin first entered the human heart, it was near where Jesus was born and here He carried His cross to die for the sins of the world. Behind me and across the garden was perhaps His tomb where He rose from the dead. There was no place more significant to our redemption or any place of records like this spot of salvation. I had visited this holy mecca for many years. I truly enjoyed experiencing God's glory and presence in this special garden. Last year, we brought our close friends to Israel for our prayer breakfast with the Knesset.

Leonardo and Mercedes had been born in Cuba. Castro had put his dad in a concentration camp for being a pastor. Once he was released, his family made their way to America. It was Leonardo's father who had gotten me connected with my ministries in Cuba. They had much to be thankful for in their lives. Leonardo had a wonderful job with a successful contracting and building company when he was suddenly let go several years ago.

Out of his brokenness and despair, God raised him up and led him to form his own company after almost losing all they had. Within a few years, his company had become one of the fastest-growing contractors in Central Florida, not just one year but two years in a row, which is unheard of for businesses. The blessings of God were not lost on this precious couple and their family. I could see God was touching them in a very powerful way as we sat near the tomb. It is remarkable when you get to see someone come to the garden tomb for the first time. I remembered as we took communion in an alcove in the garden—how emotional it was for them to take of the body and blood of Jesus so close to where He suffered and bled for us. He literally paid the price for our sins. This beautiful couple shed many tears that morning in the presence of the Lord. The sense of His love permeated the depth of our soul as we drew near to our Savior. I kept thinking how good God is and how He loves us with an everlasting love that knows no limits.

Now, I was ready to go to the tomb itself. Marie was still in her holy trance, letting God overwhelm her with His love. I decided to let her be and walk over to the tomb and wait for her there. Hardly anyone was there that morning, which made it extra nice. The busloads of tourists had not yet arrived. Yet, I could not help but sense someone had followed us from the hotel. It was eerie, but my focus was on Jesus, so I put the thought off. As I approached the tomb, walking down some steps, it appeared as just another burial site on the surface, hewn out of rock to place a rich man's body, so the Bible stated. The first time I entered the tomb a number of years ago, I was with my initial team of twenty-four. It was not as quiet as it was this morning. I remembered expecting something dramatic when I went in to see where Jesus was laid to rest. Yet, nothing unusual happened. It was actually kind of a dud for me.

I did my best to imagine and conjure up something to express the magnitude of the event, but nothing came. I was saddened and disappointed, but the next times I ventured to the tomb in the following years, I was often deeply touched and moved by the Spirit impressing upon my spirit the sacrifice and love of Jesus. After all, the Resurrection of Jesus, along with His crucifixion, are the two most important historical moments in human history. They encapsulate the entire drama of our separation from God to our restoration and reconciliation with our Creator all through His Son, Jesus. As I stood in the tomb, I felt a gentle hand rest on my back. I thought of an angel. When I turned it was Marie, truly an angel, but not of the celestial kind. Together, we pondered Jesus and His Resurrection. Jesus had brought us together for our special mission to awaken the world to His return. That thought weighed heavy on our hearts. The wonder of it increased our oneness and love for each other, forming a bond that could never be broken.

I looked into her face and thought how beautiful she was. I could not help but kiss her as we were alone in the tomb. Then I thought lightning might strike me for such an act. It was my Catholic background rising to quench this special moment of love. Marie snuggled up next to me, and I had to resist the next thoughts that raced through my body. It was time for us to leave. The peace of God had blessed our souls. Now we were off to the Mount of Olives. As we left the parking lot, our peace was suddenly jarred from us as a car struck us in the back side of our vehicle.

"Oh, man, can you believe this?" I said to Marie, while trying to get my emotions under control. I had inherited my father's curse of impatience, especially in my driving habits, so I had to stop and turn this accident over to God. "Please help me to be calm and nice," I prayed. *How easily we lose our peace in the midst of this world*, I thought to myself. When I got out of the car, people had gathered all around us on this busy street. The driver and another man came up to me and said how sorry they were. It was their fault, they assured me as I went to survey the damage. It was not too bad except the rear tire was twisted and flat.

"Let us help you," the elderly man said in such a kind voice. "We can get a tow truck for you and give you a lift back to where you are staying."

This was typical of what we had experienced since we checked into the National. Everyone treated us like a king and queen. We had been told the king of Jordan used to stay at the National before Jerusalem was retaken by the Israelis in the 1967 war. We felt like royalty in their kind charge. I thought about their offer as I went through what I needed to do—call the car rental place, get their information, and so forth. Maybe it would be easier to get back to the hotel where they would surely help us to get this situation taken care of and get a new rental to drive, and be back on the road. I poked my head into our car and asked Marie what she thought. "Whatever you think best," she replied. She still seemed fine and content. I guess I was the only one who had lost his peace.

"Alright. That sounds good to us," as I helped get Marie out of the car. "No one seems to be hurt. We will take your gracious offer." How naïve I was as I looked back on what transpired shortly after we got into their vehicle. We drove one block and as I looked up, a gun was pointed right in my face. "Be calm and say nothing," the old man said with a smile as if to infer: *we have you in our trap like a rat ready to be killed.* "You are powerless to resist."

At first I was confused. Were we being robbed? Then as I saw Marie, I realized our worst fears had come to pass. These were Islamic terrorists, fulfilling the fatwa on our lives. Who told them we were here, I wondered? My eyes flashed to see outside the car and then inside again. This was no game, but real danger. I wanted to act like a tiger, but the Lord's hand kept me from my foolishness.

Then I thought, *How could we have been so dumb as to spend a week in the Muslim section of Jerusalem after what we had been through with Fiza?* I tried to quiet my mind by stopping my second guessing the what-ifs. That would only lead to panic and frustration.

I knew Marie was already praying, so I started to pray to God for a miracle. We were in the firestorm, and only God could deliver us from these Babylonians. "May we have the faith and courage of Daniel," I prayed. "Shut the lions' mouths and keep us from the devourer." Scripture came to me that God would give me all I needed to say. I yielded my heart to God and prayed for Marie and me to be filled with the Holy Spirit. I began to claim the promises of God that we would walk through the fire and not be burned. For the God who parted the Red Sea, our escape would be a piece of cake.

It was hard to dismiss my doubts and mounting fears, but I prayed for this mountain to be cast into the sea and for God to be glorified. I held Marie's hand as we drove into the West Bank and parked behind a mosque. We were led out to the back of some building. They had not blindfolded us, which meant they did not intend for us to survive. I did not share that with Marie. A man dressed in all white with a *taqiyah* or cap on his head came to us. He read a paper he held, declaring our guilt for helping to convert a Muslim girl to Christianity. Death to the infidel was the will of Allah. We were then seated and the interrogation began.

"Where is Fiza now?" they inquired.

"I do not know," I responded, knowing Marie did know where she lived, but I did not. Marie had kept a loving connection with Fiza, who had become engaged recently while at medical school.

"You do know. She is bonded to you for life for what you did for her. Tell us the truth," he demanded.

"We are followers of Jesus. We do not lie. He is our protector, and we do not fear for He is able to deliver us from your threats, and if He does not, He still reigns as our Lord and Savior."

"Jesus will not save you," he mocked. "We believe in Jesus as well."

"Yes, but not as the infinite God-man who died on the cross to save us from our sins and rose from the dead to prove to all the world He is the King of kings, " I responded.

"Why do you hate Muslims?" he asked, ignoring my witness.

"We don't," I replied. "We love Muslims. I have several friends who are Muslims. I have seen Muslims all throughout the world. I do not hate them or you."

"Then why convert this girl to Christianity?"

"We did not convert her. We merely protected her after her family threatened to kill her."

"Do you not realize Allah will win this war? Everyone will submit to Allah in the end. Your hope is as a rope of sand. Even Jesus will bow to Mohammad when He returns," he stated.

"That will never happen. In the end, every knee will bow to Jesus and every tongue will confess Him as Lord," I boldly responded.

"Now let me tell you what is going to happen. We will lock you away for the night. Then in the morning, you will read your confession to put on video. After that, we will cut off your heads to show the power of Allah and the empty promises of your Jesus," he declared to us our fate. Then he turned to the guards. "Take them away."

The threat of imminent death awakened us to our need to share our most sacred thoughts. Like Jesus at the Last Supper when He knew He would be put to death the next day, He shared with His disciples His most intimate feelings and teachings. Now we knew it was time to tell one another how much we loved each other. Alone in a room barely large enough for two people, we turned to look each other in the eye and open our hearts. Marie was the love of my life. Without her I would be lost. My life would be empty of the joys of a wonderful wife and amazing family. We had endured countless attacks, traumas, and stress that would have destroyed the average couple, and a host of trials meant to rob us of our love and our service to Jesus, but we loved each other even more through all we had endured.

"Do you remember that day we first met years ago?" Marie asked, for it was her favorite story that we shared.

"Which time?" I joked with her.

"In America," she responded as she hugged me tight.

"How could I forget? Bart and I went to see this woman we had heard about who could help set the captives free on the Trail! I remember as if it was yesterday," as I began to tell the start of our love affair one

44

more time. The storefront was familiar I thought as we pulled up to New Beginnings Ministry.

"Recognize it?" Bart asked me.

"Yes, I do. How could I forget," I responded as I remembered the day Bart and I prayed outside Hu's grocery years back. We had been witnessing to the homeless when one of them pointed out to us that Hu's was the biggest dealer in girls and drugs. When I went to confront the owner, he blew me off and threatened to kill me. Bart and I stood on the sidewalk along the Trail and cursed Hu's store. "If he will not repent, remove him and this den of iniquity," I prayed in Jesus's name. We took His authority and power and believed Hu would be cursed and his evil would cease.

A month later we received word that Hu's grocery was closed down by a fire. No one knew where Hu was. Bart and I got a little spooked by the answer to that prayer. Wow! If it was only that simple every time we prayed for a miracle. God in His wisdom had acted swiftly and with judgment. I took a minute to pray for Hu's soul that morning.

"Lord, do whatever it takes to bring Hu to surrender His life to Jesus," I asked. It was a rather solemn request for I knew if he did not repent and believe, he would end up in the fires of hell. Dwight L. Moody, the famous evangelist, said one should shed a tear when thinking of someone lost and destined for eternal separation from God. Imagine the agony of knowing how real God is after one dies and understanding you will never be able to experience your Creator's love. Oh, the sorrow of such suffering. Jesus compared it to being burned alive forever with no hope of it ever ceasing.

My pastor friend once told me he had a man who came to visit him in his office. He had worked on the railroads. He said he died and went to hell. He saw people screaming as they burned with fire. Then he was inflamed with the brimstone of hell. He had never felt such agony. My friend asked him if he had ever experienced any real injury that he could compare it to. He undid his belt and lowered his pants. Both of his legs were scarred from a fiery accident he suffered when he was working on a train accident. He stated that did not compare to when he went to hell and burned alive. I shook after those terrible thoughts as we entered the building ready to meet this mystery woman Bart had heard so much about.

"When we walked into the ministry office, there you were. Hair in a ponytail, blue jeans and tee shirt ready for a day of battle on the streets of Orlando. I was struck by your innocent beauty. I couldn't even speak. I was tongue tied. Bart had to speak for me as I stumbled for words. Love at first sight."

"I was touched by this rugged stranger who loved Jesus as much as I did," Marie added. "We definitely had a strong sexual attraction. We had to really work at behaving ourselves."

"Yes, I almost forgot why we had come to see you. I wanted to ask you out on the spot. That cute Israeli accent made me spellbound over you. The killer was that first date. Here we were talking small talk at that fancy restaurant."

"Yeah, Outback Steak House, some exquisite place," she interjected.

"Well, we were still pretty young and living on ministry salaries. That didn't get us into the top restaurants in Orlando."

"I loved it, just being with you, hearing about your love for Jesus and you being so handsome. I was hooked from the start."

"Is that why you went to the core of our issue?" I asked Marie.

"A girl's got to look out for herself and get the guy interested. I thought that would get your attention."

We laughed as we reminisced how Marie stirred up the hornet's nest in our conversation. "All I said was, you don't remember me, do you?"

"That got my attention, but when I started to scan my memories, I came up empty. I was at a loss. I was embarrassed and had no idea how to respond. How bad was I? I didn't even remember meeting you? Talk about a turn off. I thought I had lost all chance of having a second date."

"You almost fell out of your chair when I told you we had slept together the first night we met."

"What would you expect? I had no idea who you were. You loved teasing me. Then you said it was long ago, so I did not think you would remember. I was so puzzled.

When? Where?" I began to ask.

"Think hard," you said with a smile. "Israel, small village, Jesus, prostitute ..."

"What, no way. You are Mary," I gasped. "But how?" Talk about shock. It was like getting hit with a ninety-mile-an-hour fastball in the coconut or head if you are not a baseball fan.

"Of all people you should know time travel. Jesus sent me here to work with the prostitutes after He rose from the dead and was getting ready to ascend into heaven. He told me He had a gift for me, a precious gift. I would find it in a distant land with a man I had slept with in my former days. We would have a great love and life and have a blessed family and ministry. Then, before I knew it, I was traveling forward to 1980 where we would meet. The rest is history."

I embraced her with all my heart. Yes, what a history we have had. We completed each other as one in body, soul, and spirit. "You are the best thing that ever happened to me," I said with a tone that conveyed a man's love for his woman as precious and deep as possible in their last night together.

"No," she differed. "You are the best thing that ever happened to me."

It was our favorite line that we would repeat every so often. How we needed each other now, our last night looking at a gruesome death, but what an honor to die for Jesus. We didn't want it, but we were ready to witness to Jesus as the Messiah until the end.

"God used you to bring deep healing in my soul," Marie confessed.

"No, Jesus did that long before we met," I assured her.

"Jesus did set me free, but I had a long way to go to experience the healing I needed to love the man God gave me. You made that possible by valuing me as a person in the beauty of my mind and spirit. You loved me without reservation, unconditionally, with all my sins and faults. I was a fractured human being. Jesus made me whole, but He used you to bring about the healing I desperately desired," she confessed with a passion that touched me at the core of my emotions.

"You did the same for me. Without you, I would be divorced three times and an alcoholic," I jested with her, but truly believed that would have been my fate. "Our love in Jesus Christ transformed our lives to His glory."

We knew such oneness that few couples ever achieved. Yes, we were far from perfect, but in our love for one another we were raised to a new level of living that without each other we could never have known. People often teased us that we should have our own reality television show. We complement one another with such fun and joy and crazy situations.

It was difficult to think this was the end for us. God surely had more for us to do. Yet, that is man's thoughts. His ways are not our ways. We had given our best to the Master. Jesus had carried us through so many times of failures and sins. We owed Him everything in our lives for all eternity. We were blessed to have had the life we knew together as one in Jesus Christ.

Can anyone imagine, except a former prostitute, the pain and corruption Marie had endured? Yet, she was a miracle of Jesus. She lived a full beautiful life with a loving husband of thirty-eight years, three fantastic children, and six grandchildren with more to come. How wonderful a life Jesus had given her. How she had blessed me with her spiritual strength and emotional kindness. In one sense, we both could not wait to see Jesus again.

Cinderella and the Knight, we would often tease each other with those special titles that for us described who we were to one another. She was a true Cinderella to me. The beauty of the ball with a soul to match. The dream of every man for his woman. To her, I was her knight in shining armor, who had rescued her from the hell of her former existence. Even though Jesus had actually done that for Marie, it was nice she thought of me as her deliverer from evil to a life of unlimited blessings. She saw me through the eyes of the words of Jesus who said, "One who is forgiven much, loves much." The Man who captured her soul first was Jesus, and then He graciously gave her to me. These treasures of life were rooted in her experiences in Israel before she traveled in time to the USA.

Now you know why Marie loves Israel, her home and coveted jewel. It was her place of birth where she met Jesus. She followed Him and cared for Him. Often she struggled with her emotions and what kind of love she felt. His dynamic personality and His actions of love and kindness drew her to Him. She struggled against fantasies of marrying Him. She knew this was not possible, yet His love was so overwhelming she could barely resist her thoughts of true love for Him.

When Marie came into the 20th century, she heard Helen Ready sing, "I Don't Know How to Love Him," from the musical, *Jesus Christ Superstar*. She said, "That is me," which really was her. She was that woman in real life. Even though neither of us could stand the play itself, we loved some of its music. I would often hear her humming and singing that song after we were married. I confess, at times I felt a little jealous, even though I knew Jesus's love was not for marriage. Marie's heart was given solely to me as her one and only.

Now, as we went late into the night without any possibility of sleep, we found our only peace was in the absolute knowledge that death was not an end but a glorious new beginning. We needed to have no fear, but strengthen one another in our faith in Jesus and our love for each other. It was tough thinking we would miss the kids and grand-kids. They would be alright. Their great faith would see them through. They would know where we would be in the heavens with Jesus. That brought us the comfort we needed in our hour of trial. There would be joy in the morning!

Chapter 6

DELIVERANCE AND CALL, AD 2019

"We have seen so many miracles. We know Jesus is real and is the Savior of our souls," I said softly to Marie but with tremendous conviction. "Let us pray for our captors and their salvation, that they will see Jesus in us. Our deaths will be seeds of faith in their souls. God grant us the courage to face this tribulation with love and hope. I believe He can still rescue us, but if He chooses not to, I will always trust Him." The words I spoke were not mine but Christ in me. I was weak and fearful, but in Him I felt like a mighty lion, the Lion of Judah. "He will never leave us nor forsake us. He promised to give us every word to say," as we began to recite Psalm 91 together.

Psalm 91 was a wonderful reminder that as we dwelt in the shadow of the Almighty, He would protect us from the snare of the fowler. He would be our shield and buckler. Though arrows would come at us in the night, they would not harm us. We had been like the shepherd king David, who wrote many of the Psalms. God, through us, had slain many giants and bears and defeated the demons that come at night. Jesus truly was our fortress of strength and power. We ran to Him when the enemy came at us like a lion.

We held onto each other in a deep silence as though we were our own life vests that night. If we let go, we would float away. We each could not bear being apart from the one we loved, so we held tight. We prayed for God to protect our kids and use them for His glory. All that we believed in and trusted began to flow up from our belly as rivers of living water, proclaiming our victory in Christ. Nothing could separate us from the love of God.

Then God acted. I sensed that wave of time moving me from the room. Wait I cried, I cannot leave Marie, but in an instant I was in another time, in another place. I looked up and saw three men hanging on a cross. In the middle was Jesus, covered in blood from head to toe. The crown of thorns pierced into His brow. The nails in His hands and feet nauseated me. The stripes on His back with the wounded open flesh made me want to cry out for Him to receive mercy.

His eyes were heavy with grief, staring at someone before Him. I looked to see His mother, His beloved John, and several others weeping at His feet. Then I realized Mary, the one I had seen at Jesus's feet wetting them with her tears, was bent over sobbing. Her tears could not touch His soles, but they moved upon His heart. "He who is forgiven much loves much," I remembered Him saying to Simon. Oh how Mary loved Him. She was my Marie.

I wanted to go comfort her, but I was not allowed. An angel stood by my side and told me to stay at a distance. My gaze returned to Jesus. The weight of the world was upon His shoulders. "Behold, the Lamb of God who takes away the sin of the world," John the Baptist had said that morning along the Sea of Galilee. The darkness of sin and the soul of humanity had crept into the day. The sun was no more. The Father had turned His back on His only begotten Son.

Suddenly, Jesus cried out, "Father, forgive them for they know not what they do." *Even in His suffering, He thinks of others,* I thought. How we need the grace and mercy of God for our sins. The Father would answer Jesus's prayer in a myriad of ways—for our personal salvation, but also for our families and for the nations.

I glanced to my side and there were the soldiers casting lots to divide up His clothes. The religious leaders began to mock Him. "He saved others, why doesn't He save Himself," they mocked and yelled as if to cover up their own fears.

I wanted to shout at them and rebuke them for the pain in my soul was an abyss of mourning as I saw Jesus on the cross. "If You are the King of the Jews, save yourself," they tormented Him.

There above His head was the sign in Greek, Latin, and Hebrew, declaring Jesus as the King of the Jews. The world would never understand what kind of King He was. Everyone dies for the king in our nations, but in God's kingdom, the King gives His life as a sacrifice for us. It is the wonder of His love. The King came to die but was soon to come and reign with all authority and power. His love inspired our hearts to love and serve Him. Because of His sacrifice, we could know the love of God, full of joy and hope. I would follow this King anywhere, I had promised Him years ago. He alone is worthy as tears streaked my cheeks.

Then one of the criminals hanging next to Him blasphemed Him saying, "If You are the Christ, save Yourself." The other thief rebuked him by saying, "Do you not even fear God, seeing you are under the same condemnation? And we indeed justly, for we receive the just reward of our deeds; but this Man has done nothing wrong." Then he said to Jesus, "Lord, remember me when You come into Your kingdom."

Jesus said to him, "Assuredly, I say to you, today you will be with Me in Paradise."

In that moment, His words struck me in my heart like a lance driving me to the ground. I could not stand under the force of His love and forgiveness in contrast to the betrayal He had endured. I thought, today I will be with Him in Paradise. Oh, how I wanted to go be with Marie, but I was barred from going near her. She had her part to play, and I could not change that.

The darkness increased so that from the sixth hour to the ninth hour, it had spread over the entire earth. The sun had no light and the veil in the temple was torn in two as Jesus cried out to His Father, "My God, My God, why have You forsaken Me?" For the first time in all eternity, Jesus, the Son of God, the incarnated God, the Second Person of the Trinity, of the one true God who is three Divine Persons in One Godhead, was separated from His Father. This was the worst of God's judgment that was laid on Jesus. In that moment, Jesus knew the extreme debt of our sin. Nothing as terrible as this had ever touched His Being. It was as though He was ripped from His Father's womb.

As our debt was paid, Jesus's suffering could now end. "Father, into Your hands I commit My spirit." He breathed His last. Now the way was made for the world to know peace with God. His blood had appeased God's wrath and reconciled us to the living God. His blood did for us what the blood of sheep and bulls could only symbolize. The sinless one, Jesus Christ, the only man to ever live who did not sin, became the Lamb without blemish, the Passover Lamb, who took all of our sins upon Himself so we could be forgiven and cleansed and given a brand-new destiny.

When one of the centurions saw what had happened, he glorified the Creator saying, "This was the Son of God."

I began to think of the night I had first met Jesus. Even though I had been raised in the church and taught all about Jesus, I did not know Him as my Savior. I was consumed with myself and what I could achieve with my life for my glory. Sports were my god, especially baseball. After I was released from the Cubs organization, my life collapsed into depression and ruin. Why was I born? Is there any purpose in life? How do I heal the brokenness of my life? I had lots of questions but no answers. I lived with a knife stuck in the core of my being without any relief. Something had to give. Fortunately by God's grace, my pride shattered, and I came to Jesus in whatever humility I had.

It began as I lay on my bed in the agonies of failure in my young life. The pain from the arrows of my sins ravaged my soul with aloneness and emptiness. My vanity had left me alienated and unable to love. In the depth of my desolation, Jesus came to me in the darkness of that night to light up my world with His love and hope. When I cried out to Him to take my life because I did not want it anymore, He instantly came into my room and surrounded me with His cloud of love. In His presence, my pain vanished as my sins were cleansed away. I wanted to stay with Him forever.

His love soothed and healed the wounds of my soul. For the first time in my life, I knew Jesus was real, that God loved me. He had died for me, rose from the dead, ascended into heaven, and is coming again. From that moment forward, He began to take me on the time travels through the centuries to shape me and give me understanding of the mysteries of His mission that all who would believe in Him should not perish but have eternal life. That night, He commissioned me to go to the world with His message of love, hope, and redemption. When I awoke in the morning, I was a transformed person full of His love and presence. There is no one like Jesus nor His love.

When I looked up to Jesus, they were taking Him down from the cross. Marie was there with Mary and John. Even though I knew the victory of His salvation, I felt a deep sadness in my spirit. The suffering He had endured for me and for all humanity tore at my heart for I loved Him.

The next thing I knew, I was lying in a bed next to Marie. We were not in Jerusalem, not under the Muslim threat. Where were we? Never before in my time travels did I not return to the same place I had left. This was all new to me, but I was so grateful that I wanted to shout with joy. I looked at Marie, and she was smiling.

"I know where we are. At Jason's and Machala's house in the Turks." She was right. I recognized the bedroom as soon as she said it. We sat up together. We had so much to say.

"We were at the cross. Did you see me?" I asked in wonder.

"No, I did not see you, but I knew you were there. An angel told me. I was so consumed with my grief, seeing Jesus suffer as He did, I could not look for you."

"Your tears touched His heart," I affirmed her.

"Oh, John, His death set us free. The angel told me, we would receive a wondrous gift from Jesus, and this is it. We are in the Turks safe from the terrorists. Can you believe it?" she cried with joy.

"Won't they be surprised when they come to get us. I feel bad for the guards. No one will believe that we disappeared," I laughed. "They will probably behead them in our place"

"Or lead them to believe in Jesus," she added.

"How long do you think we have at Jason's?" I wondered out loud.

"One day will be enough for me, but I hope it is weeks," she added, resting in the bed safe and secure from all harm.

Jason and Machala were long-time friends who had given us each year three or more weeks at their house in the Turks and Caicos. It was Paradise, no pun intended.

We were with Jesus in Paradise on this island of romance and peace. The house was a block's walk to the most beautiful beach in the world on Sapodilla Bay. We had spent countless hours, floating on the calm water, relaxing and being renewed by the beauty of the sun, sky, sea, and hills. God's goodness surpassed anything I could imagine at this time. His grace once more proved the salvation of our lives. We owed Him everything. He had delivered us from the fire and shut the mouths of the lions. We were grateful to serve Him in this hour before Jesus returned. That was our call from God: to prepare the way for the second coming of Christ.

The second time we went to Jerusalem, ten years ago, God sent us to seven different spots throughout Israel to pray. Each time of intercession seemed to be more powerful than the first. The most memorable was our time on the temple mount. Thirty of us had gone to Israel to scout out the land in terms of doing ministry in Israel. We ended up praying throughout Israel in seven key locations, which we had not planned, but realized at the end of our trip that is what God had led us to do.

We had gone to pray on this most sacred site where the temple and the Holy of Holies were standing in Jesus's day. When we arrived, there was a group of Asian believers already praying at a gazebo where many believe the Holy of Holies was. They invited us to join them. Suddenly, the Spirit of God came upon us. We began to cry out in prayer, speak in tongues, and prophesy. My loud voice was echoing over the temple mount. My wonderful wife suggested I lower my voice as armed guards had surrounded us. I assumed they were Muslims, but I am still not certain even today. Maybe they were angels sent to protect us? They did not ask us to be quiet but stood almost as guards around us. So, I continued with the others to speak out in the name of Jesus.

After a time, the Asians said they had to leave, so we kept praying, speaking in tongues, and prophesying, all to the glory of God. Their leader led them away, but after a hundred feet or so, she came running back to us. I asked her what was wrong. Nothing, she replied. She told me that when she had turned to look at us, she saw us engulfed in the flames of the Holy Spirit. Immediately after she said that, the fire of the Spirit stirred us up once more. We began to lay hands on one another and prophesy and cry out for God to pour out His Spirit on all Israel.

The guards continued to remain silent, standing watch around us as we kept praying. Words fail to describe the commotion and move of God upon us. I noticed that one of the men with us, J. T., was sitting weeping. Later, we discovered God had struck him blind. He was told you thought you could see, but you cannot. When I give you your sight back, then you will be able to truly see. After about a half hour, God restored his sight, and he began to see in the Spirit. This encounter with God transformed his life.

As we were praying, finally one of the guards came to me and said we needed to stop as it was time for the Muslims to gather for their Friday service. He was very gracious and kind. So, we ceased praying and began to leave. A man then came up to me and introduced himself as Bob Gibson, the son of Paul Gibson, a famous owner of a Christian television station. He had been filming up on the temple mount and saw what had happened.

As I remember, he said he had never seen anything quite like what he had just witnessed as we prayed, spoke in tongues, and prophesied. He asked who we were as we walked together down off the temple mount. I told him we were Methodists. He refused to believe me. Later, I was told he spoke about this event on his show. People called me and asked if that was us he was talking about. It was, I humbly responded.

We had six other mighty encounters during our time in Israel. We glowed in His presence when we returned to Orlando, Florida.

A week later, I was in prayer and study for about three hours when I sensed the Holy Spirit telling me to go run. I thought that was strange, but in obedience I went on my two-mile jog. As I ran along a canal near my home, suddenly the Holy Spirit began to say to me, "The return of My Son, Jesus Christ is imminent. I want you to go to the church, to the nations, and to Israel and call people to:

- Repent and believe;
- Be baptized in the Holy Spirit;
- Deny self, to take up their cross, and to follow Jesus.

Wow! I had a hard time comprehending what I had just heard. As I kept running, the significance of this message overwhelmed and puzzled me. Had I heard right? What did this mean? How was I to do this? I got home and wrote down what I had received and pondered where this would lead. I assumed, wrongly, that I would somehow fulfill this call of God at the church where I was pastor, but that was not to be. Through a series of events, God made it clear I was to retire from the United Methodist Church and begin to prepare the way for Jesus's return. This would free me to go as He directed me to all people and churches.

Within three months, I retired and launched this new ministry to prepare for Jesus's second coming. Since that time, God had put me on an adventure that is beyond anything I could ever have imagined or asked. We started a small church as our evangelism and mission base. We began a television ministry to share the message of His coming. We took in the Muslim girl, Fiza, to save her life from honor killing. This became the international story I wrote earlier about. This provided the opportunity to share the love of Jesus to millions throughout the world on secular television.

One of the major networks asked if we would give them the exclusive story of what happened in saving Fiza's life. We agreed if they would let me share the Gospel of Jesus without editing it. They concurred, so they came to our house and interviewed us for over an hour. This went out to the whole world by the internet. It can still be seen on the internet to this day. One day a close friend of ours was cleaning a pool, as was his business, and the owner of the house began talking to him about friends in Egypt. They had seen on television my testimony of Jesus and the Fiza story. These people were Muslims who were watching, and at the end of the show, they gave their lives to Jesus.

When God opens a door and you walk through it, nothing is impossible. The Spirit does miracle after miracle. There are times when I reflect on what has happened in our ministry, and I cannot believe it. I never would have imagined God would use Marie and me to touch millions of lives for Jesus, but He has, all to His glory. We came under great persecution for following Jesus no matter the cost, but God protected us throughout that year of attack. He began to send me to Israel, to the church, and to the nations.

We have seen thousands of end-time messengers raised up and are training them to go and share the Word of Jesus. I believe millions have heard the hope of Christ because of the call God gave me that day along the canal, but really it began the night I met Jesus when He told me to go into the world and tell people about Him. All of this was fulfilled in His time.

With all of those blessings He began to send me on His time travels. As I journal those experiences, I am waiting to see the mystery of all He has shown me in Eden, with Noah, in Babel, with Abraham, David, Jesus, and Pentecost. I know there is a divine puzzle within these travels, that one day the Spirit will give me the revelation knowledge to share with the world.

That night as Marie rested, I went to the beach to watch the sunset and meditate with God. I wrote this in my journal:

> The golden orb descends behind the distant jagged hills. Still, its light illuminates the crescent moon and paints the clouds with purple and pink and scatterings of white. A lone seagull crosses the sky, looking for a friend. The constant motion of the sea beckons me to race atop its rhythmic caps to distant lands. The smoky tail of a jet lines the blue ceiling to the heavens.

> Tonight the beach is filled with people. Two families have a fancy dining table with a chef fixing dinner between their house and the water—elegant, I might add. Another couple of families are having pictures taken with the setting sun as their backdrop. Others lay on their lounge chairs, silently watching the day give way to the night.

I walk to the end of the pier to escape the crowd. The clear water reveals no sharks or stingrays, only sand and grass with lots of holes, homes for crabs. As I ponder the beauty of this half hour revelation of God's glory, I try to picture the more wonderful vision of Jesus's return.

The trumpet will sound ... the sun will be darkened, and the moon will not give its light; the stars will fall from heaven and the powers of the heavens will be shaken. Then the sign of the Son of Man will appear in heaven, and then all the tribes of the earth will mourn, and they will see the Son of Man coming on the clouds of heaven with power and great glory. And He will send His angels with the sound of a great trumpet, and they will gather together His elect from the four winds, from one end of heaven to the other. Matthew 24:29-31.

It always amazes me that Jesus had a worldview since He was from a small village at the end of an empire in the middle of nowhere from the world's perspective. He said out of that worldview: "Go into all the world ... all the tribes of the earth will see Him ... the elect will be gathered from the four winds ... Jesus came not just for Israel but for all humanity and all the nations of the earth, behold the Lamb of God who takes away the sin of the world ... His glory will be seen by all people."

This coming of the Messiah will transcend all the beauty and majesty that the sunset has to offer us. Jesus's return will overwhelm our senses, as we will be taken up and receive our glorified bodies. We will be the central part of what happens in the skies of the earth. "In the twinkling of an eye we will all be changed at the last trumpet, and the dead will be raised incorruptible ... for the corruptible must put on incorruption and this mortal body must put on immortality." ICorinthians 15:52-53.

How do you paint such a picture of resurrection power, the same that raised Jesus from the dead will fill the heavens with His glory? I cannot envision what we will see and what we will say in that moment of trans-figuration. Perhaps it will be a blast of white, whiter than any white we know. When do our horses come? When do we ride with Jesus?

Now I saw heaven opened and behold a white horse. And He who sat on him was called Faithful and True, and in righteousness He judges and makes war. His eyes were like a flame of fire, and on His head were many crowns. He had a name written that no one knew except Himself. He was clothed with a robe dipped in blood and His name is called the Word of God. Revelation 19:11-13.

I cannot wait to live that sunset on this age of sin and death. Jesus brings His armies and "out of His mouth goes a sharp sword that with it He should strike the nations. And He Himself will rule them with a rod of iron … And He has on His robe and on His thigh a name written: King of kings and Lord of lords." Rev. 19:15-16.

No wonder when Jesus makes all things new; there is the river of life flowing from His throne with the tree of life, and its leaves are for the healing of the nations! The conflict Jesus brings will reap havoc on the goat nations of the earth. No one will stand before Him, but all will tremble with fear.

"Then the sky receded as a scroll when it rolled up, and every mountain and island was moved out of its place. And the kings of the earth, the great men, the rich men, the commanders, the mighty men, every slave and every free man hid themselves in the caves and in the rocks of the mountains, and said to the mountains and rocks, "Fall on us and hide us from the face of Him who sits on the throne and from the wrath of the Lamb." Revelation 6:14-16.

I rejoice that we will be with Jesus in the heavens when He returns. We are the parading army destroying all that is unholy and rebellious in the world. The cleansing of the earth will be God's answer to its cry of sorrow and abuse under the weight of humanity's sins. All creation awaits the coming of Jesus. We who are holy by His blood will see the triumph of our King. What a day of rejoicing that will be!

Believe it, expect it, and prepare for it. All the things of this world will mean nothing when Jesus returns in His glory. Let go of the foolish things of this earth and live for Jesus. In Christ's love, Evangelist John.

Chapter 7
REFLECTIONS, AD 2019

" Let's test the waters," I said to Marie to see if people knew where we were or what we had endured. "I will write on my blog what I experienced this afternoon on my bike ride. It would be fun to see how our friends respond if they thought we were in Jerusalem!"

She smiled in agreement. "We could just call the kids," she then reminded me.

"No, this will be more adventurous!" I added. I sat down and wrote these words of my miracle ride that day. I could hear mumbling from Marie, "You would think we had enough adventure for a lifetime the past couple of days."

> Dear Covenant Family,
> God often gives us little reminders, which are actually big, that increase our faith and prove to us without a doubt there is a God and He loves us. God has a plan for our lives despite all the chaos and mysteries that can seek to rob us of our faith and love for God.
>
> Two days ago, Marie and I had one of those reminders. While on vacation in the beautiful Turks and Caicos, I go for an intense bike ride each day to offset all the sitting around and eating we do. On my ride, I usually talk with

God, go over events in my life, ask God for ideas to write, and so on.

The halfway point of my exercise I call Agony Hill. It is a steep "s" curve that I fly down full speed, and then I have to ascend back up the impossible climb, which can be pure agony. This is a little-traveled expanse of roadway, so I take caution but have no fear of traffic on my wild ride down the dangerous route.

It is lined at the bottom of the sharp turn with jagged rocks and shrubbery, then there is a tidal pool about ten feet past these obstacles. When I wind down my path, I cut across the road to take the best angle and keep optimum speed. It is quite exhilarating, and I need the speed so I can coast before the next hill and my return trip.

This day, my mind was focused on the book I am attempting to outline, so I was not as cautious as I usually am when heading down the steep curve. Sure enough, as I came around the bend, there was a car heading right in my path. They must have panicked because the driver turned toward the curb right in my direction, instead of moving to the center to give me room to go around him.

In an instant, I had to decide my course of action. At my high speed, I could not break to avoid the car. Do I hit it head on, or swerve off the road into a six-foot wall of jagged rocks and then possibly flip into the tidal pool? The third option is to hit a curb on the road about six inches wide and flat on top.

Without time to debate my options, I shot onto the curb, just missing the car on my left by inches. The possibility of staying on this life line was about 0 percent. There was no way I could control the bike and not veer off into this wall of possible death or very serious injury. This is all within a second of time. I zoomed onto the curb, flew by the car and somehow did not go soaring off the curb into nature's wall. This is not a straight line on the curb, but it is bending with the road. Out of control, the impossible occurred.

In a flash it was over, and I am thanking God that the impossible has happened. (Yes, I do not wear a helmet but am in my bathing suit, t-shirt, and gym shoes.) You can imagine the result if I had barreled into that car or the immovable jagged wall. My vacation would not have ended well!

With my adrenaline pumping, I biked home in record time to join Marie at the beach where I usually share some minor adventure from my trip like a vicious dog chasing me, to the beautiful view I saw, or some new house being built. Instead, I shared with her my narrow escape from possible death or terrible injury.

She listened intently without saying a word. After I finished, she said when she left the house to go to the beach, the Holy Spirit told her to pray for my protection, so she did. We estimate it was about five minutes before my potential fatal crash. When my wife prays, God in His mercy answers!

People will say, that was a coincidence, but I know better. As my son and son-in-law have asked me several times, "Why do these remarkable events happen to you all the time?" There have been too many coincidences to disregard. I know that I know that I know God is real and has a plan for my life and for your life. Prayer does make a difference in this crazy and unpredictable world. Yes, I have had prayers go unanswered, and so has Marie. That is the mystery of life, but it does not change the truth that God is real and hears our prayers. I am thankful for a wife who knows how to pray.

You and I are in God's hands. Whatever comes, He knows and has our best interest in line for our welfare. Yes, bad things happen to all of us, some worse than others. But God always loves us, and sometimes He reminds us just how much He cares, even on a bike ride down Agony Hill. I think I may change its name to Miracle Hill. Be blessed. In Christ's love, Evangelist John.

P.S. Jesus's return is imminent. Are you ready? Are you living totally for Him, in touch with Him daily in love, in prayer, in obedience and in service?

By the late afternoon, I was getting lots of responses from my article. Everyone acted as if they all knew we were in the Turks. God used His angels to perform another miracle. Our clothes from the hotel were all at our place in the Turks, the hotel and rental car bill paid, and we had our tickets to return home. Marie and I had two weeks to rest and recuperate on the beautiful beaches of Providenciales. How awesome is our God! I have discovered if you truly yield all to Jesus and allow the Holy Spirit to guide you and obey His call to prepare the way for Jesus, one's life will be full of adventure and miracles beyond belief.

That night I went down to the beach to see the sunset and reflect on God and His love again. This is what I wrote in my journal:

Dear Covenant Family,
Last night, I experienced a sense of peace that was a gift from God. The sunset He created with the sun, clouds, wind, moon, and gentle breeze expressed the glory of heaven. I cannot describe the peace or the picture I saw from the different shapes of clouds, the majestic hues of colors, the rhythm of the sea lapping up on the shore, the veiled sun in the background, the half crescent moon above, and the gulls flying across the sky. Only God could paint such a canvas that brought me peace.

As I sat on the shore, I experienced the peace that surpasses all understanding, a peace no man can create, a peace that hung over me like an angel's breath drawing me to the throne of God. There are many types of peace. The absence of war, of strife, of inner division, of anxiety, of worry, of torment can define peace. It can also be wholeness as described by *shalom* in the Bible. It is an inner unity with God, a oneness in serving God in loving obedience, where it is a flame of fire in one's soul that cannot be divided.

The ultimate peace is knowing God's forgiveness of one's sin and rebellion. I am no longer at war with God; all enmity and hate is gone. I am reconciled with God through the blood of Jesus Christ. His love reigns in my heart and mind. It is God's gift to me in the new covenant of Jesus Christ. It goes beyond feelings. I am declared in the court of heaven that I am no longer guilty of my sins. I am set free from the condemnation and bondage of death. All my debts are paid. I am alive forever with God by His grace and pardon.

The weight of my sin has been lifted never to return. I know God, and He knows me. I have a destiny and hope that can never be corrupted or taken away. The curse of sin and death are no more. All the blessings of God are mine in the divine agreement and exchange of covenant. The wrath of God has been appeased against my soul.

I did not need last night's sunset to give me that peace. I already had it in the love of Jesus Christ, in His forgiveness and gift of eternal life. Yet, the sunset symbolized to me the peace of heaven that is free from the chaos and confusion of this world. Without this peace given to me by the Prince of Peace, last night was but a brief experience, a glimpse into eternity that will fade in the morning or with the first irritation that stirs my frustration with life.

Humanity hopes if it could bottle this peace and capture it to sell to the masses—what a relief to the human race that would be. Yet, it cannot be done. No human means can give this peace that flows from the throne of God. Since Adam's sin, this peace of God has eluded us. Jesus, the Prince of Peace, came to deliver us into the loving arms of God, to restore His peace to our soul. In Him only is this peace received and discovered.

I praise God for His peace and I marvel how we who know this peace, but let such little things of this world rob us of this truth every day. In Jesus Christ, we can now have this peace and walk in victory over those demons that seek to steal from us of our joy in Him. May you and I come to know the depth of His love that in Him alone can we have this peace of Christ that the world promises but can never deliver. When the day grows dark, may we remember who we are in Christ and what we have in Him. May we rest in Him and find our sanctuary in the glory of His presence.

I think you know where you will find me tonight.
In Christ's love, Evangelist John.

The next morning Marie and I had a powerful time of worship. She had put on some stirring worship music that invited us into the presence of God. We celebrated His glory and majesty and thanked Him for our deliverance from the terrorists. The beauty of His love inspired us to sing and pray and exalt our Creator. Jesus alone was worthy to be glorified and praised. We sensed worshiping angels fill the household with adoration. We were in the heavenlies with them, magnifying the Lord.

Marie began to prophesy in the Spirit. The coming of the Lord was near. Jesus had risen from His throne. His anointing oil flowed from His robe over the whole earth. He was preparing the world for His return. God's end-time, Ezekiel army, the dead dry bones had risen to life. He had breathed His breath into them. This army was centered in Israel, but they were also in the nations building His kingdom, fighting in the spirit, battles against principalities and powers of darkness.

God had opened the door to unite the one new man, Jew and Gentile, as one in the Lordship of the Messiah. Lights of His glory permeated Israel with His army of mighty, spiritual warriors. The nations were raging against Jesus and against Israel. The goat nations were persecuting the Jews. The sheep nations were rallying to Israel's side. The King of glory was ready to come in the clouds of heaven with His angels. When the blood moon drapes its color over Jerusalem, He will come. The earthquake will split the ground around Jerusalem, and Jesus will plant His feet on the Mount of Olives. He will enter the eastern gate, and all will bow before Him.

The weight of God's glory fell upon us as she finished her word of prophecy. Tears of cleansing washed our souls as we lay prostrate before the King. "Holy, holy, holy is the Lord of hosts," we cried. "Heaven and earth are full of Your glory." Then a sweet aroma filled the room as His anointing oil became visible upon our foreheads. The oil from His robe immersed us in His presence, and the Spirit spoke to us of our calling to prepare the way for Jesus. We both sensed we were to go back to Jerusalem for the time of His return.

As we lay on the floor, with tears on our faces, I remembered the time when I was in Zambia preaching at the end of our crusades. It was the only time I ever went to Zambia during the rainy season. My friend and partner in ministry, Dexter, had asked me to come, and the one time I had was during the rainy season. The daily rains made it impossible to hold services. For one, the people walked several miles to get to the services, and they could not do so in the driving, relentless rain. The ruts in the road made it quite dangerous for us to drive. Plus, the rain on the tin roofs sounded like thunder, so you could not hear.

When I arrived the first day, clouds were all around. It had rained once and looked as though it would rain again. I said let us go golfing before we begin the crusades tomorrow. Golf was Dexter's only way to relax on the field in Zambia. We called it counseling. Dexter needs some counseling we would joke and go off to play nine holes of golf.

"We cannot," Dexter said. "We can't golf in the rain."

"We will take authority over the heavens and command it not to rain for ten days. If it does not rain as we go to play golf, then we will know we will not have rain for ten days."

We went to the Lord in prayer and commanded it not to rain for the ten days wherever we would hold services. This was impossible in our human perspective, but with God nothing is impossible. We played golf that afternoon. No rain! It did not rain for the next ten days at any of our services. The only rain was His glory and the outpouring of the Holy Spirit.

At the last service God's glory fell in a remarkable manner. As I finished the preaching on the passage where Moses asks to see God's glory, His glory came upon us. Suddenly, everyone was on the ground, on the dirt floor weeping and crying out to God for forgiveness and cleansing, to be anointed to be His messengers. This lasted for around a half hour. When we began to rise to our feet, I noticed puddles on the ground all over the sanctuary. We called them tears of glory. We pronounced the benediction and closed the service, then the physical rain burst forth as we ran to our van to stay dry. Dexter and I looked at each other in astonishment. God is so good.

As Marie and I stood up, we smelled the fragrance of God still in the air. She gazed into my eyes and said to me what she had never shared for thirty-eight years. God had told her not to share it until He opened her mouth to speak of this wonder.

"Remember, when you paid me that night in my hut for services rendered," she asked. "You gave me twice the amount owed. I took those coins and put them away. I never wanted to use it. I did not know why, but I kept it until Jesus came to my village. Then I understood. I was to use it to buy the perfume I anointed His feet with. When I broke open the flask that day as I knelt at His feet, the aroma filled the room. Today, the sweet fragrance we smelled in our worship was the same as that oil I bought with your money."

We stood in silence in awe of that revelation. We were asking ourselves what did this mean in light of the prophecy she gave.

"God will give you the mystery this week that you have been searching to know." Marie spoke with such authority, we knew it was from God. "Study your journals of your time travels, and it will be unveiled to you."

Chapter 8

THE OPEN DOOR, AD 2019

UNITED NATION VOTE SPLITS THE WORLD OVER ISRAEL

Led by Russia and the fifty Muslim nations who denounced Israel's plans to build settlements in the West Bank, called on the UN to take away Israel's authority to rule in Palestine and return it to its rightful owners.

The United States supported Israel in her right to exist, but only a handful of nations backed the US in its attempt to stop this move by Russia and the Islamic nations to bring about what amounted to a declaration of war against Israel.

In addition, a minor article following the above, Blood Moon over Jerusalem Next Month, tried to tie the vote for military action against Israel with the prophecies in the Bible and the appearance of a rare blood moon.

"Marie," I shouted. "We need to go back to Jerusalem."

In Orlando, at the same time I was reading these articles in the Turks, my nemesis saw them as well. He imagined himself in Jerusalem meeting with the terrorists telling them with great joy, he believed this meant I would go to Jerusalem, for the blood moon would coincide with Passover. I could not resist the prophecy. With a gun in his hand, he pointed it at my picture hung on the wall. "Bam, bam, bam," he shouted. "We will not miss this time."

That morning, Marie and I decided to do our favorite pastime in the Turks. We did it every day. We took our floats to the beach and rested on the calm waters of Sapodilla Bay. We would sit in our floats and lounge for about two hours. We talked and met tourists and enjoyed the peace of endless summer.

"Do you really think we should go to Jerusalem after what happened with the terrorists?" She questioned me. "Jesus said do not put the Lord your God to a foolish test."

"You think it would be foolish to go back for the blood moon at Passover, when Jesus might return?"

"Duh, yes," she replied. "They just tried to kill us. Now you want to head back into the fiery furnace. I think any normal person would say that is pretty stupid."

I laughed. "Why don't you tell me what you really think. I'll tell you what. Let's pray and see what the Spirit says."

"So, I'm the bad guy if we don't go," she snipped at me.

"No, I want you to feel you have a say in what we do. I will submit to your answer once we pray."

"Then it's easy. We are not going."

"We haven't prayed."

"I don't need to pray. I know we should stay home."

I was frustrated. I could feel my emotions rising. Why did she have to be so adamant and unbending? What was worse is that she was almost

74

always right. I felt like this when I was in the Congo helping my missionary friends set the child soldiers free, and the rebels were shooting at us late at night in the mission house. That was the last time I was able to go to the Congo. Why did I have to be so stubborn and competitive?

"Alright, then we agree together that we will not go unless the Spirit speaks to us to go," I relented.

"Yes. You got it." She shook her head at me in disbelief.

It was difficult to rest after that. I did not want to float and relax. I was upset, but it would do me no good to press the issue. We were not going, and I did not like that. I had to let it go and let God direct us.

We had always tried to live by a couple of rules. One was we did not act unless we were both in agreement. That had worked wonders for us for years. Oneness in our major decisions had been crucial to our having such a fantastic marriage. I needed to heed that rule now. We should wait to hear from God. If He wanted us to leave for Jerusalem, Marie would hear and so would I. We would take no impulsive actions.

"Oh Lord, why is this so hard for me?" I questioned God as I lounged on my float and prayed.

"You're mad at me, aren't you?" Marie asked.

"No, I'm frustrated and angry at myself. I get these great ideas, and you shoot me down with your logic that makes sense and shows me how irrational I can be. But it would be unbelievable to be in Jerusalem for the Passover and the blood moon," I added with just a hint of manipulation. *The strongholds we struggle with from our past*, I thought to myself. *We can be rather devious and resourceful to try to get our way.*

Marie was right. It would be a foolish test. How could I think of putting her in danger again? "Sorry," I eked out. How I hated to have to apologize when I thought I was right, but I was actually wrong. Marriage is such fun.

I changed the subject to the morning headlines. "Everything in the world seems to be accelerating toward the return of Jesus. The UN gives us insight into God's timing. The nations of the earth are gathering against Israel just as the prophet Zechariah wrote they would. At some point, they will surround Jerusalem with their armies. It is going to be rough days ahead."

"And you want to jump right in the middle of all that war that will unfold. Can't you see how crazy that is?"

"No more than traveling through time to the turning points of human history. God has somehow in His mystery called us to be His messengers to the world. We are not worthy or deserving. We certainly do not have the talent as others do. Yet, we have been set apart for such a time as this."

"Time travelers for Jesus," she chuckled at its craziness. "You are right though. And I am the most blessed woman in the world to be here with you."

"We make a tremendous team, the dynamic duo for Jesus." We laughed at the absurdity, but the truth can be quite hilarious when you are over your head in stress.

"I believe Russia will strike first. It is going to happen. Why not now? It would be a blessing for us to gather in the heavens with Jesus. I cannot wait for that trumpet to sound."

We often joked we were Pan Millennials concerning the theologies of the end times. It would all pan out in the end. There were so many different interpretations of the Bible concerning the end times. When people who knew the Bible shared their views, I would say that makes sense—until I heard a different view from someone else. And I would agree that they seemed right.

I knew one thing for sure: Jesus's return was imminent like a train coming down the track. It may have been delayed, but we knew it was coming soon. It would arrive, just as Jesus would surely come.

The other significant event that we held dear was the rebirth of Israel as a nation. That miracle after 2,500 years of oppression and rule by foreign powers had come to the end in 1948, when after the horrors of the Holocaust, Israel became a reborn nation. For me that was the true north of biblical prophecy. The age of the Gentiles was ending, and the focus of God was now on Israel and the return of His Son. Human history would boil down to what happened on a small piece of land situated between three continents. Jerusalem was where heaven kissed earth and opened its window to divine revelation.

"Changing the subject, I have put my journals together and written out my conclusions on the covenants. I'm going to send them to my publisher to see if he is as illuminated as I have been to God's mysteries and how all of what is happening in the world is preparing the way for Jesus to come," I shared with Marie.

"I find it fascinating that we have missed the meaning of the two covenants with Noah and Abraham or at least we were never taught their importance in the context of relating to our postmodern world. We just focused on personal salvation but ignored the importance of the other covenants and how they come together and are fulfilled in Jesus. Maybe I'm the only one who was blind to these truths," I added.

"No, I had no idea how they interconnected nor how vital they are in combating the forces of evil today. Think about it," Marie expanded on her understanding. "Personal salvation in Jesus Christ is under attack. Even in the church body, many do not believe He is the only way to salvation. Then the family unit almost collapsed. They have redefined marriage and made sexual perversion legal. Now they are trying to do away with nations. Nations without borders. It is all packaged in the guise of compassion. Yet, they undermine the very laws and truths of God."

"If this word is to get out and influence people for Jesus, God will open the door. Whenever I think I have to push the door open, God reminds me of Zambia. Whenever we went into a new area to preach the Gospel, a miracle would pave the way for people to know Jesus is the Savior and He alone is the way to life."

As I laid back on my float, I began to remember what God had done in our mission outreach in Zambia. When I first arrived, Reverend Gene Kolonga was the leader over the six churches the Congo Methodist had planted in the Copper Belt of northern Zambia. He was a holy man of God but did not believe in miracle healings. He thought they were faked by people paid to act like they were crippled and then rise up as though they could walk. At our first evening service ever in Zambia, we held a healing time. People flocked to be touched by God. The next day, Gene got up in our service and gave a testimony. He had told his pastors not to believe in these healings. Yet, last night he was the first one to be healed. His back hurt so badly, he could barely move. When he had prayer, his back was instantly healed. He took a soccer ball and began to kick it in the air and dribble it with no back pain. Everyone marveled. That day and the rest of our time was filled with miracle healings. This spread the fire of God and built the church so in a few years, we had helped plant several hundred churches! Glory to God!

The same happened in Zambezi when we went to do crusades in the farthest part of Zambia along the Zambezi River. We joked that it was so far removed, it was beyond the Great Commission. The last night of our meetings, a blind man was healed, and a person who could not walk rose up and danced before the Lord.

Perhaps, my favorite was when we met Chief Kanyama in his palace before the Rain Festival. We knelt before the chief in honor and respect of his position. Then we talked and got to know one another. After about a half hour into our conversation someone came into the room and whispered a message to the chief. We were all sitting before him, his prime minister, policemen, and leaders along with our group of ministry people. The chief nodded but at first said nothing. After a few minutes, he asked if I would go pray for a man. It seemed he had been drinking constantly for several days. Now he had collapsed on the floor of his home. He thought he may have died.

Yes, I would go and pray. I wondered if this was a test to see if I was truly a man of God, so I began to pray silently not knowing what to expect when we got to his home. As we drove to the house, which was not a hut, but a small home, I was sitting next to the prime minister. It was his son who had been drinking. He said he is a drunkard and has brought shame upon his family. I listened and prayed, asking for more guidance. When we entered the house, a man in his late twenties was lying on his side on the cement floor. There was a puddle of drool next to his mouth. He did not move. *Maybe he is dead*, I thought. The room was quickly packed with people pressing in all around us. I was next to the man on the floor and everyone was looking to me to see what I would do. I kept praying for direction. Finally, I felt led to pray with powerful authority over this man who I could tell was not dead but unconscious from drinking.

"Cast out the demons," the Spirit said to me. I began to cast out the demon of sorcery and pharmaceuticals and the bondage of sin and death, of addiction, and any demon I could think of. The man began to stir from his stupor. He looked up at me and saw a white man. He was surprised to see me to say the least. In a minute he was amazingly sober, completely lucid. Only God could do that. I asked him if he wanted to be set free from his drunkenness. He said yes, with tears in his eyes. Then the Lord led me to have him repent of his sins and cry out to Jesus to save him. When I discovered that his wife was there, I brought them together and had him ask her for forgiveness and for her to give him forgiveness. Then his whole family gathered and we went through the act of forgiveness.

He was a transformed man, but one never knows, will it last? The next few days, he showed up at every service dressed in his best suit. The next year, when I returned to the Rain Festival, I asked about him. He was singing in the choir and doing quite well. I met with him and talked with him about his life. He was truly delivered and set free. Each year after that, I met with him. I was blessed to know he walked in the liberty of the Spirit and had not returned to his old ways.

God is a door opener. If one has the faith to walk through that door, God will do more than you can ever imagine for His glory. I was confident God would open the door for us in Israel and in the writing I had done to be received and taught to help people understand the fullness of God's word and covenant.

That night Marie had a dream of a door opening inside the eastern gate in Jerusalem at the temple mount. A man dressed in a brilliant white robe beckoned her to come. As she followed him through the gate, she was bathed in the glory of God. Then she woke up.

She nudged me and said, "We are going to Jerusalem."

Chapter 9

THE CLOCK IS
TICKING, AD 2019

After reading my internet article, he knew we were on our way to Jerusalem. Once more he emailed the terror group he had contacted just a month earlier. He emphasized not to let me escape this time. He took his gun and aimed it at my picture again. "Bam, bam, bam," he shouted. "You are a dead man."

Marie had taken a picture of the Israeli coastline as we flew into Ben Gurion Airport. We were excited but also a little fearful. We had done hours of prayer, asking for guidance, protection, and wisdom. It was harder than I thought coming back to Jerusalem, but we knew it was of God. An Airbnb had opened up for us to stay at an amazing rate, especially at Passover. We never thought we would get a ticket on Delta, but we did. The impossible had happened for us to go. We never did share with our family or friends what had transpired in our most recent visit with the terrorists. One day, I thought, I would share it with our kids and grandchildren. Would they even believe us?

"Are you ready?" I asked Marie as we prepared to land. We were both tired from the long flight, but I could tell she was tense. So was I for that matter.

"As good as can be expected," she answered as she took my hand. "When you said are you ready, that reminded me of our mission trip to China years ago when we smuggled in those 1,000 DVR videos of Jesus. We met that principal of the school on one of our prayer walks through Shanghai. She invited me to speak to the students and teach some English to them."

"How could I forget? We were carrying that box of DVRs down the street to the school, and that car was following us, going very slow as we walked. We thought we were going to be arrested. The spies had found us out and here we were in broad daylight with all these illegal videos."

"Then they pulled up next to us and rolled down their window as if to call us over to them. We were ready to run."

"Yeah to where? We were trapped. They motioned for us to come to them. Our hearts were racing. I was sweating. No getting out of this one."

"All it was, we had dropped our map and they picked it up to give it to us. They were so nice."

"That was a scare."

"It was a wonderful day. I taught those Chinese students English. They were so polite and orderly. When the principal began the class, she spoke loud and clear, are you ready? Then all the students stood as one and answered in unison, "Yes, we are ready."

"I guess we are as ready as we'll ever be. We have our armor on, and we are prayed up in the Spirit," I said, with complete trust in God and His protection.

"I just wish you hadn't written that article that implied we were traveling to Jerusalem for the Passover and the blood moon," Marie spoke with a twinge of foreboding in her accent. Whenever she was nervous she would lose her American accent and fall back into her ancient Hebrew accent. It was quite cute I thought.

"I agree, but it is all in God's hands now," I assured her as I glanced out the window.

Marie replied, "We have never felt unsafe in Israel. All the soldiers with guns and the security they have. It is safer than America."

"Oh, the only time we felt uneasy was when we traveled with Frank up to Galilee. On the way home, I knew by heart the route to Jerusalem, but he had the Waze working, and it said turn here. I did, but I knew this was wrong. Before we realized it, we were in the frontier country of Samaria, winding up into the mountains. No guardrails. Narrow road and it was if we were driving off into space. Frank was hyperventilating in the back seat."

"You wouldn't stop laughing at poor Frank."

"I wasn't laughing at him. I was nervous. Instead of tears, laughter came out. It was uncontrollable."

"He lost it when you said you were laughing so hard, your eyes were crying and you couldn't see as you drove on the edge of those dangerous cliffs along the highway."

"I never knew there were such steep mountains in Israel," I remarked, "Then when we were on the flat plains, it got somewhat scary. It was like we were in the heart of where the terrorists would train. We saw some bombed-out military vehicles. Finally we made it to the backside of Jericho, was it? Anyway, it was challenging. We told Frank we would never do that again."

"But the next night we went to that comedy show in Beth Shemesh, and Frank used the Waze, and we ended up on those mountain roads in the dark."

"I couldn't quit laughing again as Frank had another panic attack. It took us like an hour longer if we had just gone the way I knew. Let's pray we don't get lost on this trip and end up in no man's land," I said with a loud laugh.

"We are ready!" Marie smiled, but it was a nervous smile.

The wheels went down, and I looked out the window and reflected on why we were here. Russia had now joined with Turkey, Syria, Iraq, and Iran to form a coalition against Israel. Except, what was strange, Egypt, Saudi Arabia, Jordan, and Lebanon sided with Israel. The US fully supported Israel, but Europe, except for England, were in favor of the Muslims ousting Israel. It seemed to parallel Ezekiel 38 and 39 in regard to the nations against Israel. In that passage God was behind the alliances and the move of their armies. "I will turn you around, put hooks into your jaws and lead you out, with all your army, horses and horsemen, all splendidly clothed, a great army with bucklers and shields, all of them handling swords." Ezekiel 38:4.

God would bring judgment on these nations and utterly destroy their armies. *Was this the day*, I wondered? It was all leading to the return of Jesus and the creation of the New Jerusalem. How did the blood moon fit in?

Because of my Neo-Nazi nemesis, the terrorists were now on high alert for us, believing that their attack on us could spark an all-out war to bring about the end of Israel. They had my address and the neighborhood where we would be staying.

The unmasked terrorist, Baahir, sat smiling with utter joy as Kashif entered their small sanctuary in the back of the Mosque. "Why are you so joyful this evening?" Kashif asked his friend. In the background they could hear the Isha, or nighttime prayers of the Muslims.

"Our friend in America has sent us a message from heaven. Our enemies from America are back in Jerusalem," he responded as he pointed to the email on his computer screen.

Kashif could hardly contain himself as he read the words that meant death for me and Marie. "We will strike in the morning. We will shed so much blood and death among the infidels by noon the earth will shake beneath Jerusalem."

"We will give our lives for Allah. Our sacrifice will awaken the nations to attack Israel. The thunder of cannon and missles and nuclear explosions will shatter the peace of Jerusalem."

"Allah be exalted and praised. At last we will wipe Israel from the face of the earth. May His people have the courage to fulfill His promise to submit all the people and tribes of the earth to His will."

"I knew the Mahdi was coming, our eschatological redeemer of Islam. He will bring us into the paradise of Allah here among the nations. We will spark WW III and enter into his reign."

Baahir and Kahsif began to shout as one in the joy of their certain triumph over us and the Jews.

Chapter 10

THE TRUMPET
SOUNDS, AD 2019

I could hear myself saying to Marie just an hour earlier, "Today is the day!" as I now drifted higher into the heavens with the angels surrounding me. As I looked to the earth, I could see the carnage from the attack. They definitely did not come just for me. They wanted a bloodbath of death. At least thirty Israelis were scattered on the ground. I counted six terrorists dead. My soul wept for the loss of life and the futility of what had become of the perfection God created in the beginning. Paradise had been lost to the corruption of humanity. Only Jesus could restore us and His creation to the beauty and holiness that was once Eden.

My body lay in a pool of blood. The mother and baby were still crying next to me. Chaos reigned over the scene as people knelt close to loved ones wounded or worse by the reign of terror.

I wondered what would follow this mass slaughter of innocents. How would Israel respond to the brutality of these assassins? My eyes glanced eastward toward the Jordan River. What did I see in the heavens? It appeared to be a shield of angels guarding Israel's borders. These were mighty angels capable of destroying anything man could fire against them. They looked like an impenetrable barrier to missiles or rockets or even fighter jets.

The angels were linked together with shields and covered miles of sky. Truly, no weapon formed against Israel would prosper on her eastern front. So, I gazed to the west, but noticed nothing unusual. But my view carried way beyond the Mediterranean Sea across the Atlantic to my home city, Orlando. I was given a glimpse into what was unfolding on a street near the Trail in Orlando. There was Bart and his wife going door to door, asking people if they needed prayer. Bart and Ingrid were an astounding couple. Their love for Jesus witnessed to many, many people the love of the Father for the hurting and lost souls in this life. I could hear them speaking.

"One more block and we will call it a day."

"Wait. the Spirit just stirred me to a need. That house across the street. We should go there now," Bart told his wife.

"Are you certain?" she questioned.

"Yes, something bad is about to happen. Let's go quickly," he stated as they raced across the street to the house the Spirit was leading to visit.

As they moved to the house I could see inside. There was a man sitting in his front room with a gun on the arm of his chair. He looked hopeless and forlorn. The weight of sin rested heavy on his shoulders. It was massive like in the Congo, women would be loaded like mules with firewood. They would be stooped over, trudging up the steep hills for home. We prayed for so many of them at our crusades. They ached with neck and back pain. Thank God, many were healed. This man was sick with sin and desperately needed his soul healed.

Wait, who was this man? My picture was on his wall full of holes as though someone had shot it up. I looked at his face but could not recognize him. He picked up the gun and pointed it to his temple. Bart rang the bell, but he sat motionless with his finger on the trigger. Knock, knock, knock. Bart knew something was wrong. He would not go away. Finally, the man put the gun under his chair and answered the door. He was a big man. His head was shaved. He was probably forty or so. He apparently had a couple of tattoos on his arms. He didn't appear sober as he struggled to find the door knob. He opened the door ever so slightly.

Bart smiled and introduced himself and his wife. They lived in the neighborhood and were visiting their neighbors to see if anyone wanted prayer. The man seemed confused, He shook his head no. Bart usually would leave, but the Spirit had told him to go to this house. This man needed help.

"What is your name?" Bart asked.

He hesitated then mumbled, "Roger."

"Nice to meet you, Roger," Bart spoke with compassion. He knew by the Spirit and his past experience, this man was on the edge of the cliff ready to step over into the abyss.

I could read Roger's thoughts as I also tried to decipher who this man was. He had sent the email to the terrorists to kill me. Now that the deed had been committed, his purpose for living was no more. His wife had divorced him and remarried. He never saw his kids. He was alone and forsaken. He had lost his faith because of me! It was time to end his own misery.

Bart got a little brave. "I see that you are sad. Can I help?" he asked. Ingrid was silent, but in deep prayer for this lost soul.

Roger, yes Roger Martin, his family had been in one of my first churches, I realized.

He shook his head, no. "I am beyond help," he muttered.

"I was right where you are at one time in my life," Bart offered. "I was ready to kill myself. I had no hope, no friends, and no chance of turning my life around. I had no idea why I was born or if there was any reason for living at all. I could not soothe the pain deep in my soul no matter how much I drank or what drugs I took. When I was thirteen, I joined a gang, and at fifteen, I shot a man. I got arrested and was put in Juvenile until I turned eighteen. I was hard as a rock and just wanted to hurt people."

Bart had struck a nerve. In the darkness of Roger's soul, a ray of light had penetrated. He opened the door and gestured for them to enter. Bart and Ingrid sat on the couch as Roger went back to his chair. Life and death hung in the balance. Fear permeated the spiritual atmosphere as angels and demons now battled for his soul.

"I used to arrest young men like you years back," Roger commented. "You may have been one of them."

"So, you were a policeman," Bart added. He seemed to know this man.

"Yes, for ten years along the Trail. Then this preacher got me fired by telling lies to my commander. He even persuaded some of the prostitutes to back his story that I was sleeping with them and getting drug money," he lied to deny the sins he could not face. Roger's reality was one of constant victimhood and denial. He could not admit the Hyde that lived inside of himself.

Suddenly, Bart knew this man. It wasn't me who had reported Roger, it was Bart. He knew what Roger was sharing was just a smoke screen. He let it pass. He also knew that this man was the one who arrested him and treated him like dirt and faked evidence against him. Bart would let that go too.

"He must have wounded you deeply?" Bart said in reference to me, but it was actually Bart who exposed his criminal activity.

"He did. My life fell apart because of that preacher. My wife left me and took my kids. I lost my job. People wonder why we leave the church. It is because of men like that who stand in the pulpit and lie to hurting people to line their pockets with money. Wolves in sheep's clothing," his anger seething through his inability to face the truth of who he really was.

Ingrid sat there and continued to pray silently. A war was raging in that room for Roger's soul. She was determined that good would triumph over evil.

Tell him about the real Jesus, the Spirit told Bart.

"I know a man who was betrayed like you. He was the best person to ever live. He helped people and gave them God's love when no one else cared about them. But they put Him to death on a cross. It was the religious leaders who had him crucified just like that preacher did to you. His name was Jesus," Bart shared. The light of Jesus filled with hope and forgiveness penetrated the darkness of Roger's soul.

Roger put his hand to his face and rubbed his mouth and chin as he contemplated what Bart had told him. Finally, after a long pause that caused the tension of life or death to hang in the air, Roger agreed, "That's right, me and Jesus suffered the same fate."

"Jesus rebuilt my life after that night I came to him in my suffering," Bart continued honestly sharing his life story. He filled me with His love and gave me hope. He gave me a gift I could never repay. He put a man in my life, who taught me how to live like Jesus. I owe Jesus everything, and I owe my friend more than I could ever repay him," Bart spoke. The truth pressed forward into the heart of Roger.

Bart struggled to do what the Spirit was telling him to do. Give him John's name, but he didn't want to stir the fire of hatred in Roger and end the conversation. He obeyed the Spirit. "That man who helped save my life was Preacher John, who had a storefront church on the Trail." There he had identified me.

Roger's anger rose up within him. "Why, that is the man who ruined my life!" His torment and hatred spewed forth, cursing me to no end, but then something stopped him as the light of glory dispelled the darkness. "How can that be?" he questioned Bart. "Can a man be both a saint and a sinner?" he asked, puzzled by his realization that the man he hated may have truly loved him.

"We are all human and capable of much evil and much good. I can only share with you what I know about Preacher John. He loved people and gave his best to Jesus and to them," he stated sincerely with his love for me.

Tears formed in Roger's eyes. "All these years I've hated him and blamed him for ruining my life. Could I have been wrong? Was I the monster?" he asked in disbelief.

"I have misjudged many people in my lifetime. So, yes, you could be wrong, but that is not the issue. Do you want a new life birthed in the love of Jesus?" Bart questioned him like a heat-seeking missile.

"I do, but it's too late for me. You do not know what I have done. I had Preacher John killed today in Jerusalem by terrorists," Roger confessed with great sorrow and remorse.

Roger's confession shocked Bart to the core of his being, but was it true? John was in Jerusalem, but Bart had not seen the news. "Are you sure he was killed?" Bart asked, barely able to speak as he looked at Ingrid and saw tears well out of her eyes.

"It has been on television. Over thirty dead in Jerusalem near where John was staying. And I warned the terrorists."

Strange this man would think he knew where John and Marie were staying. Bart struggled to press through the pain of loss that shocked his mind. I wanted to assure Bart I was all right as I slowly ascended to heaven with the angels.

"Even if what you say is accurate, Jesus can still save your soul and rebuild your life. His love is far greater than any of our sins," Bart told the truth of what Jesus had done in his life and could do the same for Roger.

"I wish I could believe you," Roger said as he sobered up, trying to grab the hand of God reaching out to him as he struggled in the stormy waters of his despair.

"You can. He did it for me, and He will do it for you," Bart said full of hope. "Tell Jesus what you want, and He will do it for you," Bart offered the fullness of God's grace to this murderer.

Without warning, Roger reached under his chair and pulled out his gun. Bart jumped from his seat to protect Ingrid, but Roger was not about to shoot anyone.

"Before you knocked on that door, I held this gun to my head and was ready to kill myself. You have brought me hope," Roger stated with tears on his cheeks.

At that, Roger knelt on the carpet and laid his gun aside. He began to pour out his heart to God, crying out to Jesus for his personal salvation from all of his sin and wickedness. He gave Jesus his life as he repented of all he had done. He put his trust in Jesus as his Lord and Savior.

Roger, humbled and broken before God, then began to pray for his family, for his ex-wife and two kids, to come to know Jesus as their Savior. He asked for their forgiveness for the hurt he caused them. He prayed for their protection and that God would bless them and draw them near to Him.

Finally, he denounced his Nazi ideology and his hatred of John and all others whom he abhorred. He vowed to God to build up the nation of America. He asked God to use his life to build God's kingdom, to deliver him from all the demons that plagued him, and to set him free to be a new man in Jesus Christ. "Rebuild my life with meaning and purpose," he cried.

From my perch above Israel, I could see demons fleeing from Roger's body and from his house. That was as powerful a prayer I had ever heard. Bart got on the carpet with him and embraced him. One battle won. Now for the survival of Israel.

My attention turned to Jerusalem and to Marie. Could I see her? Would God let me search for her? Had she heard of what happened or of my death?

That sounded strange because I felt more alive than ever. I was free from my corrupt flesh. My soul and spirit were full of life as Jesus had life, spiritual and eternal life.

I looked east again and saw explosions in the sky as rockets and missiles began to strike the shields of God's mighty angels. Israel had no worry about who had her back. There was no mightier army on earth than the one sent from heaven. Jesus may not have called his ten legions of angels when He went to the cross, but He was using them now to fulfill His plan of redemption for His cherished people.

Where was Marie? There was our apartment. Was she there? Yes! Kneeling in prayer as I should have guessed. She was interceding for me and for the Israeli army. I wanted to tell her I was better than fine, but I could not. I could only watch and trust the Lord for her safety.

The night had fallen. Jerusalem was bathed in the crimson glow of the moon. The blood of the Lamb covered her destiny in victory. Marie was looking out her window, hoping I would come home. Then she heard a trumpet blast as clear as a note ever made in heaven. Sirens sounded for everyone to get to their bomb shelter. I could see Marie smile as explosions started to rock Jerusalem. I heard her say, "I love you, John."

Chapter 11

SENT BACK, AD 48

The words of Marie still echoed in my mind, "I love you, John," as I found myself back on earth, but I was not in Jerusalem. My last thoughts had been of my love for Marie and my desire to protect her and be with her, but I was dead—or so I thought. The terrorist had blown a hole in my chest, but now it was gone. I remembered the explosions against the angels' shields. War had exploded across the Middle East. Jesus's army was defending the eastern boundaries of Israel in the sky. Massive sheets of fire and metal lit up the heavens. No weapons formed against Israel would prevail today.

Suddenly, I heard shouting. "Stone him! Stone Him! Stone him!" The anger pierced my ears with every cry to kill someone, but who? Where was I? Desperately I tried to orient myself to what was transpiring. There was a mob of people dressed in ancient Roman attire. The words I heard had been in Greek, but I did not know the land I was in for much of the ancient world spoke Greek. Still, I understood them in my English tongue.

There, I saw a man enraged with hate, yelling, "Kill the false prophet! Kill him in the name of God!" Then men began to gather up fist-sized stones to hurl at someone in their midst, who I could not see. He was surrounded by a sea of men who had lost control and were bent on killing him. Then I noticed a rather short man next to me. I asked him what was happening. He said a man named Paul was going to be killed because some Jewish leaders from the nearby cities of Antioch and Iconium had persuaded the multitudes to stone him for his blasphemy.

Still confused, I tried to piece together where I was and what was the drama unfolding before me as I sifted through Bible passages in my mind. Yes, I was on one of God's time travels, but which one?

"This man called Paul had come to Lystra and performed a miracle," the short man continued his explanation. "A beggar who had never walked, a cripple from birth, sat on the street asking for alms. I saw this with my own eyes. Paul, with a fierce look, spoke to the beggar with a loud command, stand up straight on your feet. He leaped up and walked!"

Now, I knew where I was and what was happening. I was in Galatia, which is part of modern Turkey, in a city founded by the Romans, called Lystra. The apostle Paul was on his first missionary journey as he began to establish bodies of believers for Jesus throughout the Roman Empire. Yes, he had performed a miracle of healing the crippled man who had probably been born to an evil father, who in his corrupt thinking had taken his son and cracked his ankles after he was born so he would never walk. Instead, he would become his income as a daily beggar. This was a cruel practice in ancient days, but unfortunately could be found in modern times in the sex slave industry.

At first, the people hailed Paul and Barnabas, Paul's companion, as gods. The temple priests of Zeus then brought out oxen and garlands to sacrifice to these gods whom they called Zeus and Hermes. Paul and Barnabas became incensed that they would be called gods. They ran into the multitudes to get them to stop worshiping them as gods. They did not want fame, but only for Jesus to be glorified in the miracle.

"We are men just like you," they decried. "We have come to preach of the one true God and Jesus Christ His Son. It is time to turn away from your useless religion and the worship of false gods. There is one God, who lives, not made of wood or stone or silver. His image cannot be captured by men. This God created the heavens and the earth, the sea and all things that are in them. For thousands of years, God allowed the people of the nations to walk after their imaginations and worship demons. Yet, God in His goodness and love gave witness to His heart for humanity, whom He created in His image. Our Creator gave us rain from heaven and fruitful seasons, filling our hearts with food and gladness."

"Still, the multitudes saw Paul and Barnabas as gods," the stout man continued. "They knew only pagan ways, so they began to sacrifice the oxen to appease these gods and welcome them into their city. It was then that the Jews arrived persuading the people that these two men were demons, who led people away from God to a false Messiah. Their words awakened these deceived people of the blasphemy as the Jews picked up stones to kill Paul and Barnabas."

I now watched in horror, helpless to do anything to stop this tragedy of injustice. The men began to hurl their stones without mercy, striking Paul on his head and body. Blood started to pour from his forehead and arms as each stone struck with such force they ripped his flesh open. Paul fell to his knees, and in a moment he lay dead. The lust and anger of these murderers fell silent, just as suddenly as it arose. An eerie hush fell over the mob. They began to turn away and walk back to their homes, their demonic hatred satisfied with every blow they had struck upon Paul.

A few men then took Paul by his ankles and dragged him out of the city, purging it of the sin of these false prophets. Now the gods would be happy and hopefully bless the people of Lystra with health and prosperity. As they took Paul's limp body out of Lystra, I felt myself rising into the heavens. Then I saw the marvel of God's imagination as Paul rose next to me. Were both of us dead then? I was confused as my wounds had been healed, so I disregarded my own question as the peace of God filled my heart.

Once again I was more alive than I had ever felt in my flesh. Joy filled my face with a smile wider than the Mississippi River as I looked at Paul. Wow! I was with the apostle Paul, perhaps the greatest evangelist and church planter the kingdom of God had ever known. Paul was my favorite hero in the Bible. His teachings had helped shape me and lead me to become an evangelist for Jesus. I could not wait to talk with him. A hundred thoughts flooded my mind that I wanted to form into questions for this amazing man of God. I learned so much from this master teacher and author. I was eager to pick his brains on theology and insight into the foundation of Jesus's church.

Angels had now surrounded us, reflecting the glory of God. Suddenly, we were on what I believed to be the streets of heaven. The brilliant light was brighter than the sun, but it did not affect my eyes. I could see clearly without shading them. A rush of life coursed through my body as we approached the very throne of heaven. Beyond the light, I could see stars in all their brilliance, sparkling like diamonds in the night. I could hear beautiful singing with music that was beyond divine. Words of praise rose around the throne. "You are worthy to take the scroll, and to open the seals. For You were slain, and have redeemed us to God by Your blood. Out of every tribe and tongue and people and nation, and have made us kings and priests to our God, and He shall reign on the earth." Revelation 5:9-10.

Fiery beings, which I think were seraphim, circled the throne of God declaring the Father's glory and the glory of the Lord of Hosts, Jesus Christ. "Holy, holy, holy is the Lord of Hosts. All the heavens are filled with His glory."

Then I looked, and I heard the voices of many angels around the throne, the living creatures, and the elders; and the number of them was ten thousand times ten thousand, and thousands of thousands. Their voices thundered their praise throughout the heavens. "Worthy is the Lamb who was slain to receive power and riches and wisdom and strength and honor and glory and blessing!" The multitudes upon multitudes gathered their voices in louder refrain. Every living creature which was in heaven and on the earth and under the earth and such are in the sea, and that are in them became a symphony of praise to the Father and to Jesus. "Blessing and honor and glory and power be to Him who sits on the throne and to the Lamb forever and ever," they declared. I fell on my face before the King of glory in love and worship and adoration.

Lost in the wonder of His holy presence and in the majesty resounding in the worship of His creation, I cried tears of freedom and joy. I was alive forever more in the light of His beauty.

Enveloped in the intimacy of Him who sits upon the throne of creation, I knew the oneness of the Father and of the Son. Time disappeared as I lay at His feet amidst the splendor of His divine worshipers. I was restored in the image of my God. Peace sated my soul. When I ascended out of my prostrate position of worship I knew by His revelation that the hour was late. Jesus had risen from His throne to prepare the way for His return. Then the majesty of all this glory came to its fullness as Jesus and Paul joined me in this heavenly temple. Jesus placed His hand on my shoulder. His love penetrated my being like a cloud of righteousness descending on me and moving through every pore of my skin down into my soul.

His voice soothed my inner division. As a flame of fire I became one in my soul with the Father and Son. They truly had made their home in me. "It is time for you to go back. You have much work to do. As I am sending Paul to Lystra and eventually to Rome, I am sending you back to Jerusalem."

I could barely look up to His Majesty. My heart filled with joy as I knew I was being sent back to be with Marie and to serve my Lord in these last days. He had taken me up to the third heaven and gave me a glimpse of eternity. Now it was time to go in His name to prepare the way for my Master to return. As before in the presence of Jesus, I did not want to go from His side. His love abounded with such truth and liberty that I was captivated in His persona. This truly was a glimpse of what eternity with God would be like: no sin, no death, no suffering, no tears, but a love that completed me as God had created Adam in the beginning.

In an instant I was back in Jerusalem, standing before my apartment where I last saw and heard Marie. In the background, I could hear the explosions and feel the shaking of the city beneath my feet. I did not know what laid before me in the days to come, but I knew Jesus was with me. I could face and endure anything that would come. Little did I comprehend the enormousness of events that would shatter the nations. I had just witnessed Revelation 5 unveiled before me around the throne of heaven. Thoughts of Isaiah returned to me: "Here I am, send me." Jesus had commissioned me in heaven. "As the Father sent Me into the world, so I now send you."

I could not wait to see Marie. Rushing up the stairs, I opened the door to see her still on her knees pleading with Jesus for my safety. As she heard me enter, she turned and stood. I ran to her and embraced my love with every fiber of my being. Oh, how I loved this angel of God. Together we could climb the highest mountain and endure every test that would come before us. *How great is the Lord*, I thought as we hugged and kissed. Tears streaked our checks with joy and praise. What a holy night this was. We fell to our knees and kissed. The angels sang of the glory of God. This was a divine night that we would cherish forever as we came together in the oneness of our love.

"I thought I had lost you," she cried through her sobs of joy.

"I was lost. A terrorist shot and killed me at the café," I blurted out.

"What?" she said with curiosity and puzzlement.

"Yes, I saw you from the sky as I ascended to heaven. You were praying and said 'I love you, John.'"

"That's right. You heard me," confirming my story with astonishment.

"Then I was with the apostle Paul, and he was stoned to death," I gasped and tried to pause in my excitement but to no avail. "Then we were with Jesus at His throne of heaven. It was glorious, but I never really got to talk with Paul. In the wonder and worship I heard Revelation 5 proclaimed. I fell as a dead man in worship at Jesus's feet. Before I knew it He was sending me back to you and to earth with a mission to prepare the way."

"Whew, slow down; that is a lot to take in," Marie said as she shook her head in amazement. Then she touched my chest with her delicate fingers.

"That's where I was shot. I had a big hole with blood all over me. Jesus restored me, and now I am here with you. Does Jesus know how to make a plan or what? You and me, time travelers for Jesus, bringing us together for such a time as this." I was rambling in my excitement that was spurred by my supernatural experience.

Marie put her finger to my lips. "Shh," she said softly. "What, oh, I get it. Shh, kiss me you fool." I looked deep into those beautiful eyes and I kissed her with all the passion I had pent up within me. I could feel her heart beating beneath me. It was a kiss for the ages as her soft curves invited me into her soul.

Chapter 12

VISIT TO BETHLEHEM, AD 0

T he night air caused my bones to chill. I believed I was somewhere in the hill country outside of Jerusalem, but all I could see was a campfire down the hill. The last thing I remembered was lying next to Marie, but then I awoke in what appeared to be a shepherd's garb from ancient times. The moon was full, and the stars dazzled the dark sky as they twinkled the glory of God. What I wanted to do was to get to that fire and warm my body before I froze to death. I could see figures moving around the fire and not far were flocks of sheep.

Without warning, a brilliant glow shone around these men. In their midst suddenly stood an angel of mighty stature. I moved closer to see this marvel. Fear gripped the shepherds as they hid their faces from this heavenly messenger.

I heard the angel speak. "Do not be afraid, for behold, I bring you good tidings of great joy which will be to all people. For there is born to you this day in the city of David a Savior, who is Christ the Lord. And this will be the sign to you: You will find a babe wrapped in swaddling clothes, lying in a manger."

My heart began to pound with the realization that I had traveled in time to the birth of Jesus. Tears began to wet my cheeks as I humbled myself before God. This was more than I could imagine. I was in heaven one day with King Jesus; the next I am at the place of His first arrival on earth, born as a baby.

The last time I was in Bethlehem, I hesitated to enter as I drove my car on the back roads from Jerusalem with my worship leader on one of our visits to Israel. There was a huge sign that warned Jews not to enter the city on threat of death. I had wondered how they would know I am not a Jew? It was quite intimidating. Yet, we went forward and had a marvelous day, visiting the sights without a hint of problems.

We went to see where some believed Jesus had been born over 2000 years earlier. Now I was on foot to see the actual place of His birth with the angels singing His praise. Right on cue, a multitude of the heavenly hosts along with this mighty angel began to sing, "Glory to God in the highest, and on earth peace, goodwill toward men!" The beauty and the joy of their announcement gripped me far more than when I read it in the Bible. The love of God overwhelmed me with gratitude to my Father that He valued us so much He would send His Son to live in this evil world and then to die for us and our sins.

I began to think of the numerous Bible prophecies that promised God's Deliverer would come from heaven, over 300 of them. The mathematical probabilities gleaned from these fulfilled prophecies proved beyond any shadow of a doubt Jesus was the Messiah foretold by God's prophets thousands of years prior to His birth.

> Therefore the Lord Himself will give you a sign: Behold, the virgin shall conceive and bear a Son, and shall call His name Immanuel. (Isa. 7:14)

> For unto us a Child is born, unto us a Son is given: And the government will be upon His shoulder. And His name will be called Wonderful, Counselor, Mighty God, Everlasting Father, Prince of Peace. Of the increase of His government and peace there will be no end. Upon the throne of David and over His kingdom, to order and establish it with

judgment and justice from that time forward, even forever. The zeal of the Lord will perform this. (Isa. 9:6, 7)

And I will put enmity between you (Satan) and the woman (Eve), and between your seed and her seed; He shall bruise your head and you shall bruise His heel. (Gen. 3:15)

But you Bethlehem, in the land of Judah, are not the least among the rulers of Judah: for out of you shall come a Ruler Who will shepherd My people. (Mic. 5:2; Matt. 2:6)

And she shall bring forth a Son, and you shall call His name Jesus, for He will save His people from their sins. For all this was done that it might be fulfilled which was spoken by the Lord through the prophet, saying: Behold a virgin shall be with child and bear a Son, and they shall call His name Immanuel, which is translated, God with us. (Matthew 1:21-23)

For God so loved the world that He gave His only begotten Son, that whoever believes in Him should not perish, but have everlasting life. (John 3:16)

In the beginning was the Word, and the Word was with God and the Word was God ... And the Word became flesh and dwelt among us, and we have beheld His glory, the glory as the only begotten of the Father, full of grace and truth. (John 1:1, 14)

For I have come down from heaven to not do My own will, but the will of Him who sent me. (John 6:38)

That last verse amazed me that people could not accept Jesus was divine. The Bible clearly stated Jesus was sent by the Father from heaven. He is the only one to come from heaven as humanity's Savior. All other great men came from the earth. Only Jesus claimed to come from heaven as God's only begotten Son. He was no liar, deceiver, or lunatic. He testified to the truth. He loved and lived as no one had ever lived on this planet without sin.

I was almost delirious with joy as I realized I could follow these shepherds to see the baby Jesus. The angel and his heavenly host were gone as the shepherds spoke to one another in their haste to get to Bethlehem.

"Have you ever heard such beautiful singing?" Simon asked his delirious friends.

"Never in my life," Gideon responded. "At first I was more scared than we faced down that lion several weeks ago. I could not breathe when the glory of the Lord shone upon that mighty angel."

"When he announced the birth of the Messiah, I knew something more wonderful than I could imagine had happened," Judah spoke with tremendous joy. "How could God count us worthy of such news? I was overflowing with Yahweh's peace when the multitude of angels filled the earth with their praise."

"I don't understand how our Savior could be born a baby?" Simon questioned. "Surely, he must be a magnificent king."

"You don't know anything. Listen and believe the angel of the God. He has come to us as a humble servant of the Most High God," Gideon answered. "The anointing of King David is upon him. He will grow to become the greatest of kings in the history of Israel."

Then out of the shadows came a small, soft voice. "This baby is more than a king. He is the Son of God. I can see Him wrapped in swaddling clothes laid in a manger."

This was Simon's younger sister, Deborah. Gideon tried to silence her. "Be quiet. What do you know? You are only a girl."

But Simon spoke in her defense. "She has the gift of prophecy. Listen to her."

Then Deborah began to worship the Lord and sing praises to His Name. The aura of God's glory shone once more on the shepherds as they joined her in worship. "On this day our Savior has been born. He will bring us peace and His justice will come to rule the earth."

With that truth spoken, the poor shepherds became silent as they considered what divine majesty they had seen and heard on this cold winter night.

On the way to the manger I walked a distance behind the shepherds, pondering what this night truly meant to the world and how it fit into all I was experiencing. I had been given a glimpse of Revelation 5 and the worship of Jesus in heaven. Now I was to see Jesus enter this world as a baby. The difference in His glory spanned the majesty of a King to the humility of a helpless newborn.

In God's kingdom, humility was as great a glory as being the Ruler of heaven and earth. At the heart of Jesus was the cross where He glorified His Father and displayed His glory for all the world to see. Truly this God and this Jesus were different from all the false gods and heroes of humanity. This was a Savior I could love and follow and know in all His glory. He was my Lord who desired to know me. That truth was most difficult to fathom.

I began to wonder what God was showing me in my visit to His throne in Revelation 5. Was Revelation 6 about to follow? Were the seals of human history unraveling before my eyes? Were the four horsemen of the Apocalypse riding across the earth? Were the martyrs' prayers in heaven about to be answered in God's vengeance on those who shed their blood? Would the terrible signs in the cosmos be unleashed as they shook the earth with terror? Would the seven classes of humanity from king to slave cry out in fear for the mountains to fall on them to save them from the wrath of the Lamb who sits on the throne of creation?

Were these the last days of the last days before Jesus would return to reign over heaven and earth? Certainly, He had given me a message to awaken a world in slumber to the end times and the judgment of God that was about to fall upon humanity. Wake up and repent. Get your life in order before the living God. Cry out to Jesus to save your soul from the curse of sin and death. "For the great day of His wrath has come, and who is able to stand?"

In Jesus's glory was hope for humanity. For us who believed and lived in covenant with the Creator God, it would be a time of celebration with new resurrected bodies as Jesus had. We would be set free from the bondage and evil of our corrupted flesh. No more tears or suffering or giving into our wicked desires to sin. We would walk in the holiness and righteousness of Jesus, free from all the slavery of our flesh. What a day that will be. Our destiny was one of certain new life to live like Jesus, to love as Jesus loved, not to sin, but to live in oneness and obedience to our God. Until then we had much work to do, and mine was to awaken the world Jesus was coming.

As we approached a cave that seemed to be used as a stable for animals, the shepherds turned to one another in astonishment. Here was the baby the angels had told them had been born. Here His mother and father, Mary and Joseph, settled in to sleep as Jesus lay in a manger of straw and cloth insulating Him from the cold of the night. These men of the field fell at His feet and worshiped Him. They glorified and praised God for all they had been allowed to hear and see. What wonder this frigid night had brought the riches of heaven. The very King of creation had come to save our souls and deliver us from evil to the love of God. This was a night to rejoice and keep in our hearts as Mary did concerning all the marvels of Jesus, to ponder and reflect on this God who cared and had come to save us.

Oh, little town of Bethlehem, you have no idea what was birthed in you tonight. The root of Jesse and the seed of David had come to establish the kingdom of God. This gift of God would stir up the evil of kings and tyrants of the world to kill this dream and plan of God. King Herod would order the murder of the innocents of all the male children who were in Bethlehem and in all of the districts, from two years old and under. This horror would fulfill the prophet Jeremiah, "A voice was heard in Ramah, lamentation, weeping, and a great mourning, Rachel weeping for her children, refusing to be comforted, because they are no more." The cruelty of men to protect their power and to try to thwart the plans of God knew no bounds in our rebellious world.

Now, I thought, as Jesus prepares to come again, how the kings and tyrants of this day were promoting the killing of millions of babies and boasting of their laws that allowed them to be put to death at any age in their mothers' wombs and even after their birth. Certainly, a day of judgment was upon us. "May God have mercy on our souls," I cried.

My thoughts returned to Jesus and Mary His mother. Marie knew her as a close friend and mother. Often she would tell me of the love and comfort she brought to her. Much of her healing from the abuse of men had come from the care of Mary. Marie shared with me how this came to be.

Morning breakfast had ended. Marie was outside cleaning up, while several of the other women, including Jesus's mother were inside the home of Peter's mother-in-law on the Sea of Galilee in Capernaum, Israel. It was a beautiful day, full of the freshness of nature. The sea was calm, and the disciples were resting from a night of fishing. Jesus had returned in the morning from the hillside from a night of prayer. This was His routine of getting away from the crowds to communion with His Father. There was an aura of peace around Jesus after His night of prayer that she and the others wanted to capture by being close to Him, but they knew He needed His rest.

Without warning, a leper appeared near Marie. Then a crowd gathered. They yelled at him to leave because lepers were outcasts and forbidden to be in the town. It was the Law of God as set down by Moses. People were fearful they would catch this horrible disease. Marie looked at the leper who stood a few feet from her. His nose was eaten away as were several fingers and toes. He was a hideous sight as though he were the living dead. *How he must suffer*, she thought. She remembered Jesus's words which He had taught just a mile or so down the road on Har HaOsher, "Blessed are those who mourn, for they shall be comforted."

Jesus had explained that to mourn is to enter into the suffering of others. God is a compassionate God, and Jesus had come to enter into our suffering. How this leper had to be hurting to risk coming into Capernaum when he knew he would be driven out. He was desperate to meet Jesus and to be healed. The people took stones and began to throw them at him to banish him from their town. They yelled and screamed for him to leave. This tormented soul panicked and covered his face from the rocks hitting him.

Marie grabbed his hand and took him into the house for shelter. She shut the door and turned to see expressions of horror on the womens' faces. "A leper!" they cried. "What have you done bringing him into our house? They will burn it down. Get out. Get out," they ordered, but Marie stood between him and the angry followers of Jesus. These women had never truly accepted her into their group because of her past as a prostitute. She at times felt like a leper, but Mary had been a wonderful comfort to her. She embraced Marie as did her son Jesus. But Marie feared she, too, would be cast out.

When the women perceived that the leper would not leave, they hastily ran out the front door, leaving the leper, Marie, and Mary. She never forgot the kindness in Mary's eyes as she gave the leper a drink of cold water and some food. She thanked Mary for helping this poor man. Jesus would have done the same despite the danger of the disease. Aroused from the commotion, the disciples and Jesus came to see what was happening. Jesus stepped forward and spoke to the leper. "What do you want Me to do for you?" His words were like soothing oil to a festering wound. "Jesus, Master, have mercy on me!" he cried.

Jesus simply said to him, "Be clean." Instantly, he was healed. His skin was like the newborn skin of a baby. His nose, fingers, and toes appeared. He was whole by the power of God. He fell at Jesus's feet and glorified Jesus and thanked him with such gratitude and tender words, the angels in heaven shed tears of joy. "Now go and show yourself to the priests that you are cleansed."

"Take him to the synagogue and help him with the priests," Jesus said to Marie and to Mary.

When they left the house, the mob was ready for war. They had gathered the leaders, including the priests of the synagogue and were prepared to stone the leper and burn the house. But when they saw the leper healed, they could only stare in astonishment. "Why, he was no leper at all? How could we have been mistaken?" they murmured to themselves.

Marie and Mary smiled with joy. "Here is the leper cleansed and healed as Naamann, the great general of the Syrian army, was healed by God through the prophet Elisha."

The priests looked over the man in a careful examination. "He appears to be no leper. Were you a leper?" they asked him.

"I was, but Jesus healed me and restored me even better than I was," he replied with joy.

"Then we rejoice with you." They said this because they knew Jesus and had seen the many miracles He performed among them.

There was a wonderful celebration that day in Capernaum. The people whispered to one another, "Could this Jesus be the Messiah?" Many believed in Him.

That night many gathered in Peter's mother-in-law's house to hear Jesus speak. Marie listened with a humble heart as Jesus commended her to the people for what she had done for the leper.

> Therefore everyone who hears these words of mine and puts them into practice is like a wise man who built his house on the rock. The rain came down, the streams rose, and the winds blew and beat against that house; yet it did not fall, because it had its foundation on the rock. But everyone who hears these words of mine and does not put

them into practice is like a foolish man who built his house on sand. The rain came down, the streams rose, and the winds blew and beat against that house, and it fell with a great crash. Matthew 7:24-27.

"Marie acted as I have taught. She is a doer of the word, not just a hearer. Pray for her courage and strength to do the will of God even when the whole world is against you. Blessed are those who mourn, for they will be comforted." Jesus looked at Marie, and she thought her heart would melt from the approval shown to her by her Lord and Master. When Jesus had finished saying these things, the crowds were amazed at his teaching, because He taught as one who had authority, and not as their teachers of the law.

From that night forward, Marie was loved and accepted by the women and soon became a leader to them. How she treasured Mary's love that had first opened the door to heal Marie's heart.

Chapter 13

THE MISSING BODY,
AD 2019

The 4,000-year history of the Hebrews records numerous miracles of military victories, beginning with Abraham the father of the Hebrews. As his descendants multiplied under the covenant with God, they grew into the nation of Israel. Joshua and the fall of Jericho starts the miraculous in the Promised Land to establish their nation. This hand of God continues all the way to the 21st century where books have been written of the tales of God's deliverance from the jaws of death to the victories of retaking Jerusalem in the 1967 war.

The night that passed was another annal in those epic stories. The terror attack that sparked the missiles from Iran and Iraq recorded an astounding defense of Israel's skies. Fighter pilots recorded seeing rockets explode in midair before they crossed the border. The iron dome never fired a shot. Fifty surface to air missiles were launched after thirty Israelis had been killed in the terror attack in Jerusalem. I was one of those killed.

Not a single rocket fired landed in the Promised Land. Prime Minister Benjamin David sent word he wanted reports of any supernatural defense of his people from the military to police to rescue squads. Station 12 received the bulletin early this morning. They were alerted because the body of the American killed was missing from the morgue, and it was believed he had lived in their precinct. Lt. Ken Steinman and his partner, Robert Holtzman, were ordered to go visit my wife to see what they could find on my missing body. They were about to enter the twilight zone of faith.

Steinman had been a war hero from his duty in Gaza in the last outbreak of violence. He was an expert in tunnels. So he was the first to be called up to active duty to find and destroy these deadly passageways from Gaza into Israel. On one of their discoveries of an active tunnel, four of his soldiers were trapped by Hamas terrorists. In a daring and bold move, he was able to kill the terrorists and save three of the men that had been briefly captured. Steinman had been wounded in his leg, and he still had a slight limp, but remained in the reserve army. He wondered if he would be called up because of the attack. He was certain this would escalate into a full blown war.

Without his knowledge of Russia's new secret weapon, Steinman came to the right conclusion. The enemies of Israel believed the tables had turned on America and Israel. This hypersonic missile carried nuclear warheads and could not be tracked by defense systems. This would be a temporary advantage over the US and Israel. They needed to act while they had superior weapons that could not be defended. That hour was now!

Robert Holtzman was the opposite of his partner. He was a half empty type of guy. He was sharp witted, but his sarcasm was worse than fingernails on a chalkboard. His negativity challenged Steinman's bonding as partners. He tried, but could not bring himself to like him. Robert was an addicted gambler, who was constantly in debt. Thus, he was always looking for a quick buck, which made him an easy mark for corruption. His family had made *aliyah* from Uzbekistan when he was a teenager. He did not like Israel, and he hated Americans.

They knocked on the door of my apartment. Marie rolled over to get me to answer, but she saw I was gone. "Not another trip?" she sighed. The knocking persisted, so Marie put on her robe and asked, "Who is it?" The officers answered, it was the police. They had some questions about John Nova.

She spied through the peephole to see their badges held up high. She unlocked the door and let them enter. They introduced themselves with a very straight forward greeting. Marie invited them to sit down. "You are aware your husband was killed in the terror attack yesterday," Steinman began. "We offer our sincere condolences."

Marie struggled with how she should respond. Yes, he was killed, but he is alive. We had discussed last night it might be better for everyone to think I was dead, then they would not try another terror attack on me.

The challenge for Marie was her faith. Yesterday she had gone to her favorite Psalm 139 to find strength and comfort from the Lord. The last two verses were especially meaningful to her. "Search me, O God, and know my heart. Try me and know my anxieties; and see if there is any wicked way in me. And lead me in the way everlasting." This inspired her to be more like Jesus. She did not feel she could hide anything from these officers. Yet, how should she answer?

"Mrs. Nova, you are Mrs. Nova, correct?" Steinman asked Marie. She nodded yes. "We know you must be terribly disturbed. I find this a bit embarrassing. We need your help because your husband's body has disappeared."

Marie raised her eyebrows and acted like she knew something they did not know, which she did. Suddenly there was a noise in the bedroom. Steinman looked at Holtzman as if to say who is that? "Is there someone else here?" he asked.

"Not that I am aware of." Then I appeared through the doorway.

"I thought you were alone?"

"I did too," she replied with a sigh of relief. I had come in to rescue her.

115

"Who is this? Who are you, may I ask?"

"I am John Nova."

Steinman looked in his folder at my pictures from the scene of the shooting and in the morgue. He stared at me and then at the pictures. "Unless you have a twin, I would agree."

"No twin. But I have quite a story to tell."

"Please let us know how you are alive."

We sat down together as I shared how I was killed by the terrorist, which confirmed the eyewitness reports. Then I enjoyed telling them about seeing the angels stop the surface to air missiles. I really got excited when I told of my visit to heaven and to Bethlehem.

They listened pretty intently but seemed quite skeptical. If it wasn't for the pictures, they would have tried to put me in a psychiatric ward. There was proof. I had a huge hole in my chest in the pictures. They had a doctor's report that I was dead. They checked out my chest. Nothing, not even a scar.

"You are a walking miracle," Steinman quipped.

"Can we keep the news that I am alive a secret?" I asked.

"Why would you want that?"

"The terrorist came to kill me, even though I jumped in front of the mom. If they think I'm dead, they won't try again."

"Why do you believe the terrorist came to kill you?"

"Because several years ago, we saved a teenage girl from an honor killing, and the jihadist had a fatwa put on our lives. Somehow they discovered I was in Jerusalem. They tried to eliminate me." At that moment another knock at our door. It was Bart and Roger. They heard I was killed and flew immediately to Jerusalem to help Marie. It was fun seeing them discover I was alive, no missing body.

The officers asked who they were. I informed them Bart was my partner in ministry, and Roger was, well, a former police officer and former neo Nazi, turned to Jesus. I left out the part where he was the one that told the terrorists I was in Jerusalem because he wanted to see me dead, until he gave his life to Jesus.

Although, I still had some skepticism about Roger. My trust would have to be earned. Why was he here with Bart? But that would all be answered after the officers left. Steinman and Holtzman left for the station. While in their car they discussed me.

Holtzman thought the worst of me. "Something is rotten in Denmark. Nobody gets blown away by a terrorist and rises from the dead, sees angels, and visits heaven. Come on. There is some sorta trickery here."

"You see the pictures of him. Real life is stranger than fiction."

"Not a mark on him. He had a body double or something."

"We'll get to the bottom of it."

At that point Holtzman grabbed the radio and called into the station. "Reporting Nova is not dead, but alive. We will give more details when we arrive."

"What are you doing?" Steinman said sharply. "You know terrorists listen to our radio communications. Why would you do that? He didn't want people to know."

"Yeah, if his God is so amazing, He can take care of him. I hate these Americans."

Within minutes a secret email was sent by the jihadists to a high cabinet official, code name Z. Nova is alive. Shortly they received back from Z, "Initiate OPERATION JOB."

When the officers got to the station, they filed their report with the captain. He immediately sent the report to the PM's office. It was then shown to the PM as one of the fantastic stories concerning the military miracles of Israel. Benjamin David's interest was in the sighting of angels exploding the missiles.

Chapter 19

MARCH TO
ARMAGEDDON, DAY 1

One of the most important phone conversations in human history was taking place between President Horn of the USA and President Vladimir of Russia. They were discussing the future of Israel.

"We have the new secret weapon, Mr. President. Nothing can stop these hypersonic missiles. We have a bomb more powerful than the hydrogen bomb. Yet it leaves no radiation, just destruction. I know you are aware of this. It is no secret to you. Just like in World War II when you warned the Japanese to surrender or suffer the consequences, we are giving notice that Israel has three days to surrender, or they will be wiped off the face of the earth," Vladimir declared with the emphasis on three days before they would destroy Israel.

"We will stand behind Israel. You will bring on World War III if you do this," Horn countered.

"No war. It will end in a day. I know you must publicly support Israel. Do that and then act like you will come by her side. But do nothing and in the end, we will divide up the Middle East."

"If you attack, Israel will release her nukes. They will devastate Damascus and Tehran and Baghdad."

"Let them. We will walk in with our troops, and all of the nations will be ours. Turkey, Syria, Iraq, Iran, and Saudi Arabia will be united with us and do our bidding. They will have nothing but radiation and death. We will have the oil."

This guy is the devil, Horn thought. *They, the Christians, keep telling me about the Antichrist. Maybe he is*, he questioned himself.

"Europe will do nothing," Vladimir continued. "Yes, everyone will scream and shout and say how terrible we are. But they will not lift a finger to defend Israel. They hate the Jews. We will finish what Hitler started. Do you know the Jews think we gave them their land back so we could get them in one place to kill them all?" he laughed.

"Vlad, I am telling you not to do this. They are our ally, and we have got their back."

"I know, I know, but do not be a fool. The Muslims know we have tipped the scales with our new weapons. China has a surprise as well. The three of us can be like Rome with its triumvirate, except we will rule the world, not just the Roman Empire. Do not miss this opportunity. As my name means, ruler of the world, it is set in stone. You cannot stop it."

"Tell Israel, they have three days to surrender or it will be Hiroshima and Nagasaki all over again. This time it will be worse. They are a tiny country. Don't let a little blood turn your stomach. It is our destiny, as Stalin once said."

President Horn called Prime Minister Benjamin shortly after he hung up the phone with Vlad. He warned Benjamin what Vladimir had said to him. They have three days to surrender or their new weapon will be used. Israel will cease to exist.

"We will never lose our homeland again," Benjamin stated. "We will all die first. We would rather be extinct than be slaves as we were in Germany. I believe God will protect us."

"I believe the Bible too, but I give you my word we will not let another Holocaust happen. I vow to protect you, and you will not lose your country."

"Am I a fool to believe you? Once we surrender and give them the keys to our nation, the torture and murder would not end until we are exterminated. Better to go out fighting for what we believe in than to die like dogs in the hands of a psychotic master like the Muslims and Russia."

"Think about what I said. You have three days before they launch."

"It could be three minutes, and I would say no. Listen, we have stories coming in of angels shielding Israel. Not one iron dome missile was fired against those fifty rockets. None of them got across the border. As for me and my house, we will trust in the Lord."

Fantasy, Horn thought. He was a believer, but this was science fiction to him. If Israel did not capitulate in three days, their history as a nation and a people would be over. "Call me with your answer."

Benjamin fumed in his seat as his conversation with Horn ended. His dream the night before haunted him. He had to know what it meant. "Olga, please bring in this John Nova. I want to meet with him and his wife."

Chapter 15

THE MISSION, DAY1

The cramps in Roger's stomach had increased. Bart and I needed to catch up with each other on what had happened and where we were headed. I started to pray to get guidance on how to help Roger with these intense pains. This strong man was being brought to his knees with this physical anguish.

"What do you think is the problem? Is it physical, spiritual or both?" I asked him as he grimaced as though he were being tortured.

"Probably both, but I believe the source is spiritual. I need to know I am forgiven for all I have done. I know intellectually that Jesus took away all of my sins, but deep down I struggle with guilt and what I did to you," he confessed. I believed him.

"What I am getting in the Spirit is this stronghold is in your mind, but it is rooted in your belly. By belly, I mean the spiritual core of your being. This stronghold of false thinking needs to be torn down, but it is rooted in your life, and we need you to be delivered from this systematic bondage entwined within your being. It's like removing a tree; the stump and root system are the most difficult to get out. If the stump and roots are not dug out, the tree will grow back."

Roger nodded that he understood. "Do you forgive me for this act of terror and attempt to kill you through the jihadists?"

"Yes, and God has forgiven you. You need to forgive yourself."

"That is my stronghold."

"Speak the word out loud. Bring the darkness to light. Say 'I forgive myself for my sin.'"

"I forgive myself for my sin against God and John. I receive Your forgiveness."

I then joined him in this moment of repentance. "I take authority over this stronghold in your life. By the power of Jesus's name, I set you free from all condemnation, shame, and guilt. I command these obsessions, urges, and addictions to come out of your belly, the core of your spiritual being, and be removed from your mind. May you be transformed and renewed in the spirit of your mind by the Holy Spirit and be filled with the Holy Spirit in power and life."

Immediately tears of forgiveness, oneness, and hope flowed from Roger. All of the pent-up pain came gushing forth like a mighty river of cleansing. I had seen this many times before in Zambia, in the USA, around the world and in my own life. The mystery is that for some, they are instantly set free. For others, it is a lifetime of struggle that this freedom may only come in the resurrection. For now, I could see Roger was free from his spiritual and physical pain.

We hugged and embraced and praised God for His good gifts He loves to give to His children. Roger was truly a new creation in Christ. By the conviction of the Holy Spirit and the gift of faith, he expressed godly sorrow that leads to life as opposed to worldly sorrow that leads to death.

Bart was rejoicing with us, and I knew we had lots to do today to get back on track with what was happening. The Holy Spirit had gripped Bart when he heard of the American killed in the terror attack. He felt led to get Roger and come to Jerusalem as quickly as possible. Yes, it seemed impulsive, but he was mature enough to know this was of the

Spirit. He believed I was dead but that God wanted him to come help Marie. Now that I was alive, he knew he was right to come because we needed strong arms to help in this time of trouble.

"Two things are on my heart," I shared with them as I watched Marie give Roger a healthy meal. His gobbling it down told me God had done a substantial work of grace in him. There is perhaps no greater joy than when one is set free by the power of the blood of Jesus Christ. It is like the weight of the world lifts, and one is cleansed and pure, free all sin.

"First, thank you both for coming. You were correct in knowing the Spirit sent you and that we need your help. Now, I need you, Bart, to get hold of my kids if you will. I have this terrible burden that they need to get here asap. I believe they are in danger, and they will be much safer here. I also think they will believe we are crazy to try to get them to drop everything and come to Jerusalem. I realize they will want to talk with me, and I will, but I know it is still the middle of the night in America, and I do not want to wake them with this request. Plus, I feel I am going to have a full day and will be pressed for time." Bart agreed to try. I love to give vision, but I also love to delegate responsibilities to get the job done.

"Secondly, I feel this tremendous pull in my Spirit to go to the Wailing Wall, or *Kotel* as they say in Jerusalem, to pray. I know that sounds weird because I have never felt connected to God at the wall where so many go to pray and to encounter His presence, like Marie. So, I want us to go there after lunch to pray and see what God has in store for us."

"Man, you have to share what happened after you were shot," Bart pleaded. "What was it like to be dead and then alive, to go meet Jesus in heaven and go to Bethlehem at his birth?" He shook his head with astonishment.

"Let's eat, and I will share while we have lunch, or a second lunch in Roger's case."

"I am thankful I can eat. Praise God." I love the innocence of new believers growing in their faith. *Such joy and openness*, I thought as we went out to have lunch.

At the restaurant, Bart kept at me to share. "What was it like?"

I thought for a moment. "I haven't had any time to reflect on what happened. Holy is the first word that comes to mind—sacred, astonishing, glorious. Death was, how do I put it? Simple. It was a passing from one reality to another. I was probably in shock as I lay on the floor with a giant hole in my chest. One instant I was aware of people, then the next I ascended up to heaven with angels. I felt alive far more after death than in this reality. Maybe that is a more accurate description, alive, life as we were created to know life. Absence of pain, inner division and suffering were all gone. Safe and secure, no worries. Free, no fear. Oneness. It is rather beautiful."

"And Jesus?"

"Jesus is all Jesus, the glorious King and Son of God, worshipped and praised for the wonder He is. Loving, kind, powerful—how do you describe God? Accessible, in charge, but humble. He is life, overflowing with righteousness and holiness and beauty. Bethlehem was holy. It truly was a holy night to be there at His birth and to hear the angels sing. I came away from these experiences believing I have a mission, to prepare the way for Jesus's return. We have to get the word out that He is coming, and He is coming soon. It goes back to that call on my life along the canal when the Spirit spoke to me: His return is imminent. I believe we may be only days away. Think of it. We could be with Jesus when He descends in His glory onto the Mount of Olives and enters Jerusalem."

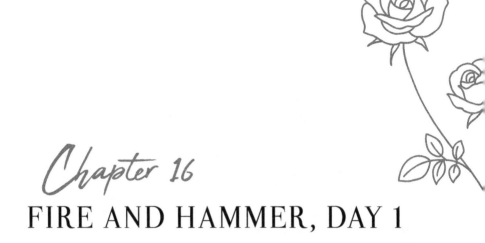

Chapter 16

FIRE AND HAMMER, DAY 1

I stand at the base of this massive wall called the *Kotel* in Hebrew or in English, the Western Wall. It is the outer base of the west side of the temple mount which served as a support for the ancient temple that no longer exists. It was destroyed by the Romans in AD 70. This holy remnant is where Jews have come to pray to the God of Abraham for hundreds of years. It is said that the walls have ears, for they hear the prayers of the Jews and are taken to God to answer. The great stones have cracks in them with pieces of paper containing the prayers of the desperate. Kings and presidents have placed their prayer notes in these slits, along with the poorest of the poor.

Marie has taken hundreds of prayer requests through the years and put them in the cracks. The saying goes, "There are people with hearts of stone, and stones with hearts of people." Marie has always connected with God at this sacred site. Strange for me, because in all of my visits to the Kotel, I have never sensed the presence of God. Even stranger, I felt compelled to come to the Western Wall this afternoon to encounter God.

As I stood looking up at this monument of stone, I closed my eyes in prayer, but I found myself in Missouri as an eight-year-old boy on vacation with my family. We were at a lodge on the White River. My parents had one room, and my brother, Mickey, who was twelve, had another room with me. My two older brothers stayed at home in Chicago to party as teenagers like to do! Mickey and I were bored of fishing, so we went scouting along the bluffs that overlooked the river. He noticed an old burnt-out hotel on the top of the bluff across from our lodge. Mickey suggested we go up and explore that building. "Sure," I said because I followed my brother's lead in everything.

I thought we were going to climb the broken, aged, concrete steps that led up the bluff, but he said no, we would climb the rugged cliff. To an eight-year-old, it seemed ten stories high and impossible to climb, but in my naivete I agreed. Up and up we went, twisting along the ledges. I never looked back but followed after Mickey as he climbed. We were almost to the top when he realized the overhang was impossible to scale. We had to go down and take the cement steps. He started back, but I stared down the steep wall we had just climbed. I became horrified and froze on the ledge. A minute earlier, I had no fear of heights; now I was paralyzed holding onto the rocks for dear life.

"Come on," he said, but I could not move. "You are going to get into trouble and me with you if you don't climb down." I couldn't speak for fear of falling to my death. He persisted in trying to lure me down, but I was not going to budge an inch. If I moved, it would be the end of me. I was only eight, and I had a whole life still to live. Finally, Mickey climbed down like a mountain goat and ran to get our parents. When my mom saw me on the ledge, she almost fainted. They called for me to come down, but I was no fool. *Come get me*, I thought.

My dad wisely figured he was not fit enough to come up and rescue me. He went to the lodge and told them of the dilemma, and within a few minutes I could hear sirens. *Surely, not for me*, I questioned. I forced myself to twist my head to see cars screeching to a halt. People got out of their vehicles on this two-lane highway to wonder at how this little boy climbed so high and now was stuck. Then the fire engine arrived, and we had quite a spectacle for these country folks to see how foolish these city people were. Several came to assess the situation. They wisely walked up the stairs to the top of the bluff as I hung on for dear life. The summer sun was beating on my neck. My palms were sweaty, and I was as stiff as a board.

At last, the firemen decided to lower a rope for me to grab onto, and they would lift me up. Fortunately, my dad surmised this would be a sure death. He convinced them to get the bucket out of the fire truck and lower one of the firemen in it to me, he would put me in the bucket with him, and the rest of them would lift us up to safety. This rescue would add a few more years of living for me unless my dad got a hold of me and spanked the life out of me. You could do that in those days, and everyone would cheer. "He had it coming," they would say. Now they put you in jail or send you to rehabilitation classes for the parental ineptitude.

How long all of this took was beyond me. Longer than I had lived according to my brain, but eventually it worked. It was one of many rescues that saved my life. To this day, I have been fearful of man-made heights, which makes no sense because that cliff was God-made, but go figure.

In my mind as I started to pray at the wall, I saw a treasure at the top of the Kotel. There was no way I could climb up this massive man-made structure of giant stones. Then, I was facing another life-or-death situation. I was twenty-two years old and had just been released from my short-lived professional baseball career with the Chicago Cubs organization. Since baseball was my god and it was now dead, I went in search of the meaning of life on the Pacific Crest Trail in Southern California. Three Minnesota Twins drove me cross country from Florida on their way to Visalia, California, to play for that city. I had my backpack and tent ready to wander the wilderness. They let me out on the side of a mountain somewhere outside of LA. If you thought my Missouri adventure was crazy for a city boy, this was a far more dangerous idea.

I had never gone camping or started a fire from sticks and twigs. Naive would be quite an understatement as to what I expected to do in these mountains, but I was determined to venture out to find God. Thank God, He had his guardian angel with me, or I would not have made it out alive. After a week of eating cold food because I could not figure out how to start a fire, the rains came. I thought it never rained in

Southern California. This torrent washed out my trail, and I was lost in the woods amid the rugged high country.

Not knowing any better, I had no fear. Why should I be afraid? No one knew where I was or that I was lost. No one would come looking for me. I had a compass but didn't know how to use it. I would keep wandering around, and somehow I would make it back to civilization. That ignorance lasted about two days. Finally, I figured if I found a stream it would go down the mountain to the ocean, and at the water edge was the highway. No sweat. I knew how to get out. My worries were over. How little I knew what lay before me.

The rains had swollen this stream into a rather swift creek. I loved walking along its edge as I made my way down the mountain. The creek ran swifter and swifter, but I had no thoughts of danger. Funny, how one dumb mistake can get you in a whole heap of trouble without you realizing it. I came to a steep bank and if I jumped down from the top of the bank to follow the creek, I could not head back up. It would be unclimbable from my vantage point, but I had to go down to follow this fast-moving water to the ocean. Down I went. No problem as I continued my hike, unaware of any danger.

Without knowing it, I was in a gorge with steep sides up the mountain. As I turned a bend, I saw there was a waterfall racing down 100 feet to a pool of swirling water. I could not go back, or up, or across the deadly water. I was up a creek without a paddle. At that time I had not found God, but He knew where I was because I prayed for help. In evaluating my predicament, I saw that there were several fir trees growing out of the rocks. I spied a large boulder in the water that if I got to it, I could climb up the bank and up the face of the gorge. Not easy, but I believed I could do it.

The problem I faced, If I went hand over hand, like monkey bars, on the fir trees' limbs, if I fell in the water, it was curtains for me. Over the waterfall I would go and plunge to my death. I was in great shape from playing ball and walking in the mountains. The more I thought about it, it was probably impossible to do what I was going to try to achieve, but I had no choice. Darkness was coming, and there was no room to camp on the bank until the morning. I questioned whether I should leave my backpack and tent behind, but I needed it to survive after I accomplished the impossible dream.

Off I went, hand over hand through the trees. My feet were dangling on the water top, pushing my boots forward toward the falls. I had about twenty feet to cover to reach the boulder. I was almost there when my backpack got tangled in the branches. I could hold on for only a few more seconds and then over the falls I would sail. In an instant, I thought I could swing myself back and forth and once free, I could fly to the boulder. Thank God, our thoughts can travel at the speed of light. So, I went for broke and swung back and forth and then let go. My hands and arms landed on the rock. My feet were in the water and being pushed by the current toward death.

The boulder was slippery, but I managed to climb on top of it and collapsed from my weary adventure, but that was the beginning. As I lay on my back looking up the canyon wall, how was I ever going to climb this massive creation of nature? Yet, it was my only way out. Summoning all of my energy, I started up the steep slope one step at a time. No rope. No experience. I only had a determination that drove me forward with the challenge to see if I would live or die. It was exhausting with no ledges to follow. Just straight up to freedom or to my fate to eternity.

I should have died, but God had other plans. As I was almost to the top, I started to reach for the next hand hold when something caught my eye. I stopped my hand just in time as it was a rattler rearing its head to strike. I slowly withdrew my hand and moved around where it lay to my safety. I did not have time to contemplate my escape from certain death. I had to focus all my energies on reaching the top. I could not let a large rattler get in my way. I moved upward with the same determination that had driven to victory after victory in my pitching career.

When a new catcher on our college team arrived and caught me in the bullpen before our first game that season, he was not impressed with my stuff. As he discussed this on the bench as I took the field, questioning how I became the winningest pitcher in college baseball the year before, our coach overheard them talking about me, and he answered the catcher's question by saying out loud, "He just wins, baby. He just wins."

Soon I was at the top. I had expended every ounce of energy I had. I ate some food and then threw it all up. My body rejected it because the fierce battle had drained me.

My mind came back to prayer at the wall. Lord, I am not climbing this Western Wall for that treasure you showed me at the top, I said. Three strikes and I am out.

"You do not have to climb it. Ask me, and I will give it to you," I heard the Spirit say to my spirit.

I asked God for the treasure. Instantly a hand gripped my shoulder. I turned to see a mountain of a man. He was an orthodox rabbi with a full red beard and curly red hair flowing from under his black hat.

"Are you the Gentile who was dead and is now alive?" he asked. He was holding a metal box. When I nodded yes, he said God sent him as His prophet to give this to me. Whoa, I was a little hesitant to receive it. After my death experience, who else was out to kill me? Bart and Roger were close by watching this scene unfold, ready to intervene.

I took it and examined it. The outside was covered with flames of fire. When I looked up, the mystery man was gone. I asked Bart where he went, and he asked, "Who?" I said, the man who gave me this box. I did not see anyone. Did you, Roger? No. Well, he was right here and gave me this fiery box. Puzzled but not surprised, I carefully opened the box. Inside was an ancient hammer that would be used to chisel stone.

Immediately, I thought of Jeremiah the prophet where God said to him, "My words will be a fire in your bones and a hammer in your hands." Then the Spirit told me, I was to give it to the Prime Minister of Israel.

My phone then rang. I answered it. "This is Olga Izmennik. I am the advisor to Prime Minister Benjamin David. He has read the report of your story and would like to meet with you and Marie this afternoon if that is possible?"

"I am at the Kotel praying, but yes, we can come."

"I am sending a car for you at this minute. Find the nearest police officer and tell him who you are, and he will guide you to the car. See you soon." With that she hung up.

What a shock to hear we were meeting with the Prime Minister of Israel this afternoon. God had prepared the way the whole time. I had to find Marie as she was praying at the women's section of the Kotel. There was a mass of people that had come to pray because of the terror attack and threat of war. As I made my way to find her, Marie was having a prophetic encounter of her own with God.

The women had pressed in toward the Wall. There was barely room to move, but somehow Marie had made it to the base of the Kotel. In this mob of people, she felt alone with God. The Spirit came upon her as a cloak of revelation. Her spiritual eyes opened to see the dream the prime minister had received the night before. The Spirit promised her the interpretation would be given to her as she spoke to Benjamin David.

Overwhelmed with God's glory, she knelt with her face to the wall. It was her protective shield from the fiery darts of Satan. This kept her mind clear to receive the Lord's message in the Spirit. She had no desire to leave this moment of intimacy, but the Spirit, once finished with the message, gently lifted her and prodded her to go find me. We met on the outskirts of the women's section. Both of us were giddy with the news that had been revealed to us. The end-time prophecies seemed to be accelerating toward the return of Jesus.

"I have exciting news to share," I started, but she interrupted before I could finish. "We are meeting with the Prime Minister," she said as she completed my sentence."

"You must have had a wonderful encounter with the Spirit to know that."

"I did. He gave me the PM's dream and the interpretation that I need to share. What's in the box?" she asked as she saw it in my hands.

"It is a treasure from God given to me by a Jewish prophet or an angel. He disappeared so I am assuming he was an angel, but I was the only one who saw him. This box is for the prime minister."

"What is it?"

"I believe it is a word from Jeremiah 23:29, where God says is not My word like fire and a hammer that breaks the rock in pieces, thus the flames on the metal box and the hammer inside. I take it to mean He has given Me His fire in my bones and a hammer to awaken the people to the return of Jesus, to break them from their spiritual slumber. It must also be for the PM to speak as His prophet to His people. Get ready; the Messiah is coming."

"Exciting times," Marie commented as we marveled in the joy of our encounters.

"Yes, and we need to find a police officer to escort us to the car that awaits us to take us to the PM's office. I got a call from Olga, the PM's advisor, that he wanted to see us concerning my report to Steinman. She has sent a car to pick us up. Let's hurry and we can catch up in the car on being led by the Spirit before we meet the PM."

We said goodbye to Bart and Roger. "Let the kids know I will call them. It is vital they get to Jerusalem."

We found a policeman who took us to where the car was waiting for us. Marie shared more of her encounter as I did with mine. We felt like a whirlwind of the Spirit had lifted us up to see the visions of God. How we were to meet the PM was beyond our abilities to do or comprehend. Both of us were convinced I had to get on television to tell the world Jesus was coming. There was no time for a book. God would lead the way as He would with the PM.

As we reflected on the incredible events of the past two days, we realized the prophecy I received years ago at a conference in Zambia had come true. Our missionary friend and partner at New Life Center in Garlington, Zambia, Dexter, laid his hands on me and began to prophesy during a mighty move of the Spirit at our annual Holy Spirit Encounter. He said as God sent Paul to the Gentiles, to kings and to the people of Israel, so I have chosen you to go to the nations, to Israel, and to the kings of nations to witness to the Resurrection and Return of Jesus.

Since that prophecy, I met many chiefs in Zambia and the Congo. I had testified to top political leaders around the world. I had gone to the Gentile nations as His witness and to Israel. I had even met our president. Now I would meet the Prime Minister of Israel. Marie and I were both humbled by what God had done through this chief of sinners. We held hands and prayed for guidance as we pulled up to the Knesset Building.

Chapter 17
THE DOOR OPENS, DAY 1

Marie and I were both nervous as Olga greeted us. "We are so glad that you could come on such short notice. Time is of the essence with all that is unfolding these days."

"We are honored to be asked," I replied as we entered the PM's office.

Benjamin David rose from his chair to welcome us. He was a middle-aged man, bald like a Caesar, and in fine shape. He had been a decorated war hero, which rocketed him to fame in Israel and eventually to her highest office. He was a shrewd politician with an intense love for Israel. Marie and I had been firm supporters of him and his policies.

"Prime Minister, these are John and Marie Nova."

"Yes, I have looked forward to meeting with you since I received your report this morning. I am anxious to hear from you what you believed happened."

"It has been quite a ride. We feel like we are in a whirlwind of adventure and historic times."

"What do you believe happened to you, and how can you help me and my beloved Israel?"

Suddenly, Marie moved by the Spirit abruptly interrupted. "I have seen your dream, and God has given me what you are asking to know."

Benjamin was stunned. "How did you know of my dream? I have told no one, not even my wife."

"The Spirit of God revealed it to me while I was in prayer this afternoon at the Kotel." She had his full attention.

"You saw three healthy and prosperous trees protected by a hand. They had loads of fruit on them. This means that you were given three days to surrender, and these days would be full of protection and prosperity for Israel. Then you saw a shadow figure rise up from the east and inject a virus into the root system of the three trees. This infection destroyed the trees and all of their fruit. The hand remained around the trees, but the trees were almost dead. The last of the three trees was shorter than the first two. Then you saw a great tree come from the heavens and the three trees came to life. This tree had a crown on top. Its branches were of iron and its leaves as two-edged swords. There was so much fruit that ordinary branches would have broken off from the weight of the abundance."

"This second and third part means this. After the three days of protection for Israel, a nation will send a virus into your computer system and crash all of your defenses. God's hand will still protect you, but you suffer three days of destruction as your enemy nations will overwhelm your army and surround Jerusalem. You will appear almost as dead. The shorter tree signifies that God will shorten the third day to save Israel. Then the Messiah will come as the King of kings to rule Israel. You will hand over the government to Him. He will rule with a rod of iron over the nations. His sword will be sharp and true with great power. The fruit of His reign will know no bounds and produce more blessings than the world could hold."

"Remarkable," Benjamin responded. "Truly, God has given you this divine wisdom. There is no one else in all of Israel who could know this. I praise God for His intervention of hope and life."

"It is not me, Prime Minister. It is God's love for Israel and His plan of salvation to deliver you from evil that Satan and his nations intend for you. The covenant of Abraham will be fulfilled."

"You are Jewish, I believe?"

"I am, and I am from the Galilee area."

"We have no record of your birth there. Forgive us, but we must be thorough in our investigations."

"That is a long story, which someday I would love to share with you."

"I may know some of it already. Our intelligence can uncover every secret. They are my eyes of God so to speak."

Then Benjamin turned to me. "What have you for me?" he asked, looking at the metal box. At that moment I realized I was to give him the box, and this treasure was not for me, but solely for him. He was to be God's voice. My mission from Jesus was not to awaken the whole world, but this one man would. God wanted to put His fire in him and His hammer in his hands.

"This treasure was given to me by a prophet or an angel at the Kotel. I was told to give it to you. The painted fire on the outside and the hammer inside are signs from God of what He did in Jeremiah. He desires to do this in you as His voice to the people of Israel. The Messiah is coming. Stand strong in your faith in the God of Abraham. Do not fear or lose courage. God is with you. When you seem to be dead, He will resurrect you in His glory." Wow! I did not know where all of that came from, except by the Spirit.

Benjamin received the gift from my hands. He examined the fire and then opened the box to see the ancient hammer. I then noticed there was fire painted within the entire box as well as on the hammer.

Marie began to weep and prophesy. All of us fell on our knees to humble ourselves in this divine moment. We were caught up in the Spirit. As Marie prophesied, there appeared a granite stone and chisel at the feet of Benjamin. As she spoke, he took the chisel and started to form the stone into a shape.

"There are two mighty, warring angels at your side, Benjamin. Michael and Gabriel are their names. They glow with the glory of God sent from heaven. Their arms are raised in worship. These angels have wings too. Their tips point toward you in splendor. God will use you to set the boundaries of Israel as promised to Abraham. The covenant will be fulfilled. He wants you to know the angel of the Lord stands with Israel. Do not faint in this battle, and do not surrender, or you will suffer untold horrors. You will lose your destiny. I will protect you and destroy your enemies. On the evening of the sixth day, we will feast together as My Son takes His bride in marriage. He has saddled His horse and is preparing to ride with His army."

As Marie finished, Benjamin ceased chiseling the stone. At first, it was difficult to discern what it was. Then we all realized it was the form of a nation. It was the expanded Israel, shaped to the biblical boundaries given in Exodus 23:31, which describes the borders as "from the sea of reeds (Red Sea) to the Sea of the Philistines (Mediterranean sea) and from the desert to the Euphrates River."

We stared in awe and silence. We dare not speak in the holy presence of God. He had given Benjamin a memorial stone to remember God was with him and Israel. Benjamin began to chant in Hebrew:

> Hear, O Israel: The LORD our God is one LORD: And thou shalt love the LORD thy God with all thine heart, and with all thy soul, and with all thy might. And these words, which I command thee this day, shall be in

thine heart: And thou shalt teach them diligently unto thy children, and shalt talk of them when thou sittest in thine house, and when thou walkest by the way, and when thou liest down, and when thou risest up. And thou shalt bind them for a sign upon thine hand, and they shall be as frontlets between thine eyes. And thou shalt write them upon the posts of thy house, and on thy gates. And it shall be, when the LORD thy God shall have brought thee into the land which he sware unto thy fathers, to Abraham, to Isaac, and to Jacob, to give thee great and goodly cities, which thou builded not..." Deuteronomy 6:4-10.

This sacred hour was chiseled into our hearts and soul. The treasures of God had been released for Israel and all of His people who followed Jesus. We all knew it in the depth of our being. We would soon see the glory of God in His fullness on earth. In my mind, I quoted John 1:14, *The Word became flesh and made his dwelling among us. We have seen his glory, the glory of the one and only Son, who came from the Father, full of grace and truth.*

It was true. The Messiah was coming to fulfill all the covenant promises God had given His people Israel and the Gentile followers of Jesus.

Benjamin's eyes were moist as he told us he wanted to hear further of anything the Lord said to us. You are my Isaiah as I humbly am Hezekiah the king, he spoke to me. He would have security protect us in these dangerous days. Then we saw the oil anointed on the stone of Israel. It was Jacob's stone from his second trip to Bethel. Surely, God had given Israel the nations of the earth, and the Messiah would rule over them forever and ever.

Chapter 18

END–TIME ARMY, 593 BC

I found myself walking along a river bank. As I marveled at the beautiful hillside and gentle rhythm of the current, I saw him. Dressed as a Jewish priest, I realized I was along the Chebar River in ancient Babylon. The man was Ezekiel. He seemed to be meditating. His head bopped back and forth as his lips moved in rhythm.

"Go ask him what he has seen," the Spirit spoke to me.

I sat next to him in silence. Then his eyes opened, and he looked straight at me. He was not puzzled but appeared to know I was a messenger from God. "What have you seen?"

> "The glory of God in a whirlwind comes out of the north in a cloud of wonder. Raging with fire engulfing itself, and brightness was all around it, radiating out of its midst like the color of amber, out of the fire. From within it came four living creatures. Their appearance was the likeness of a man. Each one had four faces, and each one had four wings. Their legs were straight and the soles of their feet were like the soles of calves' feet. They sparkled like the color of burnished bronze. Ezekiel 1:4-7.

"In the glory of His presence I fell on my face before Him as He spoke to me. 'Son of man, stand on your feet, and I will speak to you.' Then the Spirit entered me and I heard His voice clearly. He sent me to the rebellious people of Israel to speak His words of lamentations, mourning and woe." Ezekiel 2:1-3.

I was made a watchman on the wall of Jerusalem. Suddenly, in the Spirit I was in the holy city and saw the siege of Jerusalem. God was bringing a sword against Zion to bring judgment for their idolatry. He showed me the abominations in the temple. Then His glory left the Holy of Holies and lifted above the city and departed.

He told me of His love for Israel, and in a new day He would rain down blessings upon her. Out of her desolation, I will bring fruitfulness for My name's sake. The ruins will be rebuilt after I have poured out My fury. It is out of concern for My holy name that I do this so that they will know and all nations will know that I am the Lord.

"I will sprinkle them with clean water. I will cleanse them from all their idolatry. I will give them a new heart and put a new spirit within them. I will take the heart of stone out of their flesh and give them a new heart of flesh. I will put My Spirit within them. I will regather them from the nations of the earth. Then they will know that I am the Lord." Ezekiel 36:25-27.

"The hand of the Lord came upon me and brought me out in the Spirit of the Lord, and set me down in the midst of the valley and it was full of dry bones. They were very dry.

"And He said to me, Son of man, can these dry bones live? So I answered, O Lord God, You know.

"Prophesy to these bones and say to them, O dry bones hear the word of the Lord. I will cause My breath to enter into you and you shall live. I will put sinews on you and bring flesh upon you, and cover you with skin and put breath in you; and you will live. Then you will know I am the Lord.

"So I prophesied as I was commanded and as I prophesied there was a noise, and suddenly a rattling; and the bones came together, bone to bone. Indeed, as I looked, the sinews and the flesh came upon them and the skin covered them over, but there was no breath in them.

Also He said to me Prophesy to the breath prophesy son of man and say to the breath, come from the four winds O breath and breathe in these slain that they may live.

"So, I prophesied as He commanded me and they lived, and stood upon their feet, an exceedingly great army. Then He said to me, Son of man, these bones are the whole house of Israel. They indeed say, our bones are dry, our hope is lost, we ourselves are cut off."

"Therefore, prophesy and say to them, thus says the Lord God, behold, O My people, I will open your graves and cause you to come up from your graves and bring you into the land of Israel. I will put My Spirit in you, and you will live, and I will place you in your own land. Then you will know that I, the Lord, have spoken and performed it." Ezekiel 37:1-14.

"One day you will have one King and one kingdom. My servant David will be your prince forever. I will make a covenant of peace, an everlasting covenant. I will establish them and multiply them, and I will set My sanctuary in their midst forevermore. My tabernacle will be with them and I will be their God and they will be My people.

"The nations will know that I, the Lord, sanctify Israel, when My sanctuary is in their midst—forever more." Ezekiel 37:28

"Then I saw the nations from the north, the east and the south come against Israel to surround her. This will happen in the latter days. They will come against My people Israel like a cloud, to cover the land. It will be in the latter days that I will bring them against My land, so that the nations may know Me.

"I will bring judgment on these nations and destroy their armies. I will then hold a great feast. Israel will be restored to the land forever as I promised Abraham. I will not hide My face from them anymore for I will pour out My Spirit on the house of Israel, says the Lord."

As I sat with Ezekiel, I heard his words and understood the prophecies that had been fulfilled and were about to happen. I remembered a visit I had when my kids were young. I was asleep at our house in Orlando when Liz began to cough, and it awakened me. I got up and gave her some medicine and went back to bed, but I could not sleep. Then I sensed an evil presence come into my home. Its wickedness was so powerful, I became fearful for my children. I arose and anointed each one with oil and prayed over them. This demonic being seemed to stand in the hallway. I cried out to God for help. The Spirit told me to get my Bible and read the passages I was led to study.

On my knees in our living room I read aloud the book of Revelation. Still the evil remained. I was then prompted to read Ezekiel 37, the passage on the dry bones. In that instant, the evil spirit left the house, and I was given an interpretation of the dry bones. Before God could breathe His breath into us He had work to do in us. We had a form of religion, but had denied the power of God. Israel and His church were in captivity, hopeless and buried. God would raise us up with hope and freedom. New life would come into us as the Holy Spirit, the breath of God, entered us.

Pentecost had begun in Jerusalem and had spread across the world. In the last days the final outpouring of the Spirit would be in Jerusalem and upon Israel. Then the Messiah would come in His glory. When we are the most hopeless is when God does His greatest works. In our desperation, He hears our cries. The noise in Ezekiel 37 is the sound of repentant hearts weeping before God over our sins. The rattling is God's response as He begins to cleanse us and prepare us for His Spirit and His work.

The bones coming together is the oneness of the Jew and Gentile becoming the one new man. The sinews and flesh and skin is the building of God's temple with His new man. His breath is His Spirit as He comes to dwell within us and empower us to prepare for the Messiah to return. It was then I knew 1948 and the rebirth of Israel was the pivot point of end-time prophecy. It was the linchpin of preparing for Jesus to come and be received by His people and the entire world, for He is the cornerstone of God's holy temple. In Him, we will all be one.

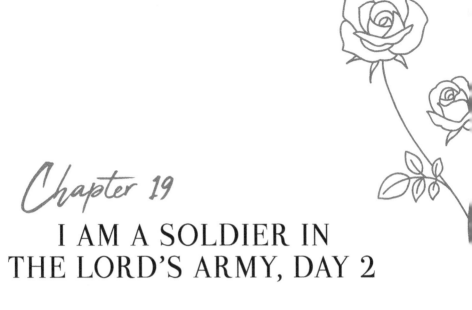

Chapter 19

I AM A SOLDIER IN
THE LORD'S ARMY, DAY 2

I awoke next to Marie in our apartment. She was lying awake, waiting for my return from my time travel. Her smile welcomed me home. Thank God for a wife who is patient and kind in the midst of chaos. She rolled over onto my chest as I began to tell her of my mission.

"I need to tell Benjamin what I heard from Ezekiel. It will give him hope and strength for the days ahead. There will be days of hopelessness. God will use this to bring His people to repentance before He comes to deliver Israel and the world from the powers of darkness.

"Marie, my entire mission from Jesus is to tell the Prime Minister His message for what will unfold in the next six days. It is not about awakening the world to Jesus's return. God has raised up an entire army in Israel and around the world since 1948 to do battle in the spirit realm. I truly believe Jesus will come on the 6th or 7th day of that dream."

Marie raised herself up on her elbows to look me in the eye. "It sounds so incredible when you say it out loud that the Messiah is coming. The first time He came, I remember everyone was discussing that it was the hour of His coming to deliver Israel. But we missed it, except for a few of us."

"Jesus said most will not be ready for His second coming. Even believers will be deceived. Our job is to get the word to Benjamin, so he can lead us through the ordeal we face until Jesus arrives in His glory. After I listened to Ezekiel, the Spirit reminded me of my experience years ago when the kids were young, and He gave me the interpretation of Ezekiel 37. It is all unfolding just as He witnessed. The dry bones are alive and fighting as His mighty army. But it is not linear as we have always thought. The prophecies are more like an intertwined spiral, rapidly heading toward the age of Jesus's reign.

"We have tried to outline them and fit them into our understanding. But God's ways are far more bound by His heavenly time. We see through a glass darkly because we cannot comprehend the multiplicity of what takes place in God's mind. I know this, God has a plan, and no one or nothing will stop it. We have got to be prepared not to lose hope or faith no matter what occurs."

We both took a deep breath. "Jesus will amaze us with His wonders not to please men, but to obey His Father. Sacrifice and death to self will be a prime part of His plan," Marie wisely stated.

Little did we know what awaited us. I needed to call my kids. Funny, they were in their thirties, and I still saw them as children in my mind. Time is a strange master of our fate. In the blink of an eye, the years roll past and begin to steamroll as one gets older.

Bart had talked with Jonathan, Ashley, and Liz, but none of them were convinced to get to Jerusalem. I wanted to call them before I met with the PM, but they would be sleeping. I would wait until they were up in the States. Now, I needed to seek the Lord and prepare for the day. It is fascinating that I never felt tired after my journeys. In fact, they seemed to energize me. Prayer and the word would set my course for the day's events. Benjamin had given us a private number to call if I had a message for him. After our time in the Spirit together, I had his trust. I may ask him for help, I thought to myself, to get my son and daughters and their families over here. Best I get alone with the Lord before I do anything else. Only God could grant me the wisdom and guidance required for today.

I went to my prayer room and lay prostrate before God as I did every morning for the past thirty-five years. It was a joy to meet with the Creator of the universe. It grieved my heart that so many people ignored God and missed out on this treasure of personal intimacy with the Lover of our soul. God is a Person with a mind, a will, emotions, and an intellect, who loves to interact with us. He created us in His image so we could talk and share our lives with him. Adam and Eve had walked in the garden with Him. In our secular culture, people mocked us who still believed in the stories of the Bible.

All I know, my journey with God has been the greatest blessing of my life. If it was fantasy, then I gladly embraced it. I tried the world's way, and that left me hopeless and alone. Jesus had carried me through the most devastating times of my life. He had rebuilt my life and given me His love. It was far more than this sinner deserved.

As I lay in His presence, His Spirit took my spirit into His confidence. I asked God about the days that were to come. He took me to Bible passages that related to what awaited me. I found myself in 2 Samuel 18 when King David's son was killed by David's trusted general Joab. How David grieved over Absalom's death even though he had betrayed David and caused a civil war. Surely, this was not what my children would do. I inquired of the Lord what He was trying to say to me, but I could not hear His answer, which was not unusual. Many times, I was given a glimpse of what was to happen, but I often failed to comprehend what God was saying to me. Only after the event did I understand what the Spirit was speaking to my spirit.

After about a half hour I was deeply immersed in His presence. I cleared my mind of my flesh that pulled me in different thoughts and brought up so many things I had to do. Our inner self is so divided, I cannot wait until I know the oneness of devotion and service and love for God that awaits us in the Resurrection. I was at peace and resting in the Lord. I found myself worshiping and praising Jesus as though I was back in heaven. It was glorious. Tears of joy and love filled my eyes as I communed with the living God. How wonderful God is that He cares and loves us and created us to spend such a moment of life with Him.

I would meet with the PM today and share with him God's word for the days ahead. Then a heavy burden came upon me for my three children and their children. I found myself weeping and crying out for their protection. There seemed to be a mighty battle taking place in the spirit realm for them by the angels of the Lord against the demons of Satan. I prayed intensely for God to send angels to cover them and drive off the demons that meant them harm. I named each one and believed in God's intervention.

In my thoughts I was back with Ezekiel after my warfare. His words were clear and true. I went over them several times so I would be precise with the PM.

I laughed a bit as I remembered how in the Spirit years ago, God had told me I would meet with kings and chiefs. I never thought it would happen. Yet, over the years I had ministered to several chiefs in Zambia and the Congo. I had prayed with political leaders, and as I shared earlier, even the President. God was true to His promises. Today I would meet again with Benjamin David and advise him as his counselor. I prayed for humility and the grace to resist the corruption that power can have on a human being. My father had often quoted the phrase to me when I was young, "Absolute power corrupts absolutely." I had discovered how true that was in my dealing with rich and powerful people. It can be very seductive and corrupting to one's soul. At the end of my prayer and study I remembered to pray for Bart and Roger. They had been a huge help to Marie and me. I knew they would take a bullet for us.

When I finished praying, I got on the internet to check my bank account to see what funds I had to help with plane tickets for the family. I felt such peace in this turbulent time of tribulation. God was with me and that made me feel secure and safe. The screen popped up for my password and into my accounts I went. My heart began to race as

I looked in unbelief. All my money was gone. I started to panic. I felt queasy and anxious. I began to sweat as this could not be. What happened? Where was our money? What could I do while I was in Israel?

Then I realized this was a terror attack on Marie and me. They had killed me, and God raised me back to life. So, they stole my money. I closed my eyes to calm my thoughts. Fear is a vicious animal. It was producing a panic attack where I could not think. I started to pray, but I could barely formulate thoughts. This was a disaster. I quoted the word, "Be anxious for nothing. Seek first God and His kingdom. I will never leave you nor forsake you. I can do all things through Christ who strengthens me. Nothing can separate me from the love of God in Christ Jesus. God is my protector. He is my fortress and stronghold."

I started to get a grip on my thoughts. Stop and let the Spirit take charge of my emotions. Take authority and know His peace. I am in a battle. What is the situation? I have lost all my money in my bank accounts. I need money to help the kids get to Jerusalem. I need money to pay my bills and to live on for the next five days.

I gave a chuckle at that last reflection. If I truly believed Jesus would be here in four or five days, what would I need money for? I could call my financial planner and cash in some stocks for temporary relief. I had credit cards with large amounts of credit to use, which would last me a month. All was well, but there was danger. The terrorists must know I am alive. How? They could have been watching Marie. Bart and Roger know I am alive. The PM and his staff know.

I called Bart and asked him to get Roger to investigate my finance attack and to see if there was a mole in the PM's office. Then I had to tell Marie so she could go to war in prayer for our protection. I still had to call the kids and the PM. I had to contact my bank. I started to feel anxious again. Take a deep breath. Breathe slowly. Focus on the victory of Christ. No weapon formed against me can prosper. All is right with God. The worse the world or Satan can do to me cannot take away God's love for me, nor could it separate me from Jesus. I could face anything with God in front, behind and around me.

I suddenly found myself ten years past with Marie in Venezuela. We had finally arrived at the farm on an island off the coast of Venezuela. It was here we would minister to about seventy leaders from the local churches. It was such a joyous reunion as I saw old friends who I had come to know through several visits to the Isle of Blessing. We hugged and embraced and smiled as we greeted one another. It was always strange to me as we tried to communicate, but I knew no Spanish and most of them did not know English. We wanted to say more and ask about families and friends and their ministries, but we could not. The only exception was when one of them spoke a little English, but it was hard. What communicated was our love for one another and our love for Jesus. These wonderful people had very little materially. They labored hard at jobs and then pastored their people with great love. They built communities of faith that were on fire for Jesus in the power of the Holy Spirit. Even though the government persecuted them terribly by stealing their valuables, cutting off their phone services to punish them for violating their impossible demands, and declaring their home groups illegal.

They demanded that every visiting pastor get a religious visa in order to minister. Then they would deny the visa when they applied for them. That had happened to Marie and me, so we came on a tourist visa. If caught preaching or doing any active type of ministry, they could arrest us and send us home and then fine the local pastor $1,500, which for them was an impossible amount to raise. So, this day we were meeting at a farm outside the town. The ten pastors and their missionary leaders had gathered secretly for us to teach and pray with them. There were about seventy of us jammed into a small farm house that they used as a church. The love just flowed from my friends. I would be so moved by their faith and love that I would often have tears of joy streak down my checks.

There, I saw one of my favorite missionaries. He was an old black man who talked to me in Spanish. Even though I never understood a word, he would keep rambling on about his family and ministry as though I knew every word. His joy captivated me, and in the Spirit I knew what he meant. After he greeted us we went inside and saw more of the people sitting in makeshift benches and chairs squeezed into the front room. Behind it was the kitchen, and outside the women were preparing the lunch meal. As I made my way to stand in the kitchen, I kissed each of the women with a holy kiss on their cheek. They were wonderful lovers of Jesus and great cooks too.

Imbrey was part Indian and Spanish, a very petite woman full of contagious joy. We visited her home once for fellowship and a meal. It was delicious, especially a coconut milkshake that was the best I had ever tasted. I told her if she came to America she could make a fortune selling this sweet nectar of the gods.

The kitchen was full of men waiting for the ministry time to start. Just as I found my spot next to the sink, we started to sing. Our praise shook the farmhouse with pleasing worship to the Lord. They had no inhibitions but sang with beauty and oneness of their love for Jesus. Now my tears really started to flow as the presence of God filled the room. I wished every person in America could come and experience the intimacy and freedom these leaders had in the Spirit. As wonderful as many churches are in America, none ever match what I experienced in these house churches in Venezuela. It would transform their worship and lifestyle in Jesus. I loved going on these trips because it inspired my faith and energized me in my passion for Jesus.

When we finished singing, Enrico our leader, called me forward to say a few words before I would preach, and then Marie would preach and prophesy. As I took hold of the small, rickety pulpit and looked into their eager faces, the anointing of God flooded my being. It was like being lifted up into the heavens. Strength and power in the love of Jesus came forth from my voice. We were one in the Spirit. I decided to say a few words of greeting and go right into my message. It was on the idol of self and how to gain victory over our inner struggles and division that can plague our soul and mind.

As I was in the middle of my message, I thought I heard commotion outside. Sara came up to me and whispered I had to stop speaking as soldiers had arrived. It happened so quickly. Two officers and five soldiers stormed into our midst. With guns raised, they shouted at us to sit and remain calm. We were told we were holding an illegal meeting and must stop. They took Enrico, Marie, and me into custody for not having the proper visas. It got rather tense when one of the pastors, a former member of the elite guard, challenged the officers, denouncing them for their action. The captain took his pistol out and walked up to Hermano. He placed the gun to his forehead and said he would shoot if anyone made a move. Hermano stood firm and did not back down, but cooler heads prevailed.

It is amazing the restraint my friends show under constant persecution by the authorities. When the government takes control of the citizens' lives, there is no recourse to resist. The frustration can build, but these men and women of Jesus are led by the Spirit and respond with love. I was very protective of Marie and would not let the soldiers touch her. That did not sit well as they then shoved me to the ground and kicked me several times. It felt as though they broke a rib, but I was only bruised. I could see fear in Marie's eyes as I looked up with my hands raised in surrender.

They put us in their Land Rover and whisked us away to the jail. They had us sit for a number of hours by ourselves, which we used to pray and praise the Lord. Then they brought us out and told us we had broken the law, but they would let us go with a warning if we would not take part in any religious activities. We submitted to their orders and were allowed to leave after we signed some papers that admitted we had acted illegally. Whew, that was a close call. Later we found out that one of Enrico's leaders had betrayed us. Earlier that week, Enrica had to remove him from leadership due to a financial discrepancy. He in turn called the security leader and told him of our plans to preach without the proper visas.

How did we find out who the traitor was? No one knew the location of our meeting except three people; one was this former leader. He sold us out as so often happens in a country that is ruled by socialists and communists. They allow little freedom of worship and need to control the population.

Our escapades continued as the next afternoon, we were having a late lunch, when we heard a loud lion like roar outside our door. They are killing the 450 pound pig for the feast this weekend we were told. Being a city boy, I had never seen this execution done, so I ran to the door and opened it.

One of the workers, who was the leader of the men's group, was swinging the limb of a tree like a long baseball bat. Whack and a thump at the back of the sow's neck and it instantly collapsed, knocked out. Then another worker ran in with a knife and stabbed it through the heart. He was obviously experienced and skilled as he instantly ended the pig's life. It had resisted their attacks for a minute or so. I thought, how do you kill such a large and powerful animal? They had struck it several times but it fought on bravely, making the sounds of an embattled beast. The final blow finished its gallant effort to live. The piercing of its heart put it out of its misery. Now we would feast with its blessing of plenty.

I watched as Manuel meticulously shaved the course hair from the sow to prepare it to be cut up into edible portions of meat. I wondered what Liz would say about all of this as she was an avid defender of animal rights. I, on the contrary, was fascinated by this process. They slit the pig open and cut off its feet, which they saved to cook and eat. The knife was long but sharp as a razor. They cracked the ribs and cut out the heart and the lungs, then the kidneys, bladder, stomach, and intestines. Blood was everywhere, pouring down the pig off the table. Next they cut out the portions of the hind legs and front legs and ribs to eat, which included the head.

I remembered doing a Jamaican wedding in Orlando and going to the reception. They had goat brain soup. I loved all the other food they served, but the soup was not too tasty for me. Would this all end one day I wondered? The lion would lie down with the lamb. We would not bite and devour each other, nor slaughter animals for food. Yet, it puzzled me if the animals continued to reproduce, where would we all live? Or like us, would there be no sexual reproduction or we would still eat the animals to enjoy the blessings of God and maintain a proper balance? I reflected that soon we would know as Jesus would make all things new. Peace and oneness would rule the day and our hearts.

That afternoon we discovered a massive storm was coming our way. All boats from the island were canceled. The planes were full, so we could not leave the island, even though we were told to depart within a day or so. That night monsoon-like rains fell drenching the ground with flooding. As I lay awake, the Spirit convicted me of my idol of self. After the soldiers had raided our Bible study, I had a few hours to process the event. I thought we should leave because we had been forbidden to minister to anyone. So, I pressed Ernesto to get us tickets on the boat or a plane to get home. He made several calls and informed me no one would go home for at least five days because of the storm.

Now the Spirit spoke to me, "Why was I trying to leave? Did I not send you to minister? Who is directing you to depart?" Then it hit me, that the idol of Self had risen up and taken the throne of my life. I was sent here to serve. Just because I could not serve the way I wanted to, I was ready to go. God had more work for me in a different manner. He would show the way. Rest and relax in Him. Enjoy the stay.

Marie and I spent the next six days ministering to a small group of leaders secretly and God ministered to us, to refresh and renew us. We had a wonderful time in His Presence. We received a prophecy from Sara, Enrico's wife, that God would rebuild us in our family concerning our emotions, in our spirit, in our ministry, and in our finances for this new year. Within six months all of this came true. We healed from our trauma with taking in Fiza, the Muslim girl they tried to honor kill. In the Spirit, we went deep in His call on our lives and new avenues of proclaiming Jesus around the world opened up to us. Then we received an anonymous gift of $10,000 to buy a new car, which we sorely needed.

Marie had blown her Audi's engine and we had no money to fix it nor money to buy another car. We were down to one car with three kids and a full-time ministry. We were able to get a used van, which had only 5,000 miles. God loves to bless His children. Now all of those concerns would be gone when we had our resurrected bodies, no sin, only complete trust in God and His provision. No sweat of the brow or toil. No pain in childbirth for no more children for the redeemed while the unbelievers would still produce children.

While we were in the airport preparing to leave Venezuela after the storm abated, I saw a display of how Christians try to live. In the hotel was an escalator. As I was prayer-walking through the lobby, I observed a young girl trying to walk up the escalator steps that were going down. She would get up a few steps and then stop and come back down to where she had been while still attempting to go up the downward-moving steps. She kept doing this over and over again as her family watched, laughing at this ridiculous sight. I thought that is the way most Christians live. They are trying to follow Jesus in their own way, in their own efforts, to climb up the escalator. Instead of flowing with the Spirit where they could cruise up the escalator that was going the right way up. How easy that is. The Spirit would just take them up to their destination.

Most believers are trying to love Jesus and live for Jesus their way, in their own strength and it is futile. Eventually the girl stopped trying to go up a downward escalator. She grew tired of trying to do the impossible in her own strength. In the Spirit, we can love Jesus and live His way. The power of the Spirit will take us to where God wants us to go. I had the courage to face whatever would come!

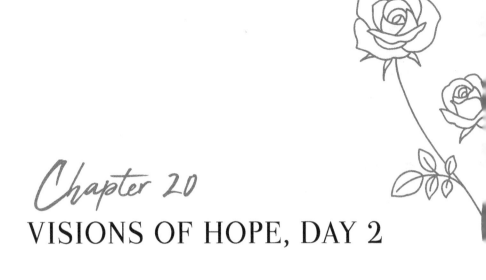

Chapter 20

VISIONS OF HOPE, DAY 2

As I waited outside the Prime Minister's office, I debated whether I should tell him about what was happening in my life: another terror attack on my money and my concern for my children and grandchildren. I had no money. Yet, he already had so much on himself. I did not want to trouble him more. Still, it was my kids who needed protection. I would let the Spirit lead me on this.

Olga greeted me again as I went in for my meeting with Benjamin. She was quite pleasant and graceful. She asked me where Marie was, and I told her she was trying to help get our family to Jerusalem. "May I be of service? I could have my assistant make arrangements," she offered.

Thank you, Holy Spirit. This could be a blessing and I would not have to mention it to Benjamin. I asked myself should I mention the attack to her also? Why not? If anyone could retrieve my money the Israelis could.

"Olga, I would love to take you up on your offer. I feel it is vital my family gets here safely. Plus, I hesitate to mention this, but I believe I was hit with a terror attack last night. All my money disappeared from my bank accounts. The terrorists must know I am alive."

"How terrible. We can help with that. I will have you meet with my assistant once you are finished with the prime minister."

I breathed a heavy sigh of relief. God had my back as I knew He did, but this was quick confirmation and an answer to my desperate prayers. I could not wait to tell Marie.

"What news do you have for me?" Benjamin asked as we greeted him.

"It is good. I know that. What I must share will seem strange, but I have to tell you what I believe God has given to me for you."

"Yesterday, after our encounter with God, I know God has blessed you with a direct line of communication from heaven. I need His wisdom and guidance. The heaviness of events press in upon me in this hour of crisis."

"I had a vision of the prophet Ezekiel," I began, omitting the fact I was a time traveler for Jesus. "He shared with me much of what is in his book in the Bible. God has a plan, and it will unfold in the next four or five days as He ordained before time began. It confirms your dream and Marie's interpretation, except it picks up after the first three days and seems to focus on the last three days."

"As you know, I must give an answer to President Horn that we will never surrender by tomorrow, the third day. We have intel that the Russians do have a secret weapon, and if our info is accurate, we have no defense to stop it."

"God has His angels standing guard, so I take hope in their defense, but after three days a sense of hopelessness will overtake Israel. Out of this desperation, the people will cry out to God and He will act to deliver Israel. The valley of dry bones has become a mighty army. God has been recruiting this spiritual dynamo since 1948. We have far more angels and warriors of the Spirit than Satan has demons and the armies of earth. So, I am confident we must not lose hope and trust that God will deliver us as He has throughout our history. I take courage from Churchill's words in WWII. Even in our darkest hour we will prevail. We must never, ever give up.

"Know that the armies of the north, east and south will strike Israel. I think it will be a terrible blow, but it will end in our triumph."

The PM nodded his head in agreement. "I was wondering who would come against us from the south, but I am no longer in the dark on this. Last night, there was a coup in Saudi Arabia. The royal family was murdered. The man temporarily in charge is a close friend to Iran and the Shiites. He will move against us with the Russians, Turks, Syrians, Iraqis, and Iranians."

"Things are moving swiftly," I added. "God knew all of these things would happen. Nothing occurs that He does not know would take place. You are like Hezekiah when Assyria came with certain destruction against Jerusalem. God will defeat the armies. It is written in Ezekiel 38 and 39. In the final hour, there will be a tremendous feast of victory," I assured Benjamin.

"I am most grateful for your help. Please continue to share with me any word you receive. You are my Isaiah, and we will see the Lord of Hosts high and lifted up as He defeats the armies of Babylon."

After I left the PM, Olga's aide met me, and we arranged for my family to be flown to Jerusalem and for the Israeli cyber-defense to see about my money. Things were looking up. I was confident all would happen as God ordained. Now, I had much to do, especially concerning my family. I will feel much better when they arrived in Jerusalem. The PM's office would get them living quarters and have them on the first flight to Tel Aviv once they were ready.

"I think there is a mole in the PM's office," Roger started. As I looked at him and heard him speak, I again marveled at the transformation of this man. He had looked the part of a Nazi and was on the point of death. Now he was vibrant, handsome, and focused on his mission to help me and prepare the way for Jesus to come.

"Why do you believe that?" I inquired.

"My sources in the military intelligence are rather certain it is a woman with the code name Z."

"The only woman I met was Olga Izmennik, but it could be her assistant or some other female that has access."

"I doubt it is a lower-level person. My guess, it is Olga who has close contact with the PM."

I shook my head. "Hard to believe. She was very kind and helpful. But if what we suspect is true, then my family is in more danger than I realized. She knows my money is gone. Do you think they will still work on getting it back?"

"Probably. It is part of the game, but don't get your hopes up. Besides, if Jesus shows up, you won't need any money."

"Well, what do we do?"

"If our military suspects her, you can bet Mossad and the PM know. They may be using her to help Israel's cause."

"Bart, what is your advice on my family?"

"We should get them here asap. You need to call them like now. First let's pray."

"Yes, I agree."

We knelt in prayer, the four of us and began to intercede to the Father for my family, for protection, for wisdom, and for protection for us in Jerusalem and for those in America, including Bart's wife and kids and Roger's. We prayed that all that was dark would come to light and every demonic spirit would be exposed. We asked for strength for the days ahead and concluded with, "Come, Lord Jesus, come."

Marie and I called our son, Jonathan, to urge him to get over to Jerusalem, but found that it was impossible for them to leave earlier than two more days.

"I know this all sounds bizarre, but I can't say more strongly that you could be in real danger," I pleaded.

"Pops, we love you and respect you, but understand our point of view. You are asking us to leave the safety of America to go to the lion's den. Not everyone is on board with leaving our jobs, our homes, and our security."

"Daniel was safe in the lion's den. All your mom and I can say is pray and let the Holy Spirit guide you. I am going to have Roger see if he can get security protection around everyone's house. Until then, know we love you and we will be praying for you. Give my love to everyone."

I hung up and turned to Marie. "They are not coming." She felt deflated. "They don't understand because they are not living through what we are. It is too much to take in without experiencing it themselves. I have to see if Roger can get them some protection."

Marie moved closer to me and snuggled into me. Tears wet my shirt. She knew trouble was coming. Her prophetic antenna was up. The canary in the cage was chirping loudly, but all she could do was pray. "I feel like it is just after the crucifixion when I gathered with Mary and the women waiting to go anoint His body. But this time, we know Jesus rose from the dead."

"That's right. We have hope in the midst of despair. We need to put on some praise music and worship. Let us fill this household with the glory of God."

At my suggestion, Marie put on some Hillsong worship music as we four gathered to exalt the Lord God. How wonderful it is to praise Him in the midst of battle. It brought to mind that the Christians sang Psalm 118 as they were marched to the Roman Coliseum to be torn apart by lions or burned alive as torched for the emperor. "This is the day the Lord has made. We will rejoice and be glad in it."

"Lord," I prayed, "give us the faith of those believers. Awaken us to the eternal and not be slumbered by the temporary. May we keep our eyes on Jesus and His plan. We have victory in Jesus Christ. The battles may rage, but the war is already won." Soon the room was filled with His glory. The heaviness of the hour left us as we put on this garment of praise. We sang and danced before our Creator. His love and power would sustain us and our families.

Chapter 21

A GLIMPSE INTO
THE FUTURE, DAY 3

W e fell asleep just after midnight. We entered the third day. Israel was quiet and safe. The PM's dream and interpretation held true, but the world was on edge. Few of us knew of the ultimatum that hung over Israel like the sword of Damocles, ready to fall. Day three would be one of anticipation. Who would blink first? For years the world had been at the precipice of world war, only to wait for all of God's pieces to be in place. The clock was about to strike midnight in the history of the human race. All of heaven watched to see what would unveil in Jerusalem, the center of God's eye.

There I was standing in the heavens with the apostle John. I saw seven angels, each with a bowl of God's wrath having been poured out over the earth in judgment for our rebellion and sin. Humanity had refused to repent of our wicked ways. It was the age of man. We stood on the earth erecting our towers of Babel, gateways to God, with a defiant fist raised, determined to create our own destiny. The seventh angel poured out his bowl into the air, and a loud voice came out of the temple of heaven, saying "It is done!"

Noises and thunders and lightnings shook the skies. A great earthquake exploded across the earth like no other earthquake in the history of mankind. Jerusalem was divided into three parts, and the cities of the nations fell as the great Babylon was remembered before God to give her the cup of wrath of the fierceness of His ire.

Babylon, the scarlet harlot of Satan and his kingdom would now feel the fullness of God's vengeance for her sins against His faithful and for its evil that encompassed the world. The angel took John and me to see the harlot and the judgment that would cast its doom across the earth. Kings and the inhabitants of the earth had been made drunk with the wine of her fornication. So we were carried away in the Spirit to see this mystery, Babylon the Great, the Mother of Harlots and the Abomination of the earth. This scarlet woman was drunk with the blood of the saints and with the blood of the martyrs of Jesus. Her figure astonished me as she was shaped by seductive evils that seduced the minds of men and women.

> She sat on a scarlet beast which was full of names of blasphemy, having seven heads and ten horns. This beast that she rides are the kingdoms of this earth throughout human history. They make war on the Lamb and the Lamb will soon overcome them, for He is the Lord of lords and King of kings. The waters that surround her are the peoples, multitudes, nations, and tongues, which will turn against Babylon and destroy her. Sin is devoured by its many children and is consumed by its own lusts and passions which pervert the laws and truth of God.

> Then another angel came down from heaven and declared Baylon the great has fallen, is fallen, and has become a dwelling place of demons. A prison for every foul spirit, and a cage for every unclean bird. All the nations have drunk of the wine of the wrath of her fornication, the kings of the earth have committed fornication with her, and the merchants of the earth have become rich through the abundance of her luxury.

Then the voice from heaven called God's people to come out of her, lest they share in her sins, and lest you receive of her plagues.

Then the kings and merchants of the earth began to mourn and lament when they saw the smoke of her burning, saying, "Alas, alas, that great city Babylon, that mighty city. For in one hour your judgment has come."

For in one hour, such great riches came to nothing. Every shipmaster, sailors and those who trade on the sea stood at a distance and cried. For in one hour she is made desolate. By her sorcery all the nations were deceived and in her was found the blood of the prophets and saints and of all who were slain on the earth.

The entire world was engulfed in the wailing and weeping of the kings, the merchants, the shipmasters, and all the people who had been seduced by the harlot and her system of evil. I had to cover my ears for the sound reverberated like a thunderous symbol in my ears.

Then we saw rejoicing in the heavens. "Alleluia! Salvation and glory and honor and power belong to the Lord our God! For true and righteous are His judgments because He has judged the great harlot who corrupted the earth with her fornication, and He has avenged on her the blood of His servants shed by her."

The twenty-four elders and the four living creatures fell down and worshiped God who sat on the throne, saying, "Amen and Alleluia!"

With the same suddenness that took me into the future, I was now back in my bed, lying safely with my bride. My head was a whirl with the sights and sounds I had seen. The God of judgment was so foreign to our culture. It was difficult to grasp what lay ahead for the world system of Babylon whose tentacles intertwined with every nation in their lust for power and dominion. The phrase, in one hour Babylon would fall, reverberated in my being. It became the focus of my experience. I had often pondered how this would happen in the practical expression of its prophecy. Because of Marie's interpretation of the PM's dream, I think I knew.

A computer virus would be released against Israel, but it would not be contained to Israel. It would spread like a horde of demons into every household and business. In one hour, the entire world economic system would collapse. Anarchy would reign. Fear would produce war and death and mass suicide. Could this possibly happen after the third day? Just as Jesus had risen on the third day to conquer evil, He would come to destroy all that were unholy and unrighteous on this earth tomorrow or the next day? The world system of wickedness would consume itself in its sins, and then Jesus would make all things new and restore what He and His Father had created in the beginning.

In the morning I would tell Benjamin what I had seen. It was frightful for human eyes to behold, but the creatures of heaven rejoiced with the martyrs that certain destruction had come to the end of the beast, the unholy city, and their kingdom of evil. The Messiah would descend to set all things right with His word and truth.

Chapter 22

ON THE EDGE, DAY 3

We could cut the tension with a knife bloodied from battle. The preliminaries of war had been fought like two heavyweights feeling each other out with only a few blows landed in the initial rounds. The end-time fighting was but one day away. It would be a fight to the death. As for me, I had a terrible foreboding of what this unique day in the history of the world would bring. There had been many battles throughout the ages that changed the course of human history, but this moment would alter time itself.

The age of sinful humanity was about to close so we could venture into a bright and glorious future. Our destiny secure in Jesus Christ, I still twinged with doubt as though something could go dreadfully wrong. I was set to meet with the PM once more. Olga weighed on my mind. Was she the notorious Z in league with the terrorists, a Russian mole trying to bring down Israel and lift Russia to become the new Rome? Marie, Bart, and Roger pleaded with me not to go, but how could I disobey my orders from heaven? My mission was to keep the PM informed, to help guide him through the unknown into the future.

I still had not given up on getting my family to come to Jerusalem. Something sinister hung in the air over them and in my thoughts. I could only do so much. Roger had some of his partners on security watch, but it was not 24/7. A terrorist could strike at any moment. If a person was willing to die for their cause, there was not a whole lot anyone could do to stop him.

The scene of Babylon had shaken me more than I realized. I was like everyone else in this world. I denied how evil we were in our systems of oppression and selfishness. I could not believe that humanity was capable of such cruelty and barbarism. Even when studies from World War II had been done where ordinary God fearing citizens could turn into Nazi exterminators, I would not accept the truth. We needed a resurrection from our culture of death. Whether it was war, crime, murder, violent abuse, or death by drugs, alcohol, or some sexual addiction, we were a race bent on destroying ourselves. If we would not kill or harm others, our own bodies took their own life in the genetic defects that brought aging, sickness, and death.

Jesus was our hope. He had conquered sin and death. He had defeated Satan and his demons. He would restore us in the perfection that God had created Adam and Eve. This was beauty and our wonderful life in the image of God. I had to keep my eyes on Jesus and the hope we would know in the days ahead. God promised to go before us. I knew Jesus and the reality of His power and knowledge. The future was full of wonders far beyond what I could imagine. It was the short, temporary suffering I wanted to avoid, but it was coming like a plague. Only Jesus had the cure.

Miss Joanna, Olga's aide, greeted me at the PM's door. How typical, the thing we fear never happens. Olga was tied up with her duties for the Prime Minister. She had arranged for the flights for my family. My money was a different story as that may take weeks to recover if ever. Their cyber-techs were focused on the coming war. My funds were a low priority, which I understood. They were the least of my worries with the coming of Jesus, money would not be an issue.

I thanked Joanna for her help. Then she said the PM had appropriated a large sum of money for me as compensation for my help. Since I did not have a safe bank account, it would be given in cash with the proper documents, explaining why and how much.

Could I meet with their people tonight near my apartment? Joanna would send me instructions on where and when to meet. I offered not to take the money. I was not asking for any, but she told me the PM insisted I receive a generous amount as per Olga. I agreed to meet them and receive the funds.

"A new adventure to share," Benjamin opened our conversation. "Tell me, how does this time travel work?"

Surprised by his knowledge of my travels, I stood in silence for a minute.

"No one is supposed to know," he helped me along seeing how stunned I was by his comments on my time travels. "But we Israelis have our ways." So much for my private adventures, I reasoned.

"I'm not sure I can explain it," I stuttered. "Of course, God does not need a machine to make it happen. I am usually asleep or in prayer, and suddenly I am in another time that concerns the future of humanity or some important past experience recorded in the Bible. My educated guess is that there is a portal that can be accessed in the time continuum. When that door is accessed and opened, one can walk through the portal at a specific time and return the same way."

"Why you?" he asked.

"I have no clue. Why did God choose David or Abraham? Only God can answer that question. It has made my life very interesting and full of blessings."

"Is it a vision?" he inquired as he pursued his curiosity as to this fascinating subject.

"No, it is more than a vision. I step into the reality of the moment. I am actually there. At least I believe I am. I often am not allowed to say anything that would impact the person or the era. Yet, I interact with the people."

"I would love to hear more about your journeys, but today is the third day and I have much to do. What do you have for me?"

"It was rather different in that I did not go back in time, but was in the future with the apostle John, witnessing the fall of Babylon. The judgments of God have been poured out by angels in heaven upon the earth. The final one is the destruction of the entire ungodly system of Babylon. The city itself has already been judged, but now its world empire will fall. As I thought through this process and went to God in prayer, I have to believe it will come in some form of computer virus from China.

"It will attack Israel and then spread throughout the world through the internet and into the cloud," I stated, still uncertain what "the cloud" was. "All stored information and backup will be corrupted and wiped out. The entire economic system will collapse within an hour. Chaos will reign. I am concerned that your whole defense system will be taken down. I have to believe tomorrow will be V-Day. It will be an earthquake like we have never seen. The foundations of world civilization will collapse. No one would have believed it possible just a generation ago, but it seems too easy today.

"The good news is heaven rejoices, for it paves the way for the Messiah to come and save Israel and His body of believers. The end of our age is at hand. You are the one chosen by God to hand over your government to the Messiah."

I'm not sure if Benjamin was in shock, but he was speechless. The trial that stood before him had become like Goliath looming over the shepherd boy. Only one steeped in intimacy with God could have the courage to look the giant in the eye and deliver a death blow to save his nation. Did Benjamin have the faith to slay the bear?

"Whatever you do, do not surrender to the unholy trinity as their armies come against you. You will be tested. Hold on to God and your faith. He will carry you through these perilous times just like He led Moses and the Hebrews through the Red Sea. Our Creator will part the sea, and the armies of your enemies will be destroyed."

"Today then will be the last day of prosperity. We face three days of destruction, before the Messiah comes. We are as best prepared for the cyberattack as we know how."

"I doubt it will be enough. It will be like 200 million demons crashing your computer defense system. I would prepare for the onslaught of the northern, eastern, and southern armies against your borders. Those will not be enough. Jerusalem will be surrounded, but the Messiah will come in the last hour to save the day," I assured him.

"The Messiah will be our John Wayne and his cavalry coming to rescue our wagon train from the Indians," Benjamin quipped, but in his heart he knew it would be much worse. The slaughter could be another Holocaust.

"It's more like God has been preparing us from ancient days of heroes from heaven who will save the human race. Hollywood has been telling us for years the end of the world is coming, except they miss the Messiah part. He will arrive in the clouds of glory with His army of angels and saints. Have you ever read Augustine's *City of God*?" I asked. "He contrasts the city of God with Rome. Instead we have Babylon and Jerusalem. One is the world system of corruption that grew out of the city of Babylon. The other is the holy city of Jerusalem and the reestablishment of God's perfect world system of truth and justice ruled over by the Messiah. We win, and if you will excuse my interpretation, Jesus already defeated Babylon on the cross. We are now just seeing the completion of His victory."

"We will know shortly who the Messiah is. I pray we do not miss Him a second time," Benjamin commented revealing his faith.

I knew to leave it alone at this point of our discussion. The die was cast, and we had to live out our part on the world stage as Shakespeare had said. What a play it is!

Chapter 23

THE BEGINNING
OF THE END, DAY 3

The call Benjamin made to President Horn was sated with turbulent waters. He informed Horn that Israel would never surrender to Russia's demands. God would deliver them from the bear and the lion. Horn tried to dissuade Benjamin from his decision. The US would support and protect them from atrocities and from losing their nation.

"No one can keep us safe at this point but God," Benjamin told Horn. "I have complete confidence in our God and His covenant promises. We appreciate your help, but Russia and her allies are bent on our destruction, and they will not pull back at this hour.

"We will be prepared for a cyberattack like one you have never known. China will unleash an army of demons that will bring down the world system."

"How do you know this?" Horn inquired, sensing a darkness that would cover the earth because of the foolishness of Benjamin's deluded faith.

"I have it on the most reliable source. Isaiah told me."

"Who is this Isaiah? A code name for one of your operatives?"

"Let us just agree he is a messenger from heaven."

"I am confused, Benjamin. What can we do for you?"

"I think it is what we can do for you? You have had our back. Now we will have yours. All hell is about to burst forth upon the world. Only the man of faith will be left standing. Please convey to the Devil, Vladimir, we reject his demands, and we know his final destiny will be a lake of fire. Godspeed, Mr. President."

With that conclusion, President Horn ordered that he be put through to Vladimir. "We need to prepare for all-out war," he told his staff. "Gather everyone, especially the military, for an urgent conference. No one has an excuse to miss."

"Hello Vladimir, I just got off the phone with Benjamin. They will not surrender."

"I see," he sounded almost gleeful in his response. "Do we have our deal?"

"No deal. We stand with Israel."

"Then the Middle East will be ours alone. So much for the Roman triumvirate," Vlad said as he hung up the phone. "Move forward with Operation Annihilation. We launch after midnight," he commanded his generals.

The message came from Z for the terrorists. Finish OPERATION JOB. They will meet on the Mount of Olives, overlooking the Jewish cemetery tonight at 8 p.m.

Chapter 24

ALLAH AKBAR, DAY 3

Marie's anxiety level seemed off the charts when I arrived home. That told me she had a message for me that had caused the canary to start chirping.

"How did it go?" she asked.

"As good as it could under the circumstances. I believe Benjamin has a powerful faith in God. He is the right man for the hour."

Not able to contain herself any longer, Marie asked me to sit down. I could tell this was serious business. "What's up?"

"Oh, besides the collapse of Babylon and the end of the world and the coming of the Messiah, let alone the release of a couple of hundred million demons, not a whole lot," she said sarcastically.

"You received a word?"

"Yes, and I need you to listen. I saw an explosion on the Mount of Olives. This Olga is Z. She wants to take you out."

I nodded in agreement. Only her connection with God and the prophecies given could have let her know our meeting tonight was on the Mount of Olives. Her words seemed true to me.

"Where are Bart and Roger?" I asked, ready to press forward with my task.

"You are not listening to me!" Marie stated strongly as she grabbed my chin to force me to look into her eyes.

"I am. That is why I need to speak to Bart and Roger. I am already with you. You are bull's eye, spot on. I am thinking ahead."

"You are? Why so agreeable?"

"Because my meeting tonight is on the Mount of Olives overlooking the Jewish cemetery and the Eastern Gate."

"You are not going to go, right?"

"I don't know. I think I have to meet with her people. They are giving us a large sum of money to help us."

"It's a set-up. Don't you see?"

"I do. We need to calm down and think this through and most importantly pray about it."

"What is there to pray about? The money means nothing. You are putting your life in jeopardy."

"Yes, but the PM wants me to go. It is his way of exposing Z. He knows everything. He secretly asked me to do this. I will be perfectly safe."

"No, I won't let you. If he has the details on her, why not just arrest her?"

"This is his way. I do not know all that he knows."

"Crazy. God has shown me what will happen. You are like the apostle Paul when the prophet told him not to go to Jerusalem, and he still went and look at what happened to him," she exclaimed, reminding me he was arrested and eventually executed.

"You didn't see me killed, did you?"

"I didn't have to. The whole area was one mass of death and debris."

"Look at it. I know you are right, but how this all plays out is in God's hands."

"Do not put God to a foolish test," she countered. "You are so stubborn."

"I am," I answered with a smile and took her in my arms and embraced her. "I also know I have a part to play in these last days and I think there is more I need to tell the PM."

"Your pride will bring your death," Marie said angrily. "Why won't you hear me?"

"I agree with all you have said, except I don't think tonight is my rendezvous with death. Bart and Roger will be there to protect me."

"Then I am going too," she insisted.

"No, you are not. I can't be distracted by your presence. I need you here, interceding for my protection. God has shown you what will happen so you can pray. You should probably send out a world-wide prayer alert. It may be the last opportunity before the computers crash."

"I already have," she said, but she did not smile fearing my fate.

I had to laugh at her ability to be one step ahead. "You knew I had to go, didn't you."

"That did not keep me from trying."

"You can be one tough cookie, or you can be the sexiest woman alive." I had to kiss this beautiful time traveler of mine. As we kissed, I was flooded with memories of our wonderful marriage and ministry. We had our trials, but we were always one in spirit and in love.

"Bart said he would be gone for a few hours," she whispered as she enticed me to the bedroom. Why not? It could be our last encounter of passion. Oh yes, I would still call the family one more time, but that could wait for now.

The night was warm from the desert wind that had blown into Jerusalem. As I stood on the Mount of Olives, I could see the Eastern Gate in the distance where Jesus would enter the city of David. It is hard to imagine He would land on this hill and split the ground in two, causing a deep divide for miles.

It would be a grand entrance full of His rightful glory, no longer hidden from His people. When He first came to Israel, He would manifest His glory in divine miracles for people who had eyes to see, but in His humanity He cloaked His glory from their view.

In the Gospel of John, which speaks of the fullness of His glory, His initial miracle of turning water into wine revealed His glory to His disciples, and they believed in Him. His greatest expression of His godly glory was on the cross as He died for our sins. Our God is like no other god in His power and in His humility. What god in human history ever came to die for us and our salvation from our sins? Only the God of Abraham came into this world first as the Suffering Servant of Israel. Soon He would come as the Lion of Judah to complete His mission for His Father as His only begotten Son.

Then one day He will hand over the keys to the kingdom to His Father, and all things will be made new in heaven and on the earth. We were on the cusp of that divine event as I embraced this magnificent scene of Jerusalem that lay before me.

The Mount of Olives

Bart and Roger were positioned near me. There were still people milling around this scenic sight. Roger and Bart knew the danger awaiting us. The PM's men would arrive with the case of money. When the terrorists moved in to kill me, they would stop them by any means necessary.

One day there will be peace, I thought. The lion and the lamb will lie down with one another. The hearts of men and women will be changed from our very DNA to the depth of our soul. No more war, oppression, division, suffering or broken relationships. We will be one in Christ and rule and reign with Him as His kings and priests. Until then, evil must be confronted and overcome with love, but sometimes with force, as the kingdom can come with violence in this sinful age. *Come, Lord Jesus, come*, I whispered to myself.

Back at our apartment, Marie wrestled with her emotions. The weight of our journey had stripped her of the emotional energy she needed to fight the fight of faith. Old demons began to stir within her soul. That wounded little girl came drifting up through her subconscious. Marie found herself watching in her mind, hearing in her thoughts that scared daughter of Eve reenacting the abuse from her father. He loomed over her like a giant volcano spewing forth its anger, bitterness, and hate. Screaming at her that she was worthless and was but a piece of dung, cussing at her with every foul word imaginable.

She saw herself crumble in her spirit. Heard herself crying and condemning herself as that wicked little girl who would never succeed in life, craving for the love of her father but never believing she was loved or lovable. Always yearning for her father to cradle her in his arms. Instead, she saw herself in the image her father created her to be: alone, unloved, empty, and as a bad person. The pain of her memories brought a flood of tears but never enough to relieve her suffering and to save that little girl.

This was when Marie would give in to depression or she would cry out to God for deliverance. She would remind herself, "That is not me. I have a new identity in Christ. I am created in God's image. I am a good person, strong and mighty, filled with the presence of God. I am healed, renewed in holiness and righteousness. I am beautiful in His love."

Then the healing oil of the Spirit soothed her wounds and brought peace to her soul. Oh, how she thanked Jesus and her Father in heaven for their gifts of restoration and wholeness. How she thanked me for comforting her and helping her realize she was a wonderful person. No need to condemn herself. She was free from all guilt and shame by the blood of Jesus.

She was one with the Father and the Son and with me. This unity brought peace to her soul. The pull of those ancient wounds in that little girl faded away, back deep into her subconscious. Like the gentle waters of a slow winding river, the Spirit of God brought her soul to rest in the arms of her Father. She saw herself as the beautiful Cinderella, who was loved by her devoted husband. Now she could live to fight this night for the love of her life, her knight in shining armor, her beloved John.

I checked my phone. It was 8:01. My heart started to pound. My palms were sweaty. I looked around. I could only see Bart and Roger in the background. I stood at a waist-high wall near some steps that led down to another pathway around the Mount of Olives. Behind was the road and the parking area. A few buses lined up down the way. A car just pulled up. Three men got out. One was carrying a briefcase. Time to roll, I thought to myself. I moved forward to meet them. The rest remains a blur to me. From behind one of the buses, a man came running toward me yelling, "Allah Akbar, Allah Akbar" over and over again.

The three men seemed taken off guard, which I thought was strange. Why didn't they turn to stop him? Instead, Bart and Roger raced at the man. Then I realized he had a suicide vest strapped to himself. As Roger and Bart leaped on him, I felt a shove that knocked me down the brick stairs. As I tumbled forward, an explosion filled the air with smoke and shredded metal. The blast instantly annihilated the bomber, Bart, and Roger. As I lay at the bottom of the steps I was dazed from my fall. I had hit my head on the cement sidewalk. The explosion rocked the air with a force of pressure that stunned me, but the blast of shrapnel and devastating dynamite went over me. Bart and Roger had smothered much of the power of the explosion.

Later I discovered that the three men had been killed as well with a number of people injured. Tragedy had rained down on us like a hail storm from hell, full of all the devil's wrath. I could not help but grieve for Bart and Roger who had taken "a bullet for me." "Greater love has no man than this then to lay down his life for a friend." I kept hearing those words from Jesus before He died for us on the cross over and over in my head.

I lay on the pavement in shock. People gathered around me to see if I was injured. Sirens began to sound the alarm of emergency vehicles racing toward us. Blood and body parts were scattered all around. I heard cries of children and adults as they suffered the loss of loved ones or of their own wounds. The Prime Minister had his evidence for Z to be arrested, but at what cost? The terrorists were celebrating my death once again. Only this cat still had a few more lives in him. Marie would be happy to see me, but both of us would mourn the loss of our dear friends and partners in ministry.

I wept for Bart's wife and children. My comfort was they would join him in three or four days. He had just gone home early. In terms of eternity, he was a few seconds ahead of their rapture that would unite them in the sky. As I tried to get my bearings and make sure I was not wounded, I felt a presence comfort me. Then I realized it was an angel that had pushed me down the stairs out of harm's way. I imagined it was the giant guardian angel God had placed by my side many years ago that people periodically had seen walking with me in my churches. In my thoughts, I thanked Him for his mercy and protection. I was one blessed man who still had a mission to complete. Low and behold, at my side was the briefcase from the PM. God never ceases to amaze me.

Chapter 25
INTO THE DARKNESS, DAY 4

Darkness had crept over the city of David like a cloud of foreboding. By the time I reached home, it was after midnight. Day 4 had begun. I was sore and exhausted. I did have a gash on the back of my head that took a few stitches, but other than that, I needed to crawl into bed and sleep. My thoughts would not calm as I pondered what events would begin to happen. Marie wanted all the details of what had occurred. We were shaken by Bart's and Roger's death.

I plopped the briefcase on the counter. Marie wrapped herself around me and would not let go. I shared with her the terror that struck on the Mount of Olives. In the midst of our grief, I told her of my guardian angel, whom I assumed was with us now. It was strange to think that an invisible figure hovered around me in my most intimate and sinful moments. I hoped he was installed with a forgetful memory disc. The secrets our protectors could tell. The thought made me all the more thankful all my sins were erased by the blood of Jesus and forgotten by God. I was not sure about angels.

"Should we call Bart's wife?" Marie asked.

"I suppose so. Although it might be best she doesn't know and she can meet him in the air when Jesus comes. It would save her and the kids a lot of pain and suffering."

"That is a strange way to look at life, but you may be right. If Jesus is truly going to arrive in two or three days, then why not hold off?"

"We can wait until the morning to decide when our heads are clear. Although, then it will be sleep time in the US. I don't know. If they identify him, then they may contact her. Although I have no idea how they could identify Bart except through me."

I did hear at the hospital that a police officer was killed. His name was Holtzman. I wondered if that was the officer at our apartment with Steinman? "It gets weirder and weirder. Just like the Bible, the stories have more intrigue than real life," Marie added. "I am crushed by Bart's death, and I am so grateful you are alive. My emotions are on a roller coaster."

"For sure. I need to rest, but my mind will not stop going over all the details of tonight, the past couple of days, and what will happen today and the next. I wonder if the PM knows I am alive?"

"I bet he knows. He seems to have a handle on everything."

"Hey, can you believe when my head began to lose its fuzziness, there was the briefcase of money next to me. I have to thank my guardian angel for placing it there for me."

"Have you opened it yet?"

"No, we might as well." The latches were snapped off from the explosion. No lock we had to solve. I opened it, and we both stared at the contents. Nothing was in it. Empty, nada. "What does that mean?" we both said together.

"It says God wanted you to know it was empty. It's a clue," Marie said in her wisdom.

"But to what?"

"The secret to who Z is," Marie reasoned.

"You're right, but why would it be empty?"

"Lots of reasons. The guys delivering it took it because they knew you would be killed and not miss it."

"Nope, then they would not have been killed by the suicide bomber. Maybe Olga took it for herself and then gave the empty briefcase to them to deliver."

"Another mystery," I added, with a tiredness that caused my mind and body to ache. "No mysteries tonight. I have to rest."

Suddenly the air raid sirens sounded. We had thirty seconds to get to a shelter. I looked at Marie. We both communicated we did not need to go to the shelter, God's shield of angels would stop these secret weapons. We went to bed and waited for what we did not know.

The Israelis did not realize these missiles would be on them in ten seconds. Vlad had ordered Operation Annihilation to start on the morning of the fourth day. On time, they were launched traveling faster than any missile in human history. They were headed to Tel Aviv, two to Jerusalem, several to secret bases within Israel, one to their nuclear underground site, and three going to Galilee. Faster than sound, they screeched toward the Golan Heights, loaded with bombs more powerful than the hydrogen bomb but would leave no radiation, just destruction. As they approached Israel, the mighty warring angels locked shields and stood against these deadly foes. To the disbelief of the Russian radar operators they vanished without warning. Puff! Gone in the armor of the Lord.

The power of these missiles struck and shook even the angels in heaven. The blast caused the ground to quake, but the defense held. Vladimir's secret weapons proved to be harmless in the face of angelic opposition. He became enraged when the report reached him that the attack had failed. "Impossible!" he screamed. "The iron dome could not stop these harbingers of death from their destiny. Israel must have another unknown defense. Give the command for the troops to advance and tell the Chinese to launch their virus. We will overrun them on the ground."

Chapter 26

THE DARKNESS
SPREADS, DAY 4

Hidden in the Huangshan mountains of China, sheltered by a massive wall of rock, the communists erected a secret cyber base. Within this military enclave existed a rather unassuming room that harbored a voracious army of 200 million demons. These coded programs were honed and disciplined through years of study, trial and error, intense research, and constant probes and attacks against the most advanced technology in the world. They were formulated and processed to attack the US, Russia, Australia, Europe, the Middle East, Canada, Central and South America, Africa, and this morning Israel. Primed and ready for launch, they would devour the defense programs of the IDF and render them useless. In the heart of this base was a room full of computers and technology that were out of the 22nd century of imagination. Yet, this was real. The command order had been received. A cluster of Chinese soldiers stood around one main computer with a small insignificant woman huddled over her keyboard.

Colonel Liu nodded at her, and she raised her index finger and punched send as the room exploded in cheers. OPERATION ABADDON launched. In an instant this demonic army went forth at the speed of light across China, like cyber sonic horsemen riding over the mountains and plains of the ancient Silk Road, across the Euphrates River, and into the cyber units of Israel.

Within seconds, these evil minions started their delicious feast on the most precious steak Israel had to offer. Codes and programs vanished in the corruption of these devils. The Israeli soldiers manning their stations watched in disbelief as their screens blurted out messages that sent them into a panic. Then there were only blank screens. Along the Golan Heights, the Sea of Galilee, the Jordan River to the Dead Sea, and the Negev, all communications and plans disappeared. The valiant soldiers of Israel were isolated and unprepared for what would be their darkest hour. The command center of Israel could not even make a phone call. The faces of generals turned white with fear. Without any notice, the Russian tanks, combined with Syria and Turkey, began to roll into the Israeli territory of the north. Iraqi and Iranian tanks pushed across the Jordan Valley. Up through the Negev came the Saudi tanks.

Massive confusion gave way to cries of the wounded torn to pieces from the heavy fire of these tanks and then the silence of death. Israeli tanks exploded into heaps of rubble filled with brave but dead soldiers. Some of the Israeli commanders called their troops to retreat. Others ordered them to charge into the jaws of death. Without any coordination, this first advance by the enemy turned into a sea of blood and slaughter. In the main cyber headquarters, a courageous tech warrior sought to fight this battle with counter measures. Instead, he released into the public internet this vast army of demons with one push of a button. Within an hour, Babylon would fall.

Sleep escaped me as my own battles raged within me. It was as if I was living in a dream and these fantastic scenes kept coming out of the pit of my subconscious. I had no control, but to walk through them and suffer the slings and arrows of fate. In the Spirit I knew God was in charge, but my flesh warred against my spirit. The deep pain that tore at my soul scourged me with a whip of nails and bone. My soul was bleeding to death. Desperate for relief, I cried out to God for His peace to soothe me with heavenly oil.

Like a cloud that brought gentle rain, the Spirit of God descended on me, and I began to think of all of the heroes in my life. My dad is playing catch with me in the vacant lot across the street from our house. I would pitch as he caught my fastball and coached me how to pinpoint control. Those were moments I would come to treasure. Then, Reverend Stoneman who mentored me in my ministry, sat beside me in prayer and study. He poured his life into me to teach me what it meant to be a man of God, devoted to Jesus, and to preach the word of God in power and boldness. Bart and Roger came fresh to me as the heroes who saved my life. There was Fiza, the Muslim girl who came to us to save her life and would not deny Jesus in the face of persecution. My missionary partners who sacrificed a life of comfort for one of untold challenges to bring the Light of the world into the darkness.

These memories were a tremendous comfort to me at a time I needed heroes to give me strength and courage. The Book of Hebrews says these heroes who are in heaven are cheering us on in this race of life to glorify Jesus. My emotions broke with rivers of praise to my God to those who taught me the Way, the Truth, and the Life.

Then there was Marie, my biggest hero, who had overcome the terrible abuse of her soul and body to become a favorite of Jesus. She left a life of sin to live a life of love to glorify her Savior. God, in the wonder and genius of His plan for me, had given me the only one I could have loved for a lifetime. He had to go back in time to pluck her out and send her to me. Thank God, He opened my eyes to this treasure beyond measure.

I had run to the stronghold of my fortress where God dwelt and met me to fill me with hope and power for the days ahead. I knew that the dawn would bring more darkness and challenges on my journey, but heroes would arise and stand with Jesus and the God of Abraham to prepare the way for Jesus to come. Little did I know that those heroes were fighting for their lives and the very existence of Israel in the black night of this end-time invasion. Alone for the moment, Steinman, the detective war hero, took out his diary and began to write a love note to his wife and children. As his life's blood poured out of his body, so flowed his expression of love for Beth and their five kids.

My Dearest Love and Beautiful Sons and Daughters,

I pray this letter finds its way to you. Forgive the stains of blood on the page, for I am badly wounded and will not survive the night.

We were overrun on the Golan Heights by Russian and Syrian tanks. What was left of my unit has retreated to Har HaOsher on the Sea of Galilee. The nuns have taken us into their care in their convent. We have no place to run or hide until the enemy finds us. It will mean certain death, but I will probably be gone before they find me.

Know that I love you all. You are so precious and the heartbeat of my soul. I wish I could be with you. I fear for the future of Israel. Our frontlines had no communication or warning. After midnight, the ground shook like an earthquake, but no missiles hit us. We were confused by the noise and shaking, but no bombs. Then the tanks started rolling into Israel and we had no warning, no orders, only confusion. Before we knew what hit us, we were scattered and beaten. It was every man for himself.

Aviel and Albert, my two former Russian friends, were by my side. We fled together down the slope of the hill. I noticed some movement to our right. It was Turkish soldiers. One threw a grenade and I pushed Albert and Aviel away. They were spared the shrapnel, but I was terribly wounded. I fear I saved their lives and lost mine. I do not die a hero, but only one who has done his duty in defense of our beloved Israel. They picked me up and carried me to this nunnery that I am told is where Jesus preached His famous Sermon on the Mount. If ever Israel needed a Savior it is now. The nuns tell me He is coming soon to rescue us, but I know our God is our Deliverer. He will send the Messiah one day to set us free from our oppressors.

My strength leaves me. I can barely write, but there is so much I want to say in love to you. Tell our children to do their duty for Israel. Our Deliverer will come. Perhaps it could be this Jesus. The nuns are very kind and love us Jewish soldiers. They truly have hearts that love. They tell me this is what Jesus taught.

The darkness is getting more black. My eyes are heavy. I feel cold. I fear this is...

Scribble shot across the page as the angel of death took this brave soldier home to the bosom of Abraham. Sister Teresa found Steinman dead with his diary open, but the pages had flipped to his police notes. She closed his eyes and covered him with a sheet. Then her curiosity took over as she read what was written. She told herself she was looking for his name and an address to send this diary to a loved one, which she was, but she wanted to read what was written in his police notes.

I heard that Holtzman was killed on the Mt. of Olives in a suicide bombing, an attempt on this John Nova's life again. I believe Holtzman was a traitor, working with the terrorists to kill the American. Olga, from the PM's office told me this.

She was working with me to expose a mole in the PM's close circle of advisers. His code name is Z. She suspects it is the Prime Minister himself. Do I dare trust her?

I wish I could warn John and Marie Nova of the danger they are in. Olga says the PM has taken them into his confidence.

Sister Teresa put the diary into her pocket. She knew she had a mission from her Lord. Get this diary to John and Marie Nova in Jerusalem and see that this man's wife receives her love letter.

Chapter 27

THE COLLAPSE OF
BABYLON, DAY 4

A s Marie and I awoke to a new day, we realized something was dreadfully wrong. Nothing worked. The power was off. The phones did not function. No internet service. I looked out our window to the street and there was an eerie silence where normally it was abuzz with traffic and noise.

It has started, the fourth day with its infection of evil. We assumed the Chinese had delivered the virus to knock out Israel's defense, but we had not thought that the entire world system would cease to exist. We should have, since I had gone to the Fall of Babylon, but God only gives us so much insight, and sometimes I missed the rest of the story.

"We won't be able to contact Bart's wife," Marie said. "We should take comfort in the knowledge that the PM's dream is unfolding as we were told by the Spirit. I pray the kids are okay and ready for what will challenge them in these next two days. We probably won't see them or hear from them until Jesus gathers us up in the sky."

The peace I had received from the Spirit in the night moved me to lift up my hero. "You are the best," I told her. "You are my greatest hero, beside Jesus," I added.

"You are my champion. My knight in shining armor. My King David, slaying Goliath."

"Does that make you Bathsheba?" Marie gave me a glare with a little romance mixed into her stare. "With my past, you could say that." I needed to hear her sense of humor. It gave me peace in the storm.

"I wonder how we will be in the age to come when we receive our resurrected bodies? No one will be married," she lamented.

"I don't know how that will all work out, but you will still be my best friend, even though you hate sports."

"You never know what I will be like when I can play as well as you. I only hope Dolce is with us."

"You will have a whole slew of dogs at your side."

"I just want Dolce."

"Yes, no one is like the diva dog," I added.

I changed the subject. "I wonder how the IDF is fairing against the Russians and Turks and Persians and Arabs. We are still in our buildings, so I gather the secret weapons were stopped by the angels. As you said, everything is coming to pass just as you prophesied. In a day or two Jerusalem will be surrounded. I wonder what Benjamin is doing? Is his faith holding?" I questioned. "Only God can keep him strong under this pressure."

"I can't comprehend what is happening around the world. No communication. No television or internet. No power. No access to money. No business. No food or water. Hey, we better store up as much water as we can." I surmised.

"There are generators that can pump us water and give us some light, right?" Marie asked.

"Probably, but for how long and to whom? Thank the Lord, Jesus is coming and we won't need any of that. You know, we have read it in the Bible and in books and watched it on television, but we never comprehended what it would actually be like."

"I for one cannot wait to see Jesus again," Marie said with joy.

In Marie's wish, a light awakened my mind to the eternal. We live in a world that is temporary. We focus on the temporary, even though the Bible teaches us to live for the eternal. But the eternal is beyond our grasp. At least for most of us. We go about our day worrying about money and food and clothes and success and relationships and rarely giving thought to the eternal things of God. But eternity does not begin when Jesus comes. It is here and now in our relationship with God.

If I could, if Marie and I could focus on God and His eternal plan for the next few days, then we would walk through the valley of death and know the love of God and one another. Our hope would not be in the temporary but in the everlasting life of Jesus Christ. I wished I had always lived for the eternal. I had tried, but not done very well. Too often fear has been my master other than Jesus. The temporary would rule my sleep and my decisions. I had held onto things that had no value in God's kingdom. I had placed importance on things that had no worth in His eternity.

My life would have been much simpler and full of the peace that surpassed all understanding had I valued what God valued. Instead, the strongholds in my mind and pre-Christ habits would take charge at times when I knew better. It was just tough to live in the eternal all of the time. My spirit was willing, but my flesh was weak. That is why I needed a Savior and God's forgiveness. We can't run from ourselves, and we have this innate ability to destroy ourselves and all that we love.

Half a world away in America, most people were still sleeping. Darkness is the hour for evil to stalk the earth. Terrorists in three cities in the US—Atlanta, Orlando, and Los Angeles—were about their father's business as they set in motion the final phase of OPERATION JOB. In their hearts, they were doing Allah's will. How deluded we can be, especially when we do not have the Spirit's eyes to see. I was thinking of Paul's prayer in Ephesians where he prays for us that God will give us spiritual eyes to see and know His revelation knowledge. I began to hum "Open My Eyes, Lord" as they started on their mission of murder. The gate was closed to cars without the access code. It was after 3 a.m., so they did not want to wait for a car to pull up and open the gate. They hit the accelerator and rammed through the gate. The crashing noise woke the two men Roger had sent to guard Jonathan's house.

By the time they realized a terror attack was unfolding, a car was speeding down the block toward them. They hardly had time to jump out of their car and raise their hand guns. They emptied their bullets into the driver's side, but within two seconds, the SUV turned sharply into the front of the house and exploded. The house perished in an instant. The two men in the SUV and the two security officers were killed. Everyone in the house was whisked away to heaven by angels. They never knew what hit them.

At the same hour outside of Atlanta, Muhammad drove cautiously with his partner, Ahmed, toward a home in the quiet suburbs of Marietta. Muhammed loved the excitement of battle as he loved his name not for the revered prophet, but for the greatest heavyweight fighter in the world, Mohammed Ali. He loved being in the fight to submit the world to Allah and now would be giving his life for this holy jihad. From their surveillance they had seen two guards in a parked car two houses down from their target. They would probably be asleep, but they could not take that for granted. They planned to kill the officers and then blow up the house of the family that had become the enemy of their jihad. What they did not know, these two guards had been highly trained navy seals and took their responsibility seriously. They were defending their country and the world against Islam. They would not be asleep on the job.

When Jerry saw the headlights come at them, he realized this could mean danger. He alerted his partner, Wes, and they drew their .45s with the intent to kill. When Muhammed turned into the driveway of

Ashley's home, Jerry and Wes leaped out of their car with guns raised and began to fire. Their bullets struck Muhammed and Ahmed with deadly force, but it was too late. The van exploded with the force of a two-ton bomb. The jihadists evaporated. The house collapsed in a heap of rubble. Jerry and Wes were blown ten feet backward but survived. Ashley and her family were in the arms of angels safely floating up to heaven.

It was just after midnight in LA. Liz's home was an elaborate estate in Hollywood. They had just seen their last guests leave. They were tired, and the kids were in bed. Going to turn on the alarm, Tom, her husband noticed it would not set. As he turned to tell Liz something was wrong, two masked men opened fire and sent him to heaven. Liz heard the shooting, but before she could react, the terrorists found her, and she joined Tom on his flight to the gates of Paradise.

Evil knows no limits when it comes to the corruption of the human heart. Abbas and Omar's pride swelled as they carried out their god's work to bring Allah as lord over the earth. They sought out the children who had awakened but were still in bed. These harbingers of the devil made certain they remained in their safe little beds for all eternity as their bullets slaughtered the innocents. They, too, joined their parents on their journey to heaven.

Abbas and Omar left the estate and were never heard of again until they stood before the judgment seat of Christ. The Book was opened, their deeds exposed, and they found themselves in the lake of fire reserved for all who had rejected the Messiah as Lord and who failed to honor Israel and value and bless the Jewish people.

Chapter 28
THE VICTORY OF
THE CROSS, DAY 4

B ack in Jerusalem, Marie and I had no idea our family had been slaughtered. We had agreed to enter into a day of worship and prayer and fasting to praise God and to seek His guidance for these last three days. After several hours of worship and praise and reading the word, Marie experienced one of her dramatic visions that opened up to her the gift of prophecy. Revelation 19:10 reads, "For the testimony of Jesus is the spirit of prophecy." Marie saw heaven opened and behold, a white horse. And He who sat upon him was called Faithful and True, and in righteousness He judges and makes war. His eyes were like a flame of fire, and on His head were many crowns. He had a name written that no one knew except Him. He was clothed with a robe dipped in blood, and His name is called The Word of God. And the armies in heaven, clothed in fine linen, white and clean, followed Him on white horses.

Now, out of His mouth goes a sharp sword, that with it He should strike the nations. And He Himself will rule them with a rod of iron. He Himself treads the winepress of the fierceness and wrath of Almighty God. And He has on His robe and on His thigh a name written: KING OF KINGS AND LORD OF LORDS.

This is the same vision John the Apostle had as recorded in Revelation 19:11–16. After that vision of Jesus, He came to earth to defeat the beast and his armies.

Then Marie saw Golgotha, the hill of the skull. In Calgary, there stood a lone cross in the fading sunlight, clouds partly shading the sun. She seemed a distance away as though she saw the cross loom over Jerusalem. The sight was where she stood with Mary, the mother of Jesus, but Jesus was not on the cross. The cross guarded Jerusalem from evil, like the cross instilled fear in Count Dracula and caused him to run away from his victim. The power of the cross was in Jesus's sinless sacrifice of Himself and in the blood He shed for our sins. The cross had done its work of redemption by appeasing the wrath of God. Out of the cross came the Resurrection and Reign of Jesus as KING OF KINGS AND LORD OF LORDS. The fruit of the cross was the salvation of our souls. It stood strong and unbending against the last grasp of evil in this world.

Jesus was coming but not as the Lamb, instead as the warrior King of the line of David. Jesus would come to claim His rightful crown to rule the nations forever and ever. Though Jerusalem would be surrounded by demons and the armies of the beast, they could not prevail. His victory over evil would bring in His kingdom of peace and justice. Satan would be bound for a thousand years. The armies of men cannot stop the legions of the beast, but the armies of Jesus will vanquish all that is wicked and corrupted by humanity. He will come on His white horse with His angels and the resurrected believers. Jerusalem will be saved. He will take His place on the throne of glory.

And I saw these thrones and they that sat on them, judgment was committed to them by Jesus. Then I saw the souls of those who had been beheaded for their witness to Jesus and for the word of God, who had not worshiped the beast or his image, and had not received his mark on their foreheads or on their hands. And they lived and reigned with Christ for a thousand years.

Marie began to speak. "Jesus has risen from His throne and will mount His white horse. It is saddled up and ready to ride. All that is left is for the armies to gather around Jerusalem. The dead in Christ will rise and afterward, we who believe will join them in the air. We will receive our resurrected bodies to follow Him into battle."

"In His mercy and grace Jesus has spared us the deep sorrow meant for us. You have one more journey to take and to share it with the PM. All will be complete, as it was on Golgotha."

As His peace rested in our soul, we were no longer divided in our minds. The oneness of Christ united us in Him and one another. It was a peace the world could never know in its fractured nature because of sin.

Outside Jerusalem, the world was in chaos and confusion. Battles raged as the armies of evil raced toward Jerusalem. Blood and death soaked the ground of the Promised Land. The covenant would be fulfilled as given to Abraham because the life of Israel was in its blood. The nations of the earth ran to and fro without an anchor. The sheep nations wondered at the Lion of Judah, but the goat nations rejoiced ,thinking the Jews and their precious Israel would be wiped from the face of the earth as promised so many times by her enemies. Yet, she always resurrected to life to bless the nations that would honor her and her people.

Sister Teresa was given one of the nunnery's vehicles to take the treasured diary to Jerusalem. In this diary, she carried the riches of truth. Despite the intense fighting, she made her way to the sacred city to deliver the holy scroll.

Chapter 29

LIGHT IN THE DARKNESS, DAY 5

I stood on the very spot where two days before the terrorists and Z had tried to kill me. The Kidron Valley lay before me with the Eastern Gate and Jerusalem in the distance. This was where Jesus would return according to the prophet Zechariah. Quickly, I realized my time travel was spanning the past and the future. Zechariah was here, and in His vision, he was seeing the future coming of the Messiah. Where we stood were the armies that would encompass Jerusalem, perhaps within hours.

Zechariah speaks, "Do you see the armies gathered from the nations, soldiers from the north, from the south, from the east?"

I could see to the south the Arab armies, to the north the Russian, Turks, and Syrian armies, and to the east the Iraqi and Iranians. The day of the Lord had come to Israel and to the world, but at the center of the conflict was Jerusalem.

"For I will gather all the nations to battle against Jerusalem ... then the Lord will go forth and fight against those nations. As He fights on the day of battle and on that day His feet will stand on the Mount of Olives, which faces Jerusalem on the east. And the Mount of Olives will split in two from east to west ... and the Lord will be King over the earth. On that day it will be one—the Lord is one and His name one." Zechariah said this with somber reflection and holy accuracy.

The Mount of Olives is where Jesus ascended into heaven and where the angels promised He would return to sit upon His throne over all the nations of the earth united in His one kingdom. Here, O Israel, the Lord your God is one.

The concept of oneness is rooted in God and His nature. The sin of Adam fractured that oneness in God's creation. Jesus died to restore it, and now He would return so we would know this oneness as God is one for all eternity. I could see in the Spirit the Jerusalem of Zechariah, and I could see in the Spirit the Jerusalem of Jesus. All rebellion and evil would be banished forever in His kingdom with its capital, the sacred city. Benjamin David needs to have no fear. Israel and Jerusalem would endure the tragedy of the three days of death to be raised to life by the Messiah, who rose from the dead after three days in the tomb. His blood would once and for all time remove the sin of the world. The angels would sing in heaven with His faithful followers as the mystery of the ages was revealed in the Son, Jesus Christ. The blood of bulls and goats were merely a temporary solution to the eternal problem of sin and death.

Jesus, in His death as King, Prophet, and High Priest, satisfied once and for the eternal demands of God's law. No more sacrifices would be required. The chains had been broken. He came to set the captives free. His truth would prevail in His court of justice. For Jesus is the Way, the Truth, and the Life. In Him is the love and glory of God for everlasting peace.

I stood and marveled at the revelation of God upon this mountaintop. His glory came down from heaven the first time in Jesus but was hidden. In another day, it would shatter the valley as His death had torn the veil in the Holy of Holies. No more division. We would all be one. I cried, "Come, Lord Jesus, come!"

When I returned home, Marie was sitting with a woman I came to know as Sister Teresa. She was a frail-looking woman in her forties but as tenacious as an alley cat. She spoke with a German accent, but I never did discover where she was born. I did find out she loved Jesus, and in her mind, she was married to Him. As tough as she was, there was a kindness and a gentleness that created in her a servant heart. Years of training had taught her to live a life of humility. She insisted on the truth. When she was on a mission, she got it done.

When she discovered Steinman's diary and read about his discoveries on Z, she knew she had to get us this information. Her skills as a nun in keeping secrets and learning secrets enabled her to find us in Jerusalem. I came to enjoy her in our short time together.

Sister Teresa had given Marie the diary and showed her his notes. She shared with us how Steinman died a hero, saving his soldier brother's lives. Her news from the front was not good. The first tree had withered and lost all of its fruit. The enemies had taken Galilee. The second tree was sure to follow, then Jerusalem.

She was a true believer in Jesus. Her faith was as strong as an oak of righteousness planted by the stream of living water. Her revelation knowledge had witnessed to her spirit we were in the Ezekiel 38 and 39 war. Jesus was soon to come. We felt the oneness of the Spirit with her. She reminded us charismatic/evangelicals that she was in the Spirit, as you like to say.

She also shared with us some Catholic prophecies about Pope Francis. The nuns believed he would be the last Pope before Jesus returned. He would be in league with the Antichrist. She was full of surprises. She wanted to deliver the diary to Steinman's wife, but first she knew she had to get it to us. Marie and I read his notes on Holtzman and Olga and the PM. He was onto something, but who was Z? I could not believe it was the PM after all we had experienced with him. It had to be someone else.

Sister Teresa had brought a light into the darkness of deception and wickedness. Steinman's diary showed the way to the truth of God but not enough to lead us home. Our lives were still in danger as long as Z was operating with the terrorists. I did not see everything clearly, but the light from the diary dispelled the darkness so that, in time, I could fully see the unraveling of the mystery of Z. Just as Jesus taught in parables, I was on the verge of comprehending the parable of Z and the defense of Jerusalem. I knew the end game, but I needed a few more pieces of the puzzle to fall into place to fully grasp God's plan.

After she left, Marie and I discussed the death of Steinman. Too many men and women had given their lives for "the cause." He was a good man with a wife and kids. His loss would leave a hole in their hearts. It made me reflect more on my heroes as I had done earlier. A sadness enveloped me as I remembered one of my favorite missionaries. He was a German, as I imagined Sister Teresa was. His life journey had begun in pain. His father was abusive and drove him out of the family house at an early age. This led him into the wilderness of sin.

His tormented soul led him to rebel against the norms of his culture. He hopped on a motorcycle and took two years to travel from the tip of northern Africa to the Cape of Good Hope in South Africa. On his escape from life, he had a terrible accident. Left for dead, some doctor repaired his broken neck. God had a plan for Hans. In his miracle healing he met Jesus. His radical heart was transformed into a zealot for Jesus. He ended up a missionary in Livingstone, Zambia, near Victoria Falls after he married his American wife, Ann. They began a feeding center for hungry children. They shared the love of Jesus and led many Zambians to love Jesus. They had two beautiful girls.

To support their mission work, Hans traded his motorcycle in for an ultralight flying machine. This is basically a kite with an engine. He once told me it was the safest means of flight in the world. He worked for an ultralight company near Victoria Falls along the Zambezi River. I met Hans through my good friend Dexter, missionary to Africa, and I stayed in Anna and Hans's house on one of my crusades in Zambia. We shared our life stories and talked about Jesus and life. I did not spend much time with him, but we became bonded brothers. Ours was one of those friendships that knit souls together as though we had always been soldiers together in the foxholes of life.

Hans gave me a wonderful gift before I left Zambia. He offered to take me up in his ultraflight and show me the Falls and the wilderness along the River. The night he spoke to me of this, I could not say no to him, even though I was scared of man-made heights, like flying in a kite-powered vehicle over the wilds of Africa. I could not sleep the whole night because I knew I would die the next day. I prayed and prayed for God to take away my fear, but in the morning I still believed I would die. When I suited up for the flight, it took every ounce of faith I had to sit in that death trap. Once we lifted up into the air, which happened very quickly, I held on so tight, my knuckles went white. My fears only abated as I saw the glory of Victoria Falls through the mist that arose from its thunderous waters.

In Zambian, the words for Victoria Falls means the smoke that thunders. We flew through the mist and over this seventh wonder of the world. God is the Master of creation. This flight left me spellbound with a new understanding of the Master Craftsman and His creation. On our way back, Hans asked me if I wanted to fly the plane, but I deferred to him. I was too frozen to my handles in fear. I insisted he fly us home. It was a treat of a lifetime. On the tips of each wing were cameras, and from them, I was given the most majestic pictures of my flight into the glory of God. My fear of heights vanished in the wonder of it all. I was cured of all that fear, and the peace of God reigned in my soul.

Our ministry in Orlando started supporting Ann and Hans in their work in southern Zambia. He would read my daily teaching I sent by email. We talked about them coming back to minister in our church. I once wrote a message on being a greased pig that inspired a short campaign on being greased pigs. One of our leaders had t-shirts made that said "I am a greased pig," which we wore in honor of Jesus. A greased pig is impossible to grab a hold of. I thought that we needed to be so anointed with the oil of the Holy Spirit, we would be like greased pigs so the devil could not grab onto our lives. Hans loved that illustration.

He wrote back, saying he wanted to be one of God's greased pigs. We sent him one of the t-shirts with the message that he was surely so slippery with the oil of the Holy Spirit, he was a stellar greased pig.

About a year later, I received word from Dexter and Dan, a member of our church and a leader on Han's ministry board, that Hans was killed in an ultraflight accident. I could not believe it. He was one of God's invincible warriors, a mighty soldier in His army. I felt sick to my stomach when I heard of this tragedy. My heart went out to Ann and their two wonderful girls. So many heroes in the Lord's service have headed to heaven before us. It is a mystery to me why this happens to the best of us, but God has His plan.

As Dexter and I shared about Han's powerful ministry and life, Dexter assured me he is just five minutes ahead of us. We rejoiced even in our sorrow that he is with Jesus, alive forever in His glory. Soon we will see him again. It hurts, but it is the peace that surpasses all understanding that keeps us from despair. It is Jesus's gift to us, that we are passing through this life, to the greater glory in the next one. Hans is waiting to welcome us home. The afternoon I heard of Han's tragic death, I was driving on the most dangerous highway in America on Interstate 4 through downtown Orlando. I was in heavy traffic going 60 mph. There was an empty lane three lanes over, so on an impulse I decided to go from the farthest lane left to the farthest lane right to take the next exit.

A huge semi-truck was in the next to last right lane. I wrongfully assumed the far right lane was empty, but I could not see on the other side of the truck. I quickly cut over going at a high speed and cut in front of the semi into the far right lane. The problem was, this lane was occupied by a large passenger truck going 60 mph. In an instant I should have crashed into this F150. Somehow the driver saved the day and avoided me hitting her at full speed by an inch.

I was in shock at what had just happened and cursing myself for doing the stupidest stunt of my life. Well, it was one of the dumbest and one of the most dangerous acts of my life. I was shook to the core, knowing

I should have had a terrible wreck and most likely dead or horribly injured, along with others. I credited the lady driver and my guardian angel for saving me from certain tragedy. The mystery of life continued that day, and it was continuing in my saga in Israel. I have asked people since that near accident, have you ever done something so foolish that the result should have been tragic, but in the mystery of life you were spared the horrific consequences that should have resulted?

Chapter 30

THE NOOSE
TIGHTENS, DAY 5

The army of Israel's enemies had crushed the IDF as it now cruised toward Jerusalem. The failure of her sophisticated defense systems due to the computer virus and the astounding well-coordinated offensive of the six-nation army created a Blitzkrieg that would soon decimate all of Israel. Amazingly, the shields held the skies clear of missiles. Every one launched had been defended by the angels of heaven. Tales continued of the miracles in the heavens against the onslaught of the six in the air. God's hand was holding, but the second tree had withered and died. In a matter of hours, the tanks and soldiers of the 666 would swarm around Jerusalem and bring her to her knees. Barring a miracle, Israel would suffer the unthinkable.

Where was the US military support? Prime Minister David had called President Horn at the initial attack, but all communication was cut off quickly by the virus. The US was helpless to act; her defense systems no longer existed. She was desperately trying to protect her shores as she labored in the dark.

Israel was cut off and alone. It was as if the world had descended into the Dark Ages. Satellites did not function. There was no communication by phone or internet. Power grids stopped working. Businesses shut down. Babylon had literally fallen in that prophetic hour. While the merchants of the earth and her kings mourned, heaven rejoiced in God's judgment. Soon the King would come to restore God's reign in righteousness.

In the midst of world chaos, Benjamin David had sent a car to bring Marie and I to his office once more. He was desperate for any word we could give him. For he knew Israel had at best twenty-four hours to survive as a nation. The barbarian horde would be at his gates, and they would show no mercy. Generators had kept his offices at the Knesset functioning, but most of Israel lay in darkness. It was a somber mood that hung in the air when we entered his headquarters. Fear and anxiety reigned in the hearts and minds of their leaders. They tried to deny the inevitable, but reality dictated that they had hours left.

The never-again mantra of Israel that they would die to the last person before surrender was becoming reality. The leaders tried to think of how they could guard their families and nation from the horrors of defeat that would await them. They envisioned mass death squads killing their children, raping their women, and destroying all the greatness they had built in one generation. How could God allow this to happen? They silently asked themselves. This would be worse than the Holocaust of World War II. The words of the prophet Daniel echoed in their minds:

> "At that time Michael, the great prince who protects your people, will arise. There will be a time of distress such as has not happened from the beginning of nations until then. But at that time your people—everyone whose name is found written in the book—will be delivered.
>
> Multitudes who sleep in the dust of the earth will awake: some to everlasting life, others to shame and everlasting contempt.
>
> Those who are wise will shine like the brightness of the heavens, and those who lead many to righteousness, like the stars for ever and ever.

But you, Daniel, close up and seal the words of the scroll until the time of the end. Many will go here and there to increase their knowledge."

Then I, Daniel, looked, and there before me stood two others, one on this bank of the river and one on the opposite bank.

One of them said to the man clothed in linen, who was above the waters of the river, "How long will it be before these astonishing things are fulfilled?"

The man clothed in linen, who was above the waters of the river, lifted his right hand and his left hand toward heaven, and I heard him swear by him who lives forever, saying, "It will be for a time, times and half a time. When the power of the holy people has been finally broken, all these things will be completed."

I heard, but I did not understand. So I asked, "My lord, what will the outcome of all this be?"

He replied, "Go your way, Daniel, because the words are closed up and sealed until the time of the end."

"Many will be purified, made spotless and refined, but the wicked will continue to be wicked. None of the wicked will understand, but those who are wise will understand."

"From the time that the daily sacrifice is abolished and the abomination that causes desolation is set up, there will be 1,290 days.

Blessed is the one who waits for and reaches the end of the 1,335 days."

As for you, go your way till the end. You will rest, and then at the end of the days you will rise to receive your allotted inheritance." Daniel 12:1-13.

It was difficult not to focus on the first verse of chapter 12 that the worst suffering ever would come upon Israel since the beginning of nations. The rest of the chapter promised hope, but they were staring at the death and destruction that had already come upon them.

I had been with Daniel when he penned those prophetic words. I knew God would deliver His people from certain death as He had parted the Red Sea to save them from the Egyptian army, but it was hard to believe that the waters of death would part again as they had for Moses and the Hebrews.

I had seen with Zechariah just that morning the armies encamped around Jerusalem prepared to eliminate the city of David. Then, I saw the glory of the Messiah descend and destroy the armies with a mighty earthquake by the hand of the Lord.

When I met with Benjamin, I told him of my vision with Zechariah. I encouraged him that God would act and not surrender to the nations of 666. Alas, it was almost impossible to disperse the cloud of despair from his eyes as he faced the inevitable. His enemies would have their boots on their necks. They would slaughter the Jews. In the heartache of this hour of tribulation, he told me they had discovered the mole in his office that had betrayed him and the nation of Israeli. It had been Olga. She spied for the Russians and had conspired with the terrorists to undermine his nation.

They had already executed her for her crimes. When I heard this news I wanted to shout no! She was innocent. She was the scapegoat to protect and hide the real Z. My mind raced with confusion and I resisted the urge to confront the PM because I could not believe he was Z. How did I know Steinman was right in his assessment of the situation? We were falling down the rabbit hole and there appeared to be no bottom.

It was as if reality had faded into a nightmare, or was it reality had broken into our dream to show us the evil that confronted us and the hopelessness of humanity without God's intervention. All the efforts of mankind had failed since the Garden of Eden to rescue us from our sins. God was showing us our need for Him. No human effort could save us. God alone was our Deliverer. In the mysteries of the prophets lay the answer to the maze of death we were trapped without an escape possible. I thought of all the scapegoats throughout human history, who had hid the truth of the wicked masterminds behind the veil. The greatest scapegoat of all time was Jesus Christ, led out to slaughter as an innocent Lamb to take away the sin of the world. He had to come again to save us.

That afternoon Marie and I felt alone. Bart was dead. We had no communication with our family in America. We tried to pray together but failed to connect with the Lord. I decided to retreat to our bedroom for some solo prayer time with God. I found myself at the Last Supper with Jesus and His apostles. It was His last night alone with them. He was teaching them great truths from the very throne of God, instructions they would need for the days and life ahead of them. It was an intimate time of love and prophecy as they celebrated the Passover Meal. What was Jesus thinking and feeling, knowing He would be the Passover Lamb the next day, sacrificed on the cross for the sin of the world? His knowledge of the future had to be a dilemma for Him to face His suffering, but it was also a blessing because the reality of His salvation far surpassed all He would endure.

But this was no myth. It was real-life history. God had become a man. The suffering and death He would endure was genuine. The lashes would scourge His back. The crown of thorns would bleed His brow. The nails would pierce His hands and feet. He would be separated from the oneness of His Father, which would cause Him to cry out in pain and desperation.

His love for us was authentic. He gave His life in humble surrender even when He had the power to destroy all of His enemies and not suffer a single blow. No greater love in creation was His display of submitting to the will of His Father to set us free from the wrath of God. He was the Suffering Servant of Isaiah. Yet, there was a traitor amongst them as He spoke. Judas sat next to His Lord, knowing he would hand Him over to the authorities to be put to death. He had seen the miracles, heard Him teach with authority and truth, and experienced His love. How could he do such a thing as betray the only innocent Man in human history, who knew no sin? It strikes at the core of our wickedness. The heart is deceitful above all else. We are capable of the most heinous crimes.

I wondered what Jesus thought as He washed Judas's feet. Could there be a more wonderful act of humility? Did He pray for his salvation, or did he know his fate was sealed to hang himself in the horror of what he had done, in betraying the Son of God? I found myself weeping for Judas. For just as Jesus represented humanity on the cross, Judas was the image of our worst nature. Maybe I was crying for myself or Jesus too. The events of my life had overcome me in this hour of temptation. Could I say with Jesus, "Thy will be done, Father?"

The influence and power of a father cannot be overstated. It is at the heart of the troubles of our culture. Much of the pain we endure is the failure of a father to love his children and to properly express it. We are all on a journey to know our father's love, some more than others. Jesus knew His Father's love. That was one of His most powerful strengths and why He could go to the cross for the love of His Father, knowing how faithful His Father was to Him. Jesus endured the rejection of humanity because He knew such wonderful intimacy with His Father. In my insecurities, I knew the love of my Father. I was blessed with a great dad. Flawed, yes, unable to communicate his love for me and I for him, but he sacrificed his life for me. I remembered after I had come to give my life to Jesus, I desperately desired to express and say the words I love you to my father and to hear him say it to me. Why was it so hard to say those words? What caused such a barrier that made it like an impossible challenge to achieve?

Then one day on the driveway as I was saying goodbye after a nice visit, I said to him, "I love you." Those three simple words contained enormous power. I could not believe I had spoken to him the words, I love you. Even more wonderful was he said them back to me. Why had he or I waited all those years to utter those beautiful words? Why would it still be so difficult to say once the barrier was broken? It motivated me to say it to my kids every day when I dropped them off at school. Why was that so unnatural when it should be the most natural of expressions?

Jesus showed us the way to His Father and His love for us. To know that the God of creation loved me and died for me in His Son transformed my life. Even though I could not comprehend all that that meant, it created in me a new heart and a contrite spirit and released in me a willingness to serve and love Him with all of my heart. I would need all of that courage and love in the hours of trial as we would face the terror of evil's last grasp at survival in God's creation.

Prime Minister David gave the orders for the Levitical priests to erect the tent of David on the temple mount. It was to be placed where the gazebo on the mount was located near the Dome of the Rock, where it was believed the original Holy of Holies was in the temple. If he was forced to surrender, they would sign the ceasefire in the tent of King David. This was where they worshiped 24/7 in the ancient days of David and placed the ark of the covenant. This sacred site was the forerunner of the temple his son Solomon would build. David, because he was a man of war, had been forbidden by God to build God's house.

The modern-day priests of Judaism were ecstatic. To them, this was the fulfillment of prophecy in the book of Amos and the preparation to rebuild the true temple of God on the site where Abraham had been ordered by God to sacrifice Isaac, his son.

Instead, God intervened to spare Abraham's son and provide His own sacrifice. This foretold that God would send His only begotten Son, Jesus, to be our sacrifice for our sins. For God did not spare His Son as His supreme expression of love for us.

"In that day 'I will restore David's fallen shelter—I will repair its broken walls and restore its ruins and will rebuild it as it used to be, so that they may possess the remnant of Edom and all the nations that bear my name,' declares the Lord, who will do these things."

The materials were already to go to the temple mount. It had been these priests' mission to have secured all the necessary items that David had in his tent. Now they needed an armed escort to go up the temple mount and erect the tent.

They contacted the musicians and singers so they could immediately begin the worship and sacrifice. The Messiah's coming was imminent.

In the Muslim quarter in Jerusalem the Mufti met with his leaders to plan the takeover of Jerusalem. They knew that the Israeli IDF had been defeated. Now it was their time to reclaim their new capital.

Rumors were abuzz that the Jews were going to secure the temple mount for some kind of religious demonstration. The Muslims would be ready for any such blasphemy against Allah. This was their Mount, Al-harim al-Sharif, the noble sanctuary, where Mohammad was transported from the sacred mosque in Mecca to the Al-aqsa during his Night Journey. It was also the site of the Dome of the Rock where they believed Abraham brought Esau to be sacrificed on the rock, which now was within their holy mosque. Leaders were instructed to gather their armed warriors and to recruit their people to gather at the Al-harim al-Sharif after lunch. They would storm the mount and drive out the Jews. Never again would a Jew be allowed to walk this holy site. In their hearts, they believed their Messiah, the 7th Madi, would arise from the Muslim world to submit all the earth to Allah.

Chapter 31

Z, DAY 6

M arie woke with a start. She had seen a great stone strike the army of six, and its resounding effect had made her jump up in bed. The stone became a great mountain and filled the whole earth. Jesus is coming. He has hurled from heaven a stone not made with hands. It will break into pieces the armies and kingdoms of the earth. His kingdom will arise and stand forever over all the earth.

We could hear the rumbling of tanks in the distance as the army of six approached Jerusalem. First came the Iraqis and Iranians, the Persians of old from the Jordan valley, then the Arab Saudis from the south out of the Negev, and finally, the Russians, Turks, and Syrians arrived from Galilee in the north. In two days, they had swept across Israel, and their prize sat before them like a jewel that had been coveted for seventy years. It was in their grasp, and they lusted for her like a harlot lying before them. What was left of Israel's IDF stood on the ancient walls of the Old City. They would fight to the last man. This was the end of a dream of almost 2,500 years, born only a generation ago in 1948 as the restored nation of Israel. In some ways, it was miraculous they had survived this long, surrounded by enemies who hated them and rewrote history to accuse them of being a colonial power in their own land, which they had established almost 2,000 years before the Muslim Arabs swept up from the south to conquer and claim this land as their own.

Those within the walls of Jerusalem prayed and hoped for God to do His miracle. Others hoped the Americans would come in their military might to save them. Many followers of Jesus believed He would descend on the Mount of Olives to destroy their enemies.

One of the key questions was, would Israel launch her nukes? Few knew that the virus had wiped out any possibility of firing them. The cyber army of Israel was frantically trying to devise a cure for the Apollodon virus. If they failed, Prime Minister David was considering surrender. Thus, the erection of the tent of David, which would symbolize the life and faith of Israel. In surrender, they would survive. His worry was, would President Horn live up to his promise? Without communications between the nations, he had little faith he would or could act to defend Israel.

Once the walls were breached, there would be no possibility of controlling the horde that hungered to take Jerusalem. The horrors imagined would become a reality of slaughter that would surpass the day the Romans took Jerusalem in AD 70 when the blood of the Jews ran ankle deep throughout the city.

Marie and I wondered about our family, not knowing they were safe in the heavens with Jesus. This was the 6th day. The third tree withered and lost her fruit. We believed the great tree of the Messiah would come. We imagined He had mounted His white stallion and had gathered His army of angels, soon to call up His army of believers and then descend to the earth. We took comfort that we would see our children and grandkids probably today in our resurrected bodies with Jesus. Multitudes from 400 generations of believers would be transformed in the blink of an eye, dressed in white robes of purity and holiness, cleansed in the red blood of Jesus.

We heard a knock at our door. It was the PM's security force who came to bring us to him for one last visit. I needed to warn him they still had a traitor in their midst. Yes, it could be him, but I still could not accept Steinman's conclusions. If he was Z, it was the greatest deception in the history of humanity since Judas betrayed Jesus. As we drove to the Knesset, we could see Jerusalem was in disarray. Chaos abounded. Refugees and families from the outskirts of Jerusalem were fleeing into the city as the barbarian six approached. Most of the people living toward Tel Aviv and Galilee and even Jericho had not the time to run. The armies swept passed them on the road to Jerusalem. Jesus had told the people to flee from Jerusalem when the Roman army would come to destroy it, and many Christians were saved from destruction by obeying Him in AD 70. In Jeremiah's day, they were told to stay in the city, and they would live. That held true as well. There were no prophecies about the day of wrath, but my impression was to stay in Jerusalem.

As we waited in the outer office of the PM, I happened to pick up an article on Benjamin David and his life. He was born in Rome and his family made *aliyah* when he was twenty. He was educated at Oxford. He was never married and was a war hero. As I read about his college days at Oxford, the article said he was an excellent fencer. He was so outstanding, his nickname was Zorro. I dropped the magazine when I made the split second connection with Zorro and Z. That gut feeling told me he was Z. There was no longer any doubt in my mind.

Was everything about him a façade? How could God's hand seem to be so strong upon his life? What about the prayers, the dream, and the prophecies? Then it hit me. Jesus, the heir to David's throne, was coming to reign forever and ever. Before King David became king, Saul from the house of Benjamin was king. He loved Israel, but his pride failed him. God's hand had been upon Saul, but our Creator determined his pride would not submit to God's redemption plan. He required a man after His own heart. That was David. Now the Son of God of the line of David would be King of kings.

Prime Minister Benjamin loved Israel as Saul had, but his pride would try to stop the redemption plan of God. As God removed Saul, He would replace Benjamin with Jesus. I turned to Marie and whispered to her that Benjamin was Z. Her eyes lit up. Fear tried to grip both of us, but we rebuked it in the authority of Jesus. We had to have clear heads and sound thinking, void of fear to hear God's voice. This was zero hour. We were on the precipice of Jesus's return. We needed courage and faith like Joshua going into the Promised Land.

As we sat down with Benjamin, I couldn't tell if I was to be Samuel the prophet confronting Saul or Nathan declaring to David, "Thou art the man" in his sin with Bathsheba. That reminded me of Pilate and Jesus when he said to the mob, "Behold the Man!" This was said in Zechariah 6:12–13, concerning Joshua, a type of Jesus as the high priest:

> "Behold, the man whose name is Branch: and he shall grow up out of his place; and he shall build the temple of Jehovah; even he shall build the temple of Jehovah; and he shall bear the glory, and shall sit and rule upon his throne; and he shall be a priest upon his throne; and the counsel of peace shall be between them both." Zechariah 6:12-13.

The Prime Minister was not Jesus, but a false king or fallen king, but I did not think he was the Antichrist. He certainly could be a type of the Antichrist. My heart pumped adrenalin through my arteries as I struggled on what to do. Marie and I both were praying in the Spirit in one half of our brains while the other half began to engage Benjamin. I did not feel I was any of the prophets but was merely completing the mission Jesus had given me.

"We appear to have lost the war," he began without any betrayal or fear of who he was and what he was about to do.

"That is what the prophets Zachariah, Ezekiel and Daniel tell us, that Jerusalem will be surrounded and it will be a time of terror, but God will deliver His people," I began, pleading for him to remain faithful. "The angels still guard your skies. The Messiah will come and destroy these armies. You must not give up hope. That is what Isaiah told King Hezekiah. Your entire history is of God miraculously destroying your enemies."

I could see he was not hopeful. "I have commanded that the tent of David be erected on the temple mount. They are already worshiping

God as we speak. If we do not surrender, then we will be annihilated. Once our gates are breached, no one can save us. Signing a peace treaty in the tent of David will show the people we will endure."

My courage to confront Benjamin was failing me. Suddenly Marie stood up to Benjamin and stated as boldly as one could, "You had them killed, didn't you? They are all dead. Our family was wiped out by your twisted evil mind. You are Z!" The Spirit of the Lord had entered her and showed her the murder of our family.

I leaped to my feet in rage, thinking to kill the Prime Minister, but his security was ready and stopped me before I could act. I struggled with the strength of three men, but I was no match for these trained agents. They had me down on my knees and handcuffed before I realized what hit me.

"We know the truth. Steinman wrote of your betrayal and Holtzman's betrayal too. You murdered Olga and my family. Why?" I cried out.

"Take them away and hold them until I decide what to do with them." Even his voice was different, cold and void of compassion. He had lost his way, and Satan had taken hold of him. His destiny would be one of Saul to die on the battlefield.

The agony of hearing my family exterminated, and for what? To take away my faith and turn me from God? To hide Benjamin's secret of doing whatever it took to save Israel? He did not need to ravage me and Marie. This revelation tore at my soul like a bull goring his prey. My intestines were ripped open in grief, and my blood poured out from my body.

Marie expressed her brokenness with sobbing and tears. The fruit of her womb had been torn to pieces by evil men who wanted power to gain their will. She wept for her children and grandchildren.

For comfort I kept repeating what my father had said weeks after my mother died. She is only five minutes ahead of me. My family was but a few minutes ahead of us in terms of eternity. We would see them in the course of hours. They are better off than we are. Those words and thoughts helped ease our sorrow, but nothing to deliver us from the knowledge they had been brutally murdered. I cried as Jesus on the cross, "My God, my God, why have you forsaken me?" I heard Marie pray, "Though you slay me, I will trust in my Redeemer."

If we were right, the third day of tribulation would be shortened by Jesus. For Marie and me, it could not come soon enough. The war had ripped out our desire for fighting. We cradled each other in our arms for comfort. In that moment, evil had triumphed.

Meanwhile in the throne room of God, the Father and Son were communicating in the Spirit how this day of wrath would unfold. We, as humans, could not comprehend how God is three Persons in One nor how He moved from the realm of heaven to earth as they were two different realities. One was spiritual without sin and the other was physical and corrupted by sin. God transcended all of His creation, but He can interact within both dimensions.

The great tree of life placed His crown on His head and prepared to leave heaven to reign on the earth. His branches were of iron to rule the nations and His leaves full of truth, laden with the fruit of lives devoted to Him. He would put an end to the corruption of sin. Heaven and earth would then flow together as one as it was in the beginning when there was no rebellion. The excitement built in heaven as the creatures: seraphim, angels, saints, and all that dwelt in and around the throne prepared for the climax of world history. They sang to the glory of God and declared His praises. The angels formed their units, ready for war, as did the martyrs and the rest of the saints, who would be joined in the sky by the resurrected faithful. All of the prophecies were now flowing together as one mighty river rushing to the side of Jesus to come in His cloud of glory.

All of creation groaned under this weight of sin that Adam had committed. It longed to be set free to be restored to its oneness with God without the evils of disobedience. This groaning was causing signs and wonders in the heavens and on the earth. The world was so divided, more than any other time since Babel, that they could not communicate to one another what they saw happening on their side of the world. The virus had made certain of that ultimate division.

The gateway to God we had invented through technology had been our undoing. None of our resources could stop the events of prophecy. Human ingenuity was limited. Only God could save us, but that did not prevent Vladimir and Benjamin and the other corrupt world leaders from trying. In their evil minds they were on the verge of victory and ushering in a new age of *man*. Little did they know it would be short lived.

Chapter 32
LOOK TO THE HEAVENS, END OF DAY 6

Standing on the temple mount, I see crowds of Muslims gathering down the steps to the north, and I could hear the chants and prayers of thousands of Jews at the Kotel. Singing and praise echoed across the mount from inside the tent of David while hundreds of Jews enveloped the tent of David on the outside to join in worship. Tension filled the air as Muslim and Jew looked to their God to destroy one another and for their prophecy to triumph. Once more in history, it seemed the Jews would become the defeated foe and be crushed by the foreign invaders. Only this time there would be no one left to resurrect from the ashes.

Suddenly, the history of this nexus flashed before me. I saw Abraham standing on Mount Moriah with Isaac bound on the altar of sacrifice. I heard the words of the Lord promise to supply His own sacrifice of salvation for humanity, which would be Jesus. Then David appeared, crowned as king of Israel. I heard God's words, telling him on his throne his Seed would reign forever and ever. His Son, Solomon, would build the first temple on this holy site of sacrifice, and the ark of the covenant would dwell in the Holy of Holies of the temple. The glory of God would rest upon the ark. Sacrifices would be made on the altar until the true sacrifice, His Son, would die on the cross for the sin of the world.

I saw Solomon fall on his face before the living God, as His glory filled the temple. No one could move in the majestic presence of the Lord of Hosts, the true King of Israel, Jesus Christ.

Then hordes of Babylonians came rushing in to burn the temple, but the glory had already departed, only to appear again in God's only begotten Son, Jesus Christ, as He dwelt in human flesh among His people. History repeated itself before my eyes as the Romans came and conquered Jerusalem as Jesus had predicted in AD 70. They over-turned every stone of the temple and soaked Jerusalem in Jewish blood.

Jesus promised to return in His glory as God. He prophesied that they would not see Him again, until they said, "Blessed is He who comes in the Name of the Lord!" As he wept over Jerusalem rejecting Him as King and Savior He cried out, "If you, even you, had only known on this day what would bring you peace—but now it is hidden from your eyes. The days will come upon you when your enemies will build an embankment against you and encircle you and hem you in on every side. They will dash you to the ground, you and the children within your walls. They will not leave one stone on another, because you did not recognize the time of God's coming to you."

Now the day of His return had come. The Romans had done their evil deed. The new army of six had encamped around the walls of Jerusalem, but they would be destroyed by Jesus and His heavenly army.

As I finished my thoughts, I heard come from the worship in the tent of David a loud voice pray, "Blessed is the Messiah who comes in the name of the Lord."

My eyes shifted to Benjamin as he prepared to enter the tent of David. Word spread that a helicopter would fly in the new world ruler. Vladimir of Russia would come to sign a peace covenant with Israel, representing the six nations. Benjamin relished the thought that he had made a brilliant move to save Israel. The Jews, under the pressure of defeat, would be stirred to action by the tent of David, erected and activated for worship. They had to believe in themselves in order to survive. The covenant with Russia and her allies would be more than a treaty, but the entering of an unbreakable pact that would ensure the life of Israel under the protectorate of Russia. Israel would become a vassal of the evil empire and the surrounding nations, but she would survive.

The Daniel 9 covenant is included in Daniel's vision that God gave him through the archangel Gabriel in answer to Daniel's prayers for what would be the future of Israel and God's people. It is the famous seventy weeks determined by God and given to Daniel so they would know the faithfulness of their God.

> "Seventy "sevens" are decreed for your people and your holy city to finish transgression, to put an end to sin, to atone for wickedness, to bring in everlasting righteousness, to seal up vision and prophecy and to anoint the Most Holy Place.
>
> Know and understand this: From the time the word goes out to restore and rebuild Jerusalem until the Anointed One, the ruler, comes, there will be seven 'sevens,' and sixty-two 'sevens.' It will be rebuilt with streets and a trench, but in times of trouble. After the sixty-two 'sevens,' the Anointed One will be put to death and will have nothing. The people of the ruler who will come will destroy the city and the sanctuary. The end will come like a flood: War will continue until the end, and desolations have been decreed. He will confirm a covenant with many for one 'seven.' In the middle of the 'seven' he will put an end to sacrifice and offering. And at the temple he will set up an abomination that causes desolation, until the end that is decreed is poured out on him." Daniel 9:24-27.

For 2,500, years Jews and Christians have tried to interpret these sacred words in various fashions. The problem they faced was God sealed up their meaning until now. The other issue is we do not see time as God sees time. His prophecies of the end times are multi-layered and thus far too complex for human understanding. Only divine revelation can give a semblance of knowledge, and even then, we see through a glass darkly. We attempt to give a linear timeline to nail down the dates of Jesus's return through Daniel 9 and other words of prophecy in the Bible. God does not see time in linear terms because He transcends time. He determines time. He is the Lord of history. He allows us to know what He knows only when we need to know. His desire is that we know the season of His Son's second coming. In fact, He expects us to know that season. Only the unbelievers should be left in the dark.

Here, on the Temple Mount, Marie and I were witnessing the hour of Jesus's return. I turned to her to ask what she was thinking. She nuzzled close to me as best she could with our hands cuffed together. "I am grieving over our family and the horror of how evil the human heart can be. Yet, I know Jesus is riding His white horse, ready to come make all things new. We will be with Him and our loved ones in the twinkling of an eye."

"Until then, we all have our parts to play," I added in a sadness that forbade the hope of glory.

The noise in the Muslim crowd increased with a terrible fervor. Then a shout blasted forth. "Fire." A barrage of rifles sounded as the mob stormed the barricades. Israeli soldiers and worshipers fell wounded or dead. Chaos took over the temple mount as people fled or stood still in shock. The IDF returned fire and a hundred Muslims fell, only to be trampled by a thousand faithful, rushing to tear down David's tent and drive the infidels from AL-Harim al-Sharif.

I looked at Benjamin who had not entered the tent. I saw him nod in our direction. Our guard raised his gun to shoot us dead. Instead, we vanished before his eyes.

Marie and I found ourselves ascending up to heaven. Our handcuffs were off, and we were holding hands. We gazed into each other's eyes to see each other full of joy and love. We knew this was the glorious beginning, the promise of a new age in the history of humanity. In the distance we heard a trumpet sound.

"One day is as a thousand years."

Chapter 33

THE COMING OF
THE LORD, END OF DAY 6

In the distance, as we looked down from the heavens, Marie and I could see the temple mount. We could hear men shouting, "Allah Akbar, Allah Akbar," amidst the rapid shooting of their rifles. Men and women lay dead across the stone pavement. The tent of David was tattered and torn. The rabbis and priests who refused to run to safety were butchered and slaughtered like the fatted calf. Turbaned fanatics stood among them, proclaiming the victory of Allah.

"There is only one God, Allah, and one prophet Mohammed. Allah has given us his sacred mount and his sacred city, Jerusalem."

Prime Minister Benjamin had escaped with his security force down the ramp on the Western Wall, and Israeli soldiers guarded the exit. Occasional shooting persisted, but the battle was short-lived. The Mustif and his men had won the day.

As we rose in the sky, we began to see bodies of people rising with us. A great company of saints as far as the eye could see were being gathered up to Jesus.

Then we saw the cloud of glory with myriads of angels surrounding the brilliant splendor of the King. As we approached the Lion of

Judah, the last trumpet sounded, and in a twinkling of an eye we were changed. We suddenly had new bodies that were incorruptible, clothed in immortality. The glory of the Lord filled us with the majesty of our God. We had become like the Heavenly Man. The last Adam had breathed His life-giving spirit into us. We now bore His image, full of His power and beauty. We had become spiritual beings, freed from our corruption, dishonor, and weakness.

The heavens were filled with the wonder of the new creation Jesus had promised. The sting of sin and death had been swallowed up in victory. Once again humanity could taste the fruit of the tree of life.

There beside us were our children and grandchildren. Above us were our parents, who had been raised from the dead out of their graves at the first trumpet blast. The joy of the Lord overflowed our souls as we embraced one another in the love of Christ. Instantly, we knew what our family had suffered at the hands of the jihadists, but there was no grief. The peace of God consumed our thoughts. We were one in the spirit as Adam and Eve had been one at the dawn of human creation.

The idolatry of self had been replaced by the true worship of the living God. All inner division had vanished with our flesh. In our resurrected bodies the intimacy of love replaced our shame and condemnation. We had no fear of exposure of our sinful past. All was gone in the glory of our King Jesus.

Without words, we could know the thoughts of Jesus and one another. We knew we needed to align for battle. Jesus emerged from the cloud of glory on a magnificent white stallion. His angels were seated upon their steeds, and then we were mounted on the horses of the heavens. All was in order. There was no confusion, while chaos reigned on the earth below. The armies of Satan had breached the gates of Jerusalem. The houses of the Jews were rifled with plundering soldiers. Women were ravished. Half the city had already been taken, just as Zechariah had prophesied.

The day of the Lord had come. Jesus descended upon the Mount of Olives that overlooked the Eastern Gate across the Kidron Valley. As His feet struck the earth, a massive quake exploded across the Valley from north to south as half of the mountain gave way to the power and majesty of Jesus. We found ourselves riding with Jesus in this glorious moment. A darkness came over the land. Yet, we could see that a fountain of living water had erupted in Jerusalem rushing to the Jordan River and to the west, the Mediterranean Sea.

The fire of the Lord went forth from His mouth and dissolved the flesh of the army of six as they stood on their feet. Their eyes dissolved in their sockets, and their tongues dissolved in their mouths in the terrible judgment of the living God. Panic swept through the city and across the land as the enemies of Israel turned on one another to kill and murder. None of those opposed to the Holy God of Israel were left standing. All were consumed in the fiery judgment.

In a flash, our spiritual horses took us over the Valley of Jezreel. This expansive and fertile soil funneled the armies of the beast and the kings of the earth toward Jerusalem. There, I pointed, showing Marie and our family, the most hideous beast. For though he was a man, we saw in the spirit his true nature. He was like a dragon with one horn, but with the face of a gargoyle. Filth spewed from his mouth as he ordered the kings of the earth to battle. This army had followed on the heels of the army of six. It consisted of the kings of the earth who ruled the goat nations and had joined forces with the Antichrist to defeat the Messiah.

The Faithful and True, who judges in the righteousness of God, made war on these deceived leaders. As He rode, His eyes were like flames of fire and on His head were many crowns. He was clothed with a robe dipped in blood. His name is the Word of God. Out of His mouth went a sharp, two-edged sword that struck the nations with His judgment. In His fierceness and wrath, He consumed them as the Almighty God. As the armies fell as dead men before Him, we could see written on His robe and thigh KING OF KINGS AND LORD OF LORDS.

An angel standing in the sun cried with a loud voice for us to gather for the supper of the great God. We would dine on the flesh of the captains, the flesh of mighty men, the flesh of horses, and of those who sat on them, and the flesh of all the people, free and slave, both great and small.

The beast was captured with the false prophet who worked signs in his presence, which had deceived all those who had come to worship the beast and his government. On those who worshiped the one who symbolized the age of man and the false religions of the world, we could see the mark of the beast.

The beast and false prophet were cast alive into the lake of fire burning with brimstone. The rest of the rebels were killed with the sword of the Spirit which proceeded from the mouth of Jesus who sat on the white horse. The birds of the air swooped down to eat of their flesh.

In an instant we sat together as one family to eat manna from heaven. Loud voices from a great multitude in heaven cried out "Alleluia! Salvation and glory and honor and power belong to the Lord our God!"

Worship and adoration broke forth in our hearts as we joined with the heavenly hosts as they spoke with the sound of thunder, "For true and righteous are His judgments, because He has judged the great harlot who corrupted the earth with her fornication; and He has avenged on her the blood of servants shed by her."

I looked around me to see the martyrs of Jesus dressed in the white linen of His purity. At last, His truth and justice prevailed. The prayers of the martyrs and their question to Jesus in Revelation 6 had been answered. "How long, O Lord, holy and true, until You judge and avenge our blood on those who dwell on the earth?"

Another chorus of praise arose from heaven, "Alleluia! Her smoke rises up forever and ever!" Declaring the complete fall and end of Babylon, Satan's wicked and evil system of rebellion among the nations of the earth.

Then before my eyes a scene of worship unsurpassed since the beginning of time unfolded like a scroll. It was mystical in its divine glory as the twenty-four elders and the four living creatures fell down and worshiped God who sat on the throne, saying, "Amen and Alleluia."

Then the voice of one representing God who stands at the throne of God declared, "Praise our God, all you His servants, and those who fear Him, both small and great!" Then the resounding voice of a great multitude united in the oneness of their praise thundered forth as the sound of many waters cascading with the force of a thousand atom bombs, shaking the heaven and the earth, "Alleluia! For the Lord God Omnipotent reigns! Let us be glad and rejoice and give Him glory, for the marriage of the Lamb has come, and His wife has made herself ready."

Our hearts leaped within us as we heard this declaration for eternity had enveloped the chosen Bride of Christ into His arms of love and wonder. I saw us shining in the garments of fine linen, clean and bright reflecting the righteous acts of the saints.

God's faithfulness poured out in His blessings upon His Bride as we feasted together in the oneness of His love. We knew that this testimony expressed the spirit of Jesus's prophecy. The Messiah had come to take His bride into His glory and fulfill all the prophecies of His Word.

The celebration of this marriage feast shook the heavens and the earth being the consummation of the long-awaited mystery of God promised in the garden after the fall of Adam. Our Father would send His Savior, His only begotten Son, to deliver us from the curse of sin and death and the bondages of Satan. The joy and freedom that beat in our hearts overwhelmed us with His love. The day of salvation had finally come in all of its fullness. For we had known in part as one sees through a dark glass. Now we knew in full the love and hope and wonder of our God.

The peace and purity that united our new resurrected lifestyle with Jesus and the Father culminated in the holiness of our Lord in us. We were one in His love and glory. Free at last, free at last, thank God, we were free at last! No one or nothing could ever harm us again. Our corrupted nature is gone, no longer held back by our idol of self. Jesus and the Father truly reigned on the throne of our lives. Satan was bound for a thousand years. No temptation could reach our minds or seduce our souls. Pure, unadulterated love enveloped our hearts—no inner division, only complete unity. Paradise was restored.

Yet, not for everyone. There were still a billion or more souls on earth under the curse of sin and death. They lived in a quiet war against King Jesus. They knew of His authority and power, but refused to bend their will to His. One of them was my grandson!

Chapter 34

JESUS REIGNS,
THE 7TH DAY BEGINS

As I reflected on the events of the sixth day, I had always struggled with the concept of the 1,000-year reign of Jesus. I supposed it was the challenge of understanding events not bound by time within our framework of time. It seemed illogical that Jesus would return, bind Satan for a thousand years, then let him loose again to raise up a final rebellion of the nations against the rule of Jesus. Why was that necessary? It made no sense.

As I pondered these thoughts, it came to me, God's heart was that none should perish. If Jesus had returned and made all things new as Revelation 21 and 22 described, then they would all be lost. Here was a thousand years for men and women to repent and believe. A thousand years is but a day to God. The wait was worth the salvation of those trapped in darkness.

For now, Satan would be bound for that millennium. Jesus would reign, and we would witness to those who had not yet believed. This further spoke to me that this 1,000 years, with Satan and his demons rendered helpless, would demonstrate the corruption within the unregenerate human heart. There would be no excuses for humanity that our only hope for salvation was God in Jesus Christ. As it was for now, we saw the most spectacular triumph of Jesus over Satan. When He was crucified, He paraded Satan through the streets of heaven as the Roman emperors humiliated the generals, chiefs, and kings they defeated in battle, marching them through the streets of Rome. The people threw rotten food at them as they were caged, naked and chained like beasts. All manner of insults mocked them. However, in heaven, it was more of a display of victory over evil and the triumph of the King over rebellion.

Out of the heavens, an archangel came hurtling to earth and laid hold of the dragon. There was no battle but more like a giant grabbing the scruff of the neck of a small dog. Granted, Satan, in the form of a dragon, was no tiny animal, but he appeared so as the supreme power of God as in this angel lifted Satan off his feet and then was bound with chains of spiritual iron. This messenger of God took the golden key to open the bottomless pit, a realm of such darkness and terror; it cut off all contact with God and hope. The black void was cold as ice, but the frozen waste land burned with fire. He opened the door to this hellish creation of God and cast the dragon into the bottomless pit.

He then sealed the entrance so that no spiritual being could enter or leave. The deception of the nations had ended. Babylon was no more. Now Jesus would establish the seventy sheep nations of the earth to rule His kingdom for the next thousand years. All the goat nations were no more. Their right to rule was revoked because of their failure to be in covenant with Jesus and to bless Israel.

Jesus had descended in His glory upon the earth. By defeating the army of six and the rest of those nations that had joined them to destroy Israel, He sat on His throne of glory with all of His angels beside Him. The nations of the earth gathered before Him with their kings, chiefs, presidents, and prime ministers, representing their governments. With one swift move of His hand, Jesus separated the sheep nations from the goat nations, the sheep on His right and the goat nations on His left.

Jesus began to address the sheep nations who had defended Israel and had based their laws and government on the New Covenant sealed by the blood of Jesus and the Laws of God. With a voice loud enough to encompass the world, He spoke to them. "Come, you blessed of My

Father, inherit the kingdom prepared for you from the foundation of the world: for I was hungry and you gave Me food; I was thirsty and you gave Me drink; I was a stranger and you took Me in; I was naked and you clothed Me; I was sick and you visited Me; I was in prison and you came to Me."

From His right came the voices of those who ruled the sheep nations saying, "Lord, when did we see You hungry and feed You, or thirsty and give You drink? When did we see You a stranger and take You in, or naked and clothe You? Or when did we see You sick, or in prison, and come to You?"

Jesus, sitting as King with His head crowned with many crowns, the most humble of men, spoke with such compassion, even the goat nations melted before His voice. "Assuredly, I say to you, inasmuch as you did it to one of the least of these My brethren, you did it to Me."

In a flash, as though there was a huge screen across the sky, movies of ships and planes being loaded with goods passed before our eyes. Women and men carrying baskets of grain and food, medical supplies, clothing, and tents, with tears of compassion, filled the cargo holds with an abundance of these goods. Then hungry, starving children were given bowls of food. Nursing mothers were given enough nourishment to feed their babies. Doctors risked their lives to treat the sick and diseased. Fevered babies were made well. Lepers were made whole, and blind eyes were given sight by doctors in surgery. Those who were hopeless in prison were visited by the friends of loved ones and pastors. The naked were clothed and strangers provided a place to sleep with shelter over their heads.

My eyes filled with tears of joy as I watched countless thousands of servants sacrificing their time, energy, money, and sometimes lives to help the least of those whom many nations did not care or value. When we looked at the faces of these poor and suffering victims, we saw the face of Jesus. My heart ached with love as I witnessed these miracles of hope spring forth into life. Then I saw their armies and politicians and leaders and rabbis and pastors surrounding Israel with acts of love.

They showed they valued the Jews as they valued their own loved ones. Each one of the Israelis were cared for and supported in war and peace. Hands joined in oneness for these fellow brothers and sisters.

All races, tribes and covenant nations embraced the Jews as their own, fulfilling the call of God to bless Abraham and his descendants. I was filled with such pride for these nations and their people as they labored and loved the nation of Israel.

Then Jesus turned to those on His left, the nations who had rejected Jesus and His covenant. They had persecuted the Jews and never repented. They sought to destroy the nation of Israel and wipe it from the face of the earth. Across the sky we saw images of rejection and persecution. Concentration camps of Jews being put to death through torture, gassed in chambers of horror, raped ,and murdered. Every ounce of decency was denied the Jews.

Ships fleeing in the night refused refuge in the goat nations. Leaders mocking the Jews. Soldiers were striking the Jews, driving them from their homes. Many left to die in the cold and darkness. Families were separated from one another, with children weeping and mothers crying. There was no end to the evil. Nations refused to feed their own people, starving them to instill their own warped vision of power. The hungry and thirsty were denied the simplest of food and drink. People were imprisoned without justice. The sick were denied medical treatment, and strangers were left to die in poverty.

The goats showed no compassion or care for humanity inflicted on the least of these, never hearing their cries. The goat nations tried to defend themselves before Jesus, but to no avail. His justice was swift and hard as He spoke to them. "Assuredly I say to you, inasmuch as you did not do it to one of the least of these, you didn't do it to Me. Send these away into everlasting punishment, but the righteous into eternal life."

It was then that the seventy nations of God and His kingdom were established. Each resurrected leader immediately went to their nation to establish Jesus's reign. I saw thrones appear over these sheep nations.

Jesus ordered each ruler to have judgment over the faithful nations. It was as if Jesus was the head of a body. The brain sends messages instantly to billions of cells in that body. Once received, they respond immediately to the message from the brain in remarkable obedience. Each cell knows its duty and does it without hesitation. God's brilliance demonstrated in the most glorious manner.

Then appeared the souls of those beheaded for their witness to Jesus and for the Word of God, who had not worshiped the beast or his image, and had not received his mark of covenant on their foreheads or their hands. They would live and reign with Christ for a thousand years. Thus, in a second, the faithful saints who had prepared themselves in living the Sermon on the Mount, who had gone to the nations of the earth to witness to Jesus and make disciples, who had given their lives in faithful service to our Lord became priests of God and of Christ and will reign with Him for a thousand years.

As Jesus sat on the throne of His judgment seat, the most remarkable moment in this young age of the millennium occurred. I watched as Prime Minister Benjamin David of Israel was brought before the King by two mighty angels. The archangel Michael, protector of Israel, announced that the prime minister was now to hand over the rule of the government to Jesus. If I had been in my old nature, I would have been full of wrath and anger at the man who had my family murdered. Instead, I understood the man's heart. Yes, he had sinned terribly in betraying Jesus and me for that matter, but his intent was to save Israel at all costs until the Messiah would come. He was more a Saul than a David, but now Jesus was accepting him before His throne.

The glory that shone forth from Jesus was the splendor of God. His grace beckoned Benjamin to come and to do his duty as the prime minister of Israel. This official and legal act was of vital importance in following the laws of God to transfer the kingdom into Jesus's rule. Here the Son of Righteousness would take His rightful place on the throne of the nation that would oversee the nations of the world. Jesus's reign would begin, as a son of Saul and a son of David handed Him the keys to Jerusalem to symbolize the succession of authority.

Benjamin came forward and knelt before Jesus. He appeared humble and contrite, knowing the foolishness of his actions in the last days. As he gave Jesus the key to the kingdom, Benjamin began to change. His fleshly body became a resurrected vessel of Christ. In the twinkling of an eye, Benjamin, murderer and deceiver, became one of the resurrected children of the living God, co-heir with Christ. The glory that manifested the majesty of Jesus filled Benjamin to overflowing with the light of salvation. I rejoiced in his redemption. In this age there was no need for words, for sin was no more for the resurrected followers of Jesus. Love and holiness pervaded our community of faith in the oneness of our Lord's glory.

Jesus took the key and rose from His throne. All of us were bathed in His wondrous glory. We knelt in homage and love before our King. God had created us to follow a leader. In our sin, we had corrupted that gift into a selfish desire to oppress and dominate our fellow man. Free from such evil, we gave our devotion and loyalty to the only One who deserved our faithful service. The oneness that had been lost in the garden was restored to us as we were truly one new man, a holy temple filled with the presence of God. In the silence of this sacred moment, we heard the Father speak from heaven: "This is My beloved Son in whom I am well pleased."

Spontaneous songs of worship began to rise from our hearts in all of the tongues and languages of the world. The beauty of this worship filled the earth with joyous praise. All the creatures of heaven and earth declared, "Worthy is the Lamb to receive glory and honor and thanksgiving. He alone will reign forever and ever over the kingdom of our God."

An explosion of adoration echoed through the heavens and around the globe as if waves of glory and love danced from our hearts to exalt our King and Lord. As I looked upon Jesus, my heart exploded with love and devotion to Him as I repeated the words of adoration to my Savior. This became the crowning hour of redemption for the human race. All who believed in Jesus and had entered into the new covenant by His blood knew Him, and He knew us in the wonder and riches of heaven.

Jesus reigned as King of kings in Jerusalem in His holy temple. Order was established throughout the earth, and of His kingdom, there would be no end. His truth and His justice would now prevail in the hearts of men and women as the tree of life began to grow in the center of Jerusalem. From Jerusalem its roots started to stretch to the nations and to every capital, the gift of life became a reality as its leaves were for the healing of the nations until all would be one under the reign of Jesus the Son of God.

In the aftermath of such wonder I sat with my family and friends in the warmth of our love. I could not help but marvel at the life I had had with them, one of blessings, love, heartache, and adventure. The memories started to float into my mind like clouds of enchantment. I began to explore them in the ecstasy and agony of my past life. In my mind, I could see the hand of God guiding every one of my steps. My vision became so clear I could see the beauty and the darkness of all that had transpired in my life.

As I marveled at the wonder of Jesus and this new millennial age, in the dark corners of some of the nations fermented evil in the hearts of a few men and women. In them, the seeds of rebellion had been planted in their wicked hearts.

Chapter 35

THE CONGO

The lush forest surrounded us with God's glory. The steep hills disguised as mountains zig-zagged the countryside. I could not help but think this was the garden of Eden. God had sent me to visit Adam years ago in one of my time travels.. The beauty and innocence remained in this corner of the northeast province of the Congo, except all innocence had been wiped away by twenty-five years of warfare and the rape of a child's youth, as thousands of boys and girls had been enslaved by the rebels to fight a war that would never be won.

Marie and I bounced along the dirt roads of the Congo, if you could call them roads. We were with our friends, Alice and Ashley, missionaries to the beloved people of the Congo. They spent much of their efforts rescuing the lost generation of these child soldiers. These seemingly infants were stolen from their villages, given guns, and filled with hatred through drugs and alcohol. They were the human shields for the adult men and women whose value to their generals far exceeded those of the children. Their innocence would never be restored to them, as violence and sex would crush their spirits and send them to a prison that had no key. When one looked into their eyes, all you could see was a hopeless gaze that spoke volumes of their deep despair.

Alice and Ashley had saved many of these lost children. They had made a dent in the rebels' army. So much so, the top general demanded a meeting with Ashley to demonstrate the high cost inflicted on his troops. It would be a dangerous rendezvous for Ashley. If the general saw fit, he could have him killed on the spot. There were no good guys in this part of the world, only devils who fought for dominion over the treasures of the vast riches buried in the hills and mountains of the Congo.

It was getting late in the day. We had only traveled thirty miles into this paradise after eight hours of bumpety bump jarring on this main highway. I joked with Ashley, if he could get a helicopter we could have saved seven hours of hell. Often the ruts grew so deep they swallowed whole cars. The clay, slick with rain, made driving almost impossible, like sliding on ice. We had barely two lanes to drive with sheer drops of 500 or more feet on the side of the steep terrain. Along one bend was a damaged truck from a mudslide. The dead driver lay along the hillside. One of the more sobering sights that could prophesy what was to come.

Suddenly, the road vanished into a river. As we moved forward in our Land Rover through the swift-flowing current, abreast to us were cannibalized vehicles that never made the crossing. I wondered if there were crocodiles or hippos in these waters. They were in the mountains of Zambia. I assumed the sound of deep-throated mating cries echoed the rule of their domain.

We had left a temporary camp of 30,000 refugees the day before. Endless blue United Nations tents created a village of hopelessness where entire families lived after they had lost almost everything from rebel raids, who drove them from their villages to this wasteland. The women had been raped. Their children were stolen to become soldiers. Those men who fought back were slaughtered with bullets and machetes. Yet, here these refugees were in the darkness of humanity protected by the United Nation military, or so they thought.

Two weeks after we had ministered to thousands of these suffering casualties of war, the rebels swooped in to rape, murder, and steal what little they had left. The UN soldiers were not allowed to defend them. When the rebels approached, all the soldiers were ordered to the fort in the city of Goma. They were not allowed to engage in battle. The rebels knowing this, brazenly marched in to satisfy their lusts without fear of reprisal.

They would do this offensive once a year to show their muscle and to fortify their stranglehold on the land. It gave them a sense of purpose, masquerading their real motives of greed and power. Once they got what they desired in children, women, and money, they ran back to the hills of Eden to rest and make plans to terrorize the local villages. This was the game that had been played for twenty-five years. The leaders of Goma put up with this tragedy because they had 25,000 soldiers in their city buying their goods and making the few very rich while the rest suffered in the poverty that permeates much of Central Africa.

A year earlier, one morning before dawn, I awoke to the sound of worship rising from the villages nestled in the valleys of this once paradise. We stayed in a tent on the top of a hill. Through the early morning fog I could see the fires burning throughout the surrounding valleys. The people were worshiping God with sounds as if they were angels. The glory of God rose throughout the land in these guarded hills, sheltering the people in their own little world. The worship was so magnificent, I knelt in prayer and praised with them the God of creation. I imagined God rejoiced and wept over His people who still loved Him and exalted him in the midst of endless warfare.

By the time we forded the river in our Land Rover and rose to the top of a mountain we could see our mission village down the hill. It had a few huts and small houses along the only road through the village with footpaths that led to more huts. There was a small school house and a meeting lodge and one church with a thatched roof and concrete block walls. They had a rugged soccer field with two wooden poles without a net for a goal. Their soccer ball was made of rags and twine, but oh how they loved to play.

We had a meeting with the chief the next morning and then one with the rebel general in the afternoon. Tonight we would rest and sleep in our tents, one for Alice and Ashley and one for Marie and me. After we set up our tents, we made a fire and cooked dinner. The air was heavy with a dampness that kept the foliage green and beautiful. We were near the Ituri Forest, so there were a variety of trees, such as mahogany, ebony, and iruho. The steep hills and mountains mixed with savannah, and rivers made for a wonderland of nature.

To the north of us was the Ituri Forest where the pygmy tribes lived. Most of Congo consisted of the Bantu people. We would be seeing the chief of the Ngala tribe. I had met him a year before and had a nice friendly visit in his home.

For Marie and me, this was our first mission trip together as husband and wife. We felt like we were on our honeymoon. It was this night that we conceived our first child in the wilds of Africa. We always said Jonathan received some of his safari DNA from the Congo.

Since we met in Orlando, Florida it was love at first sight. Of course Marie had the advantage on me, since Jesus had sent her from His day to mine to meet and marry me. We laughed that I never had a chance. It was predetermined I would be hers and she mine forever.

I remember the fire of our camp kept increasing as Ashley stoked it with wood. I could see in Marie's eyes a fire burning as well. It was quite romantic in this Paradise. We were determined to get to bed early. Ashley and Alice joked about the wild noises of the rainforest. We smiled and said good night. We had such an amorous feeling between us, we could not resist the passion that pulled us close together as one. I was enticed by her full auburn hair that lay across her shoulders, curled and fresh with the scent of lilac.

As I pressed my lips to hers, the fire grew within us. "There are times when I feel you possess my soul in the beauty of your love," I whispered to her as I gazed into her soft beckoning eyes. She smiled and gently said, "It brings me such joy to see you so alive."

Later, we lay side by side with Marie nestled against my chest. "God's gift of family will be one of our treasures," I said to her.

"He did tell Noah in His covenant of family with him and his descendants be fruitful and multiply," Marie replied as I caressed her hair.

"Such beauty has never been seen by man or me," I spoke as I looked at her. "You do take my breath away." She pulled closer to me and kissed me. That was the beginning of our first of three children. We would refer to this night as the tent of meeting.

The next day we awoke to the dawn of God's glory. We were tired from the drive and late night, but refreshed by the presence of God. We marveled how close we felt to God when you have no television, phones, cars, and commotion of the modern city. You are surrounded by the magnificence of God's creation in what seemed to us His pure innocence.

Our time with the chief went well. He warned us about meeting with this General Moses who had led the rebel army for over ten years. He was shrewd and wicked with a keen mind. He hated that Ashley and Alice had been liberating his child soldiers. Expect an intense confrontation, the chief warned us. This inspired us to spend much time in prayer after we left the chief. We cried out to God for Him to be glorified in our meeting. We prayed for protection and wisdom and that more children would be set free. As one, we proclaimed the mountain of unbelief to be cast into the sea and the general and his soldiers would come to Christ. We asked the Lord to use us to plant the seeds of salvation in their hearts.

Words of prophecy flowed from Marie. She saw a camp with many soldiers; then suddenly a great fire spread throughout the camp. Ashley reached into the flames and pulled out a fiery brand. He ran out of the camp down the hill. When he opened his hand to grab the hot ember, he was not burned. The brand turned into a jewel of great value.

In the afternoon several of Moses' adult soldiers met us at the edge of the village and took us deep into the hills and forest. Ashley and I went with them as the ladies stayed to minister to the people of the village. We rode in an almost new United Nations Land Rover. Our guards carried AK-47 rifles with belts of ammo around their shoulders and backs. They also had revolvers on their belts. They wore camouflage uniforms with spit-polished boots. They were young, probably in their twenties, but seemed like seasoned fighters.

I was tense being surrounded by guerillas who could easily kill us and have our bodies disappear. Being Americans did give us a greater sense of protection and that our wives were left behind to report us missing if it came to that, but there was no law out here, just the rebels. When we arrived at the camp, we stood outside an open tent, probably stolen from the United Nations. The camp was filled with armored vehicles and Land Rovers. These guys were well supplied and fed. I was impressed and realized the truth: they controlled this territory. They were the law.

Ashley and I were sweating in the hot sun of the equator. We were high up in elevation, so it was cool, but the sun was like a torch on my neck and face. Ashley would take the lead. I was to be his wingman.

Finally we were called into the tent. We were surrounded by ten soldiers as we came before the general. He was probably in his mid-forties. There was not an ounce of fat on him. His arms and chest were muscular. He was a fighter of the first degree and knew how to rule with authority.

He actually greeted us with a warm welcome and offered us some beer or tea, but we kindly declined. That brought him right to business. With a voice that exuded confidence and control, he spoke directly to Ashely. "Your good deeds are ruining my young soldiers. I cannot allow this any longer. Let me show you one of my fighters, who, because of you and your wife, is no longer fit for service. He loves this Jesus and will not kill any more."

A child of about eleven was brought into our midst. He looked glassy-eyed as though he was drugged. Our hearts broke over the loss of his innocence and the thought of the thousands of young boys and girls through the years who were never allowed to grow up. Most died early or lost all sense of decency. The girls, if they survived, would become the sex slaves of the camp.

"Since this one is of no use to me, I will have him killed right here. Then you can take him home to this Jesus." A soldier stepped forward and drew his pistol.

"Wait!" Ashley cried. "Let me have him alive."

The general put up his hand to stop the soldier, but the man fired point blank at the general. Shot through his temple, the general fell dead to the ground. It was a coup, an assassination. For an instant everyone froze as we were all stunned. Then all hell broke loose. Each soldier pulled up their weapons and began to fire at each other. We were in the middle of this firefight. The soldier who had killed the general was wounded. Bullets raced all around us. The sound of these rifles and guns was deafening. I lost all awareness of what to do or what was happening.

Ashley grabbed the child and shouted, "Run!" It was as if a wall of angels stood around us. Not one bullet struck us. We dashed to the Land Rover we had come in. The keys were in it. The three of us jumped in, and Ashley took off in a tear.

Fortunately, before he had become a missionary, Ashley raced off-road vehicles and four wheelers. Before I knew it, we were down the hill from the camp. I looked back and saw no one. They were killing each other just as in the days of Jehoshaphat when the three armies of Syria, Moab, and Edom turned on one another and slaughtered themselves.

By the time we reached the village, my head had cleared. Ashley said they probably had planned to blame the assassination on us. Thank God, He had other plans and guided us to safety. , Ashley and Alice knew the child soldier with us by the name of Charles. This brand plucked from the fire would become a mighty evangelist and church planter in the Congo in the years to come. He was a precious diamond in the hand of God. I loved how Marie's prophecies came to life!

Chapter 36

BETRAYAL OF THE BRETHREN

Then there was the darkness. the wilderness journey that almost shattered our marriage. Two years after Jonathan was born, I was to go to Zambia to help my best friends, Dexter and Susan Green, plant churches in the Copper Belt.

Marie had led a women's retreat with over 200 women from our church. It was a powerful time in the Lord, but one woman was offended by her. She then lied to some leaders about Marie. Three days prior to my trip to Zambia, the leaders had a secret meeting about my wife. Then the day I was to leave, two leaders came to my office and told me about the meeting that concerned Marie. They said I needed to get her in line because of what this woman said. Her husband was a rich contributor in the church, and they did not want him to be offended. I had just finished preaching three services and needed to get to the airport when they cornered me in my office.

They very politely disguised their troubles with Marie, but behind it, I could tell something sinister was brewing. Just two weeks before, these same leaders and about eight other elders in the church told me what a fantastic job I was doing. There was no better church in all of Miami they told me. I did not take their rebuke of Marie with a good attitude as my focus was on the crusades I would do in Zambia. When I arrived home to pack, Marie was quite worried about where I had been. She asked about the meeting, and I said I was in a rush not to miss my plane.

"What was it about?' she inquired, but I put her off, which told her it was about her.

"It was nothing," I replied, trying to avoid the pain I knew she would suffer. I kissed her and was off to Miami International for a thirty-hour, grueling flight and lay over time to Ndola, Zambia.

The crusades were beyond powerful. God did more than we could ever ask. We saw miracle healings of sick babies to blind eyes being opened. Hundreds gave their lives to Christ. Hundreds more were baptized in the Holy Spirit. Evangelists and future pastors were raised up. Many churches would be planted. Near the end of the crusades I poured my heart out to Dexter over what these leaders had done. I could not hold it in any more. They believed a lie about Marie because they wanted to believe it. I was angry and wanted to put these leaders in their place. Almost all were very successful businessmen with strong personalities.

I was once told by a pastor friend, the most dangerous person in the church is a successful businessman who was not filled with the Holy Spirit. How true that came to be in my life. I thought they were all about Jesus, but I soon discovered they were more about themselves and their own agendas than about Jesus and His kingdom.

When I returned home exhausted from my travels, all Marie had thought about for two weeks was what had been said about her. She had heard from other ladies, wives of these men, what had taken place. Being a Bible believing follower of Jesus, she went to the woman and confronted her with her lie. That was a disaster. The woman denied her falsehood and tried to turn the tables on Marie that she was lying. Then this woman told her husband, who supported her lie. This led the church into a storm of hurricane proportions.

As soon as I put down my suitcases in the hall of our house, Marie went at me with her hurt and pain. I had little energy to give her. The devil took my weakness and brought division into our lives. "Where was my knight in shining armor?" she cried. "How could you not defend me? I have witnesses that can prove she is lying. You don't want to confront them because you are afraid they will leave the church," she protested.

The toughest job in the world besides being a pastor is being the wife of a pastor. Marie is a strong, loving woman all out for Jesus. She could take a lot of grief from people, but this straw broke her back. We were at a very large church that did amazing ministries in missions, with the children and youth, and with social outreach as well as hundreds of souls saved. We had grown to almost 4,000 members, but it all seemed like fluff to me now.

Seeds of division had been sown years ago between our church and our school of over 700 children and youth. On the surface we were on fire, but strongholds of religion and controlling spirits were at work to undermine our unity. There was a strong spirit of sexual sin that had never been confronted by the pastors or leaders. Sexual sin with the youth pastor and some of the young men in the church had been covered up by a former pastor who was involved in terrible sin with mostly single moms. His wife had threatened to leave him, but all of this had been covered up by the hierarchy. The dam was about to break. I had many prayer warriors doing battle for Marie and me and the church. They were determined to see our people repent and humbled before God to restore the unity of the Body and release the power of the Holy Spirit.

A special meeting was called for the Personnel Committee as these leaders wanted to discuss me before those who determined if the pastor should stay or leave. These men had been my friends for years in this church and had just recently told me what a super job I was doing. How fickle are the hearts of men! I was so naive. I was completely unprepared for how vicious this night would become. These were my friends. Surely when push came to shove they would support me. How wrong I was.

The nine-member Personnel Team gathered. I was to sit in the room and hear each one of the leaders share about me. The wind, not of the

Spirit, but of the devil came rushing in one by one. Shock and awe could not compare to what was hurled against me. I was the worst pastor. I should resign. I had lied and hidden from the people the debt of the school. I should leave and become an evangelist. My time at this church is over.

Every time I wanted to defend myself and challenge their accusations, the Spirit told me to remain silent as Jesus had done before Pilate and the religious leaders. I could not believe what I heard from these Christian men and my friends.

I once was told by a great pastor at one of the largest churches in America after he resigned, when he was asked if he would ever go back to that church as its pastor, his reply, "Even Jesus was only crucified once."

When all was done the committee voted for me to stay 5 to 4. Several of them had been warned before the meeting, they had better vote me out. They buckled and voted nay. I went home unable to think or function. I was like a soldier who had been knocked unconscious by an explosion. I do not remember driving home. Marie greeted me at the door. She tried to comfort me and at the same time get from me what had happened.

I could not say. The daggers in my back took my speech away. I was shell shocked. Betrayed was written across my forehead. I could not comprehend what my friends had done to me. They really did not care about me at all. How could they turn on me? Three weeks ago, I was their hero. Now I was a miserable failure.

In my heart there was a wedge between Marie and me for the first time in our marriage. She conveyed to me I had let her down and not defended her. Instead, I had deserted her to please these men who did not even support me. "Where was the man I had married?" she asked. The pain froze my brain. I had nothing to say. To ease my pain, she seduced me into bed. It was not our most joyous union.

I was still dazed and shattered. I felt a failure in my marriage and in my ministry. I could not shut my mind off from thinking and hearing those men and their debasing words. Is that what they truly thought of me? I could not accept it. I did not sleep one second that night. Early in the morning, I went to church and lay in the chapel. I cried out to God for strength and for direction. But my prayers did not lift beyond the ceiling of this sacred place. Yet, God carried me through the day and the next day. On Sunday I had to preach. Fear consumed me that I would show up, and everyone would be gone.

To my relief all the people came and God carried me on His shoulders through the services and into the next week. Marie and I survived, but it gave us some scars that we carried with us. Fortunately, God had given us an unbreakable bond. Our love held against the winds that battered our home. The storm came, and we did not fall. We knew deep in our hearts we could not live without each other. Two months later she surprised me with the news she was with child. We were a family of three about to become four.

Chapter 37

ROMANCE IN CUBA

Powerful waves crashed against the seawall of Havana Harbor as Marie and I strolled along the main avenue along the coast. Wonderful sights surrounded us. The colonial fort, heroic statues of freedom fighters, cannons, a festival with salsa music in the air, and the colonial façades with beautiful ironworks outlining the streets and buildings. The oldest cars from the '40s and '50s rolled by, a reminder of the communist takeover. Now they were nostalgic memories of better days that added to the romance and magic of this central port of call in the Caribbean.

We could see couples holding hands, others kissing in the shadows. It made our hearts soar with passion and love. Our walk from our hotel was meant to refresh us after an exhausting series of ministries in the churches and at the Camp Canaan Retreat center. God had moved mightily upon the pastors, missionaries, and people. Fresh visions for ministry inspired countless people to step out in faith to achieve what was impossible with man but possible with God.

The movement of the Spirit in Cuba had multiplied the church beyond comprehension despite the intense persecution they faced from the government. The communists had tried to kill my friend in Cuba three times. My other good pastor friend had been in a concentration camp when his son was born. Like ancient Rome, no amount of suffering imposed by the government could stop what God was doing. Marie and I loved ministering with the Cuban people. Their hunger for God made teaching, preaching, and ministering so easy. Thousands had been baptized in the Holy Spirit, and they would go forth to spread the Gospel. Cuba was an island on fire for Jesus and ready for His return.

The main church in Havana welcomed us with such love, it caused us to love them even more. The morning Marie and I ministered in the services, hundreds were healed of sicknesses, disease, and infirmities. So many swamped the altar, we could hardly move and pray over them, but God's Spirit touched each one of them. The memories of Cuba kept flooding my mind as I reflected on my family in my resurrected body. I could see the Hotel Nacional of Cuba as though it was yesterday. Marie and I rested for two days in luxury on this seafront resort.

This famous hotel, erected in 1930, dominated the turquoise, crystal-clear waters of the harbor of Havana. Within its walls, this gem nestled in paradise captured the magnificent 500-year history of Cuba. The royal palms rose to the sky, standing guard to welcome all who come to enjoy its romance and beauty. "The Pit of Wishes," or Wishing Well, sits alongside the road walkway that leads to this entrance into the soul of Cuba. The legend says you will receive your desires by holding hands over the well and asking for your dreams to come true.

Marie and I held hands over the well and prayed for the conception of our third child. We laughed because this was the same hotel my parents had stayed in 1951 when they took a boat from Miami to Havana. The story was this was the ship where my older brother was conceived. We would watch their black-and-white home movies that were taken on their trip. We saw the same hotel, the same waterfront, the same statues, and the same cars, only looking sixty years younger on the screen!

As we walked into the ornate Hotel Nacional, a life force drew us into its history of people that spoke of lives and destinies that have dined and slept within its wonder. A display of famous people tell of which rooms they stayed in. There was Brando, Churchill, Johnny Weissmuller, Frank Sinatra, and the captivating beauty, Ava Gardner, whose alluring gaze transcends the generations of famous actresses. Her picture on the wall beckons one to the seduction of sirens encountered long ago by Odysseus in the isles of the Mediterranean Sea.

In a few steps, we were led into the open garden that released the elegance of the Nacional's charm, with its fine-kept lawn, flowers, and people seated around tables, sharing their lives in deep conversation. An arrow pointed us to La Barraca where we sat serenaded by the *soperos*, three amigos that warmed our hearts with romance. We toasted my parents in honor of their visit, almost sixty years earlier. Then we walked hand-in-hand to the edge of the hill that overlooked the sea. Cannons pointed outward, entrenched ready to fire on the American ships in the Spanish American War of 1898. We continued to the trenches, dug during the missile crisis of 1962 that almost brought us to the brink of World War III with the Soviet Union.

To the left along Malecon Avenue we saw the monument to General de Brigade Henry M. Reeve. Further down is the monument to the victims of the USS Maine sunk in 1898. Two cannons lay atop, with black iron chains linked over them. Below on each side were empty fountains tarnished with beer bottles and debris.

As we wandered to the Cueva Taganana, or Tangnana Cave, we saw more cannons and trenches. It inspired me to believe men are always looking for a cause to fight for. Marie and I shared our desire to tell the world of Jesus. This was the war to end all wars and bring peace to the soul of humanity. In front is the Cuban flag proudly waving in the sea breeze with a large sign that reads Cuba. Water flows over the rocks before the flag and cascades down into a pool on the Malecon Boulevard that runs ten lanes wide along the sea wall.

As we looked across to the bay, the open sea came to us in waves that rolled in and crashed against the jagged rocks. In desperation, they expend their last energy, determined to leap the sea wall and spill onto the walkway. In the moonlight, it is a majestic scene of power and life. On the waterfront we can see lovers nestled on the wall half hidden by concrete posts sharing secret kisses as the waves crash against the walls.

The sirens are calling to Marie and me to share our love in a passionate kiss that takes our breath away.

Gathering our composure we return to La Barraca where we only have eyes for one another. There is a mystical power in gazing into the eyes of the one you love. It is like the joining of two souls with one heartbeat for each other. Captivating and enticing spring to my mind. It creates a deep hunger to become one in body and spirit.

"God has blessed me far more than I deserve," I said to Marie, trying my best to express my love for her. "If I had never met Jesus, I wouldn't have you and our children, a family of love, hope, and faith to withstand the storms of life. Look at the treasure God has given me in you. I owe Him everything. How you bless me. I feel my heart could burst because of you. Just your smile inspires me."

Marie took my hand. "You bless me more than you know. Your love has made me whole. Think of where I was without Jesus and then you. There is no meaning in my life without you. Your love healed my soul and made me realize I am a good person. That is a treasure I will cherish forever."

"You are so beautiful, my love. Can we capture this moment and hold it in our hearts forever?" At that I moved over and kissed her soft lips. I was soaring like an eagle in the heavens. I wanted to get so close to her that nothing could ever part us.

"You are the only woman I have ever loved and given my whole heart to," I spoke tenderly to reveal my true emotions.

"But you were engaged once?" she questioned.

"Yes, but because of you, I know I did not love her. You are my love forever."

"And I yours. You alone have my whole heart, mind, body, and soul. I could love no other but you. You are God's gift to me, and I love you."

That night, our third child was conceived at the Havana Hotel to complete our family until we would have a multitude of grandkids. God's covenant with Noah had come to us through Jesus Christ: be fruitful and multiply. Because of God's blessings and promises, we had multiplied in our physical family but also in our spiritual children we helped give birth throughout the world.

To be fruitful and multiply was inherent in the covenant God gave to Adam in the garden and then to Noah and Abraham. The seed of His love in us could not help but produce fruit and increase in the physical and the spiritual realm.

Since we had gathered with Jesus in our resurrected body, we knew millions of spiritual children in the new millennium on earth. There was no need for introductions, for when we encountered one another, we knew who they were. It produced such joy and celebration. I think there was a continuous rejoicing among the resurrected.

The beauty of God's plan surpassed anything we could have imagined. How could we convey this to the people who had not believed and not been transformed? This would become one of our main purposes in these next 1,000 years: to see God's forever family be fruitful and increase.

Chapter 38

THE VISIT

I saw now I needed to visit my grandson and tell him of the love of Jesus. It was so clear to me as the day I time traveled and found myself with Cleopas as we walked the dusty, dreary road to Emmaus, a town seven miles outside of Jerusalem. Suddenly, a man joined us out of nowhere and asked us what we were discussing on our journey. For we seemed quite downtrodden.

"Have you not heard what happened these past days in Jerusalem?" Cleopas, my companion, responded.

"What things?" the stranger answered.

Our minds could not believe this one was ignorant of how Jesus had been crucified, so we told him of our sorrow. "God's mighty prophet, Jesus of Nazareth was murdered, hung on the cross. He had done great and wondrous miracles and taught the Word of God as no other to the people. The chief priests and our rulers delivered Him to be condemned to death and crucified by the Romans. We believed and hoped He was the promised Messiah sent by God to redeem Israel. Now on the third day after His death, our female friends went to His tomb this morning and claimed it is empty. They saw angels who told them He was alive. Our friends ran to the tomb and went inside and saw it was vacant, but they did not see Jesus anywhere."

The stranger shook his head as if mocking us for our lack of understanding. "You are foolish in your thoughts and slow of heart not to believe in the prophets that spoke of the Messiah. Did they not tell you that the Christ must suffer these things and then enter into His glory?"

His words stirred our minds as if, please tell us what you know. He began to expound to us the words of Moses and all the prophets, revealing to us the scarlet thread that wove its way through the Scriptures concerning Jesus as the Messiah. The stain of sin can only be washed away by His blood. God gave the Hebrews the Law to teach them how to prepare for the Lamb of God who would take away the sin of the world. Our Creator gave them laws of sacrifice for the blood of bulls and sheep to be a temporary act of forgiveness to appease the wrath of God. But do not think that their blood would be eternal, he told us.

Christ came to die once and for all time for the sin of humanity. As the sinless Son of Man and the divine Son of God, He alone could fulfill the Law of God concerning sin and death. He did what the first Adam could not do, live a sinless life; thus He could be the blameless Lamb sacrificed for sin. He became the Second Adam to establish God's kingdom. As the suffering Servant of Isaiah, by His stripes we are healed.

He then quoted the great prophet who saw the Lord of Hosts in the temple:

"He was despised and rejected by men. A Man of sorrows and acquainted with our grief. We hid our faces from Him; He was despised and we did not esteem Him. He bore our griefs and carried our sorrows. Yet we esteemed Him stricken. Smitten by God and afflicted. He was wounded for our transgressions. He was bruised for our iniquities. The chastisement for our peace was upon Him, and by His stripes we are healed.

All we like sheep have gone astray; We have turned, every one, to his own way; and the Lord has laid on Him the iniquity of us all. He was oppressed and He was afflicted, Yet, He opened not His mouth; He was led as a lamb to the slaughter, and as a sheep before its shearers is silent, so He opened not His mouth." Isaiah 53:3-7.

As he spoke to us, it was as if the very heavens opened and the revelation of God poured into our souls and minds. As this man of knowledge quoted the prophets further, we now understood why Jesus had to suffer and then rise again. Our hearts were no longer heavy but full of joy. Jesus was the Messiah. He had fulfilled all Scripture as He had once told His disciples He would do, and on the third day He would rise again.

How foolish we were not to see and believe. We were blinded by our ambitions to make Him king and us rule with Him. Our hatred for the Romans stopped us from understanding the Word of God and hearing rightly the words Jesus had spoken to us. Cleopas remembered three distinct times on the road to Jerusalem Jesus told them He would be betrayed and handed over to be crucified and He would be resurrected on the third day.

As night drew near, as we approached Emmaus. The stranger acted as though He would keep on his travels, but we begged him to eat with us and stay the night. We hoped we would hear more of his insight into the mysteries of God's truth, hidden from us since Adam. That night became a time of covenant between us. We entered into the sacred meal as he took bread, blessed it, broke it, and gave it to us. In that treasured moment, our eyes were opened, for we saw this was Jesus risen from the dead. As we went to praise and worship Him, He vanished. Oh, how our hearts burned within us. We were like men dying of thirst being given living water poured forth from the fountain of His life.

We could not sit still. In the wonder of the hour, we gathered our belongings and rushed back to Jerusalem to the eleven apostles to tell them of our glorious encounter. When we arrived, with great joy we told them of Jesus and His words. As we broke bread in the covenant meal He had given us, our eyes were opened as we knew He was Jesus, risen indeed!

So, it would be with my grandson, I hoped. He had missed Jesus. Even though he was raised in the church, joined the church, and was baptized, he had never given his heart to Jesus as his Savior. But it was not too late. We, the resurrected ones are here to witness to all that Jesus was the Messiah. I had to believe Jason's eyes would be opened as Cleopas's were on the road to Emmaus.

Strange, the earth was still the earth for another thousand years. Yet, I was not the same. My resurrected body felt no pain and never grew tired or sick. The inner division of fears, worry, and anxiety was gone. The idol of self is no more a plague upon my soul. I was alive as Jesus was alive after His Resurrection.

I was immortal and incorruptible. My sole desire was to love and serve Jesus. The intimacy enjoyed with God could never be described in human language. The oneness with God was as a flame of fire that could not be divided. My heart was purer than pure. I could travel at the speed of light. I could eat whatever I liked because my lust for food or money or power had faded with the corruption of my flesh, replaced by the wonder of perfection. All was in order. I did not take offense. I never feared. I only loved to give love without lust or manipulation.

I found my grandson's home, and in an instant I was at his door from Jerusalem to Orlando. I did not miss the long, taxiing plane flights where my feet swelled and jet lag nagged at me for days. The time never changed for us in our new bodies. We were always on God's time. The beauty of God's creation shone in my mind and heart like the eternal glory of God. I enjoyed passing through doors into a room, but I thought I had better knock at Jason's door. I was at peace when he answered the door, but he was not. Alone and without family, he had grown angry at being left behind. Beside the marvels of Jesus and the evidence of the resurrection, he refused to believe in Jesus. His heart was as cold as stone on a winter's day.

I stepped forward and embraced him with love. He welcomed me in but was reserved. I detected he thought I was there to berate him and condemn him that he had not been transformed.

"What have you been up to?" I asked, even though I knew he was not working at his usual job. The earth may not have changed, but the world had. The justice of Jesus had caused a whole reorganization of cities, states, and nations. In this new order of community, the unredeemed people struggled to find their place. Sin still abounded in their hearts and lives. They lived almost in a twilight zone of shadows and fear. One would think everyone would choose to believe in Jesus and be transformed, but that was not the case. The hardness of heart in sinners is not a problem of logic, but a spiritual resistance to the God of truth. As though they were trapped in a worldview that would not adapt to the new reality of Jesus as the ruler of the world.

Despite the glory of His presence and the millions of resurrected believers traveling around the world, interacting with the unsaved, they still denied their need for a Savior. They could not gain victory over the prison of their thoughts and unbelief. The conviction of the Holy Spirit was absent in this millennial age. We, the resurrected, were to be the conduits of salvation to the lost. Thus, here I was to gain the trust and confidence of my grandson, believing that by my love for him, I could open his heart to Jesus and to life.

"Have you seen my father?" he asked. "He has not visited since his death and resurrection. I was away the night they were murdered. I wonder about Mom and my brother and sister. Why haven't they come? I hear of others, in-betweeners we call ourselves, who have seen their families."

"Big daddy," he cried. "I am so alone. I cannot bear the pain. One day we were all a big happy family. I snuck out one night from home, and the house is blown up by terrorists. Jesus came back, and where am I?" Big Daddy was the name I took from the movie *Cat on a Hot Tin Roof* for being grandpa. I loved that movie, and everyone thought I was crazy to choose it, but the grandkids never gave it a second thought! I could see his spirit was crushed. His grief had produced a prison of shame, guilt, and anger. Until he knew he was loved, the wall to his soul would never be breached.

"I miss you," I said with kindness. "It must be so difficult not knowing what has happened with your family. They all miss you and wonder why you are not with them."

"Then why have they not come to see me? I hear you can travel in an instant to anywhere on the planet. Why don't they come?"

"I do not know, but I am here. Perhaps they are trying to figure out why you are not with them."

"Why aren't I?" he questioned. "I thought I was a believer. Why was I not gathered up in the sky with all of you?"

"You know that answer, I would think. You choose to close your heart to Jesus. He never knew you."

"I knew Him. Wasn't that enough?"

"No, it is not." I said softly. "When I was your age, I had been taught all about Jesus, but I had not given my life to Him in repentance and faith. I had head knowledge of who Jesus was, but not true faith. Even the devil knows who Jesus is, but that does not save him. You have to truly believe in Him and give all of yourself to Him, to come to Him in humility and desperation that only He can save you from yourself and your sins."

He looked sad and distraught. "But you know all of that. You heard it a thousand times at home, at church, at school, with your friends."

"So many of them are still here. What went wrong?" he cried.

"Too many families gave their children religion but never Jesus. Our culture deceived them. They loved sin more than the Savior. The love of the world seduced them into a false belief. Deep down, they wanted to be their own gods. I was the same way until my life fell apart. In my aloneness and brokenness, I cried out to Jesus and gave Him my life. You can still do that," I encouraged him gently without manipulation.

"I do believe in Jesus. It's just that I don't know what is stopping me from crossing that line to give Him my whole heart."

"I cannot do it for you. Faith must be your own trust in Him." I placed my hand on his shoulder as he dropped his head. "It cannot be out of emotion or a desire to be with the family. Your will needs to surrender to Him. Open that door of your heart, and He will answer."

In that instant I knew his heart bowed to Jesus. His eyes filled with tears as he asked Jesus to take his life for His glory. "Do with me what You please. I do believe. I do surrender," he cried.

Suddenly, the room filled with a brilliant light. There stood Jesus in all His glory. Jason and I fell at His feet in love and worship. "I have come to take you home, Jason," Jesus said.

The beauty of that moment seared into my mind for an eternity. Jason transformed from his corrupt earthly body to one like the heavenly Man. He was freed from sin and death, alive forever more with Jesus and all of us. The wonder of Jesus. I could not help but praise my Lord and King.

As we traveled to Jerusalem in what seemed like a nanosecond, I was filled with joy at the thought of this prodigal's homecoming. He was not much of a prodigal since he had not left his family to squander his inheritance on sinful desires, but he had wandered from Jesus. Now he was one with Him and with all of us. They say there are no tears in heaven, but I felt a few drops crease my cheeks as we arrived at Jonathan's house.

Chapter 39

THE IDOL OF SELF

The celebration of life as God has life continues in the new millennium in abundance. The tree of life became rooted everywhere in the nations. Its fruit was full of life. One serving a day of this delicious nectar brought an ever-increasing awareness of who we are in Christ. The love and intimacy of this new life took us to depths of joy and understanding incomprehensible in the old nature.

When Jason and I arrived at his father's mansion, we celebrated with an abundance of love and joy. His dad threw the party of the ages now that his son was home. They hugged and embraced. The smiles that lit their faces reflected the riches of heaven. We were one as a family, complete in Christ and complete in one another. The unity and love exploded into the revelation of God's glory. The Father and Son dwelt in us and with us, and the light of Their presence outshone the sun because all darkness had vanished in the glory of the Word.

"This is so cool, Dad," Jason stated. "We just thought to be here and in an instant we traveled 6,000 miles."

"The joy I feel with you resurrected makes me even more whole," Jonathan replied.

"After my transition to my glorified body, God gave me a glimpse into my old nature. I saw the corruption of my flesh intertwined with that idol of self on the throne of my life. I was appalled by who I had been. I truly wanted to be my own god."

"Thank the Lord, all that is past. We are totally free to live as we were created."

"But, there are millions still in bondage to that sinful nature. I believe I am to help them get set free. As I was reflecting on how to do that, I went to Big Daddy's journals and found this written several years ago. I remember him preaching on this."

I thought about what Jason was about to read. I wrote this at a time of tremendous trial in my life. I had fallen into sin. I could not get victory over my temptations. I knew if I did not master it, this sin could destroy me and ruin all I had lived for in my family and ministry. It was a battle for my soul. I cried out that I could not serve Him with this in my life. They were the same words I had uttered to Jesus on the night of my conversion when He came into my room and set me free from sin and death. That night Jesus reached into my mind with a laser beam of light and removed my struggle for five years, only for it to return at a season of great stress. Then, in desperation I asked once more for a miracle.

Jason began to read aloud from my journal:

> I had a wonderful experience as I was exercising and worshiping the Lord in the late afternoon. In my usual manner, I pray and talk with the Lord as I do my step machine for twenty minutes. Suddenly, out of nowhere, the Spirit reminded me this January was forty years since I met Jesus Christ. For me, it was the most dramatic experience of my life. It transformed me from an agnostic at best to one totally in love with Jesus as I realized He was truly God in human flesh, who died on the cross, rose from the dead, and is coming again.

> In this encounter I realized for the first time Jesus loved me as He entered my room and surrounded me with what

I came to describe as a cloud of love. He took away all the emotional pain of my life, all the heartache and confusion, and best of all, every sin I had ever committed.

In this new freedom of salvation, I began my incredible journey of getting to know Jesus through the Word, by the Spirit, and numerous experiences that confirmed to me my experience with Jesus was the most real moment of my entire life. It propelled me to become an evangelist for Jesus.

As I continued to worship God as I exercised, I was captivated by the thought of forty years, forty being a significant number in the Bible, especially forty years.

In the Hebrew Bible, forty is often used for time periods, forty days or forty years, which separate "two distinct epochs." Rain fell for "forty days and forty nights" during the Flood (Gen. 7:4). ... Several Jewish leaders and kings are said to have ruled for "forty years," that is, a generation. The Jews wandered in the wilderness for forty years. Moses was on Mt. Sinai forty days and forty nights. Forty often denotes a period of trial and testing.

I thought I had not been in the wilderness for forty years, but then I realized I had been in the wilderness for at least the last forty days. My transition from pastor/evangelist to evangelist had not been an easy one. Numerous stressful situations and traumas had impacted my life. I struggled with obsessive thoughts and sinful patterns. Yes, I had been in a spiritual wilderness without comprehending that truth.

Out of the week of prayer and fasting, I had several powerful breakthroughs in the Spirit. One was the realization that Self had placed itself on the throne of my heart, soul, mind, and body. It was the root cause of my struggle within my soul and mind. Yes, Jesus was still all to me, but self in its pride is deceitful above all else. I had yielded the throne of my being to self.

It was the idol of self that had to be removed to regain the spiritual life I had been given by Jesus and the Father. Self-satisfaction, self-fulfillment, self-gratification—all these concepts showed me, Self had reasserted itself in my life. I went into a time of reflection and confession and repentance. God, in His way, did what I was helpless to do; He removed self from the throne of my being.

I prayed for self to be crucified from the throne of my mind, soul, spirit, and body. I asked Jesus and the Father to sit on the throne of my mind, spirit, soul, and body. This became a daily exercise during the week of prayer and fasting, but it was more than an exercise. It was a cry of desperation that I could not serve God as I desired unless self was removed and Christ was King of my life.

At some point that week, God acted. Incredible peace came into me. All obsessive thoughts and temptations faded. I was free. My sense of joy and love rose to new levels. Jesus and the Father reigned in my life. The wilderness journey had ended. I was alive more than I had ever been.

I told Marie, I have never loved God more. I never loved her more than now. These are two healthy signs of a heart and soul freed from the bondage of self. I actually felt like I cared more for others than myself. I have been full of the oneness Jesus promised in His John 17 prayer. I was all in for Jesus.

For me, out of the wilderness meant that this year would be a year of blessing beyond measure. What greater blessing than to be in love with the Father and Jesus and to be in love with my wife and family and friends!

I share this journey because God's gift for me is the same gift He offers to you. Only the Holy Spirit can bring you into this gift. Our part is to hunger and thirst for God, recognize the conviction of the Spirit, yield to His call, and receive the glory. With Jesus and the Father on the throne of your soul, mind, spirit and body, those sins you struggle with will disappear because the root has been removed. It is the most wonderful and glorious season of my life. It can be for you too!

When Jason finished reading, I added to what he had read. "You know Jason, the greatest challenge I have discovered in life is to get victory over that inner core of my being, that is self-centered, proud, manipulative, and deceitful. If this idol of self is not conquered, it will destroy your relationships, fill your mind with tormenting thoughts and desires, and end up ruling your life.

"In our resurrected bodies we have been set free from that inner beast, those that God is sending you to love and share with Jesus, battle that idol of Self daily, often minute by minute, and they are trapped in the deceit of their worldview that serves that golden calf.

"The challenge is to love oneself which is good, but to recognize the difference between self-love and self-glorification. We are vain creatures created to love self in the context of humility and dependence on God. If the Father and Jesus sit on the throne of our soul, mind, body, and spirit, we will learn to have healthy relationships and rule over that sin principle that has infected the very heart of who we are.

"Again, we have been liberated from that sin nature, but the unredeemed are still in the battle of their lives. Until they respond to the call of God's grace in Jesus, they will never be set free."

Jason got it. "Until we gain a true opinion of who we really are and stop denying reality, but face yourself in the mirror, we cannot get the victory."

"That is correct." I shared with him a story that taught me that lesson.

I was reading Dickens's novel, *The Tale of Two Cities*, when an older man called me to come in for some counseling. His wife had an accident that left her without the ability to have intercourse. He was struggling with how to cope with his dilemma because he still longed for affection and physical love. This wise man asked me, "What do you do when you have a legitimate need, but your partner is incapable of meeting that need? I do not want to seek a mistress or go into pornography. I love my wife. I know there are fates far worse than death that tempt me to fulfill my valid need."

I remember nodding to him and agreeing, "There are prisons that capture a man's soul. If one is not careful, there is no escape."

I thought of that marvelous book by Dickens. In the end the main character takes the place of a man in prison awaiting death. He sacrifices his life so this man can go free. He lives out Jesus's call to lay down our lives for a friend as the greatest expression of love, as Jesus did for us. That is literally death to self.

I have learned that the greatest good I can do is to deny self, take up my cross, and follow Jesus. For this older gentleman, this would demand a cost that few are willing to pay, but he was because he loved his wife. He later shared with me how difficult it was to count that cost daily, but he was able to do it because he loved his wife, and Jesus and the Father were on the throne of his life.

Once Jesus reigns in your life in that manner, this gift that only He can do in your life, needs to be nurtured and cherished, because it is a freedom that brings a peace the world can never give. It is worth its weight in gold.

That is why our new life in this millennial age is so beautiful. There is no idol of self to battle. We are resurrected believers, restored to uncorrupted beings as Adam and Eve were before they sinned. Somehow God has fixed it so we cannot sin ever again. Our love for Jesus is pure and holy and satisfies our soul. It is the tree of life.

Chapter 90

THE PRODIGAL
GOES BACK

Time is the allusive mystery that has plagued humanity in our striving to measure and control life. For the unredeemed, time continued as it had for millennials. They aged with each passing second. Their bodies grew older, and they got sick and died. Despite science and its amazing attempts to clone, to create cures, to slow down the aging process, the curse of sin and death still prevailed. Not so for the resurrected followers of Jesus. A thousand years was but as a day to them. Forty to fifty years was but an hour, for we lived outside the boundaries of time that the unbelievers of humanity could not escape.

In this dual system of time, those on the earth, outside the kingdom of God, grew restless with their separation from the treasures and riches and health of the redeemed. This bred jealousy and envy, anger, and hatred of Jesus and His kingdom. Hidden organizations of resistance arose. They began to attempt to devise weapons that could harm the resurrected bodies of His followers. They looked for a leader who could unite them in their rebellion. Those who did not turn to Jesus for salvation became consumed with evil. The hardness of their hearts drove them to self-destruction. The idol of Self reigned over them.

It was to these lost souls that Jason decided to go back into their world to share with them the love of Jesus Christ. He knew their destiny was death and eternal separation from God. He agonized over this senseless rejection of Jesus in their lives. Jesus knew of this growing rebellion but allowed it in His love for them. He chose certain ones of the redeemed to go and express His love for the unrepentant. Jason was one of the chosen evangelists. Thus, he embarked on his mission to those he lived with before his transformation.

Many had already died. The others had aged remarkably. As he entered their old hangout at The Parliament House, he saw the desperation and hopelessness on their faces. Being in the spirit, he could discern through the laughter and drunkenness he heard. They medicated their pain with the lust of their unregenerate souls. He did not pity them because he knew they longed to love and be loved. Once he had been seduced in the gay and lesbian lifestyle. When he was twelve, a new charismatic youth pastor had molested him and several of the other boys at a very vulnerable season of their lives.

This dark secret he could not tell anyone, not even his father. It was this perverted penetration of his soul and body that created a hunger and obsession to find love in men. As hard as he fought against the desire to be loved by other males, he could only hold out for so long. Within his being, this sinful seed took root, not of his own choosing. Then it became a lifestyle where he found love and acceptance. In the culture before Jesus's return, a great moral war arose within the body of Christ and within society to accept this as normal.

He never did get set free despite all his hours of prayer and crying out to God. Why was I attracted to men? What is this demonic creature within me? Of course he had to hide it from his Christian family. They would not love him but reject him. At times the pain was unbearable. Once more he would give in to his passions. The guilt increased. He often contemplated suicide. An opportunity came to talk privately with the head of a ministry that promised deliverance from homosexuality. Full of hope he sat and bore his soul to this man.

At the end of this liberating discussion to finally bring the darkness to light, this leader kissed him and took him to bed. That was the cliff of doom for Jason. There was no hope for him with God or Jesus or the church. He gave in and left his family to enter fully with those like him. The battle for freedom did not go away. His new open lifestyle had shadows that followed him. He hated himself as he indulged in the sexual perversion he wanted to believe was wrong, but it was the only thing where he could find relief from the constant fever to be loved. The sexual satisfaction was off the charts.

When I came to him after the resurrection of the believers and he gave his heart to Christ, he had instant deliverance. The idol of Self vanished. He was not just a new creation; he was like Jesus. The corruption of his soul was gone. Liberated from the inner division and darkness the light of Christ brought him the peace of God he had always longed to know. Those inner voices no longer tormented him.

Sin and temptation could not touch him. The lustful desires and unfulfilled love did not exist. He was loved and could give love in all the holiness that God intended. He had high hopes to share this with his old lovers and partners. No fear, no worries, no anxiety, only complete freedom to love was in him. He had no hidden agenda.

Jason was not the first resurrected, heavenly man to come into the Parliament House. His persona of light and love was not missed by those in the bar. Soon every eye was on him as he took his seat at an empty table. He was an intruder in this establishment where men and women came to hook up with likeminded lovers. Disdain, curiosity, and a shunning from others marked him as one not welcome, but Jason was not in the bondage of his past. He only had love, not judgment or condemnation. He knew the deep inner struggles of their lives. He came solely to share the choice of Jesus and life.

Soon two elderly men invited themselves to sit with Jason. They came to play with him and mock him but also were attracted by his persona of masculinity. After they introduced themselves a lively discussion followed.

"My lover here ran to be the president of the United States of America. Christians shouted vile accusations full of hate at him. Don't tell us about this Jesus of yours when His followers would never accept us into their fold."

"What they did was unacceptable and wrong, but we are all flawed individuals who do things we should not. Still, many who claim to be followers of Jesus are not. Remember the Israelites in Isaiah's time. They worshiped in the temple, sacrificed their sheep for the forgiveness of their sins, prayed and rejoiced before God. Isaiah wrote in his first chapter that God hated their religious acts. He told them not to pray because of their sinful lifestyles. He would not listen to their prayers. Yet, He called them in His love to repent. Though their sins were as scarlet, He would make them whiter than wool."

"Are you saying our love for each other is not authentic?'" he asked as they showed their wedding rings.

"Jesus said in the last days, do not be deceived. We are easily deceived and rationalize away our sins. He said it would be a time when the people would change the laws of God and replace them with their sinful laws. Repentance is genuine humility before God. It is having an accurate opinion of who we really are. Jesus tells the church in Laodicea they saw themselves as rich and holy, but they were wretched and poor, in need of seeking God's forgiveness."

Jason continued further. "I know your life. Before I gave my soul to Jesus, I lived the life you live. I can only say that what Jesus did in me demonstrates that He is true and righteous, full of love for us. His way is the only way to salvation."

"You mean our way is wrong. That is the same old garbage of hate they preached at us."

"Think about it. We all long to be loved. I know your impulses and desires for men. You believe your love is authentic and it is, but it is being expressed in the wrong way. That is why we all are sinners in need of Jesus. We do what seems right to us, but it leads to death. I am free and will never struggle again. The obsessive thoughts and yearnings are gone. I am loved and can give love in holiness and truth."

"You are trapped in a lie forever," he countered with anger and bitterness.

"That is your choice to believe, but I tell you, my transformation is real. You can have what I have for all eternity. There is nothing that can match it in this world. It is life and hope and love—all you have ever wanted and more. You will be changed in the twinkling of an eye."

They shook their heads in disgust, but a crowd had gathered around them and heard the words of life. In their loneliness and pain, they hungered for this truth to set them free, but they were afraid. The peer pressure on them was enormous. If they were wrong in their choice for Jesus, where would that leave them? Their flesh fought hard to resist. It cried out to be satisfied. The idol of Self would not die easily.

Chapter 41

SPIRITUAL WARFARE

The ornate court of the proconsul Sergius Paulus on the isle of Cyprus in the city of Paphos filled each day with citizens of Rome and Cypriote patriots seeking favors from their ruler. The spacious hall sported the busts of Caesar and Jupiter and Venus. The frescoes told stories of lust and power.

On this day in the year of our Lord AD 45, stood an evil man, a sorcerer and false prophet by the name of Bar-Jesus, son of Joshua. He entertained the proconsul with works of magic and miracles. Possessed by a powerful demon, he gave prophecies that came true. He had earned the ear of Sergius with such wisdom as a seer of the future. Into the room walked Paul, the apostle, on his first missionary journey into the Roman Empire. Accompanied by Barnabas, they came to proclaim that Jesus was the Messiah of both Jew and Gentile.

The church at Antioch, inspired by the Holy Spirit, fasted and prayed, then laid hands on Paul and Barnabas to send them out as the first missionaries to Cyprus and then into Asia Minor or modern day Turkey. While in Cyprus, Paul worked many miracles. His fame came to be known by the proconsul, and he had the two brought to him to hear what they had to say. Jealous of the attention Paul and Barnabas received, the sorcerer moved to retain his influence on Sergius. In a jealous snit, he tried to silence Paul with his false wisdom and foolishness.

Paul would have none of this demonic trickery. Filled with the Holy Spirit, Paul boldly confronted the impostor. "O, one full of all deceit and all fraud, you son of the devil, you enemy of all righteousness, will you not cease perverting the straight ways of the Lord?"

I had arrived a few minutes earlier from the millennial age. Time traveling brought me into such diverse and tense situations of history. I marveled at Paul's strength and courage. His words were stinging and exposed the wickedness of this false prophet. Paul's loyal faithfulness to Jesus convicted me with his intense and cutting words. How he was led by the Spirit to speak the truth against the forces of evil. He held nothing back, while I remembered in humility how in my day we were so meek and mild, afraid to speak with such power.

He knew how to take authority over the devil and his minions. He was not afraid of man but only feared God. He continued to belittle this demagogue. "And now, indeed, the hand of the Lord is upon you, and you shall be blind, and not seeing for a time." Immediately a dark mist fell on Bar-Jesus and he began to stumble around, seeking someone to lead him by the hand.

Helpless and feeble, he had fallen victim to the judgment of God for his sins. I had seen blind eyes opened in Zambia in my crusades, but never had I seen a manmade blind by the power of God. The fear of the Lord came upon every person in the court. The expression of God's glory stunned the crowd. The proconsul could not comprehend what Paul had done, but he realized that the God of Paul in Jesus Christ was real. I had seen the same response all around the world in our meetings when the miracles of God broke forth in wonder as the lame walked and the babies burning with fever were healed.

"Paul, I believe in your Jesus. For no mortal could do such a sign." In that hour, he gave his heart to Jesus and a new body of believers was born on that day.

I could not help but rejoice in the majesty and mystery of God. Paul saw me and smiled. He remembered me from our time when we went to heaven after he was stoned to death in Lystra. Then God raised him from the dead as He did me after I was murdered by the terrorist. We never had a chance to talk in that meeting, but now we would spend as much time as my travel allowed. I shared with Paul the return and rule of Jesus in Jerusalem.

"I thought for sure Jesus would come in my day," Paul emphasized to me. "I had no idea it would be another two thousand years. Yet, a thousand years is but a day to the Lord."

I told Paul of the wonders of our resurrected bodies, how we were like Jesus and could travel the world in an instant. Our bodies were immortal and incorruptible. Jesus reigned in Jerusalem as the King of kings. Soon all things would be new as Jesus promised. I thanked Paul for his lesson in how to fight the good fight of faith, to defeat the powers of darkness, and to be bold for Jesus. I confessed I lacked such faith at times. I would need to use what I had learned in the final days of Satan's release from the prison of the bottomless pit.

Before I went back, I knelt before Paul and asked him to lay his hands on me, so I would be filled with the Holy Spirit, to act in courage as Paul had to conquer my spiritual enemies. The sacredness of that moment meant the world to me. To have this mighty man of God pray for me impacted my soul. I once vowed that whenever I had the chance for great men and women of faith to pray for me, I would ask them and receive. I thought of my bishop friend in Cuba and the heavenly man from China, who were like Apostle Pauls to me, how they had laid hands on me and prayed the fire of God into my bones. Now, the one and only Paul of the Bible imparted God's fire into my soul. God never ceased to amaze me with His precious gifts that I did not deserve.

Cruelty was in the air as I arrived back in Orlando. The Gospel of Jesus had stirred up the demons of hate and vengeance. It was the classic battle between good and evil. Jason was right in the middle of it! He had returned to witness the love of Jesus, but Mr. B. and his friends would have none of the generosity of God. Their wounded souls so crippled by the cruelty of humanity caused them to bite the very hand of love that reached out to them. Jason had no fear, for he knew Jesus and his transformed body were impervious to their attacks. Complete security is a marvelous gift of God to those who believed. He had been totally healed by the power of the resurrection, but not these wounded souls.

Hurt begets hurt. It loves to bite the hand that could heal. Led by Mr. B., they could only use words to try to harm Jason. Words are mighty weapons. They can bless or curse, shape a life to love or cripple a mind to hate. But in the perfect love of Christ, free of the corruption of the soul and flesh, words are impotent darts quenched by the shield of faith.

I moved cautiously into the midst of the angry mob to support Jason. The smell of fear and evil oozed from their bodies as they surrounded us. "Time to shake the dust from our feet," I said, but Jason would not give in to their empty threats.

"I know the agony of your hearts. The rejection. The cry I just want to be loved. Accept me for who I am is all you desire." His passionate words began to pierce their darkness and soothe their wounds. "It is in coming to Jesus that you become human in the fullest intent of God. All of us want to be whole and live in peace with the freedom to love. That is Jesus's gift to all who will give Him their heart."

"Stop!" Mr. B shouted. "Enough of your manipulation. God created us as we are and now He turns His back on us. Jesus has redeemed you but forsaken us. We do not need a Savior like that. Leave us alone."

"Alone? Are you not tired of being alone in your pain? Jesus suffered and died for you. He knows what it means to be alone in our grief and sorrow."

The miraculous began again. Two then three people received their new, resurrected bodies. Their aura of light glowed against the darkness. People began to murmur in connection with this transformation. Then another and another, until Mr. B. and his followers had had enough. They stormed out of the room. The rest followed, except those who had become followers of Jesus.

Chapter 92

LESSON LEARNED

I t was around 4 a.m. when the email arrived from Grovar. One sentence: Pastor Blake, our brother, Godfrey, has died.

I had not been to Zambia for several years after traveling to this beautiful land for sixteen years in a row, sometimes twice a year. In those crusades, I had met many wonderful people and made lots of friends. One of the tribal groups we ministered with were the Lundas of northwest Zambia, and they spilled over into Angola and the Congo. Over a million hardy and rugged people lived among this tribe. They were loving and friendly, many new in their faith with Jesus.

Chief Kanyama had become a dear friend. Dexter and our evangelism team had traveled to his remote village for four consecutive years. It was far out on the frontier of civilization, deep in the hills and valleys of this ancient land.

The drive to their village was on a two-lane strip of asphalt that had not survived the rainy seasons of Zambia. Huge potholes had been created by the rain and from the weight of the copper trucks that barreled along from the mines. It was twelve hours of stop and go, and dodge the craters that could destroy your vehicle. One of the more amusing parts of these journeys was along the road; young children would stand waiting for cars to come. There would be several potholes blocking the way. They would have makeshift shovels and mounds of dirt. For a few pennies, they would fill in the holes so you could continue on your journey.

Once you paid them, they shoveled their dirt into the holes, pounded it down, and off you went. As soon as you were gone, they would dig up the dirt, and voila, the potholes were restored until another car would come and pay their toll. Everyone knew their game, so some would kindly pay the price, but others would storm out of their cars and chase the kids away. Once these disgruntled drivers left, the children would be back, manning their station. It gave them enough pennies to purchase the food they needed to survive. We were glad to help them most of the time!

It was in the village of Kanyama, I met Godfrey. He was a sharp young man with a beautiful family. He was educated and spoke five languages. As headmaster of the local school, he was highly respected. He had a deep faith in Jesus, nurtured by the missionary families that had come from England before the turn of the 20th century to northern Rhodesia.

These missionaries were the offspring of a London surgeon, who left the riches of England for the wild country of the Lunda tribe. His wife and two children died on the walk through Angola to the Lunda people. The call of God comforted his sorrow but challenged his faith. He found his only hope was in Jesus. After they crossed the mighty Zambezi River, they came to a ridge that overlooked the largest tributary of the Zambezi called the Lungwebungu River. It was at the heart of the Lunda people's land. For four generations, these descendants of this surgeon labored with the Lunda people but with only minor success.

Then the grandson of the doctor had an encounter with God. He was baptized in the Holy Spirit and suddenly what took decades to achieve, now took weeks. Converts by the thousands came to Jesus. Hundreds of churches were planted, all without the aid of the mission's denomination in England that condemned these Spirit-filled believers as heretics and cut them off from their home in England. Yet, the missionaries prospered in the Spirit while almost dying without proper funding, but God supplied their needs. It was out of this great revival Godfrey had come to know Jesus as a child. Raised up in the biblical faith of Jesus and the power of the Holy Spirit, he became a leader of men and women for Jesus.

On my journeys to Kanyama, Godfrey would come to be my translator when I preached at the Rain Festival. This is where the tribal leaders and people would gather to thank God for the harvest and to pray for the rains to bring in the next year of crops.

My heart wept when I read the email, so simple yet it captured the life of these precious people. They lived and died like all the families of the earth. Because of the lack of nutrition and very few medical supplies and doctors, their harsh life brought death often at a young age. I took comfort in the truth Godfrey had lived his life for Jesus and his people. He was with Jesus forever. He was better off than all of us, yet it was still a time to grieve his loss.

The chief's son had sent me the email. They were close friends. It touched me that he would think to write me the news of his death. I would only stay with them a week at a time, but when you labor in the Spirit with people who love Jesus and are totally committed to Him, length of time does not matter. You enjoy the oneness of love and come to treasure men like Godfrey. He would be a tremendous loss to the community, but God would raise up another, then another and another. We are all servants of the living God used for His glory.

Now, in eternity with our resurrected bodies, Marie and I went to Zambia. I loved this new mode of travel—no thirty hours of planes and layovers. In an instant, we left Jerusalem and were in Kanyama. The first one to welcome us was Godfrey. Even though he lived in Jerusalem like most of the resurrected, he came to his home village to evangelize his friends who had not surrendered to Jesus. We had a celebration of welcome with hugs and embraces with him and his wife, Betty. She at one time had been the chief, but she had a vision from God to bow to her brother to be chief. She was a godly woman who was a mighty prayer warrior.

Marie had not met them nor their family, so it was a joyous time with old and new friends, rejoicing in our oneness in Jesus Christ.

Most of the people had become followers of Jesus since the resurrection. The witch doctors had seen the power of God through the transformation of the believers, but a few still held to their old ways of devil worship. They had hypnotic control over their followers. The people were rooted in false worship and lived in the spirit realm. They had not been corrupted by secular humanism. They believed in curses; thus they lived in fear. If the witch doctor cursed you with sickness, you got ill. If he came against you with a curse of death, you died.

One time, Godfrey and I, along with my Zambian evangelist friends, were driving in our van near Kabompo, Zambia, a day's drive from Kanyama. We came over a ridge in the road and headed down toward Chikata Falls on the Kabompo River. Earlier that day we went to the Kabompo River at the ferry crossing. Large crocodiles were sunning on the banks. Not far away, people were swimming in the wide flowing waters near the crocs. I asked about the danger of the aggressive Nile crocodiles. Were the people not afraid? No, my friends said. I inquired if anyone got attacked. Oh yes, they replied nonchalantly, several are eaten every year. *Why go swimming*, I thought to myself. But it is their way of life. Just like we have tens of thousands killed and maimed by car accidents every year. Why drive a car?

As we approached the falls far from the town of Kabompo, I saw a witch doctor walking along the road and pointed him out to Godfrey and my friends. He was quite an intimidating picture. He was tall and muscular, dressed in his bright, colorful outfit as though he was prepared for war. He held a hatchet in his hand. His head had a bonnet of feathers like an American Indian headdress. He had a loincloth on with no shirt. He was a powerful demonic figure as he chanted curses at huts he was passing. Everyone seemed afraid of him.

I said, "Let's go and talk to him about Jesus," even though I was somewhat hesitant as he waved his tomahawk in the air at the people in their huts. There are no officers of the law in this remote area. The witch doctor could be the law. None of my companions wanted to go witness to him. They still had much of their African roots in them and believed in the power of the witch doctors to curse and do harm to them and their family.

I egged them on and said, "Let's pray and seek God's guidance." As we prayed, he turned toward us and proceeded to approach us, shouting and chanting in his Lunda language. My friends cautioned me about getting out of the van to talk to him. If I got out, my translator, Godfrey, would have to come with me. Being led by the Spirit, I hopped out of the vehicle as the witch doctor stood about ten feet from us. I was praying in the Spirit for protection and power. I remembered the apostle Paul and how he confronted the sorcerer in Antioch on my time travel.

I introduced myself and said I had come a long way from America to tell people of the great news of Jesus Christ, God's Son from heaven who came to set us free from sin and death and fear. In Him, all curses could be broken, and he could know the one true God. Suddenly, an intense anger came upon him as he glared at me with unholy fire. He raised his hatchet and spoke some words I did not understand. I turned to ask Godfrey to ask what he said, but he had run back into the van when the man had raised his tomahawk.

I stood my ground as though I was facing a bear. I had been told never run, or they will think you are game to eat. Since my interpreter was missing in action, I began to pray in the Spirit toward the witch doctor. He began to step toward me, to intimidate me, but I took authority over him and the demon that possessed him. "I command you, son of the devil, be still and come out of this man. I set you free in the name of Jesus Christ."

Immediately, he dropped his ax and fell to his knees. He cried out with an evil gurgle of pain. Then he fell as though he was dead. Villagers who had watched from afar came running up to us. My friends joined me from the van. They feared he had died. His body lay limp, but I could see he was breathing. "Be gone, spirit of Satan. Hear the word of the

Lord." His body started to shake uncontrollably for about a minute, which seemed forever. Then he stopped, and peace came over him.

"In the name of Jesus you are free from your bondage. Now give your life to Jesus and live to serve the one true God." I saw a demon-like creature rise from his body in the spirit. Then he sat up, calm and full of joy. The people began to shout and praise God. I asked Godfrey in his native language to lead him to the Lord and to tell him what it means to follow Jesus. After he was done, we gathered the people, and I preached about the love and salvation of Jesus Christ. That day, many came to Christ, many more were healed, and a new church was planted in this village outside of Kabompo.

The witch doctor gave me his ax as a gift, which I gave to my young son at the time, but kept it away from him until he was older lest he attack his sister with it!

Now, as we laughed about that incident, there before us was the former witch doctor in his resurrected body with his wife and family. They had come with Godfrey; since that day they had become good friends, and the devil man became a preacher and pastor of that church and a great evangelist for Jesus.

Chapter 93

REUNION

The rugged mountains of Guatemala rose steep into the sky with beauty and grandeur. Our mission team had been dropped off on the side of a road in the wilderness of the Nebac Indians. We started on a dirt trail that led high into the mountains lined with volcanoes. Jonathan, my son who was only eleven, and Bart, my partner in ministry, along with several others were going to three villages that had little knowledge of Jesus. One village had a small church built by one man, the only believer in the village. Every Sunday, he would hook up his sound system to a battery to broadcast the Gospel throughout the village with his sermons. No one ever came to worship.

A missionary doctor, Tom Dubois, had recruited us to go with him into these uncharted mountains, to plant churches in these villages. It would be an arduous journey climbing the mountains and breathing in the high altitude, resting in our sleeping bags while plagued by biting gnats that left us with swollen hands and faces. God was with us as we walked these ancient hills populated by the Nebac Indians, isolated from civilization. The last village we went to had never seen a white man. The hills were filled with pagan altars and witch doctors who ruled the people with fear and demons. It was an adventure of a lifetime, heading into this pristine wilderness full of marvels that inspired us with the presence of God.

The lush vegetation and age-old trees spiraling up the mountainsides reminded me of the world before the fall. We saw thundering rivers and cascading waterfalls that spoke of the glory of God. At times the silence of the deep forests drew us into the quiet heart of God. We could hear His voice in the majesty of the still, noiseless beauty of nature. Bart and I had decided to return in the millennial age to see what the seeds of the Gospel had brought forth to these humble people who received the Gospel of Jesus Christ and began to worship the one true God. Roger had also come with us. Our first stop was at our last village in the wilderness where we slept in a horse barn and took our baths in a horse trough. Only God and the frigid water kept us from getting worms or parasites.

We sat together on the same ridge surrounded by the steep mountains. The glory of God's creation still shouted out His praise. We bathed in its beauty and reflected on those last days in Jerusalem where Bart and Roger had saved my life on the Mount of Olives. Z had tried to assassinate me with a terrorist attack, but Roger and Bart tackled the assailant. In the melee, the bomb exploded, and they were killed. I thanked them over and over again for their brave exploits.

Then we talked about their families and life in the millennium. Bart's wife and kids were fine, and so were Roger's. His ex-wife was still unredeemed, but he continued to go and witness to her. We marveled at the grace of God in all of our lives. Roger thanked God for his resurrected body that did not have his Nazi tattoos. The peace that he knew in Jesus and the wholeness of his mind and body made him forever grateful to his King. Bart had changed little, except for his glorious body. He enjoyed his family and all the blessings that flowed from the throne of God.

We talked and laughed about our adventures across the world smuggling DVRs into China, going on safari in Zambia, and flying over Victoria Falls in an ultra-flight, which reminded me I needed to see Hans and all of my missionary friends from Zambia and the Congo, especially Dexter and Susan. At last we went to the three villages we had visited years ago. They were mostly deserted. Almost all of the people had become followers of Jesus and had been taken up to Jesus when He returned. Strange how many of the villages were empty, but the big cities were full of people—the contrast in lifestyles in humble communities to the rush-and-tumble of city life where secular humanism had won the day before Jesus came back to reign.

Bart and Roger and I went into these villages and shared the Gospel to those left behind. Most of the people knelt before the Lord and gave their hearts to Jesus. The auras of light chased away the darkness, and we had wonderful celebrations of life. We decided after this adventure for Jesus, Bart and I would go back to all the villages and towns and cities we had gone to share Jesus throughout the world to see whose hearts were ready to surrender to Jesus. Once more we joyfully praised God that our travel time was in an instant and not hours of flying and delays and sleeping in airports. Life was a breeze compared to the sinful world we had left. Wherever we went, people received the love of Jesus and came to the new life of the resurrection!

Chapter 44

GOOD GIFTS
FROM GOD

I loved hearing my son Jonathan preach and teach. One, because I was proud of him as I was of all my children and grandkids, but also because he loved Jesus and knew the Word of God. He was anointed by the Spirit to preach the Good News. One of my favorite sayings I picked up from him was, God loves to give us good gifts. It would be so wonderful to me when I heard that reminder every so often. My Father desires to bless me. This morning in prayer, I began to reflect and dialogue with my Father on His good gifts to me and how grateful I was.

Whenever I preached at churches or on the mission field and shared my testimony, I often said if I had not met Jesus, I would have been divorced three times, would have been an alcoholic, missed out on my beautiful family, and achieved nothing for God or humanity in my lifetime. However, Jesus delivered me from that life of misery and through Him my Father gave me good gifts that are beyond anything I could imagine or ask for. First and foremost is my love relationship with God and Jesus, and then my fantastic family including my love affair with Marie.

If those were not enough, God has always provided for us on a pastor's salary. He has healed us, protected us from evil attacks and danger, given us His righteousness and holiness, sent me to the ends of the earth on adventures to tell people about Jesus, surprised me with miracle after miracle in healing others, in finances, in friendships, and in carrying me through the dark valleys of life, including my failures and foolish mistakes and decisions.

In the midst of this wonder, unexpected surprises have come my way so that my son and son-in-law comment on why all these marvels happen for me from the simplest to the grandest gifts from God. I plucked this gem from my journals as to a time of one good gift that I had never dreamed would happen. It was not even on my radar.

Yesterday was a glorious day because out of the ashes arose the glory of God. The day before we had our team meeting on our April 21 event, Combating Anti-Semitism, we were discouraged and ready to call it off because we could not get the speakers to commit, and this had put us way behind schedule. We stopped and prayed, crying out to God. He would have to open a door, or we would not do the event. Then I felt led to exhort us that we were going forward to bless Israel until we were told to stop by the Holy Spirit.

Added to this struggle, I came down with a head cold and felt terrible. After the meeting, I went home to bed discouraged and down. After midnight, I got up to check my messages. One of our new leaders on our Jerusalem-Orlando team, Bonnie, had sent me an email. Bonnie has a worldwide ministry, supporting Israel, and is a true God-inspired activist for Jesus and Israel. She had volunteered to send our invitations to President Horn, his son-in-law Thomas, Sandra Black, the woman credited with leading President Horn to the Lord, and Ari Berstein, one of the president's Jewish advisers to speak at our event.

This list of speakers had come to us from a conference call I was blessed to be part of from the White House on the president's executive order combating anti-Semitism. Since our upcoming event was on the same theme, I wrote our liaison to the White House, Eve Trudy, if one of the four or all four on our conference call would come to our event in April months before, but had not heard anything.

In answer to our prayer at our meeting that morning, The White House called Bonnie that night and said they were interested in having the president or one of the staff I mentioned, come and speak! Wow! A call from the White House. Talk about changing the atmosphere from despair to exaltation. We called an emergency meeting, and everything fell into place. We went from no attendees to the president who would come, and this would bring in the governor of Florida and other prominent leaders who love Israel.

I asked Marie, how does this happen? Every time I want to quit these meetings to bless Israel, God does something miraculous. When I think I can relax and let go, God has me on another adventure! I am continuously learning to trust God and not try to make things happen. I am constantly amazed at what God does beyond anything I can imagine.

Thus, the President did attend our celebration to bless Israel and to unite together to combat the evil of anti-Semitism. This persecution of the Jewish people is rooted in Satan and his plan to stop the Messiah from coming to save us. The children of Abraham are God's chosen people, the apple of His eye, called to bless the nations of the earth. Thus, they became the main target of the devil and how they have suffered terribly through the ages and in almost every nation where they fled.

The event became a national story. We got to meet the president, his family, the governor, and many more leaders who love Israel. It was the gift of a lifetime, but more importantly through ministries like Ezra International, Bridges for Peace, Cru, Proclaiming Justice to the Nations, and many more ministries that sponsored and attended our event, we helped combat the anti-Semitism that was rapidly spreading on our college campuses and in our cities and even some churches.

We held our event on the National Remembrance Day of the Holocaust. We were able to raise $200,000 to help educate our children and remove the anti-Semitic teachings in some of our schools in Florida. God is so good. Who would have thought it, that this self-centered, untalented human being who cannot do anything but pitch and hit a baseball could be part of such a great adventure for Jesus and Israel?

Yet, there was more in that there was a greater gift from one of my closest friends. At the celebration, an attempt was made on the president's life. In the confusion of the attack by a radical terrorist group of jihadists, called the Allah Glory Brigade, James West laid down his life to save me and the president. James was a successful businessman, who was head of our security that worked with the secret service on our event against anti-Semitism.

Before the president was to enter the ballroom to speak, we held a VIP reception for our biggest supporters to meet and greet the president and take pictures. Horn was a gracious man who loved the limelight and to mingle with people who loved America. A mole in the White House discovered the plans for the president's arrival and reception. His hatred of the president moved him to leak the information to the terrorist group. They in turn devised a plan to kill the President. Working as servers for our breakfast, they hid within the service room suicide vests to blow up the president. It was a simple plan, yet plausible if one was willing to die to act it out.

As we were entertained by the president and his wife, these American-looking terrorists managed to put on these explosives and storm the room. The secret service closed ranks around the president as they heard the commotion outside the reception room. One of the terrorists was about to make it through when James tackled him, and the bombs went off, killing my friend with the terrorist. If he had gotten through the doors, everyone in the reception would have been wounded or killed. We were devastated by James's death. His gift of life made him a hero, but his love for us and the president made him a legacy for Jesus. "No greater love is this, than to lay down one's life for a friend."

All of this was in God's strategies to prepare the world for the return of Jesus. When you align yourself with God's plans, there is no limit to what God will do. Be encouraged, live for Jesus, and expect good gifts from your Father in heaven. Get on your face and thank God with a grateful heart for all He has done for you! If you think the life before Jesus's return was full of good gifts, just wait for the millennial age!

Chapter 45

THE WEALTH OF
THE NATIONS

As I was rejoicing in the good gifts God loves to give His children, I found myself whisked away in time to ancient Jerusalem. Before me stood the magnificent temple of Yahweh built by King Solomon, the son of David. This Phoenician design given by God to David, spared no expense. Six hundred talents of gold covered the walls and ceilings. The finest timber of cedar from Lebanon lined the floors and walls. The Holy of Holies separated the outer chamber from where God will dwell in His glory. The altar of sacrifice was in the outer court. In all its grandeur, this first temple built in Jerusalem was considered one of the great wonders of the ancient world.

God had blessed Solomon's father, King David, with military victories that united and expanded Israel's borders. Treasures poured into Israel from Persia, Babylon, Egypt, Ethiopia, Syria, Edom, and Moab. The wealth of the nations caused Israel to become the most prosperous nation on the earth at that time.

When God asked Solomon what he desired, he answered, wisdom and understanding. Because Solomon requested these humble gifts, God promised wealth beyond measure to Solomon and his kingdom. The Queen of Sheba lavished Solomon with gifts of spices, precious stones, ivory and gold.

Now I watched as the priests brought up the ark of the covenant, which contained the tablets of the Ten Commandments, which the Lord wrote with His own fingers. After the priests placed the ark in the Holy of Holies, the cloud of glory descended into the temple and filled the entire house of God. The cloud of His Presence was so thick that the priests could not minister. Solomon cried out, "The Lord said He would dwell in the dark cloud. I have surely built You an exalted house, and a place for You to dwell forever." No one could stand in the presence of God; everyone, including the king, fell to their knees and covered their faces before His glory. From this moment on, the gifts of God in the form of the wealth of the nations poured into Israel.

The wealth of gold that came to Solomon weighed at least twenty-five tons a year. Out of this gold, he made 200 large shields of hammered gold, plus three hundred smaller shields of hammered gold. His throne was made of ivory overlaid with gold with twelve lions guarding the throne. Nothing like this had ever been made in any nation for any king. All of this and more was because God had made a covenant with Abraham, then Moses, and then David to bless Israel and to bless the families and the nations of the earth through Israel, for we know God loves to give good gifts to His children.

As I lay on my face in worship of the Lord God, I imagined King Jesus sitting on His throne in heaven and all of creation worshiping Him. All of this majesty and splendor in Jerusalem was but a forerunner of the millennial glory that I knew in the return of Jesus.

Zechariah the prophet saw this day when he wrote that the wealth of the surrounding nations would be gathered together; gold, silver, and apparel in great abundance. The people of the nations would come to worship Jesus in Jerusalem as their King, as their Lord, and as their Savior. All of this was being fulfilled in the millennial age, but it had started years before Jesus returned in His glory.

I remembered being with my team at the ancient village of Capernaum on the Sea of Galilee. Here was the center of Jesus's ministry. Peter and several of the disciples were fishermen on the Sea of Galilee. His mother-in-law had a house on the shore of this sparkling lake in the north of Israel. Out of Capernaum and the surrounding villages Jesus performed many of His miracles and taught the multitudes of the truth of God. Near Capernaum was where He gave His apostles and the crowds the greatest teaching ever given to humanity in His Sermon on the Mount. That was where Sister Teresa had nursed Holtzman before he died and found his notes to expose PM Benjamin and brought them to us to warn us of the danger.

On my first trip to Israel, I took a few moments alone in this recon-structed village where tourists from around the world visit. I was out-side the entrance where the buses parked. As the people walked past me, I heard the different languages of the nations being spoken. They came from Japan, India, Mexico, Norway, Germany, Brazil, and more. I marveled at the realization that Zachariahs's prophecy was already happening. The nations of the earth were coming to Israel to worship Jesus. They were bringing their treasures and leaving their money in the land of Jesus.

Besides this, Israel was economically prospering with all of her new inventions and innovations in technology and agriculture. For such a tiny nation, they were out-producing almost all the nations of the earth and, in turn, fulfilling the covenant given to Abraham to bless the nations of the earth.

Marie came up to me and asked why I was smiling. I told her I was witnessing the prophecies of God unfold before my eyes in the multi-tudes coming to Israel because of their love for Jesus and the God of Abraham. How magnificent it was to be alive in the land of Israel, to walk where Jesus walked and to see the prophecies of the Bible blossom as beautiful flowers for us to see and smell the fragrant aroma of our God in all His glory. Jesus saw all of this when He got alone with His Father to pray through the night in the hills just above us. This had to inspire His courage to face the horrors of His death on the cross. The Word says He went to the cross because He knew the joy His death would bring to all who would believe in Him and come to the Father in salvation.

He knew all of this would happen as we are seeing it now. Then I shook my head, meaning I do not think many of them realize what is happening. They are not making the connection that their trip to Israel is as much fulfillment of Scripture as is the *aliyah* of the Jews coming from the nations of the earth to settle in their cherished homeland. Both rivers of faith were coming together as one in the Promised Land.

Marie nodded in wonder. Tears welled up in her eyes as she remembered her life not far from here, where she met Jesus. She had wetted His feet with her tears and dried them with her hair and kissed them in her love and adoration for her new found Savior. The depth of her love for Jesus had no floor or ceiling. She came to know Him as God who became Man to love her and set her free. He gave her a new life that led to our love and family. Truly God created us to be fruitful and multiply in His love and blessings.

It was after Marie met Jesus that He began to go to every village and city, sharing the glad tidings of the kingdom of God. She and several other women began to travel with Him. They had all been delivered and healed of evil spirits and infirmities. Their newfound joy was especially contagious to the women they met. These humble women ministered to Him in the most holy service as the nuns do today. They set themselves apart for Jesus to care for his need to eat and clean. This set Jesus free to focus on His call from His Father.

He would go about Israel to plant the seeds of salvation. He was the sower of the Word of God. For He was and is the Word. He taught in parables to reveal the mysteries of God's kingdom to the people. They loved Him for His authority and love that He gave to them.

As we finished the day at Capernaum, I shared with Marie how clearly I could see at this moment the mysteries of God that were revealed in Scripture tied to Jesus and the Jewish people. What had begun in Israel with Jesus went out to the Jews and the Gentiles to all the nations of the earth. Now as His return would soon happen, all the promises of God were coming full circle back to Israel, preparing the Promised Land for the Promised One of the Father. I lamented with Marie that I felt sad in my excitement because so few seemed to realize the dimensions and consequences of His return. They were asleep and unprepared for what would take place in a few short years when He came back.

We had to do all we could to awaken the church and the nations to the coming day of judgment. Marie nuzzled up to me and said, "Do not fear. God has raised up His end-time army to prepare the world. We just have to listen and obey His call for us. In that truth we have our peace and rest in Him. We are not the Messiah, only His humble laborers working in the fields of harvest." To that compassionate insight I said Amen and goodnight to my beautiful bride. She encapsulated Cinderella in all of her storied life, and I loved her all the more for her wisdom and charm.

Chapter 96

FAMILY

Our mansion in heaven was not a glamorous palace like some had taught from the Bible. It was a nice house with plenty of room for all of our family. I had done a study on the concept of mansion in heaven from John 14:1 and 2. "Let not your heart be troubled; you believe in God, believe also in Me. In My Father's house are many mansions; if it were not so, I would have told you. I go to prepare a place for you." I came away with the concept of a room, not a mansion. In other words, Jesus was saying there is room for you in My Father's house. We have a place in the family of God to be loved and to live in the light of His glory.

We have a destiny of hope in Jesus Christ. We are safe and secure in Him, in our relationship with God and one another. That is what we discovered in this millennial age. It was wonderful to have that blessing of a room in God's house. Plus, there was no worry, but only joy in the Father's gifts.

We gathered around the piano as a family, all the kids and grandkids, with Marie playing an old song she composed when our firstborn, Jonathan was around two. We were laughing and full of joy as we sang: "I stinky in the morning, I stinky at noon, I stinky in the evening, and I stinky real soon. They call me the stinky boy, the stinky, stinky boy." This was in reference to his taking his diaper off and spreading his smelly waste around the house. Nice treat from our strong-willed son.

Jonathan was a good sport as he sang with us. Of course we were in the millennial reign of Jesus, so all was done in love and good fun. Then Marie shared her story of the Snuggle Bunny that she invented as a bedtime tale for the kids. Mr. Snuggle Bunny was a make-believe rabbit that got into all kinds of trouble but managed to wiggle his way out of every drama. He would then nuzzle up to his family, and all would be well in the end. We thought of creating a children's series on Mr. Snuggle Bunny but it never developed with a growing family and a busy ministry.

The other satire that always came up was I could never sing on key. I had this booming voice, but I didn't even know what a key was. At church, we made sure my mic was turned off when the worship in song started. I would joke that when I was in heaven I would sing with the best of them. I would fit right in with Scripture because in Revelation the angels spoke with a loud voice. We laughed because we believed the reason God sent me into the wilds of Africa is because there were no mics or amps, and everyone could hear my voice at great distances. I roared like a lion!

God made me for adventure. I was watching a television series called *Poldark*. The main character was Ross Poldark. He and his wife led this adventurous life in Cornwall, England, after he fought in the Revolutionary War on the side of the British. One night after we had seen another show in the series, I said I feel like Poldark. He goes from one adventure to another. In this particular show, he said to Demelza, his wife, after they finished an adventure, I am done. No more adventures for me. I am going to lead a quiet life as a country gentleman. Of course, in the next scene he is on his way to France to rescue his friend who was captured in the war with France.

I remembered I had a similar experience with God and a new adventure. I could not help but share that event with the family as we snuggled together in the love and the joy of our intertwined lives. The night had been full of the wonders that happen in the darkness of the African jungle. The guards at the Mogumbo Lodge had awakened us at 2 a.m. to tell us the hippos had come out of the Zambezi River to graze on the rich grass near our tent. The four of us had come to Livingstone to meet Dexter before we started our crusades. In the morning, we would go search for the majestic animals of Africa on a day safari. James, Chris, and Felipe, and I had arrived this morning from our twenty-four hours of travel.

Tired and weary, we had gone to bed early with orders to the guards to come wake us if the hippos came to feed. Sure enough, there they were as large as mid-sized sedans. Six of them eating the luscious savannah grass along the Zambezi River. Another mission team of young girls joined us to watch the hippos under the full moon. Their hair were in curlers as they were dressed in sweatshirts and pajama bottoms. They were from Alabama and spoke with a true southern drawl.

I held a flashlight in my hand, flicking it on and off at the hippos to get their attention. They were only about thirty feet from us, but the guards had guns, so we felt safe. Suddenly, the hippo I was flashing my light at, snorted like a bull and scraped his huge paw along the ground as though it would charge. One of the girls asked the guard, "Are hippos dangerous?"

"They will kill you," he replied, deadly serious.

Then the hippo had enough of my teasing. It looked up and charged at me. Everyone turned and ran for cover. Curlers went flying. Screams pierced the night. Everyone was running as fast as they could. Our hearts were pumping adrenaline through our veins. We dashed to our tents, but realized they were no deterrent to the great behemoths racing after us. The entire group of them were on our heels when we came to the swimming pool and all of us jumped in except me.

Why would we be safe in the pool? I reasoned. Hippos love water. I ran to the other side of the pool and then into the restaurant lodge. James, Chris, and Felipe were underwater, hoping for the guards to save them. The girls were soaked and shaking. The guards were nowhere to be seen as the hippos stopped at the pool with no desire to get wet. They simply turned around and walked away into the dark. It seemed they enjoyed having the last laugh on us.

Dexter, who had stayed in his tent because he had taken many teams to this place and seen the hippos a dozen times, heard the commotion and came to see what was up. He found me laughing near the pool as everyone dragged themselves out of the water soaking wet. No one was laughing but me and the hippos.

"I figured we were safe with the guards and their guns. I never thought they would run for their lives and desert us."

"Can I tell you something," Dexter said with a little smirk on his face. "Those guards may have guns, but they are too poor to afford bullets."

My face turned ashen as I realized we could have all been killed. Hippos are the most dangerous killers of the African beasts. They kill more people than any of the animals that roam the plains and swim the rivers of Africa.

"Tell us about the time you and Dexter got squeezed in your van between two bull elephants," one of the grandkids shouted.

"We will save that for another time," I replied.

Now we were all on an endless adventure with Jesus in the 1,000-year reign. Jason was in the middle of it as His evangelist. Marie and I never knew what God had in store for us, but we were enjoying our time with the love of family. It is wonderful because there are no relationship problems or challenges in our resurrected bodies! What a contrast to the past age. Even though Marie and I had a storybook marriage, we had our battles. Both of us were strong willed and driven to success. My sinful zealousness to win did not help our relationship. Often I had to remember the relationship is more important than being right. It was a long, hard lesson for me to learn.

From the start of one of our planning meetings, Marie had jumped in to show the cost we would pay if we did not get a top-notch speaker. The Broadmoor Hotel would charge us more than we could afford. Without a dynamic orator, we would never attract enough people to pay all of the expenses. We had set a cut-off date, and we arrived at that day with no speaker. I was leading the meeting, and I wanted this event to succeed, even though I had wanted to stop it many times out of frustration. I was going on four crusades in the next two months. It would be easier for me to call the event off. Yet, I believed God had called us to put it on.

As Marie spoke, focusing on all the negatives, I could feel myself getting angrier and angrier at her. In my mind, she was ruining the meeting. Besides, what was everyone thinking of us as she was opposing my position? Not a good situation! In her mind, she was protecting me from being foolish in proceeding with the event. She was merely pointing out the inevitable failure if we went ahead.

I held my tongue to let her speak. I did not want a blow-out in front of all of our friends and partners in the ministry. The meeting was slipping away, and I could not rally the troops to recruit the people we needed to make it a success, even if we agreed to still host it. That was when we went into prayer to petition God's intervention. When we got home, I was exhausted from my cold and exerting all my energy to save the meeting from defeat. Marie acted as if nothing was wrong. I told myself to remain quiet, but she asked me something about the meeting, which moved me to tell what I was honestly feeling.

"I could barely control my anger," I said. "I was so upset with you."

She gasped with surprise. "I couldn't tell you were mad. I was only trying to ask questions to help us see our situation." Now she was getting upset at me because she felt she had disappointed me, which was the last thing she wanted to do.

"It's not your fault," I replied. "The problem is within me. I should not react that way. You have a right to your opinion."

"Especially since several agreed with me," she answered. Her voice reflected a rising tension.

"It will be impossible to rally the troops now," I added with a sharp bite of disappointment.

"So that is my fault?" She was puzzled by my sarcastic remark.

"No, you needed to say what you did. That's why I did not cut you off."

"I feel like we are back at that one church, where people tried to control us and keep us from expressing the truth."

"I'm telling you, the struggle is not you, but me." But the damage had been done.

"Fine, I won't go to the meetings anymore. I'll do the lunches, and that is it."

"So, now you are deserting me just when I need you the most!" My loud voice is getting louder with my anger. I am burning mad. All this venom had built up in me like an overheated boiler ready to explode. We had not had a fight like this in a long time.

Early in our marriage, before we learned to better communicate, once a month that venom would move us to bite and devour each other. I found myself back in that prison of relational bad habits that we had overcome.

"I'm done with the team. I don't want to get in your way. I was only trying to ask questions, not undermine your authority."

"You did a poor job of that. Just leave before I say things I shouldn't say." She stood there determined not to leave now. "Go, I feel sick and I need to rest," but she kept badgering me. I knew I should stop, but my emotions were out of control.

"Just like you not to support me when I need you the most." I shot more venom into her veins.

"Oh like all the times you chose the church people over me and did not defend me, but bowed to their crazy demands. You love to please people." She bit back like a cobra.

"Will you please go?" My venom was about to strike for a death blow. I thought of the time I laid my whole ministry on the line to defend her and split the church. How could she say I did not defend her?

Too late. "Oh yea, like this weekend when I stood with you helping you through your depression. I put up with all of your misery." I attacked like a cottonmouth.

That bite drew blood. She stormed out the door with an almost fatal stab in her heart. The anger, the sickness, and heaviness crushed me. I hated myself for losing it with her. Marie was the love of my life, but now I had hurt her and she had also wounded me deeply. The hell with it all. Forget the event and forget her.

That night she slept upstairs as we did not talk. I went to God in prayer, asking forgiveness for my Neanderthal behavior. I could be such a beast. It was in the middle of the night I asked the Father and the Son to get back on the throne of my mind, soul, heart, body, and spirit. I did not want to miss any area where I failed and told the idol of self to get off the throne.

Then I went to my emails and saw that the White House had called Bonnie. I did not sleep the rest of the night, thinking of all we had to do since God had come through in His miracle working power. Early in the morning I got out of bed and prayed for Marie to forgive me. Before I did anything that day, I had to make things right with Marie. That was usually terribly hard for me to do because I hated to lose, but now the peace of God had returned to me. I went upstairs and tried to humble myself. "Can we not both admit we failed? I am sorry for all I said and did."

"I could not handle that you were so angry because you thought I was opposing you."

"I know. That was why I struck such a nerve. It was so bad of me. Forgive me?"

"Yes, forgive me." In the presence of the Spirit all was at peace. It was rarely that easy, but God worked His wonders in both of us. Then I told her of the exciting news, and out of the ashes we arose with a mighty sense of His love and glory.

Thank God, those times of venom were gone forever. Only peace and love and oneness reigned in us and with each other. No hidden motives or agenda. We were fully and completely new creatures in Christ. As we gathered the family for prayer, there were five extra littles one with us. "Who are they?" I was asked.

"They are the ones we never got to hold in the past life. This one is Marie's and my first that she lost in her early pregnancy. Her name is Julia. These two are Liz's from her two miscarriages. This one is so special; her name is Jennifer from an abortion in my early twenties. Our fifth is from Marie in her time before Jesus. God has healed our hearts and reunited us with these treasures that we thought we lost long ago. More love because of the grace and mercy of our God."

I took Marie's hand and looked into her eyes. Our union is more beautiful than ever. I said to her, "You truly are Jesus's Cinderella. Out of the darkness and pain of injustice, He delivered you and gave you the most treasured of lives. I thank God for you every day."

"And you, my knight in shining armor," she said as she looked at our family of covenant blessings. We praised God for His covenant with Noah and His promise to bless the families of the earth.

Chapter 97

THE WILDERNESS

Millennial Reign

O ne of the great joys of having a resurrected body like Jesus's was there was no need to exercise. There was no weight gain or loss. My new body was a perfect functioning machine of glory. Yet, I still loved to work out. Our bodies were created to work for the pleasure of God. Thus, I regularly spent time alone exercising this glorious creation. This morning I got on my rowing machine and put on worship music to sense the wonder of God's presence. I came to love this time of worship and exercise as I pushed my body hard and listened to the songs of praise often to the rhythm of the music.

As I heard a beautiful voice sing one of my favorites, "What a Beautiful Name," I found myself overwhelmed in His presence. Then a worship leader began to witness to the overflowing move of the Holy Spirit in his life. This was before the return of Jesus. I found myself in tears of glory exalting the name of Jesus.

Then, over my shoulder, I sensed something. I gazed back behind me, as I rowed faster and faster, and I saw a golden lampstand. Its flame was brighter than the sun. As I then looked forward at the rowing machine, the plastic wheel of water that rotated as I pulled on the tee-shaped handle began to spin dramatically with a supernatural energy.

Fiery water started to shoot from the wheel and cover me with the Spirit of God. The power of His glory lifted me up. Suddenly I discovered myself time traveling into the distant past.

THE YEAR AD 30

The stark desert of the Judean wilderness lay before Him. Jesus had come to seek His Father in prayer and fasting among the wadis, cliffs, and plateaus in this land of desolation. Led by the Holy Spirit into this wasteland, it was here that He would not only meet God but would be tempted by the devil.

Forty days and nights had passed, Jesus ate nothing. He was famished with hunger, but being filled with the Holy Spirit, He had a strength beyond His physical needs. In these weeks and hours of loneliness, He had been sustained by the presence of His eternal Father. Jesus knew His time had come to begin His three years of ministry to do His Father's will. He would discover much pleasure in obeying His Father, but He would also endure the savageness of men and suffer torture and rejection by those to whom He had given life.

I came tumbling into my time travel at the end of Jesus's forty days. The sheer heat and oppressive desolation of the hills and desert caused me to marvel that Jesus or anyone could survive for forty days without food. There He stood a short distance away as I watched Him pray. I was hidden by a corpse of jagged rocks. He appeared weak and drawn in body but alive in the Spirit. It was then that the devil came upon Him and said, "If You are the Son of God, command this stone to become bread."

Jesus looked directly into Satan's eyes and spoke with authority. "It is written, Man shall not live by bread alone, but by every word of God." The force of Scripture Jesus quoted pushed Satan back in the spirit. He realized this was no mere mortal he had come to seduce with his wiles.

Stirred to combat, the devil took Jesus up on a high mountain and showed Him all the kingdoms of the world in a moment of time. I found myself atop the precipice with them. "All this authority I will give You and their glory; for this has been delivered to me since the fall of Adam. I will give it all to You; if You will worship before me, all will be yours."

Satan's audacity and pride betrayed him. To think that the Son of God would prostrate Himself at the feet of Satan and worship him was pure vanity and disillusionment. Jesus rebuked Satan sharply. "Get behind Me, Satan! For it is written, You shall worship the Lord your God and Him only shall you serve."

I reflected that Jesus used those same words, "Get behind Me, Satan," to Peter when Peter tried to persuade Jesus not to go to Jerusalem and die for us.

In a flash, we were at Jerusalem on the pinnacle of the temple. "If You are the Son of God, throw Yourself down from here."

Satan then quoted from the Psalms to Jesus. "For it is written: He shall give His angels charge over you, to keep you, and In their hands they shall bear you up, lest you dash your foot against a stone."

Jesus answered Satan's twisted use of Scripture with the Word: "You shall not tempt the Lord your God."

Knowing his battle was lost, Satan slipped away into the night, only to return at a more opportune moment.

Here I was on the high point of the temple with Jesus. He was exhausted, but He had done what Adam had not. He did not sin, nor would He ever sin. In His perfection, He would be the Lamb of God without blemish who would take away the sin of the world.

Jesus looked past the walls of Jerusalem to Calvary where He would be nailed to the cross and die for my sins. I wondered what His thoughts were at this time, but all I saw was a smile that broadened His face, full of joy and celebration. His eyes lit up with the satisfaction that He had done His Father's will.

Millennial Reign

I hurled back through time and space to a dark and foreboding chamber. Two figures were before me. The first I knew was Satan. The other man I came to know as Mr. B.

"Sign on the dotted line, and all I promised you will be yours forever," Satan tempted him as he slid his finger across the signature line of a contract.

"I will not age from this moment forward. I will grow in power as the leader of your covens. I will reign with you over the human race forever. I will gain riches and glory, and every worshiper will bow before me. I will not get sick or die." Mr. B. summarized the promises of Satan.

"Yes and much more. You will become what no person in history has ever done. You will rule over every nation of the world. Even the angels will look upon you with wonder." Satan gleamed with delight as Mr. B. took the golden pen into his fingers and signed the document. At that moment, he lost his soul to the prince of darkness. Fear caused me to shiver that this person would pledge his loyalty to Satan. I abhorred this traitor to God and humanity. I knew in my heart he would suffer in the lake of fire forever with Satan. The date he wrote was before the return of Jesus.

Marie stood in the den as I appeared before her. My aura of light seemed a bit darkened. "Where have you been?" she inquired. "It must have been some trip," she added as I paused without answering. "You look somewhat shaken."

I nodded my head yes. I walked over to her and gave her a deep, deep hug. I needed to be reassured we were in our resurrected bodies, and all was well with our souls. The thought of such evil I had witnessed shook even my unshakable body.

"I was with Jesus in the wilderness while Satan tempted Him. It was glorious and inspiring to watch the Son of God defeat Satan on his home turf. But, then I went to another wilderness, the desert of one's soul. I saw a man sign his destiny away to Satan for what could never happen. Yet, he was so deceived he believed Satan would conquer Jesus."

The futility of the human soul without the truth of God is the saddest of all destinies. Yet, the struggle within the soul of one who knows God can rise to the point of desperation. It is when God takes one into the wilderness, as the Spirit led Jesus, that God desires to teach us His ways and who we are.

In seminary, one of my teachers called it the "dark night of the soul." Hosea the prophet said that God led the Hebrews into the wilderness to teach them how to sing. I remembered thinking to myself that in all the years I knew Jesus, I had never known a dark night of my soul nor had I learned to sing.

Then one day the Lord spoke to me so clearly in my prayer time. I had gone through a difficult season. My thoughts had been plagued with obsessive desires and compulsions I could not control, which led me into sinful actions. I would then cry out to God for forgiveness for I truly hated the sin I had done, but I could find no relief. Day after day the muddled thoughts came upon me, and I looked for ways to escape, but none came. I cried out to God I could not serve him with such chains upon my mind and body. Deeper and deeper I sank into bondage.

I went back to the night I met Jesus. In the love and wonder of that encounter, I told Jesus I could not serve him with the sinful afflictions in me. He reached into my mind with what seemed like a laser of light and delivered me from my bondage. Now it had returned to enslave me. I could not tell Marie for the shame of it. Yet, this demon would not relent its attacks upon me. I was in the wilderness, and I did not know it. God was trying to get my attention to teach me to sing, but I could not hear His voice in my pain and confusion.

At last I went into a week of prayer and fasting. I found peace for my soul. Then one day I realized the inner torment was gone. I was free. In that divine moment the Spirit spoke to me. I had been in the wilderness of sin because I had wandered from His kingship. I could not hear His voice, for I had quenched the Spirit. I still loved Jesus, but His reign in my soul had vanished. My flesh, that carnal nature of the old self, had taken the throne. The idol of Self took charge of my life.

In the midst of my prayer and fasting, God answered my cry for freedom. I was liberated in a moment of surrender and a work of God's grace. Jesus and the Father were back on the throne of my soul at the very core of my being. The voices of temptation ceased. My mind was at peace. When the shadows came, I prayed that simple prayer, "Father God and Jesus sit on the throne of my life. Idol of self, get off the throne of my life." As long as I nurtured my being with prayer and the Word, with love and obedience, I walked in such victory and peace, I realized I had learned to sing in the wilderness.

Chapter 98

CONFLICT, 445 BC

T he journey had been filled with anticipation. For Nehemiah, a sacred Jew, going to Jerusalem, the holy city, pulled him to its bosom like a baby to his mother. This was the eternal city of God that anchored the Jews to the covenant and to the promises of prosperity and wholeness. In a word, *shalom*. Even though the trip was filled with danger from Shushan to Jerusalem, Nehemiah knew God's peace. The Spirit of God had filled him with certainty of purpose. He was to go to Jerusalem to rebuild the city and establish it as the capital of Israel once again.

His miraculous encounter with the king affirmed to him that God was intimately involved in this enterprise. King Artaxerxes gave him the authority to complete the task of restoring the walls and the temple and the city itself. In addition, He provided the riches and ability to do all that was needed. The legends, the holy teachings, the mystical call of this treasured city secured by King David, underscored the gigantic task before Nehemiah. This was like Troy to the Greeks. The romance of its existence, the importance of its influence, and its power over the future of the Jewish people could not be overstated.

Jerusalem stood for all the Jews believed and hoped for in God. It was His city and symbolized His love for the Jews and His promise to restore them to their destiny. They had squandered their heritage through disobedience and idolatry. Nehemiah would see that this would never happen again to God's people. The Jews were His chosen ones of all the nations and people groups of the earth. They were to be His light to the nations to illuminate the nature and character of the one and only God, the Creator of all things. The darkness of the Gentiles blinded them to God. It was their mission to reveal God to them and bring them the gift of salvation.

The call of Nehemiah weighed heavy on him. To many, he was the Messiah figure who would deliver the Jews from death to a new life centered in Jerusalem. Every Jew in captivity longed to return to Jerusalem. He was to pave the way like Moses and Joshua had for the Hebrews from Egypt to the Promised Land. When he arrived at Zion, he had not anticipated the opposition that arose against him from the Gentiles who had invaded his land and made it their home. They were threatened by Nehemiah and his mission. They devised every trick to stop him from doing what God had told him to do: rebuild the city for it to be a home to God's people once again.

At first, they tried to seduce Nehemiah, but they soon realized that would not work, so they strategized a plan that would bring certain failure. They went to the authorities and lied against Nehemiah to undermine his reputation and purpose, telling them he had come to rebuild the ancient empire of the Jews and threaten the Persian Empire. They wrote a letter to the new king saying Nehemiah was trying to build his own empire and worked against the Persians. At first it stopped him, but nothing could stop God and His plan of salvation that through the descendants of Abraham would come the Seed of salvation to the Jew first and then the Gentiles.

Here I was, back in time, standing at the broken wall and burned gates of Jerusalem with Nehemiah. Men and women were laboring tirelessly to rebuild the wall under the danger of attack and death. As one put a stone back in the wall, another stood guard with spear and sword in hand. Night and day, these people of God broke their backs to build the new Jerusalem in defiance of those ignorant of God and His ways. I could not help but think this is the same in my day in the future millennium. The resurrected Jesus looked to the coming down from heaven of the New Jerusalem, while the unredeemed of the nations worked to prevent the final stage of God's plan to complete the restoration of humanity to being fully human as Adam and Eve had been before sin entered their heart and the world.

I hoped they would only see God in His love and purpose, and then they could work together to build His kingdom. Instead, in their fear, feeling threatened in their loss of power, they came against God and Nehemiah. No persuasion would change their mind-set. They were blinded by their worldview of God and His plan of redemption.

The final details were in place. The reconstruction of the wall and the gates of Jerusalem was completed in record time. It was miraculous and unimaginable that they finished so quickly the impossible task that had stood before them. They had withstood the opposition. They had fought off their foes, and now they would dedicate the wall and the city to the glory of God. Standing next to Nehemiah at the Guard Gate, which was the last gate to be hung into place, I realized what a giant of a figure he was in God's plans. Without his faithful determination, Jesus might never have been born to die for us and lead us into the New Jerusalem.

Nehemiah was proud of what they had accomplished for God. They would celebrate what they achieved. In my day, it would be like the winners of the Super Bowl being handed the Lombardi Trophy. The triumphant team had lived with a single purpose. They spent all of their energy and time to win the game. They left every ounce of exertion on the field. When the gun sounded, they were exhausted but exhilarated for what they had done.

Nehemiah was the leader, the hall of fame coach, who willed his team to victory. Yet, this was no temporary victory. It had eternal implications. The glory of men fades and has no value in God's kingdom. Jesus is the Alpha and Omega of creation and life. He is the eternal one, restoring to us eternity of life that has true value and meaning established by God.

The sound of the trumpets called the people to hear Nehemiah declare the glory of God recaptured for Jerusalem. The mission to rebuild had been finished. The city was once more the center of life for the Jew. Never again would they lose their call of God to be His light in the darkness of the world. They would love and obey God and His law, preparing the way for the Messiah to come.

Little did Nehemiah know that this was just one piece in the tapestry of God. He could not imagine that the Jews would lose their way again and reject their Messiah. Still, God loved them and would use them to bless the families and nations of the earth with His salvation in Jesus Christ, born a Jew. They and the Romans would put Him to death as the suffering Servant of Isaiah, but He would rise on the third day. The fountain of His New Covenant of redeeming blood would flow from Jerusalem to encompass the world with His love and hope to restore humanity to the life God had intended from the beginning.

New Millennial Reign of Jesus
As I rejoiced in Old Jerusalem with Nehemiah, Jason was preparing the way for Jesus and the New Jerusalem as he shared the Good News of Christ to the unredeemed on earth. How he longed to communicate the truth and promises of God so these lost souls could come into the oneness he now knew. He prayed for the words and wisdom to express how the aloneness of that inner struggle was no more, once he gave his heart and life to Jesus. This aloneness was more than loneliness. It was the root of the loneliness that plagued the heart and soul of humanity. The inner division tore apart the peace of God and left it tattered in pieces in the soul.

Constantly pulled in different directions, the peace of God could not exist in the corruption of rebellion in the human heart. Jesus had described this struggle in the Sermon on the Mount when He said we try to serve two masters. In the end, we can only serve one—either God or the idol of self. We were helpless to put ourselves back together again in the oneness of creation. Only God could do this work of grace in us through Jesus Christ, and even then, it would not be complete until one received his or her resurrected body as Jason had.

Now he knew the oneness of God's love that created the peace of God that could never be lost. This sense of aloneness was gone. No inner voice of self-interest that went against the desire to love and obey God could be heard. No anxiety or fear that had plagued his soul and mind existed within him. This gift of peace and harmony was for all who would repent and believe in Jesus as their Lord and Savior. Jesus alone could be Master of one's life and destiny.

Nothing could compare to the beauty of this new life. Sin had vanished. It was not even a concept that could enter the new resurrected life. We have freedom and liberty to love as we were created to love without shame or guilt, perfection in all of its ideals. Paradise lost was now paradise regained in the transformation of being like Jesus in every sense, except we were not God but created in His image.

The temptation that grabbed hold of Adam to be like God in the garden did not exist in concept or desire. All corruption of the human soul had been eradicated. Only the purity of heart, oneness of purpose, and service joined with God in eternal relationship completed us as human beings.

Chapter 99

ONE LOVE

I have had but one love, my Marie. Her sweet innocence captured my heart the day we met. Now in our new, resurrected bodies, our relationship had changed. No more man and wife, we were still family. I treasured that, reflecting on our love that had aged like a fine wine.

YEAR 1985
I remember the first time I told her I loved her. We went to a dinner theater to see *Cabaret*. When I tried to pay for the tickets with her standing beside me, I had to search for some more money in my wallet. I had miscalculated the cost. Fortunately, I found a twenty-dollar bill hidden in the fold of the wallet. What a disaster it would have been if I had come up short. Years later, we would talk of that night with laughter and how we probably would have never had another date if I had not found that extra money to purchase the tickets.

The night was one of those rich moments when two people connect with each other and forge an unbreakable bond. We ate and held hands while we watched a wonderful performance of the saga of two people struggling to love in the horror of Nazi Germany. After the show we went for a walk down Park Avenue in Winter Park, near where I had gone to college. We found ourselves on the beautiful Rollins Campus after we had been chased out of Genesis Drive on the other side of Lake Virginia.

Several magnificent estates hug the lake side. They were known for the mansions and the peacocks that strutted the back dirt roads along the lake. At night, the gates would be locked, so we had to sneak around the fence to walk the dusty paths to see the gorgeous birds full of plume and feathers. Suddenly we heard the night watchman coming, and we had to jump the fence to escape his eye. Our hearts were pounding, while I feared I had made another blunder that was supposed to be our romantic night together.

Along the shore we came upon an old dock. It was in disarray, missing several boards, but we managed to walk out to the end of the pier. We sat on the edge with our feet dangling over the end without fear of gators coming by for a quick meal. The moon was full without a cloud in the sky. Its light reflected on the calm and peaceful water. The gentle breeze drifted across our cheeks. Our hearts were anything but peaceful, pounding with excitement.

We shared our dreams for ministry and serving the Lord. In the back of my mind, I kept thinking about the Song of Solomon and the beautiful maid who loved her husband. How they gave themselves to each other in the love ordained by God. The wonder of that gift drew me close to her. At last I looked into her beautiful brown eyes. Her long hair, curled to perfection, felt soft and silky as I pulled her close to kiss her. Our passion lit up the sky like fireworks as we embraced. With our faces nose to nose and cheek to cheek, I told Marie I loved her. She replied with words of love. That night we decided to marry. God blessed us with a union of wonder as we wed and began to live our lives as one.

"What are you thinking?" I heard Marie ask.

I smiled at her. "Nothing," I kidded her. "Just remembering the night on the dock when I first told you I loved you."

She still had that sparkle in her eyes. Like diamonds of infinite worth, her love and joy spoke through those big, oval beauties that let me gaze into her soul. How easily she could entice me!

New Millennial Reign of Jesus
It was strange now. No more romance and marriage in the millennium. God had other plans. But it was not a sad emptiness. We had a new type of love that was deeper and richer than anyone without a resurrected body could comprehend. Now we had a spiritual union abiding in us that took the place of our once-physical passion. In the perfection of our immortal and incorruptible bodies, we did not lack, nor were we ever frustrated. Oneness in that perfect peace enabled us to commune in a way that fulfilled our heart's desire.

We still hugged, but there was no physical attraction, just warmth and contentment. I still treasured that night as a golden memory forever etched in our oneness.

"You did not go with Jason?" she questioned, knowing I had not as I was sitting with her.

"No, it is his call to obey as Jesus directed him. I cannot wait to hear his story. It is a wonderful thing to not have to worry or feel pressure to succeed. Perfect peace is one of the best gifts Jesus has given us."

"It is," she replied as she sat close to me. "Do you think we can go back to that dock on Lake Virginia?" Wow, I had her daydreaming of that night.

"I don't see why not. All we have to do is think about it, and we will be there."

"I have a better idea. Let's go somewhere we have never been."

"I like that. What are you imagining?"

"How about Rome?" Poof, we were there overlooking the Tiber River at the top of the river walk stairs. We gazed at the ancient bridges that spanned the legendary river. We saw the steeples of the great churches that spiraled the skyline of Rome. Majestic and inviting was this mythical city.

"I always wanted to go to the Spanish Steps," Marie said and instantly we stood at the base of the stairs. Behind us was the Fontana della Barcaccia or "Fountain of the Boat."

"Folk legend tells the saga of a fishing boat left grounded at this very spot during a tragic flood of the Tiber River in the 16th century. It was designed by Pietro Berini who was a member of the renowned artistic family Berini."

"Aren't we impressive," I replied to Marie's acute insight into history.

"Over there to the right of the steps is where John Keats died in 1821. The house where he lived is now a museum dedicated to the famous poet."

"You stinker! You planned this trip all along. You've been studying the history of Rome."

"What makes you think that?" she teased. "Did you know the unique design of the Spanish Steps, built in 1723 to 1725, attracted artists and poets, which in turn drew beautiful women, who came hoping to be chosen as models. This, in turn, lured rich Romans and travelers," she mimicked the voice of a tour guide. "Thus, it became a crowded gathering spot for all ages and classes of people." We broke out laughing as she posed like a beautiful model.

We looked up the steps full of people sitting and talking, drawing and sketching, some conversing with the resurrected. Suddenly, before our eyes, one of the unbelievers transformed into glory. We should not have been surprised because this happened all over the world on a regular basis. The resurrected speaker was probably one of Jesus's evangelists like Jason.

Yet, the power of the transformation impressed us even more than the ancient staircase that led up to the Trinità dei Monti church that dominated the view to the Piazza di Spagna. Instead of thinking us up the 136 steps, we climbed each one. When we reached the top, we were not out of breath because of our perfect bodies. That was an added blessing we enjoyed.

"How about the Coliseum? Did you study up on that wonder of history?"

"Of course," she replied as we found ourselves inside this Roman marvel. "The Colosseum is also known as the Flavian Amphitheatre because it was begun by the Emperor Vespasian in AD 72 of the Flavian Dynasty. It is situated in the center of Rome just east of the Roman Forum. It could hold up to 80,000 spectators and averaged around 65,000 throughout its history."

"What a remarkable achievement," I added as I envisioned the crowds of Romans cheering on the gladiators in their death matches.

"Yes, they used it for gladiator fights, and even sea battles, animal hunts, and the reenactment of famous battles. On a sad note, some of my friends were probably martyred here," she said, referring back to her days in ancient Israel with Jesus and the people she knew, who took the Gospel to Rome.

Eerily, we began to hear strange voices rise up from the dust and inner chambers of the Coliseum. "Oh, my Lord," I shuddered. "I can hear the prayers of the martyrs rising up to heaven as they cried out to Jesus before their deaths."

"They would sing Psalm 118—'This is the day the Lord has made, let us rejoice in it.'"

"What faith! What courage they had. They were going to be burned alive or fed to lions and tigers. Yet, they sang to their Savior in praise. They knew their destiny."

"God answered their prayers then, and He just recently brought revenge on Satan to fulfill their prayers' purpose."

"How long must we wait?" I muttered beneath my breath quoting from Revelation.

An awareness then came over both of us. Rome had been the bastion of Babylon before it moved to London, then to Washington, DC. Babylon had fallen, but keepers of the darkness still lurked in Rome, London, DC, and many of the major capitals of the world. Their secret aim was to overthrow Jesus and reestablish Babylon in Jerusalem.

"There is much evil here. Do you sense the witches and warlocks?"

"I do. They are casting spells at us at this very minute, but they have no power to harm us. We are immortal and cannot fall to their wickedness."

"We came here for a purpose, did we not?"

"Yes, I believe the day is almost over for us."

"And a thousand years for them. They must be generational descendants of the Druids and Satanic worshipers. How long have they persevered against the love of Jesus?"

"This must be one of their key sanctuaries."

"It should not surprise us with the Catholic presence here. This was one of the original battlegrounds where Jesus's followers contested against the spirit of Babylon. This was Satan's headquarters in my lifetime in Israel."

"If I did not know that Satan and his demons were bound in the bottomless pit, I would swear they were lurking all around us."

"It is rather beautiful that we have no fear of evil, knowing we are invincible to their temptations."

"But what are we to discern in this presence of evil? Perhaps we are to take the Gospel into the heart of their lair?"

"Look over there. Do you see that dark cloud in the spirit? It hovers over that church building."

"I think we should take a gander to find out what lies within."

Inside the church, it was dark. We could hear chanting below us in some hidden chamber.

"Do you hear that?"

"Satan, Satan, Satan, Prince of Darkness, hear our cries. Come to us. Liberate us. Once more rule the earth. We are here to serve you. There are covens throughout the earth waiting for you to come and lead them."

"I know that voice. Who is that?" I whispered to Marie.

"What's more, why are they meeting and what do they hope to achieve? Listen."

It was a man talking to another man. The voice was familiar, but I still could not remember who it was. "I can sense his chains breaking. I hear him knocking on the doors to the bottomless pit. His time has come to be free. He will lead us and his demons in the rebellion. Once Satan is released, we will rise and he will reign over humanity and the world."

"How foolish they are," I stated.

"How evil. One final rebellion will come. The Lord's response will be swift and eternal."

"What should we do?"

"Let's go into their secret chamber and confront them."

The room was spacious as we appeared before these human devils. They looked surprised as they saw we were of the resurrection. Our aura of light illuminated their meeting quarters. There were over a hundred of these Satanic worshipers. Deceived by their own inner corruption, they were trapped in their darkness to worship the defeated foe of Jesus.

"Welcome," the voice of the one I knew said to us.

Now I remembered. He was the man who ran for president to whom Jason had witnessed the Gospel. Boldness gripped my soul. "Why do you chant such evil? Why do you resist the love of Jesus Christ?"

"Why do you believe the lies?" he responded as he removed the hood from his head that guarded his face. We could see his countenance. He exuded a bitter and hardened gaze that reflected a spine-tingling evil. He had taken on the look of his master.

"I must warn you of your fate. Those who reject Jesus to serve the Dragon, will suffer the fires of hell forever and ever. You have no chance of overthrowing Jesus. You must know that. Why resist His love and offer of forgiveness? Jesus is all powerful and all knowing. He knows what you are doing. That is why He sent us to give you perhaps one last opportunity to reject Satan and come to Christ."

"You are the ones deceived. Soon Satan will break free from his bondage and rise to deliver us and regain his kingdom."

I shook my head. Marie took my arm. "You have done all we need to do and say." She then began to prophesy. Her words flowed like a fountain of life against the spirit of death that permeated the room.

"Satan is the father of lies. His roars have been silenced. He no longer prowls the earth but is chained in the frigid darkness that burns like fire. The last rebellion will come and all of creation will see the final mystery of God unfold. The heavens will cheer the destruction of the beast and all of his followers. The time is imminent. Repent and give your heart to Jesus or suffer the terrible consequences of your hardened hearts."

Suddenly, auras of light sprinkled through the chamber. New believers had been transformed by her words. Their resurrected bodies threw off the black robes and put on the garments of praise. They began to sing to the glory of Jesus. At their song of praise, the others cowered backward in fear of the majesty and authority of the King. The room filled with worshiping angels declaring the holiness of Jesus. Twenty of the devil worshipers had become those of the resurrection. Our mission complete, we joined them in the alleluias of adoration and love to our Jesus. The light of glory grew brighter and brighter, which drove the deceived out of the room.

Abandoned by these lost souls, we united in the oneness of our worship to Jesus. It felt like all of Rome shook with His thunder and exploded in His lightning. I could see in the spirit the streets of Rome. People fell to their knees, and thousands sang the new song of Jesus. All across this pagan city, auras of light appeared and increased in volume until all of Rome burned with His fire.

Then the angels of heaven began to shake the heavens with worship. We could hear thunder from Jerusalem, exalting Jesus as King of kings and Lord of lords as lightning streaked the sky. It was a virtual fireworks display for all the earth to join as one in the song of salvation. Auras of light lit the jungles of Africa to the rice paddies of Asia to the valleys of Europe, to the mountain ranges of South America and the plains of North America.

Millions of souls came into the kingdom that last night. It was the latter-day rain of the great harvest reaped from the sowers of Jesus, the fearless evangelists who took the Gospel to the ends of the earth. It was twenty-four hours to us, but a thousand years had passed. The angel of the Lord had opened the bottomless pit. Out of the darkness came a cloud of evil. Within its vapors stalked the devil and his demons.

Chapter 50

THE REBELLION

End of Millennial Reign of Jesus

The foul smell of brimstone drifted with the dense cloud of the devil and his demons. Let loose by God, Satan is determined to win back his kingdom on earth and reestablish Babylon in Jerusalem as the throne of his reign. It was on the outskirts of that ancient center of evil, Babylon, that the angel of the Lord had opened the bottomless pit and unchained the red dragon. For a thousand years he had planned to retake his right to rule the world. All he needed to do was to get one son of Adam to sin. Then he would recapture his legal right to be king instead of Jesus.

Surely, out of the billions of resurrected believers, one would succumb to his wiles. It would be the final test of God's plan. He knew if he could deceive just one, it would render the blood of Jesus powerless. Satan would write his own new covenant and enslave the sons and daughters of Adam forever. Out of the pit, Satan rose in all of his treachery. He came forth out of the cloud of evil to address his demons. The growing ugliness of Satan in the isolation of the bottomless pit had removed any hint of disguising himself as an angel of light.

His fierce countenance resembled a red dragon in the spirit realm. His claws were as sharp as a razor. His plates of lies covered his body. His eyes were like flames of fire. His feet were covered with turmoil and division. His waist was girded in deception. His shield quenched the spirit of faith. His sword contained the teachings of secular humanism of the new age of progressives. Surrounding him were his demons chanting day and night of his vainglory.

Satan was ready for battle. He had waited centuries to recover his destiny. He instructed his demons to fly out to the capitals of the world and find his followers to gather his army against Jerusalem. He knew that many kings and chiefs had rebelled in their hearts against Jesus. His covens of worshipers had prepared to storm the gates of heaven, beginning in Jerusalem. He called out in the spirit of evil, the one he had left instructions for before he was bound in chains. In his demonic scriptures he had written of the one who bore the mark of Cain on his soul. He would have the spirit of Nimrod to first take Babylon and then spread the web of wickedness to the nations. He was the one who had aspired to be the president of the United States of America.

From the four corners of the earth, the descendants of Gog and Magog gathered for battle. Satan rejoiced in the knowledge that the world had no standing armies. Only his human soldiers had weapons. Surely Jerusalem would be the first of many capitals to fall.

"Strike at the heart," Satan ordered his troops of demons and worshipers. "Remove the King and the rest will flee."

He then turned to his spies. "Has any of the resurrected given in to our temptations?"

"Not a one. They appear to be immune from all temptations as if they cannot hear our seductive voices."

Satan snarled at the report. I will find one, he thought to himself. He began to scan the nations, looking for a choice prospect he could separate from the pack who was weak. "Find me the brightest star among the resurrected, who once was mine."

That night, Marie was in prayer, alone in her room. The windows were open as she spoke to the Lord of her intense struggles. Never had she felt the presence of evil as she did this night since her resurrection. Images of her past life so long ago forgotten and forgiven flooded her thoughts. They were thoughts that plagued her of the men who used her and paid her and the shunning and gossip she had endured from the women of her village.

Shame began to creep into her memories. She felt as Jesus did on the eve of His betrayal. She agonized as she sweated great drops of blood. She loved her Savior Jesus. Yet, the pull of darkness haunted her soul. "Why, Lord, is this happening?" she questioned. "I cannot fail you. Send an angel to help me."

Her room was full of the most vile demons trying to tear down her defenses. The spirit of guilt and the spirit of fear attacked her innocence. Lust and shame came against her. "I am the daughter of the King," she told them. "There is no condemnation in Christ Jesus. I am alive in Him forever. No weapon formed against me can prosper," she spoke with authority.

Still the onslaught continued. When these demons fled, others would arrive to torment her. Then the spirit of pride seeped into her tower. "Yes, you are his daughter. The most beautiful of all the women in His kingdom. You are His treasure. You alone should be His bride. He desires you above all the others," he whispered.

Vanity came next. "You have served Him faithfully. You have sacrificed and suffered for Him. Go to Him. Give yourself to Him. Share in His glory. All the creatures of heaven and earth will worship you. Your name will be above all other names."

"Be silent," she commanded, but the demons could tell she was uncertain now. Perhaps a crack in her armor, they thought. This urged them to tempt her more.

"I need you John. Come to my rescue," she pleaded to the heavens.

At last Satan came himself to lure her into his kingdom. "How precious you are, my dear. You are the rarest of beauties. Come with me, and I will show you the kingdoms of the earth. Together we will reign over all the world. Eat of my fruit that will bring you life forever as my queen. He will not come to save you. I will treasure you as the highest and most beautiful in all the land."

Marie saw herself adorned in satin and lace with a royal robe and scepter. All bowed before her as she walked with her king. The riches of all the wealth of the nations lay at her feet. She could have this and more if she surrendered to his charm. All that she had denied herself to serve Jesus would now be hers.

She looked at Satan, but she saw the grandest of kings, handsome and majestic—the highest of all beings in heaven. *How could this be,* she wondered. He is pleasant to my eyes. He is full of grandeur. His splendor rivals the galaxies of suns and planets.

Before she could think another thought, I appeared on my white horse ready for battle. "Be gone, you vile and evil being," I spoke to Satan with all authority and power. The dragon turned his tail and fled to his armies outside of Jerusalem. Marie collapsed into my arms, exhausted and confused. Her shield of faith dented and tarnished. "You are safe, my dear. Rest in my embrace. The war is almost over. You were the last battle, and we have won."

"Where were you? I was desperate. I felt I was ready to give in to his wiles."

"Jesus would not let me come. Some of His ways are still a mystery, but you are safe. All is as it should be. Jesus trusted you with our eternity."

Then the voice of Jesus spoke dearly to our hearts. "Well done, good and faithful servants. Enter into the joy of your Master."

Immediately we found ourselves at the feet of Jesus. The beauty of His eyes drew us close to Him as we worshiped our King and Lord. His love and peace enveloped us. The perfection of His glory softened our hearts and inspired us to praise.

Chapter 51

WAR FEVER

Year CC999, Millennial Reign of Jesus

The armies of Satan marched as one across the breadth of the earth. Demons relished the bloodlust they inspired in the hearts of men and women. The unredeemed humans enjoyed the ecstasy of marching to the drumbeat of war. It produced a fever of death, to kill the redeemed and reclaim their nations.

For a thousand years they suffered at the hands of Jesus and the resurrected. The saints had been the kings and priests that ruled the land. They were second-class citizens in their eyes, forced to grovel under the resurrection leadership who held the power. Their "enemy" could not be harmed. They were always right. They enjoyed the privileges of the riches of heaven. It was time to set things right, so with the rise of Satan, they had their leader and their cause to storm the gates of Jerusalem.

Encamped on the four sides of the holy city, they stirred up their fever for battle. Daily drills of combat and nightly drinking and dancing to the drums of war made them eager to fight. But how? The temptation of the innocent one had failed. The resurrected could not be hurt by any weapons they possessed. The demons knew the angels and humans were far superior than their forces. What was Satan's plan?

Meanwhile, the resurrected army of Jesus gathered without fear. They had full knowledge that their foes would be utterly defeated. Instead, they spent hours in prayer, crying out for the souls of the unredeemed to be saved from the wrath of God. Jesus, in His love for the lost, gave them every opportunity to come to Him. A few had, but the others were blinded by the deception of Satan and the war fever that possessed them. Jesus was patient. He knew when the last to be delivered from the bondage of sin had snuck over to their side. The hearts of the others had gone beyond redemption.

My family and I gathered to pray and wait upon the Lord. Marie shared with them the horror of her struggle. "I thought those days of temptation and sin were over. I believed in our new bodies; we could not disobey God. Yet the presence of evil brought me to the edge. I fought hard, but if John had not come, I may have fallen."

"No, you would not. Your shield remained up. You fought the fight of faith and won as Jesus did in the garden. Your heart is God's heart."

"It is, but I felt capable of sin. I had not sensed that since we were glorified with Jesus."

"The Lord had a purpose in it. He knew your struggle and bid me stay with Him as the demons came against you. When Satan entered, He allowed me to go. We still need each other. Your warfare is but a prelude to the final battle of Revelation 20."

I turned to Jason. "We met an acquaintance of yours in Rome. He was the high priest of Satan, praying for his release from the bottomless pit. Our confrontation sparked the worldwide revival the night before the 1,000 years ended."

"Who was it?"

"The man who ran for president, Mr. B. Thank God, he did not win the nomination. The darkness has overtaken him completely. He is Satan's right hand man for humanity, the leader of his covens across the world."

"I failed, then, in my attempt to give him the Gospel."

"No, that would be like saying Jesus failed with Judas and his betrayal. Each person is accountable for their choice of who would be his or her master. You did all you could."

6030 BC
The family faded from my view, replaced by God sending me on a time travel to almost as far back as one could go in human history. Two men were dressed in animal skins arguing face-to-face. Then one of them turned to walk away, but the other man stooped down and grabbed a rock. In a reckless impulse, full of hate, he ran upon his adversary and struck him in the head with a deadly blow. I watched in horror as the wounded soul fell to the ground with his skull crushed. The murderer turned him over to see if he still had breath, but there was none. His life force, the breath of God, had left him cold and lifeless.

A terrible dread came over the killer as he realized what he had done to his brother. He looked around in all directions to check if anyone saw what had happened. At first, I thought this was Moses with the Egyptian he murdered, but I quickly knew it was Cain and Abel. I followed Cain as he went to his home, filled with fear. What would God think and do, he wondered. I have done a terrible deed unworthy of a son of Adam. He agonized, not over his brother Abel, but of what might become of himself.

Then I heard the Lord say to Cain, "Where is Abel your brother?"

Cain replied, trying to hide his shame, "I do not know. Am I my brother's keeper?"

I wanted to yell yes you are. I realized in that moment, little had changed with sinful humanity. I was witnessing in Cain and Abel what we were living with the resurrected and the unredeemed. The anger, the spirit of murder, the desire to dominate my brother was still at work in the human heart of those not yet glorified. They were coming after us in this fever of war to gain their wicked way.

God had warned Cain earlier of what he would do if he allowed sin to rule his soul. The story told in Genesis 4, tells us that Adam and Eve acquired a man from the Lord. The name Cain means acquired or possessed or even spear in the Hebrew. After Cain was born Eve had another child called Abel. His name means breath or breathing spirit. Abel grew up to be a keeper of the sheep and Cain a farmer. These two brothers seem to be very different. Abel was faithful in his worship of God, obedient to God's ways, while Cain was unruly and proud and jealous. He wanted to live life his way.

God loved them both. He received Abel's worship with joy, for he sacrificed to give of the firstborn of the flock and of their fat as God taught him. God gave Abel credit for his offering and forgave his sins. God did not respect Cain and did not accept his worship, for it was not as God had instructed him to do. Cain brought God an offering of fruit from the ground. It was what he had grown in the same manner Abel brought in sacrifice the labor of his hands in the sheep. Yet, that was not right in God's eyes that Cain brought fruit instead of a lamb. God was setting forth the distant truth that God would send His Son as the Lamb of God to die for our sin. Cain dishonored that truth with his sacrifice, and thus, his heart was not right with God or his brother. Trying to convict Cain of his sinful heart, God confronted Cain and warned him of his danger.

"Why are you angry? Why has your countenance fallen?" God questioned him. "If you do well will you not be accepted? And if you do not do well, sin lies at your door like a vicious animal ready to ensnare you in your anger. Sin's desire is to have you in its teeth to kill you. You need to rule over sin."

But Cain would not listen to God. Instead, his jealousy grew into a rage. For he could not stand that God accepted Abel but not Cain. His pride came up against God in his desire to control and dominate his brother. This gave rule to sin as Cain murdered his brother.

God continued to bring Cain to genuine repentance. "What have you done? The voice of your brother's blood cries out to me from the ground?" I could not help but think of the martyrs' cries arising from the dust of the Colosseum in Rome.

"Now you are cursed from the earth, which has opened its mouth to receive your brother's blood from your hand." I thought how grieved God was with His creation of humanity. Adam sinned. Now Cain murdered his brother. God's family was dysfunctional from the start. We were still sinning and killing each other in our minds and hearts and actually spilling our blood.

God then pronounced the curse upon Cain, "When you till the ground, it shall no longer yield its strength to you. A fugitive and a vagabond you shall be on the earth."

Cain cried out in his selfishness and in his pain, "My punishment is more than I can bear! Surely You have driven me out this day from the face of the ground; I shall be hidden from Your face; I shall be a fugitive and a wanderer on the earth, and it will happen that anyone who finds me will kill me."

How deeply embedded in us are our fears from our sin, I thought. Our selfishness had already become the idol of our lives in Cain. He cared more about his own life than the life he had taken and the woundedness of those who loved Abel. Sin always brings judgment and consequences. How we fight against that to defend ourselves. Our only hope is the blood of Jesus and the forgiveness of our sin.

God in His love for Cain acted to protect him. "Therefore, whoever kills Cain, vengeance shall be taken on him sevenfold." God put a mark on Cain, lest anyone finding him should kill him.

The mercy and grace of our Creator is endless in His love to pursue us and lead us not into temptation, but to deliver us from evil. The mark of Cain was now upon the most corrupt of humans in Mr. B. Though he was in partnership with Satan, God loved him, and it was not too late for him to come to Jesus in humility and repentance. At that moment I prayed for Mr. B. in this last hour of hope to believe in Jesus and to give his life to him. In him, I saw the history of our sin and judgment. Adam was driven by God out of the garden of Eden. Cain was driven from the land. Now the unbelievers would be driven from Jerusalem to the fires of hell.

In the waning hour for the last of humanity, I saw hope. God was merciful and gracious. The fever of war would end in this millennium. No more war, no more conflict, tears, sorrow or dominance. All things would be new in the eternal kingdom. We would truly love God and one another as we, the resurrected, already were. We would have forever peace and oneness within our soul. I found wonderful comfort in the truth that one day there would be no more hatred in all of creation. Only God's love and peace would prevail for all eternity.

As I returned to Jerusalem, Satan and Mr. B. were debating the next move against God. They were tenacious in their belief they could defeat Jesus and God. They just couldn't decide how.

"What weapons do we have that can defeat the invincible?" Mr. B asked Satan about his newly formed army.

"Spiritual weapons that can pierce their shields and armor," he replied with anger, incensed that this mere mortal should challenge his wisdom.

"That is fine for your demons, but what of my kings and their armies of men? Though our soldiers are as numerous as the sand, we cannot compete with the glorification of Abraham."

"Why do you fear? They are an army of love," he scoffed.

"I have found those who love in truth have much power."

"I know that those who go to war with evil and rage in their hearts usually win. We are full of wickedness. We will breach their defenses and destroy their temple and crucify their king once again. But this time He will not rise from the dead."

"You really believe He rose from the dead? If He did, then He is the Messiah."

"Oh, He did come out of the tomb on the third day. He is the Savior of the world, but I am the Prince of Darkness. I have stood before the throne of God. I know His weakness. He is kind and gentle like a Lamb. He is eager to forgive, but His strength cannot withstand what I have planned."

"Then tell me what you know that you have not shared with me."

"I do not trust men. I hold to my secret, lest you be lured away to His side. You will see the fullness of my power," Satan raged and stood on his hind legs and spread his wings to display his vanity and might. Mr. B. stepped back in terror.

The prayers of the saints in that moment pierced his soul with God's grace. He saw Satan for who he was. If he could win tomorrow it would only mean slavery for him and his men. He realized he was on the wrong side. Jesus was his only hope. How could he tell his army the truth of Jesus? God's astounding grace worked a miracle. Before Mr. B. could speak a word, he transformed with the aura of light reserved for the resurrected. For his heart he had given to Jesus.

Satan's eyes flashed with revenge. The traitor must be destroyed. He breathed the deepest of breaths and hurled a fire ball of death at Mr. B. Yet, when the smoke cleared, Mr. B. was gone.

In his new glory of light he soared through his troops telling them to turn to Jesus. By the thousands, the auras of light appeared surrounding Jerusalem. When the last of the soldiers surrendered to Jesus, the heavens opened. Divine fire, in a blaze of glory, descended and consumed the demons and the soldiers who had not given their lives to Jesus.

Chapter 52

DEFEAT AND JUDGMENT, THE SEVENTH DAY ENDS

The spiritual wings of Satan betrayed him as Jesus took him by his neck and thrashed him to the ground. He whined like a child caught in the act of a naughty deed. He tried to fight back, but he had no power. Humiliated and defeated, he was taken by Jesus and cast into the lake of fire for all eternity.

The sulfur burned the devil as he would be tormented day and night forever. Around Satan were his demons crying out in horror. There was the beast and his false prophet suffering from the terrors of brimstone and the burning fire as hot as the sun. The unholy trinity that had attempted to replace the Holy Trinity of God, Father, Son, and Holy Spirit, would forever be damned with no parole, an eternity of misery for all the suffering they had caused humanity. The rebellion of heaven and earth was no more. Now the final cleansing of the heavens and earth would take place with the great white throne judgment.

Only the holiness of God would remain. No sin or death or unrighteous would exist in the final kingdom of Jesus. The curse would forever be removed. The blessings and riches of heaven would be shared with the resurrected saints of Jesus Christ. There would be no more hate in His creation.

Before me stood a majestic throne of brilliant white. Upon it sat the holy and righteous Judge of humanity, Jesus Christ. In His robe of crimson and white, crowned with many crowns with the Book of Life at His side, He viewed the scene that surrounded Him. Around the throne behind Him, the resurrected saints in their robes of white and aura of dazzling light, stood in somber joy, knowing the last of the rebels would find their dreaded destiny before the King they refused to honor or follow. Above the throne circled the seraphim in their fiery splendor reflecting the Son of God's glory. Beside them were the angels of God, messengers and guardians of the Father God.

Before the throne the defeated and humbled rebels of humanity stooped with sloped shoulders and weary faces. Terrified of their Master, never accepting His love, they awaited their fate, to be sentenced to an eternity of fire and separation from the love of God. No worse torment could be imagined in all the universe.

AD 55
As Jesus opened the Book of Life, I found myself in chains in a dark prison in the city of Philippi. Beside me was a man rejoicing in praise of God. Though shackled in chains, he smiled at me as though he was free from all the trials and tribulations of this world. As I looked at him, I could not help but to rejoice with him, although I was a little mystified in my time travel predicament. In all of my journeys at this moment in time, I was sent to prison to be with Paul, so I rejoiced despite the aching of my wrists and discomfort of the cold damp chill of the dungeon. Why not? Jesus had won. Satan was defeated. The seventh day of the millennium had ended, and we were about to embark on a new age that could never be rivaled by any age of creation yet known.

All things would be new in heaven and on earth. I rejoiced in the wonder and mystery of God's plan as my thoughts drifted from Paul to Jesus and His salvation. The fulfillment of God's redemption story had arrived. Paul was sharing the Good News of Jesus with Roman guards who were captivated by his presence. Soon Rome itself would know the seeds of life. The tree of life would be planted and bring forth a bountiful harvest of the poor, the rich, soldiers and merchants The long journey of redemption that ignited at the cross and filtered into the prisons and arenas of Rome to the humble huts and mansions of this world had at last come to the final judgment.

Our freedom had begun on a cold night in a stable with the humble birth of Jesus to a young couple beginning their family. Mary and Joseph, chosen by God to raise up God's greatest treasure, His only begotten Son. Mary would hold these moments dear in her heart.

The life of Jesus in a human family would be a long and arduous journey, but it was God's design for us to grow up healthy and strong, to be fruitful and multiply in every aspect of life. He would come to know and love the God of creation in the warmth and security of a stable home, develop relationships that could withstand the storms of life, and to build a new community of faith that would bless the nations.

From the humblest beginnings, Jesus grew in wisdom, knowledge, and stature. He would do His Father's will, to please and obey Him as a loving Son. He would go into this world of darkness and suffering to set the captives free with His love, with His truth, and with His authority and power. Wherever He went He brought His Father's compassion, mercy, grace, and love. He would confront evil in every form of deception, oppression, and death. He would be a Man of sorrows, rejected by His own who knew Him not. His Light would overcome the darkness. He would not sin or surrender to the evil of Satan or of humanity. Instead, He would bring out the good in all who followed Him, created in God's image, to discover their potential as sons and daughters of the living God. He would be rejected, tortured, and crucified by the leaders of the Jewish and Gentile world.

Yet, He would rise on the third day to take His rightful place at God's right hand. He would rule over all of heaven and earth. He would return to be the King of nations and of His kingdom there would be no end, full of truth and justice and righteousness. Jesus Christ, the hero of humanity, from the lowest of beginnings, was to be crowned the Lord of lords, to touch the hearts of men and women, to win their loyalty with His love and restore us to the glory that God created us to know before He spoke creation into being.

The words of Paul to the guards awakened me from my thoughts. The guards were kneeling in repentance and faith, crying out to Jesus to save their souls from sin and death to a new life in Him. Thus, the kingdom of Christ would spread from prisons to pulpits, from village to town, to princes and paupers, and finally to nations and the world. The resistance of hardened hearts would melt in the truth and promise of His love. The eternal destiny of lost souls would come alive in their newfound Redeemer's love.

Jesus's voice spoke with such authority and conviction. His countenance of love could not have expressed more compassion as this holy Judge pronounced on the rebels their just sentence to the lake of fire.

> The earth and the heavens fled from His presence, and there was no place for them. And I saw the dead, great and small, standing before the throne, and books were opened. Another book was opened, which is the Book of Life. The dead were judged according to what they had done as recorded in the books. The sea gave up the dead that were in it, and Death and Hades gave up the dead that were in them, and each person was judged according to what they had done. Then death and Hades were thrown into the lake of fire. The lake of fire is the second death. Anyone whose name was not found written in the book of life was thrown into the lake of fire.

The time had come for every knee to bow and every tongue confess that Jesus Christ is Lord. All the saints knelt before their King as did the seraphim and angels and all the creatures of heaven. As one, they declared the glory and reign of Jesus Christ, the Son of God. How thankful we were that our names were written in the Lamb's Book of Life.

In the lake of fire, even Satan, the beast, and the false prophet, together with the demons and rebels of humanity knelt in the fire to declare

Jesus as Lord. You could hear the snarls that Satan and his hosts of wickedness growled as they were forced to admit that Jesus had won our freedom.

At that moment the fiery new birth of creation spread over the heavens and the earth until all was brand new, even greater than the day God first spoke His creation into existence.

Chapter 53

ALL THINGS NEW

In the beginning God created the heavens and the earth. In the beginning was the Word, and the Word was with God, and the Word was God. For by Him all things were created that are in heaven and that are on the earth, visible and invisible, whether thrones or dominions or principalities or powers. All things were created through Him and for Him. And He is before all things, and in Him all things consist.

At the end of the white throne judgment, Jesus spoke the word of creation. The heavens and the earth corrupted from the sin of Adam and of his descendants exploded in the fiery creation of God as we, the resurrected, watched from the third heaven beside the Father's throne. Then a new heaven and new earth came forth by His word. Pure and holy, uncorrupted and glorious, shining in the wonder of Jesus's Light.

We descended from the throne of God within the New Jerusalem coming down out of heaven from God, prepared as a bride adorned for her husband. This holy city would be the symbol of Jesus's new kingdom, the antithesis of Babylon and the evil that had ruled the world for millennials. It would be the center of The Way of His life as was established before the fall of Adam. Truth and justice, holiness and righteousness would unite all people and creatures in His love. Peace would reign from this time forward and forever more.

Then a loud voice from heaven declared, "Behold, the tabernacle of God is with men, and He will dwell with them, and they will be His people. God Himself will be with them and be their God. And God will wipe away every tear from their eyes, there will be no more death, nor sorrow, nor crying. There shall be no more pain, for the former things have passed away." When I heard these wondrous words, I marveled at what I had lived through in my life. What God had intended and promised to His people from Adam to Noah to Abraham to David to the Gentile world had come to pass. All things were new. We had labored to prepare the way for Jesus to return. Now we were reaping the abundance of a new and glorious life.

Moses had built the tabernacle in the wilderness at God's instruction where he would meet with His Deliverer. David had his tabernacle where the ark of the covenant dwelt with the presence of God. The Word became flesh and tabernacled as Jesus with His people. Then Jesus and the Father sent the Holy Spirit to tabernacle with us and in us. Now we, the resurrected, would tabernacle with God the Father and with Jesus for eternity.

We rejoiced as one people as the majesty and splendor of Jesus and His new creation unfolded before us. In New Jerusalem, we stood before His throne. Jesus clothed in His righteousness and holy beauty, looked upon us with His love and authority, and said:

> Behold, I make all things new. It is done. What was planned from the beginning has come to pass. I am the Alpha and the Omega, the Beginning and the End. I will give of the fountain of the water of life freely to him who thirsts. He who overcomes shall inherit all things, and I will be His God and he will be My son.

> Never again will the unholy be free to corrupt our world and our life. We will live in the oneness of God's creation, knowing one another and being known. Without fear or shame or guilt, but in complete love, truth and honesty

will we dwell together. For all has been restored to reflect
the image of God and the genuineness of His Being.

Worship broke forth throughout the heavens. Singing and dancing with
wondrous joy in praise of Jesus as the Lamb and the Lion upon His
throne. In this treasured moment, I was suddenly transported to one of
my last trips to Cuba. We were on the Isle of Youth in a district conference where the bishop was with us to preach. He is a man that is bigger
than life, full of the Holy Spirit and completely free in his expression
of God's love and truth. I was singing and dancing with the worship
leaders. The people crowded into the temple, standing along the aisles,
flowing out into the streets. Peering through the open windows, there
is always room to dance before the Lord in Cuba as David danced. It
was as though heaven had come down into our worship. Emma, one of
our favorite worship singers, was leading the praise. She not only has
a beautiful voice, but her heart is full of love and compassion for Jesus
and the people. We were all caught in the glory of God. I closed my eyes
and gave all my heart to God in worship. I could hear the rejoicing of
the worshipers as my heart opened to love and adore Jesus.

There is nowhere else in the world I would rather be in worship than in
Cuba. The believers have such hunger for God, it oozes out of the very
pores of their being, crying out in song and dance to the Lord. Their
oneness and rhythm in the music is like no other. It is a thing of beauty.
As Emma sang, her husband, Ariel, smiled as he played the drums. The
trumpets sounded with the guitars. The worship team sang in adoration. Emma encouraged us to lift our voices to the Lord. I could hear
people singing in the tongues of the nations as if all the world had
joined us in glorifying our God.

When I opened my eyes back in heaven, here was Emma leading the
creatures of heaven in worship as she had in Cuba. I had such joy in
seeing her and then Ariel on the drums near the throne of Jesus. It was
as if rivers of joy flooded my soul and cascaded out of me in worship.

I remembered that night the bishop preached on Jesus healing the paralytic. First He forgave his sins, and then, when the religious leaders

grumbled against Jesus, that only God could forgive sins, Jesus raised up the crippled man. He picked up his pallet and walked away completely healed in body and soul. How beautiful it was for all us to be in heaven with Jesus, totally healed of all of our sins and sicknesses. We were one in love and unity with the Father, Son, and Holy Spirit and with one another. We walked in the liberty of His love as did the paralytic that day when Jesus touched Him.

YEAR 2019

That night back in Cuba, the bishop had called me to the front with him after he had ministered to his people in power and might of the Lord. The pastors of the district had fallen in the Spirit before the Lord in surrender and in love. So had most of the people by the time he called me to his side. I was deeply humbled by his words of blessing about me to the congregation. Twenty years earlier, I had been the only one to support him in Florida and ask him to preach at my church. A great move of the Spirit had taken place with many healings and salvations. I will never forget seeing one of our leaders who was told he would never walk again, rise out of his wheelchair and walk. He never went back to sit in that chair. It was like a surreal moment as I watched him rise up in his own strength and walk.

The revival of God swept into our school where the young people wept at the altar to be set free from the hardness of their hearts. It was that day that our daughter Liz came to us with her friends and asked for prayer that they would be baptized in the Spirit to follow Jesus with all of their heart. That was such a special time, but short-lived as religious people in our church and school rose up against the move of the Spirit. When God's Spirit is poured out on His people, it often gets messy as the tares try to silence the wheat.

As I stood with the bishop, he asked if I remembered what I said to him, but I did not. He said I asked him how much money he needed for his people in Cuba. He said $15,000. I then called our treasurer to send them the money via Western Union through Canada. He said he never forgot how we blessed him and stood with him when they had nothing in Cuba. It helped propel them to build up their missions in Cuba and to spread the fire throughout the world for Jesus. He then stepped toward me, and as his custom, he struck me on my chest commanding the Spirit to fill me with God's Presence. I had closed my eyes in anticipation of this moment, but when he struck me, even with my eyes closed, I saw him and the glory of God in a brilliant light as clear as if my eyes were open. I went down in the Spirit as God's glory filled me to overflow with praise and love for Jesus.

Now in heaven, I saw the same people of Gerona with Emma and Ariel singing before the throne. There was Pastor Jose and Mercedes his wife. Wow, there was the bishop and Maritza, his wife. Marie and I embraced them in the love of Jesus and celebrated the reign of Jesus before the throne of God.

The worship became a thunderous ovation of love and adoration to our King as we watched a trickle of water begin to bubble up under His seat of royalty. Soon it became a river of life that moved from Jerusalem to water the earth with His glory and life.

Chapter 59

COME, LORD JESUS, COME

The river of life flowed from under the throne of the King and His Father. The Lamb looked with joy upon this pure beauty, beaming with life, for along its banks grew the tree of life. The abundance of life in the new heaven and new earth reflected the heart of God in fruitfulness and multiplication. This tree of life had been in the garden from which Adam ate. Now all of creation would take pleasure in its fruit and how it ministered to the needs of humanity. Every month, this tree bore its fruit to feed the soul of the people with everlasting life. The tree connected with the fertile soil of the earth to yield all God had to offer. No more toil or sweat from the brow of men and women under the hot sun for the redeemed. The oneness of the tree united with us in giving us a mighty harvest. The leaves of the tree of life brought healing to the nations. For the endless wars had left scars upon men's souls and upon the land. The nations needed the balm of the Lord to restore them to oneness. The curse that plagued us was no more. Endless blessings came to us like manna from heaven. Every day, the glory of God was new to us. We surrounded the throne of God and of the Lamb with love and a servant's heart to worship our Lord.

We saw the face of God in the Lamb seated on the throne. With no more sin to hide His face from us, we drew our strength and courage from our King. We were branded in the Spirit with the name of God on our foreheads, marking us as His own. Suddenly, I found myself prostrating before the throne of God at the feet of the Lamb. Next to me was Marie and around us I could see the apostles, Peter, James, John, and Paul. We were immersed in worship, declaring the holiness of our Lord Jesus with the creatures of heaven. Holy, holy, holy, is the one word to describe our King. The sacredness of the moment carried me to the temple with Isaiah and the Lord of Hosts. Then I was with Peter in his boat when the holiness of Jesus convicted him of his sin. Finally, there I was in Revelation, when the resounding songs of all of heaven and earth gave praise to our Holy Savior.

I was full of joy, knowing Jesus and the knowledge of our glorious future that Jesus had created for us to live in love with Him and one another. Night ceased to cover us with darkness. Nor did we need a lamp or the light of the sun for the Lord God's splendor shone forth His Light. In His majesty and glory we reigned with Him forever and ever.

YEAR AD 90

I found myself with Marie back in time with John as he wrote the last words of the Bible in the book of Revelation. We sat by candlelight at his side as the Spirit inspired him to give us the words of the one who is faithful and true. The Lord God of the holy prophets sent His angel to show His servants the things which must shortly take place. Then the voice of the One who sits on the throne with His Father spoke. "Behold, I am coming quickly. Blessed is he who keeps the words of the prophecy of this book."

Marie began to prophesy over John. He laid down his quill and knelt in the presence of Jesus, as Marie spoke. "The words of Daniel tell us the prophecies of Israel and His people. The words of John foretell the prophecies for the entire world for Jew and Gentile, for king and merchant and pauper and priest. The mysteries of God are revealed in the prophecy of Jesus. For in the last days the book will be unsealed. We will see the signs from heaven reveal the coming glory of the Son. Every knee will bow and every tongue will confess Jesus is Lord. We will dwell with Jesus in His love forever and ever."

These prophetic words were spoken over the one Jesus loved. John had been His faithful witness for over sixty years. The devil had John boiled in oil, but he did not die, for Jesus had ordained he would write the last book of the Bible. This aged saint of God had run the race with grace and beauty. His time to join Jesus was near at hand. To me, John was the mightiest of prayer warriors. He had recorded in his Gospel the most precious of prayers from Jesus, the high priestly prayer of chapter 17 where Jesus prayed to His Father before His arrest in the garden of Gethsemane. It was one of love, intimacy, and intercession for His apostles and for all who would come to believe in Him. I could not help but think of the global prayer movement that had arisen in the last generation before Jesus would come as an answer to Jesus's prayer, one that John would have rejoiced.

That was fifteen years before Jesus would return. God had sent us to Israel to pray through the land. Although at the beginning of our venture, we did not see how the wonder of God would direct us in our mission. The year before, Marie and I were sent to spy out the land, as we jested with each other. The Lord had given a team to visit and minister in Israel and to gain a perspective of what He was doing in the Promised Land to prepare for Jesus's return.

We had made connections with the Global Prayer Movement as I shared earlier. They had founded a center in Jerusalem to pray day and night in prophecy and music as King David had developed three thousand years prior in his tent of meeting. Twenty-four seven, musicians would play and singers sing praises and prophecies to the Lord. In the book of the prophet Amos, God had promised to reestablish this prayer and worship before the return of the Messiah. Now it has come to grow from those ancient seeds to encompass the world in prayer and worship.

Believers not only prayed in their own time zones twenty-four hours a day, every day of the week, but there were twenty-four time zones across the world. Therefore, day and night prayer would ascend to the throne of God as Luke told of Jesus's prophecy that a worldwide prayer movement would be occurring when He came again. His prayer movement, inspired by the Spirit, grabbed the hearts of young and old, but especially the teenagers and those in their twenties. Houses of prayer sprung up across America and in the nations of the earth.

Now we brought a team to Israel on our second trip to join this house of worship in prayer and prophecy. The day we visited, we had planned on spending several hours, but in God's providence, we were there to engage in an intense battle in the heavens over the holy city of Zion. Musicians were playing in harmony with the prayers of the worship leader as we gathered our team inside their chapel. Immediately the Spirit awakened us to His presence. We knew something extraordinary was about to unfold. Many of us fell on our knees and then laid prostrate before the Lord. The heaviness of His glory pressed upon us and drew us into that glorious intimacy that is beyond the veil.

Marie started to prophecy, and the room grew silent except for one keyboard player playing in the background. Marie seemed to be with Daniel in ancient Babylon as she spoke of his prayer in chapter 9 of his prophetic book. Beside her as she cried out the words of the Lord, I saw the angel Gabriel clothed in the glory of God. Marie started to confess the sins of His people Israel and those who followed Jesus Christ. This repentance was uttered in the desperation of Daniel for the Jews and the holy city. It was a deep cry of the Spirit in words of a language unknown to us.

Then, we heard Gabriel proclaim the seventy weeks given by God to Daniel through this mightiest of archangels:

> "Seventy weeks are determined
> For your people and for your holy city,
> To finish the transgression,
> To make an end of sins,
> To make reconciliation for iniquity,
> To bring in everlasting righteousness,
> To seal up vision and prophecy,
> And to anoint the Most Holy.
> "Know therefore and understand,
> *That* from the going forth of the command

To restore and build Jerusalem
Until Messiah the Prince,
There shall be seven weeks and sixty-two weeks;
The street shall be built again, and the wall,
Even in troublesome times.
And after the sixty-two weeks
Messiah shall be cut off, but not for Himself;
And the people of the prince who is to come
Shall destroy the city and the sanctuary.
The end of it *shall be* with a flood,
And till the end of the war desolations are determined.
Then he shall confirm a covenant with many for one week;
But in the middle of the week
He shall bring an end to sacrifice and offering.
And on the wing of abominations shall be one who
makes desolate,
Even until the consummation, which is determined,
Is poured out on the desolate." Daniel 9:24-27

Stunned by the revelation of Gabriel, we were silent for a half hour. Then Marie declared the seventy weeks were almost complete. The return of Jesus was imminent. Prepare the way of the Lord.

In these final years, God would raise up a generation of John the Baptists, who would end the desolation. The idolatry of secular humanism and its destruction had been determined. When the beast arises and comes on the wings of abomination, then you shall know that Jesus is soon to come in the cloud of glory. It was then we were taken into the heavens over Jerusalem to see the battle of God's angels led by Michael the archangel of Israel against the demons of Satan. This supernatural warfare awakened us to the truth that what was happening in the physical realm was but a reflection of the war in the heavens.

The speed of the angels and demons astounded us as we stayed in a sacred oneness of prayer for victory over the powers of darkness. Fireballs of atomic particles struck the demons and cast them down into dry and arid places, reserved for the fires of hell. Swords of the

Spirit clashed with the swords of Satan causing lightning strikes over the city. Michael hurled a thunderbolt of fire against the Prince of Persia. It struck him squarely in his body. Immediately, he was in chains and rendered harmless. The demons saw the capture of their leader and fled into the darkness of space.

Shouts of victory and praise rose from the victorious angels. They bowed before Jesus seated on His throne. The eastern gate in the walls of Jerusalem opened in a symbolic gesture, beckoning the King to enter as Jesus rose from His throne. The oil of anointing poured forth from the robes of His garments until the saints of the world were saturated in His power and glory, anointed to go forth into battle to prepare the way of the Lord.

The heavens exploded in the brilliance of God's light as the darkness over Israel vanished. God's promises for the children of Abraham, secure in the holy covenant, were now released over Israel. Soon their King would come and all would see their Deliverer come out of Zion. All Israel would be saved.

We began to pray the simple prayer of Revelation 22, "Come, Lord Jesus, come."

ETERNITY

The King of glory had come as He promised to reign for 1,000 years. Now that age has ended. The last rebellion of Satan and his followers had been quenched. All those who had rejected Jesus had been judged and cast into the lake of fire forever. Jesus reigned as King over the heavens and the earth. The keys of His kingdom had been handed over to His Father. The dawn of a new age of eternal peace and glory was at hand. We testify to this coming revelation and triumph of our Lord, Jesus Christ.

Cinderella and the Knight stood together arm-in-arm to behold the wonder of a new kingdom, vast and endless to explore without the limits of time or chains of a fallen world. In the perfection of God and

His creation they would know as God knows and love as God loves in the oneness of His intimacy and glory!

"Come Lord Jesus, come!"

ALL PROCEEDS AND DONATIONS FOR BLAKE'S NOVEL
WILL GO TO HIS MISSION WORK AROUND THE
WORLD AND IN CENTRAL FLORIDA.

GO TO BLAKELORENZMINISTRIES.COM TO DONATE
AND/OR PURCHASE MORE BOOKS.

THANK YOU.

CPSIA information can be obtained
at www.ICGtesting.com
Printed in the USA
BVHW070626291021
620229BV00001B/1

9 781662 831829